Books by Ernest Hemingway

NOVELS

The Torrents of Spring
The Sun Also Rises
A Farewell to Arms
To Have and Have Not
For Whom the Bell Tolls
Across the River and into the Trees
The Old Man and the Sea
Islands in the Stream
The Garden of Eden
True at First Light
A Farewell to Arms: The Hemingway Library Edition
The Sun Also Rises: The Hemingway Library Edition

STORIES

In Our Time
Men Without Women
Winner Take Nothing
The Fifth Column and Four Stories of the Spanish Civil War
The Short Stories of Ernest Hemingway
The Snows of Kilimanjaro and Other Stories
The Nick Adams Stories
The Complete Short Stories of Ernest Hemingway

NONFICTION

Death in the Afternoon
Green Hills of Africa
Selected Letters 1917–1961
A Moveable Feast
The Dangerous Summer
Dateline: Toronto
By-Line: Ernest Hemingway
A Moveable Feast: The Restored Edition
Green Hills of Africa: The Hemingway Library Edition

ANTHOLOGIES

On Writing
Hemingway on Fishing
Hemingway on Hunting
Hemingway on War

Ernest Hemingway

THE SUN
ALSO RISES

THE HEMINGWAY LIBRARY EDITION

Foreword by PATRICK HEMINGWAY
Edited with an Introduction by SEÁN HEMINGWAY

SCRIBNER

New York   London   Toronto   Sydney   New Delhi

SCRIBNER

An Imprint of Simon & Schuster, Inc.
1230 Avenue of the Americas
New York, NY 10020

First Scribner trade paperback edition February 2016

SCRIBNER and design are registered trademarks of The Gale Group, Inc., used under license by Simon & Schuster, Inc., the publisher of this work.

For information about special discounts for bulk purchases, please contact Simon & Schuster Special Sales at 1-866-506-1949 or business@simonandschuster.com.

The Simon & Schuster Speakers Bureau can bring authors to your live event. For more information or to book an event, contact the Simon & Schuster Speakers Bureau at 1-866-248-3049 or visit our website at www.simonspeakers.com.

Interior design by Brooke Zimmer

Manufactured in the United States of America

11 13 15 17 19 20 18 16 14 12

Library of Congress Control Number: 2014378813

ISBN 978-1-4767-3995-3
ISBN 978-1-5011-2196-8 (pbk)
ISBN 978-1-4767-3996-0 (ebook)

Contents

Foreword

It is very difficult for a poor swimmer in the cold water of an arctic sea to take even a partial measure of that large portion of the literary iceberg that lies beneath the surface in a masterpiece of world literature such as *The Sun Also Rises*!

In chapter 14 Jake Barnes, the first-person narrator, says this about himself:

> I was reading a book by Turgenieff. Probably I read the same two pages over several times. It was one of the stories in "A Sportsman's Sketches." I had read it before, but it seemed quite new. The country became very clear and the feeling of pressure in my head seemed to loosen.

Then, after a page and a half of philosophizing, which he distrusts in the dark after he has turned off the light:

> I turned on the light again and read. I read the Turgenieff. I knew that now, reading it in the oversensitized state of my mind after too much brandy, I would remember it somewhere, and afterward it would seem as though it had really happened to me. I would always have it.

With regard to the above two passages I refer the serious reader for enlightenment to the publications of an Iranian literary scholar, Shahla Sorkhabi Darzikola. From her I learned that it was Sherwood Anderson who first introduced Hemingway to Turgenieff, not Sylvia Beech. There are many more revelations from this Persian expert, but you must read them yourself. Please don't be put off by the sometimes awkward

English of Darzikola. More and more as the whole world comes online, excellent insights expressed in awkward English will be the norm, and there is a profound need for a mechanism in the scientific review process to deal with this. Hemingway put it this way: "English, or what it is we all speak."

And what are we to say regarding Jake's lack of enthusiasm in chapter 2 about Robert Cohn's suggestion they take a trip to Uruguay, inspired by W. H. Hudson's *The Purple Land*? Ford Madox Ford, after he had moved to America, wrote a preface to *A Farewell to Arms* in the 1930s that contains the following:

> The three impeccable writers of English prose that I have come across in fifty years or so of reading in search of English prose have been Joseph Conrad, W. H. Hudson . . . and Ernest Hemingway. . . . Impeccable each after his kind! I remember with equal clarity and equal indefinableness my sensation on first reading a sentence of each. With the Conrad it was like being overwhelmed by a great, unhastening wave. With the Hudson it was like lying on one's back and looking up into a clear, still sky. With the Hemingway it was just excitement. Like waiting at the side of a coppice, when foxhunting, for the hounds to break cover. One was going on a long chase in dry clear weather, one did not know in what direction or over what country.

When they worked together in the 1920s, it was Ford who recommended Hudson to Hemingway as writing the best English prose, and I do know something about the relationship between my father and Hudson. In his library in Key West he had the 1922 hardcover edition of Hudson's complete works, which he must have purchased when he was still living in Paris and which he took with him to Cuba when he moved there in 1939, the year Ford died. For some reason, he left behind his copy of Lord Grey's *The Charm of Birds* in Key West. Viscount Grey of Fallodon, besides being an aristocratic patron of Hudson (who spent many happy days with his beloved birds at Grey's fishing hut in the valley of the Test, a classic trout chalk stream of which it was said that even God could not buy a day's fishing on the Test), made what was perhaps the most important decision in modern history. As Foreign Minister of what was still then the United Kingdom of Great Britain and Ireland, he decided in the autumn of 1914 that his country should declare war on

Germany because of a treaty obligation to defend the territorial integrity of Belgium. Joseph Conrad, in his story "An Outpost of Progress," mocks a Belgian serving in King Leopold's private fiefdom (with the ironic name of Congo Free State) for being an officer in an army whose safety was guaranteed by all the great powers of Europe. This was the very treaty that Lord Grey felt obliged to honor.

One must not think that Hemingway, because Jake Barnes shows no enthusiasm for a trip to Uruguay, did not pay a great deal of attention to everything Hudson wrote. Hudson's generation was the first to have to deal with Darwinism, and what Hudson finally put together again for himself—a transcendental acceptance of a one-and-only life in the natural world as far away as possible from the stone, steel, glass, and asphalt of the megacity—was much appreciated by my father. He might write eloquently of Paris, the City of Electric Light and the Eiffel Tower, but his heart was with the Basques at Roncesvalles. Hudson himself, a very masculine man, under the stress of economic necessity as a penniless immigrant to London from the pampas of Argentina, wrote an eloquent and very convincing pamphlet entitled *The Value of Breast Feeding, by a Mother Who Knows*!

Patrick Hemingway

Introduction

Literature is writing that engages and endures. It is meaningful, not simply remarks, as Gertrude Stein once told my grandfather when he was a young man. Ernest Hemingway came to define literature in his own way. He believed that a writer should create an absolute truth out of fiction that feels so real it actually becomes a shared experience with the reader. *The Sun Also Rises*, a tale of expatriates living in Paris after World War I, achieves this standard of excellence and remains one of the great novels of the twentieth century. Hemingway's lean, modern prose style makes the story as accessible today as when it was first published in 1926.

From the moment *The Sun Also Rises* was published, it was a success. The exotic locales of Paris and the Festival of San Fermín at Pamplona as settings for a complex love triangle involving a beautiful woman captured the imaginations of readers. For me, what is remarkable about the book is that it continues to resonate so strongly with readers. In his book *After the Lost Generation*, John Aldridge wrote that "for members of my generation, the young men born between 1918, roughly, and 1924, there was a special charm about Hemingway. . . . The words he put down seemed to us to have been carved from the living stone of life."[1] Many people, often complete strangers, have told me what a powerful influence the book had on them when they first read it in their youth. It left them with a desire to see the Paris of Jake Barnes and Brett Ashley and watch the bullfights at Pamplona described so vividly in the novel. This was my own experience, too. I first read *The Sun Also Rises* as a freshman at Dartmouth College in a seminar on the Great American Novel, along with books by Hawthorne, Melville, and Fitzgerald. I loved the book when I read it. I was completely taken with the unrequited love between Jake and Brett, and the camaraderie and importance of friends, despite their faults. Most of all, I was fascinated by the bullfights and the energy surrounding the Festival of San Fermín and Jake's fishing for trout on the Irati River and communing with nature. A year later, I went to Pamplona to run with the bulls. It was as moving as Hemingway wrote it—especially the bullfights, which played as a powerful ritual, a dangerous and even beautiful form of art.

As a young man, I was impressed by the repeated emphasis in the novel on the need to pay the bill—to take care of one's own affairs—and by Jake Barnes's ability to make his way in the world. At eighteen, I myself did not have any practical plan for how to do that. When I read the book today, nearly thirty years later, I am more taken with Count Mippipopolous's statement to Jake Barnes about the importance of getting value for your money and knowing how to live well. Just weeks before his untimely death, my uncle Jack, to whom *The Sun Also Rises* is dedicated, and I had lunch at La Goulue in Manhattan. He told me with an ironic grin how he finally could afford to live the way he had lived his entire life. Living well is not just about having money.

The Sun Also Rises has inspired many books and countless articles.[2] There is even an entire book about these books and articles.[3] Scholars continue to analyze the novel and its complexities. *The Sun Also Rises*, like the Muse herself, moves people differently. For example, Woody Allen, who portrays Ernest Hemingway as a caricature of himself—an irony I dare say my grandfather would have appreciated—in his movie *Midnight in Paris*, clearly was inspired by *The Sun Also Rises*. One of the main premises of the film appears to take its cue directly from Jake Barnes's advice to Robert Cohn: "Walk the city at night, see what happens . . ."

The Sun Also Rises shows us that we don't always choose the ones we love. Among the passages that Hemingway ultimately cut from the book (included in the second and third appendices to this edition) are poignant descriptions of Brett's alluring qualities and how they utterly captivate Jake, especially when he is in her presence. Sometimes love just happens, and it does not always end happily. Brett's affairs with Jake, Cohn, Mike Campbell, and even Pedro Romero are hopelessly entwined and tragically sad. Love triumphs over all but leaves carnage in its wake. For Jake Barnes, wisdom is gained at the expense of heartbreak.

This new edition of *The Sun Also Rises*, which includes early drafts and deleted chapters, allows the reader to understand how Ernest Hemingway conceived his remarkable first novel. First novels are different from those written later in one's career. There is a heightened sense of expectation, an aura of unrealized promise, and a pressure on the writer to get right something he has not done before. Hemingway was twenty-six years old when he began to write *The Sun Also Rises* (see image on back cover), and he was not entirely sure how to go about writing his novel. He had been writing fine short stories and journalism for years, but had not completed a novel. During the spring and summer of 1921, while living in Chicago, he had started to write a novel based on his own experiences, one that would include "real people talking and saying what they think."[4] He brought it with him to Paris and in the spring of 1922 showed it to Gertrude Stein, together with his other work. Stein later recalled that she found it wanting and contained too much description, and she recommended that he start over.[5] This novel was lost on December 2, 1922, at the Gare de Lyon in Paris, along with most of the other unpublished stories and poems Hemingway had written until that time. With the best intentions, Hadley had gathered the manuscripts—both the originals and the carbon copies—to bring to him in a suitcase that was tragically stolen from her train compartment even before the train left the station for Lausanne.[6] While we will never know exactly how that early novel read, it was not a masterpiece, as Stein and Hemingway himself later recognized. Hemingway was still maturing as a writer, and Paris in the 1920s would prove to be an extraordinary training ground for him. The expatriate community in Paris included an amazing assortment of artists: the painters Joan Miró and André Masson, the photographer Man Ray, and writers like Ezra Pound, James Joyce, T. S. Eliot, Ford Madox Ford, and many others whom Ernest Hemingway got to know.[7] At the same time, the bohemian lifestyle did not always rest well with Hemingway. Some of the material that he cut from the beginning of *The Sun Also Rises* disparages Montparnasse and many of the people with whom my grandfather spent time in the local cafés (see Figure 2).

It was Gertrude Stein who encouraged Hemingway to experience the bullfights at Pamplona, which he first visited in 1923 (see Figure 3). The supplementary material in this volume begins with Hemingway's description of that first visit, which Joyce Carol Oates considers one of the best American essays of the twentieth century.[8] When he returned to Pamplona the following year, he ran with the bulls and mock-fought young ones in the ring (see Figure 5). He was even "gored" while attempting to assist his friend Donald Ogden Stewart, a story that made its way into the *Chicago Tribune* (see Figure 6).[9] Of course, he also went to many bullfights (Figures 4 and 7). That same year Hemingway had outstanding trout fishing on the Irati River. His fishing license is one of the few tangible items still preserved from his trip into the high country (see Figures 8 and 9). Little did my grandfather know that the stream would be ruined by loggers the following year and that the fishing would never be the same again. It was primarily the 1924 trip with Hadley and Donald Ogden Stewart that inspired Hemingway to write about fishing the Irati in *The Sun Also Rises*.

The critical success of *In Our Time*, his first book of short stories to be published in America, and the need to establish himself as a writer added pressure, which he later described:

> I knew I must write a novel. But it seemed an impossible thing to do when I had been trying with great difficulty to write paragraphs that would be the distillation of what made a novel. It was necessary to write longer stories now as you would train for a longer race. When I had written a novel before, the one that had been lost in the bag stolen at the Gare de Lyon, I still had the lyric facility of boyhood that was as perishable and as deceptive as youth was. I knew it was probably a good thing that it was lost, but I knew too that I must write a novel. I would put it off though until I could not help doing it. I was damned if I would write one if it was what I should do if we were going to eat regularly. When I had to write it, then it would be the only thing to do and there would be no choice. Let the pressure build.[10]

That pressure was already mounting by the middle of June 1925 when my grandfather again started to write a novel, entitled *Along with Youth: A Novel*.[11] Perhaps it was an attempt at recalling his first lost novel. However, after making a brief start and reading F. Scott Fitzgerald's fine new novel *The Great Gatsby*, he decided that it was no good.[12] It was only after the events of the Festival of San Fermín at Pamplona the next month that my grandfather knew he had a new and exciting subject for a novel. Hemingway said that he finally began *The Sun Also Rises* in Valencia on his birthday, July 21, 1925, shortly after the Festival of San Fermín had come to a close. He started off writing on loose sheets of paper (see Figure 13). After two days he had already written thirty-one pages and switched to filling notebooks with his narrative (see Figure 14). He wrote furiously, filling up seven notebooks and completing the first draft in two months.[13] He wrote in Valencia, Madrid, San Sebastian, and then Hendaye (see Figure 10) on the southwestern coast of

France. Finally, on September 21, 1925, in Paris, he completed the last page of the first draft (see Figure 16). He later remembered that he thought he wrote too quickly.[14] The manuscript shows that he made many revisions, a task he called the most difficult of his life. He poured himself and his experiences into the novel, and improved the story the best way he knew how—by inventing it.

It is well known that *The Sun Also Rises* is a roman à clef based on actual events and people from the summer of 1925 when Ernest, Hadley, and several friends, including Duff Twysden, Harold Loeb, and Donald Ogden Stewart, went to Pamplona for the Festival of San Fermín (see Figure 1).[15] Remarkably the first draft of the manuscript begins by using real names for the characters: Duff Twysden as Brett, Hemingway as Jake Barnes, and Harold Loeb as Robert Cohn.[16] The real-life protagonists were none too happy with their portrayals, and one remarked that the novel should have been entitled "Six Characters in Search of an Author—With a Gun Apiece."[17] By the next summer, his book nearly complete, Hemingway was back in Pamplona with a new *cuadrilla* (see Figure 12). While much has been made of the real-life basis for the characters and plot, I do not think that the comparison is as important to readers today. Besides, most of the key elements of the book are invented: Harold Loeb was not the middleweight boxing champion of Princeton, Hemingway was not emasculated during World War I, and Duff Twysden did not sleep with a bullfighter that summer of 1925. The drafts included in the supplementary material of this edition show how quickly Hemingway transformed the plot and its characters into fiction.

It is fascinating to see that the novel started out as a story about the corruption of a bullfighter (see Figure 13). It began not in Paris but in Pamplona, at a hotel where two Americans are watching a bullfighter prepare for the afternoon's *corrida*. Hemingway revised several times the powerful opening scene of the bullfighter surrounded by his handlers yet utterly alone. In one draft he emphasizes the tremendous sums that the bullfighter would make and how his life would change quickly if he were successful. Finances figure in the corruption of his youth. But as the story came into focus for Hemingway, the bullfighter becomes the character most true to himself and a perfectionist in his art.

Hemingway realized that in order for the reader to understand what happened in Pamplona, it was necessary to know what happened in Paris. He changed the emphasis of the story. He thought first of the bullfighter as the hero, then Harold Loeb, Jake Barnes, and even Brett Ashley, until finally there was no hero at all. For the most part it appears that Hemingway composed the story as he wrote. It is only well into the story, at the end of the third notebook, that he wrote a chapter outline (see Figure 15). By this time he had a clear understanding of the general progression of the book, and, except for a few minor deviations, he then followed the rough outline.

In the early stages of the novel Hemingway wrote to Gertrude Stein:

> Never worked so hard. Sometimes till 4 o'clock in the morning from after dinner and sometimes like now—it's about 4:30 am and I couldn't sleep so got up and writing now and then start. It certainly is funny how your head, I mean my head, can go most of the time like a frozen cabbage and then it can give you hell when it starts going. Have been so pleased to find it still functions.[18]

Shortly after completing the first draft of his novel, Hemingway took a trip to Chartres in late September, where he wrote a poignant foreword (see Figure 17 and Appendix II) and reflected on possible titles in an eighth notebook (see Figure 18 and Appendix IV). The foreword, which he never published, shows the profound impact of World War I on the protagonists, as well as on the writer himself:

> There is only this then to say that this generation that is lost has nothing to do with any other younger generation about whose outcome much literary speculation occurred in times past. This is not a question of what kind of mothers flappers make or where is bobbed hair leading us. For whatever is going to happen to this generation of which I am a part has already happened.

Gertude Stein's remark "You are all a lost generation" became a renowned statement characterizing the generation of people who came of age during World War I. The effects of wars on the people who fight in them would be a major theme in Hemingway's literary work. In a famous passage from *A Farewell to Arms*, Hemingway wrote:

> If people bring so much courage to this world the world has to kill them to break them, so of course it kills them. The world breaks everyone and afterward many are strong at the broken

places. But those that will not break it kills. It kills the very good and the very gentle and the very brave impartially. If you are none of these you can be sure it will kill you too but there will be no special hurry.[19]

Characters from *The Sun Also Rises* who were in the war—Jake Barnes, Brett Ashley, and Mike Campbell—are broken physically and mentally. Brett loses her first true love to the war, and no number of liaisons fills the void.[20] Mike Campbell is an alcoholic and Jake is physically wounded, though the specific nature of his wound is never described in the book. In an interview with George Plimpton, Hemingway said that Jake Barnes was not emasculated; his testicles were intact and not damaged, so he was capable of all normal feelings of a man but incapable of consummating them.[21] It was a very particular type of wound of which Hemingway had learned while he was at the Italian front.[22]

My grandfather's statement that everything that was going to happen to his generation had already happened would be profoundly sad if it were not proven by his own life to be utterly untrue. Obviously Hemingway did not know at twenty-six years of age the amazing things he would later accomplish and write about. He reflects again on Gertrude Stein's statement about the Lost Generation in his last book, *A Moveable Feast*, when he looks back on this time in his life. He criticizes Stein for too easily labeling his generation and changes his opinion from the one he expressed in the unpublished foreword.[23]

Hemingway wisely cut the foreword, never developing it beyond the first draft. In fact he added the quote from Gertrude Stein as an epigraph in a late draft only in order to contrast it with the quote from Ecclesiastes (see Figure 20). The inclusion of Stein's quote is important for its underlying conviction that the people who served in World War I were acutely affected by what we now call post-traumatic stress disorder. The post-traumatic stress of war remains a worldwide phenomenon and is a sadly relevant point of reference for readers today.[24] The war is hardly mentioned in *The Sun Also Rises*, though its presence and effects simmer beneath the surface.

From about Christmas 1925 through much of January 1926, Hemingway typed out and revised the manuscript in Schruns, Austria. He tried switching the novel to third-person narration (see Figure 19 and Appendix II) but found that it fell flat, lacking the liveliness of Jake Barnes's first-person narration.[25] He tightened the manuscript by rewriting passages and occasionally adding sections. There was also a great deal of offhand commentary that he cut, examples of which appear in Appendix II. A particularly interesting part that Hemingway revised several times is the waiter's commentary to Jake about the man who was gored during the running of the bulls. The passage echoes the actual goring and death of a young man at the Festival of San Fermín in 1924, one of the first known deaths resulting from the running of the bulls at Pamplona.[26]

By January 28, 1926, Hemingway was back in Paris, en route to New York.[27] After a six-night journey across the Atlantic on the *Mauretania*, he arrived in the city on February 9 and met with Horace Liveright the next day to break his contract with Boni & Liveright. Soon afterward he met with Maxwell Perkins and signed a contract with Scribner, his lifelong publisher. Perkins was so keen to take Hemingway on as a writer that he did not even read the manuscript for *The Sun Also Rises* before drawing up the contract, which included publishing his satirical parody *The Torrents of Spring*. Hemingway continued to revise the novel when he returned to Paris and Schruns (see Figure 11), finally sending off the completed revisions to Perkins from Paris on April 21, 1926.

As Patrick Hemingway observes in his foreword, Ernest Hemingway was inspired by literature as well as personal experience. There are many, often humorous, literary allusions in the book. Jake remarks on Cohn's perception of W. H. Hudson's *The Purple Land*, with its madcap amorous and macho escapades in the Banda Oriental (and underbelly of gritty reality that was apparently lost on Cohn), as a guidebook to what life holds. It is a very funny insight into the depths of Robert Cohn's romanticism and foreshadows his outrageous behavior later in the book.

Another literary influence was F. Scott Fitzgerald's *The Great Gatsby*, which Hemingway had read not long before he began to write *The Sun Also Rises*. Hemingway and Fitzgerald first met in a bar in Paris in 1925 and they continued to see each other in Paris and to correspond. Fitzgerald was very taken with Hemingway's short stories and actively promoted him to his own publisher, Charles Scribner's Sons. In April 1926 in Paris, Hemingway wrote to Fitzgerald about his new novel, joking about its relation to *The Great Gatsby*:

I have tried to follow the outline and spirit of *The Great Gatsby*, but feel I have failed somewhat because of never having been to Long Island. The hero, like Gatsby, is a Lake Superior Salmon

Fisherman. (There are no salmon in Lake Superior.) The action all takes place in Newport, R.I. and the heroine is a girl named Sophie Irene Loeb who kills her mother. The scene in which Sophie gives birth to twins in the death house at Sing Sing where she is waiting to be electrocuted for the murder of the father and sister of her, as then, unborn children I got from Dreiser but practically everything else in the book is either my own or yours. I know you will be glad to see it. *The Sun Also Rises* comes from Sophie's statement as she is strapped into the chair as the current mounts.[28]

After all of Fitzgerald's help securing Hemingway's new contract with Scribner, Hemingway sent a copy of the galleys to him. Fitzgerald, in turn, wrote Hemingway a long letter with significant criticisms.[29] He admonished Hemingway for lazy writing and the inclusion of snide remarks in the opening chapters, warning him that an author cannot play with a reader's attention. Fitzgerald urged him to critically edit the beginning of the book before it went to press.[30] Aside from the opening chapters, however, Fitzgerald was deeply impressed with Hemingway's book. He particularly loved the part where Frances Clyne eviscerates Robert Cohn—high-society subject matter that was the focus of much of his own writing. It is the kind of smart lecture you might expect Dick Diver to get in *Tender Is the Night* or one that could have come out of the mouth of Zelda Fitzgerald. Fitzgerald knew this terrain, and he was impressed that Hemingway got it spot-on. While he thought that Hemingway's treatment of Jake Barnes's war injury was somehow slightly flawed—more like a man in a moral chastity belt—on the whole he found the book to be superb. Hemingway took the advice of his friend and colleague and cut nearly the entire first two chapters. These chapters are included in their entirety in Appendix III. Publicly, however, Hemingway always downplayed Fitzgerald's influence and constructive criticism, even claiming falsely in *A Moveable Feast* that Fitzgerald's advice came after the book was finished. When *The Sun Also Rises* was published to much acclaim, Hemingway wrote to Fitzgerald joking that it could be titled *A Greater Gatsby*.[31]

Maxwell Perkins, on the other hand, had reservations about deleting the opening chapters and suggested working some of the material into an author's introduction.[32] After cutting the first sections, Hemingway also questioned starting the book with Robert Cohn and wrote a false start about this decision (see Appendix II). It was during the rewrite that Hemingway added the remark "Do not think that I am very much impressed" after Robert Cohn's boxing title, setting the strong personal tone of the book that is part of its power.[33] This addition is a small but characteristic example of the careful revisions made to tighten and improve the first draft.[34] Once Hemingway finalized his revisions in the galleys, he had no doubts about cutting the beginning and was certain it was the right decision.[35] The original first chapters of *The Sun Also Rises* contain valuable information about Brett Ashley, Jake Barnes, and Robert Cohn, but I think most readers will agree that leaving them out was the best editorial choice.

The title of the opening chapter—and perhaps the novel, at first—was "Cayetano Ordonez, 'Niño de la Palma,' " the original name of the bullfighter. However, once Hemingway switched to the notebooks, the working title penned on the cover of each was *Fiesta: A Novel*. In the unpublished foreword he considers *The Lost Generation: A Novel*, in reference to Gertrude Stein's comment to the garage owner, but decided against it because he did not want to use a foreign-language word or its translation for the title, stating that *perdu* loses part of its meaning in translation to "lost." Hemingway said that he usually chose the title of his books at the end, and that the Bible was an especially good source for titles. This was true of *The Sun Also Rises*, whose title is taken from the Old Testament; the passage in Ecclesiastes is quoted at the beginning of the novel. It was one of five biblical titles that he considered (see Figure 18 and Appendix IV).[36]

The Sun Also Rises is a special book in the Hemingway canon, as there is not another novel quite like it in his oeuvre. The story that comes closest is "The Butterfly and the Tank," which John Steinbeck called "one of the very few finest stories of all time."[37] Despite its hollowed-out and emotionally exhausted characters, the way that *The Sun Also Rises* is written feels fresh and engaging. It remains a great work of literature that will continue to delight and inspire readers for generations to come. With this new Hemingway Library Edition, the reader is better able to understand how Ernest Hemingway conceived and wrote his first novel, how he turned imperfect reality into a near-perfect work of fiction.

Seán Hemingway

This book is for Hadley
and for John Hadley Nicanor

"You are all a lost generation."

—GERTRUDE STEIN IN CONVERSATION

"One generation passeth away, and another generation cometh; but the earth abideth forever. . . . The sun also ariseth, and the sun goeth down, and hasteth to the place where he arose. . . . The wind goeth toward the south, and turneth about unto the north; it whirleth about continually, and the wind returneth again according to his circuits. . . . All the rivers run into the sea; yet the sea is not full; unto the place from whence the rivers come, thither they return again."

—ECCLESIASTES

BOOK ONE

— 1 —

Robert Cohn was once middleweight boxing champion of Princeton. Do not think that I am very much impressed by that as a boxing title, but it meant a lot to Cohn. He cared nothing for boxing, in fact he disliked it, but he learned it painfully and thoroughly to counteract the feeling of inferiority and shyness he had felt on being treated as a Jew at Princeton. There was a certain inner comfort in knowing he could knock down anybody who was snooty to him, although, being very shy and a thoroughly nice boy, he never fought except in the gym. He was Spider Kelly's star pupil. Spider Kelly taught all his young gentlemen to box like featherweights, no matter whether they weighed one hundred and five or two hundred and five pounds. But it seemed to fit Cohn. He was really very fast. He was so good that Spider promptly overmatched him and got his nose permanently flattened. This increased Cohn's distaste for boxing, but it gave him a certain satisfaction of some strange sort, and it certainly improved his nose. In his last year at Princeton he read too much and took to wearing spectacles. I never met any one of his class who remembered him. They did not even remember that he was middleweight boxing champion.

I mistrust all frank and simple people, especially when their stories hold together, and I always had a suspicion that perhaps Robert Cohn had never been middleweight boxing champion, and that perhaps a horse had stepped on his face, or that maybe his mother had been frightened or seen something, or that he had, maybe, bumped into something as a young child, but I finally had somebody verify the story from Spider Kelly. Spider Kelly not only remembered Cohn. He had often wondered what had become of him.

Robert Cohn was a member, through his father, of one of the richest Jewish families in New York, and through his mother of one of the oldest. At the military school where he prepped for Princeton, and played a very good end on the football team, no one had made him race-conscious. No one had ever made him feel he was a Jew, and hence any different from anybody else, until he went to Princeton. He was a nice boy, a friendly boy, and very shy, and it made him bitter. He took it out in boxing, and he came out of Princeton with painful self-consciousness and the flattened nose, and was married by the first girl who was nice to him. He was married five years, had three children, lost most of the fifty thousand dollars his father left him, the balance of the estate having gone to his mother, hardened into a rather unattractive mould under domestic unhappiness with a rich wife; and just when he had made up his mind to leave his wife she left him and went off with a miniature-painter. As he had been thinking for months about leaving his wife and had not done it because it would be too cruel to deprive her of himself, her departure was a very healthful shock.

The divorce was arranged and Robert Cohn went out to the Coast. In California he fell among literary people and, as he still had a little of the fifty thousand left, in a short time he was backing a review of the Arts. The review commenced publication in Carmel, California, and finished in Provincetown, Massachusetts. By that time Cohn, who had been regarded purely as an angel, and whose name had appeared on the editorial page merely as a member of the advisory board, had become the sole editor. It was his money and he discovered he liked the authority of editing. He was sorry when the magazine became too expensive and he had to give it up.

By that time, though, he had other things to worry about. He had been taken in hand by a lady who hoped to rise with the magazine. She was very forceful, and Cohn never had a chance of not being taken in hand. Also he was sure that he loved her. When this lady saw that the magazine was not going to rise, she became a little disgusted with Cohn and decided that she might as well get what there was to get while there was still something available, so she urged that they go to Europe, where Cohn could write. They came to Europe, where the lady had been educated, and stayed three years. During these three years, the first spent in travel, the last two in Paris, Robert Cohn had two friends, Braddocks and myself. Braddocks was his literary friend. I was his tennis friend.

The lady who had him, her name was Frances, found toward the end of the second year that her looks were going, and her attitude toward Robert changed from one of careless possession and exploitation to the absolute determination that he should marry her. During this time Robert's mother had settled an allowance on him, about three hundred dollars a month. During two years and a half I do not believe that Robert Cohn looked at another woman. He was fairly happy, except that, like many people living in Europe, he would rather have been in America, and he had discovered writing. He wrote a novel, and it was not really such a bad novel as the critics later called it, although it was a very poor novel. He read many books, played bridge, played tennis, and boxed at a local gymnasium.

I first became aware of his lady's attitude toward him one night after the three of us had dined together. We had dined at l'Avenue's and afterward went to the Café de Versailles for coffee. We had several *fines* after the coffee, and I said I must be going. Cohn had been talking about the two of us going off somewhere on a weekend trip. He wanted to get out of town and get in a good walk. I suggested we fly to Strasbourg and walk up to Saint Odile, or somewhere or other in Alsace. "I know a girl in Strasbourg who can show us the town," I said.

Somebody kicked me under the table. I thought it was accidental and went on: "She's been there two years and knows everything there is to know about the town. She's a swell girl."

I was kicked again under the table and, looking, saw Frances, Robert's lady, her chin lifting and her face hardening.

"Hell," I said, "why go to Strasbourg? We could go up to Bruges, or to the Ardennes."

Cohn looked relieved. I was not kicked again. I said good-night and went out. Cohn said he wanted to buy a paper and would walk to the corner with me. "For God's sake," he said, "why did you say that about that girl in Strasbourg for? Didn't you see Frances?"

"No, why should I? If I know an American girl that lives in Strasbourg what the hell is it to Frances?"

"It doesn't make any difference. Any girl. I couldn't go, that would be all."

"Don't be silly."

"You don't know Frances. Any girl at all. Didn't you see the way she looked?"

"Oh, well," I said, "let's go to Senlis."

"Don't get sore."

"I'm not sore. Senlis is a good place and we can stay at the Grand Cerf and take a hike in the woods and come home."

"Good, that will be fine."

"Well, I'll see you to-morrow at the courts," I said.

"Good-night, Jake," he said, and started back to the café.

"You forgot to get your paper," I said.

"That's so." He walked with me up to the kiosque at the corner. "You are not sore, are you, Jake?" He turned with the paper in his hand.

"No, why should I be?"

"See you at tennis," he said. I watched him walk back to the café holding his paper. I rather liked him and evidently she led him quite a life.

— 2 —

That winter Robert Cohn went over to America with his novel, and it was accepted by a fairly good publisher. His going made an awful row I heard, and I think that was where Frances lost him, because several women were nice to him in New York, and when he came back he was quite changed. He was more enthusiastic about America than ever, and he was not so simple, and he was not so nice. The publishers had praised his novel pretty highly and it rather went to his head. Then several women had put themselves out to be nice to him, and his horizons had all shifted. For four years his horizon had been absolutely limited to his wife. For three years, or almost three years, he had never seen beyond Frances. I am sure he had never been in love in his life.

He had married on the rebound from the rotten time he had in college, and Frances took him on the rebound from his discovery that he had not been everything to his first wife. He was not in love yet but he realized that he was an attractive quantity to women, and that the fact of a woman caring for him and wanting to live with him was not simply a divine miracle. This changed him so that he was not so pleasant to have around. Also, playing for higher stakes than he could afford in some rather steep bridge games with his New York connections, he had held cards and won several hundred dollars. It made him rather vain of his bridge game, and he talked several times of how a man could always make a living at bridge if he were ever forced to.

Then there was another thing. He had been reading W. H. Hudson. That sounds like an innocent occupation, but Cohn had read and reread "The Purple Land." "The Purple Land" is a very sinister book if read too late in life. It recounts splendid imaginary amorous adventures of a perfect English gentleman in an intensely romantic land, the scenery of which is very well described. For a man to take it at thirty-four as a guide-book to what life holds is about as safe as it would be for a man of the same age to enter Wall Street direct from a French convent, equipped with a complete set of the more practical Alger books. Cohn, I believe, took every word of "The Purple Land" as literally as though it had been an R. G. Dun report. You understand me, he made some reservations, but on the whole the book to him was sound. It was all that was needed to set him off. I did not realize the extent to which it had set him off until one day he came into my office.

"Hello, Robert," I said. "Did you come in to cheer me up?"

"Would you like to go to South America, Jake?" he asked.

"No."

"Why not?"

"I don't know. I never wanted to go. Too expensive. You can see all the South Americans you want in Paris anyway."

"They're not the real South Americans."

"They look awfully real to me."

I had a boat train to catch with a week's mail stories, and only half of them written.

"Do you know any dirt?" I asked.

"No."

"None of your exalted connections getting divorces?"

"No; listen, Jake. If I handled both our expenses, would you go to South America with me?"

"Why me?"

"You can talk Spanish. And it would be more fun with two of us."

"No," I said, "I like this town and I go to Spain in the summertime."

"All my life I've wanted to go on a trip like that," Cohn said. He sat down. "I'll be too old before I can ever do it."

"Don't be a fool," I said. "You can go anywhere you want. You've got plenty of money."

"I know. But I can't get started."

"Cheer up," I said. "All countries look just like the moving pictures."

But I felt sorry for him. He had it badly.

"I can't stand it to think my life is going so fast and I'm not really living it."

"Nobody ever lives their life all the way up except bull-fighters." *Jacky*

"I'm not interested in bull-fighters. That's an abnormal life. I want to go back in the country in South America. We could have a great trip."

"Did you ever think about going to British East Africa to shoot?"

"No, I wouldn't like that."

"I'd go there with you."

"No; that doesn't interest me."

"That's because you never read a book about it. Go on and read a book all full of love affairs with the beautiful shiny black princesses."

"I want to go to South America."

He had a hard, Jewish, stubborn streak.

"Come on down-stairs and have a drink."

"Aren't you working?"

"No," I said. We went down the stairs to the café on the ground floor. I had discovered that was the best way to get rid of friends. Once you had a drink all you had to say was: "Well, I've got to get back and get off some cables," and it was done. It is very important to discover graceful exits like that in the newspaper business, where it is such an important part of the ethics that you should never seem to be working. Anyway, we went down-stairs to the bar and had a whiskey and soda. Cohn looked at the bottles in bins around the wall. "This is a good place," he said.

"There's a lot of liquor," I agreed.

"Listen, Jake," he leaned forward on the bar. "Don't you ever get the feeling that all your life is going by and you're not taking advantage of it? Do you realize you've lived nearly half the time you have to live already?"

"Yes, every once in a while."

"Do you know that in about thirty-five years more we'll be dead?"

"What the hell, Robert," I said. "What the hell."

"I'm serious."

"It's one thing I don't worry about," I said.

"You ought to."

"I've had plenty to worry about one time or other. I'm through worrying."

"Well, I want to go to South America."

"Listen, Robert, going to another country doesn't make any difference. I've tried all that. You can't get away from yourself by moving from one place to another. There's nothing to that."

"But you've never been to South America."

"South America hell! If you went there the way you feel now it would be exactly the same. This is a good town. Why don't you start living your life in Paris?"

"I'm sick of Paris, and I'm sick of the Quarter."

"Stay away from the Quarter. Cruise around by yourself and see what happens to you."

"Nothing happens to me. I walked alone all one night and nothing happened except a bicycle cop stopped me and asked to see my papers."

"Wasn't the town nice at night?"

"I don't care for Paris."

So there you were. I was sorry for him, but it was not a thing you could do anything about, because right away you ran up against the two stubbornnesses: South America could fix it and he did not like Paris. He got the first idea out of a book, and I suppose the second came out of a book too.

"Well," I said, "I've got to go up-stairs and get off some cables."

"Do you really have to go?"

"Yes, I've got to get these cables off."

"Do you mind if I come up and sit around the office?"

"No, come on up."

He sat in the outer room and read the papers, and the Editor and Publisher and I worked hard for two hours. Then I sorted out the carbons, stamped on a by-line, put the stuff in a couple of big manila envelopes and rang for a boy to take them to the Gare St. Lazare. I went out into the other room and there was Robert Cohn asleep in the big chair. He was asleep with his head on his arms. I did not like to wake him up, but I wanted to lock the office and shove off. I put my hand on his shoulder. He shook his head. "I can't do it," he said, and put his head deeper into his arms. "I can't do it. Nothing will make me do it."

"Robert," I said, and shook him by the shoulder. He looked up. He smiled and blinked.

"Did I talk out loud just then?"

"Something. But it wasn't clear."

"God, what a rotten dream!"

"Did the typewriter put you to sleep?"

"Guess so. I didn't sleep all last night."

"What was the matter?"

"Talking," he said.

I could picture it. I have a rotten habit of picturing the bedroom scenes of my friends. We went out to the Café Napolitain to have an *apéritif* and watch the evening crowd on the Boulevard.

It was a warm spring night and I sat at a table on the terrace of the Napol-itain after Robert had gone, watching it get dark and the electric signs come on, and the red and green stop-and-go traffic-signal, and the crowd going by, and the horse-cabs clippety-clopping along at the edge of the solid taxi traffic, and the *poules* going by, singly and in pairs, looking for the evening meal. I watched a good-looking girl walk past the table and watched her go up the street and lost sight of her, and watched another, and then saw the first one coming back again. She went by once more and I caught her eye, and she came over and sat down at the table. The waiter came up.

"Well, what will you drink?" I asked.

"Pernod."

"That's not good for little girls."

"Little girl yourself. Dites garçon, un pernod."

"A pernod for me, too."

"What's the matter?" she asked. "Going on a party?"

"Sure. Aren't you?"

"I don't know. You never know in this town."

"Don't you like Paris?"

"No."

"Why don't you go somewhere else?"

"Isn't anywhere else."

"You're happy, all right."

"Happy, hell!"

Pernod is greenish imitation absinthe. When you add water it turns milky. It tastes like licorice and it has a good uplift, but it drops you just as far. We sat and drank it, and the girl looked sullen.

"Well," I said, "are you going to buy me a dinner?"

She grinned and I saw why she made a point of not laughing. With her mouth closed she was a rather pretty girl. I paid for the saucers and we walked out to the street. I hailed a horse-cab and the driver pulled up at the curb. Settled back in the slow, smoothly rolling *fiacre* we moved up the Avenue de l'Opéra, passed the locked doors of the shops, their windows lighted, the Avenue broad and shiny and almost deserted. The cab passed the New York *Herald* bureau with the window full of clocks.

"What are all the clocks for?" she asked.

"They show the hour all over America."

"Don't kid me."

We turned off the Avenue up the Rue des Pyramides, through the traffic of the Rue de Rivoli, and through a dark gate into the Tuileries. She cuddled against me and I put my arm around her. She looked up to be kissed. She touched me with one hand and I put her hand away.

"Never mind."

"What's the matter? You sick?"

"Yes."

"Everybody's sick. I'm sick, too."

We came out of the Tuileries into the light and crossed the Seine and then turned up the Rue des Saints Pères.

"You oughtn't to drink pernod if you're sick."

"You neither."

"It doesn't make any difference with me. It doesn't make any difference with a woman."

"What are you called?"

"Georgette. How are you called?"

"Jacob."

"That's a Flemish name."

"American too."

"You're not Flamand?"

"No, American."

"Good, I detest Flamands."

By this time we were at the restaurant. I called to the *cocher* to stop.

We got out and Georgette did not like the looks of the place. "This is no great thing of a restaurant."

"No," I said. "Maybe you would rather go to Foyot's. Why don't you keep the cab and go on?"

I had picked her up because of a vague sentimental idea that it would be nice to eat with some one. It was a long time since I had dined with a *poule*, and I had forgotten how dull it could be. We went into the restaurant, passed Madame Lavigne at the desk and into a little room. Georgette cheered up a little under the food.

"It isn't bad here," she said. "It isn't chic, but the food is all right."

"Better than you eat in Liège."

"Brussels, you mean."

We had another bottle of wine and Georgette made a joke. She smiled and showed all her bad teeth, and we touched glasses.

"You're not a bad type," she said. "It's a shame you're sick. We get on well. What's the matter with you, anyway?"

"I got hurt in the war," I said.

"Oh, that dirty war."

We would probably have gone on and discussed the war and agreed that it was in reality a calamity for civilization, and perhaps would have been better avoided. I was bored enough. Just then from the other room some one called: "Barnes! I say, Barnes! Jacob Barnes!"

"It's a friend calling me," I explained, and went out.

There was Braddocks at a big table with a party: Cohn, Frances Clyne, Mrs. Braddocks, several people I did not know.

"You're coming to the dance, aren't you?" Braddocks asked.

"What dance?"

"Why, the dancings. Don't you know we've revived them?" Mrs. Braddocks put in.

"You must come, Jake. We're all going," Frances said from the end of the table. She was tall and had a smile.

"Of course, he's coming," Braddocks said. "Come in and have coffee with us, Barnes."

"Right."

"And bring your friend," said Mrs. Braddocks laughing. She was a Canadian and had all their easy social graces.

"Thanks, we'll be in," I said. I went back to the small room.

"Who are your friends?" Georgette asked.

"Writers and artists."

"There are lots of those on this side of the river."

"Too many."

"I think so. Still, some of them make money."

"Oh, yes."

We finished the meal and the wine. "Come on," I said. "We're going to have coffee with the others."

Georgette opened her bag, made a few passes at her face as she looked in the little mirror, re-defined her lips with the lip-stick, and straightened her hat.

"Good," she said.

We went into the room full of people and Braddocks and the men at his table stood up.

"I wish to present my fiancée, Mademoiselle Georgette Leblanc," I said. Georgette smiled that wonderful smile, and we shook hands all round.

"Are you related to Georgette Leblanc, the singer?" Mrs. Braddocks asked.

"Connais pas," Georgette answered.

"But you have the same name," Mrs. Braddocks insisted cordially.

"No," said Georgette. "Not at all. My name is Hobin."

"But Mr. Barnes introduced you as Mademoiselle Georgette Leblanc. Surely he did," insisted Mrs. Braddocks, who in the excitement of talking French was liable to have no idea what she was saying.

"He's a fool," Georgette said.

"Oh, it was a joke, then," Mrs. Braddocks said.

"Yes," said Georgette. "To laugh at."

"Did you hear that, Henry?" Mrs. Braddocks called down the table to Braddocks. "Mr. Barnes introduced his fiancée as Mademoiselle Leblanc, and her name is actually Hobin."

"Of course, darling. Mademoiselle Hobin, I've known her for a very long time."

"Oh, Mademoiselle Hobin," Frances Clyne called, speaking French very rapidly and not seeming so proud and astonished as Mrs. Braddocks at its coming out really French. "Have you been in Paris long? Do you like it here? You love Paris, do you not?"

"Who's she?" Georgette turned to me. "Do I have to talk to her?"

She turned to Frances, sitting smiling, her hands folded, her head poised on her long neck, her lips pursed ready to start talking again.

"No, I don't like Paris. It's expensive and dirty."

"Really? I find it so extraordinarily clean. One of the cleanest cities in all Europe."

"I find it dirty."

"How strange! But perhaps you have not been here very long."

"I've been here long enough."

"But it does have nice people in it. One must grant that."

Georgette turned to me. "You have nice friends."

Frances was a little drunk and would have liked to have kept it up but the coffee came, and Lavigne with the liqueurs, and after that we all went out and started for Braddocks's dancing-club.

The dancing-club was a *bal musette* in the Rue de la Montagne Sainte Geneviève. Five nights a week the working people of the Pantheon quarter danced there. One night a week it was the dancing-club. On Monday nights it was closed. When we arrived it was quite empty, except for a policeman sitting near the door, the wife of the proprietor back of the zinc bar, and the proprietor himself. The daughter of the house came down-stairs as we went in. There were long benches, and tables ran across the room, and at the far end a dancing-floor.

"I wish people would come earlier," Braddocks said. The daughter came up and wanted to know what we would drink. The proprietor got up on a high stool beside the dancing-floor and began to play the accordion. He had a string of bells around one of his ankles and beat time with his foot as he played. Every one danced. It was hot and we came off the floor perspiring.

"My God," Georgette said. "What a box to sweat in!"

"It's hot."

"Hot, my God!"

"Take off your hat."

"That's a good idea."

Some one asked Georgette to dance, and I went over to the bar. It was really very hot and the accordion music was pleasant in the hot night. I drank a beer, standing in the doorway and getting the cool breath of wind from the street. Two taxis were coming down the steep street. They both stopped in front of the Bal. A crowd of young men, some in jerseys and some in their shirt-sleeves, got out. I could see their hands and newly washed, wavy hair in the light from the door. The policeman standing by the door looked at me and smiled. They came in. As they went in, under the light I saw white hands, wavy hair, white faces, grimacing, gesturing, talking. With them was Brett. She looked very lovely and she was very much with them.

One of them saw Georgette and said: "I do declare. There is an actual harlot. I'm going to dance with her, Lett. You watch me."

The tall dark one, called Lett, said: "Don't you be rash."

The wavy blond one answered: "Don't you worry, dear." And with them was Brett.

I was very angry. Somehow they always made me angry. I know they are supposed to be amusing, and you should be tolerant, but I wanted to swing on one, any one, anything to shatter that superior, simpering composure. Instead, I walked down the street and had a beer at the bar at the next Bal. The beer was not good and I had a worse cognac to take the taste out of my mouth. When I came back to the Bal there was a crowd on the floor and Georgette was dancing with the tall blond youth, who danced big-hippily, carrying his head on one side, his eyes lifted as he danced. As soon as the music stopped another one of them asked her to dance. She had been taken up by them. I knew then that they would all dance with her. They are like that.

I sat down at a table. Cohn was sitting there. Frances was dancing. Mrs. Braddocks brought up somebody and introduced him as Robert Prentiss. He was from New York by way of Chicago, and was a rising new novelist. He had some sort of an English accent. I asked him to have a drink.

"Thanks so much," he said, "I've just had one."

"Have another."

"Thanks, I will then."

We got the daughter of the house over and each had a *fine à l'eau*.

"You're from Kansas City, they tell me," he said.

"Yes."

"Do you find Paris amusing?"

"Yes."

"Really?"

I was a little drunk. Not drunk in any positive sense but just enough to be careless.

"For God's sake," I said, "yes. Don't you?"

"Oh, how charmingly you get angry," he said. "I wish I had that faculty."

I got up and walked over toward the dancing-floor. Mrs. Braddocks followed me. "Don't be cross with Robert," she said. "He's still only a child, you know."

"I wasn't cross," I said. "I just thought perhaps I was going to throw up."

"Your fiancée is having a great success," Mrs. Braddocks looked out on the floor where Georgette was dancing in the arms of the tall, dark one, called Lett.

"Isn't she?" I said.

"Rather," said Mrs. Braddocks.

Cohn came up. "Come on, Jake," he said, "have a drink." We walked over to the bar. "What's the matter with you? You seem all worked up over something?"

"Nothing. This whole show makes me sick is all."

Brett came up to the bar.

"Hello, you chaps."

"Hello, Brett," I said. "Why aren't you tight?"

"Never going to get tight any more. I say, give a chap a brandy and soda."

She stood holding the glass and I saw Robert Cohn looking at her. He looked a great deal as his compatriot must have looked when he saw the promised land. Cohn, of course, was much younger. But he had that look of eager, deserving expectation.

Brett was damned good-looking. She wore a slipover jersey sweater and a tweed skirt, and her hair was brushed back like a boy's. She started all that. She was built with curves like the hull of a racing yacht, and you missed none of it with that wool jersey.

"It's a fine crowd you're with, Brett," I said.

"Aren't they lovely? And you, my dear. Where did you get it?"

"At the Napolitain."

"And have you had a lovely evening?"

"Oh, priceless," I said.

Brett laughed. "It's wrong of you, Jake. It's an insult to all of us. Look at Frances there, and Jo."

This for Cohn's benefit.

"It's in restraint of trade," Brett said. She laughed again.

"You're wonderfully sober," I said.

"Yes. Aren't I? And when one's with the crowd I'm with, one can drink in such safety, too."

The music started and Robert Cohn said: "Will you dance this with me, Lady Brett?"

Brett smiled at him. "I've promised to dance this with Jacob," she laughed. "You've a hell of a biblical name, Jake."

"How about the next?" asked Cohn.

"We're going," Brett said. "We've a date up at Montmartre."

Dancing, I looked over Brett's shoulder and saw Cohn, standing at the bar, still watching her.

"You've made a new one there," I said to her.

"Don't talk about it. Poor chap. I never knew it till just now."

"Oh, well," I said. "I suppose you like to add them up."

"Don't talk like a fool."

"You do."

"Oh, well. What if I do?"

"Nothing," I said. We were dancing to the accordion and some one was playing the banjo. It was hot and I felt happy. We passed close to Georgette dancing with another one of them.

"What possessed you to bring her?"

"I don't know, I just brought her."

"You're getting damned romantic."

"No, bored."

"Now?"

"No, not now."

"Let's get out of here. She's well taken care of."

"Do you want to?"

"Would I ask you if I didn't want to?"

We left the floor and I took my coat off a hanger on the wall and put it on. Brett stood by the bar. Cohn was talking to her. I stopped at the bar and asked them for an envelope. The patronne found one. I took a fifty-franc note from my pocket, put it in the envelope, sealed it, and handed it to the patronne.

"If the girl I came with asks for me, will you give her this?" I said. "If she goes out with one of those gentlemen, will you save this for me?"

"C'est entendu, Monsieur," the patronne said. "You go now? So early?"

"Yes," I said.

We started out the door. Cohn was still talking to Brett. She said good night and took my arm. "Good night, Cohn," I said. Outside in the street we looked for a taxi.

"You're going to lose your fifty francs," Brett said.

"Oh, yes."

"No taxis."

"We could walk up to the Pantheon and get one."

"Come on and we'll get a drink in the pub next door and send for one."

"You wouldn't walk across the street."

"Not if I could help it."

We went into the next bar and I sent a waiter for a taxi.

"Well," I said, "we're out away from them."

We stood against the tall zinc bar and did not talk and looked at each other. The waiter came and said the taxi was outside. Brett pressed my hand hard. I gave the waiter a franc and we went out. "Where should I tell him?" I asked.

"Oh, tell him to drive around."

I told the driver to go to the Parc Montsouris, and got in, and slammed the door. Brett was leaning back in the corner, her eyes closed. I sat beside her. The cab started with a jerk.

"Oh, darling, I've been so miserable," Brett said.

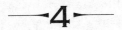

The taxi went up the hill, passed the lighted square, then on into the dark, still climbing, then levelled out onto a dark street behind St. Etienne du Mont, went smoothly down the asphalt, passed the trees and the standing bus at the Place de la Contrescarpe, then turned onto the cobbles of the Rue Mouffetard. There were lighted bars and late open shops on each side of the street. We were sitting apart and we jolted close together going down the old street. Brett's hat was off. Her head was back. I saw her face in the lights from the open shops, then it was dark, then I saw her face clearly as we came out on the Avenue des Gobelins. The street was torn up and men were working on the car-tracks by the light of acetylene flares. Brett's face was white and the long line of her neck showed in the bright light of the flares. The street was dark again and I kissed her. Our lips were tight together and then she turned away and pressed against the corner of the seat, as far away as she could get. Her head was down.

"Don't touch me," she said. "Please don't touch me."

"What's the matter?"

"I can't stand it."

"Oh, Brett."

"You mustn't. You must know. I can't stand it, that's all. Oh, darling, please understand!"

"Don't you love me?"

"Love you? I simply turn all to jelly when you touch me."

"Isn't there anything we can do about it?"

She was sitting up now. My arm was around her and she was leaning back against me, and we were quite calm. She was looking into my eyes with that way she had of looking that made you wonder whether she really saw out of her own eyes. They would look on and on after every one else's eyes in the world would have stopped looking. She looked as though there were nothing on earth she would not look at like that, and really she was afraid of so many things.

"And there's not a damn thing we could do," I said.

"I don't know," she said. "I don't want to go through that hell again."

"We'd better keep away from each other."

"But, darling, I have to see you. It isn't all that you know."

"No, but it always gets to be."

"That's my fault. Don't we pay for all the things we do, though?"

She had been looking into my eyes all the time. Her eyes had different depths, sometimes they seemed perfectly flat. Now you could see all the way into them.

"When I think of the hell I've put chaps through. I'm paying for it all now."

"Don't talk like a fool," I said. "Besides, what happened to me is supposed to be funny. I never think about it."

"Oh, no. I'll lay you don't."

"Well, let's shut up about it."

"I laughed about it too, myself, once." She wasn't looking at me. "A friend of my brother's came home that way from Mons. It seemed like a hell of a joke. Chaps never know anything, do they?"

"No," I said. "Nobody ever knows anything."

I was pretty well through with the subject. At one time or another I had probably considered it from most of its various angles, including the one that certain injuries or imperfections are a subject of merriment while remaining quite serious for the person possessing them.

"It's funny," I said. "It's very funny. And it's a lot of fun, too, to be in love."

"Do you think so?" her eyes looked flat again.

"I don't mean fun that way. In a way it's an enjoyable feeling."

"No," she said. "I think it's hell on earth."

"It's good to see each other."

"No. I don't think it is."

"Don't you want to?"

"I have to."

We were sitting now like two strangers. On the right was the Parc Montsouris. The restaurant where they have the pool of live trout and where you can sit and look out over the park was closed and dark. The driver leaned his head around.

"Where do you want to go?" I asked. Brett turned her head away.

"Oh, go to the Select."

"Café Select," I told the driver. "Boulevard Montparnasse." We drove straight down, turning around the Lion de Belfort that guards the passing Montrouge trams. Brett looked straight ahead. On the Boulevard Raspail, with the lights of Montparnasse in sight, Brett said: "Would you mind very much if I asked you to do something?"

"Don't be silly."

"Kiss me just once more before we get there."

When the taxi stopped I got out and paid. Brett came out putting on her hat. She gave me her hand as she stepped down. Her hand was shaky. "I say, do I look too much of a mess?" She pulled her man's felt hat down and started in for the bar. Inside, against the bar and at tables, were most of the crowd who had been at the dance.

"Hello, you chaps," Brett said. "I'm going to have a drink."

"Oh, Brett! Brett!" the little Greek portrait-painter, who called himself a duke, and whom everybody called Zizi, pushed up to her. "I got something fine to tell you."

"Hello, Zizi," Brett said.

"I want you to meet a friend," Zizi said. A fat man came up.

"Count Mippipopolous, meet my friend Lady Ashley."

"How do you do?" said Brett.

"Well, does your Ladyship have a good time here in Paris?" asked Count Mippipopolous, who wore an elk's tooth on his watch-chain.

"Rather," said Brett.

"Paris is a fine town all right," said the count. "But I guess you have pretty big doings yourself over in London."

"Oh, yes," said Brett. "Enormous."

Braddocks called to me from a table. "Barnes," he said, "have a drink. That girl of yours got in a frightful row."

"What about?"

"Something the patronne's daughter said. A corking row. She was rather splendid, you know. Showed her yellow card and demanded the patronne's daughter's too. I say it was a row."

"What finally happened?"

"Oh, some one took her home. Not a bad-looking girl. Wonderful command of the idiom. Do stay and have a drink."

"No," I said. "I must shove off. Seen Cohn?"

"He went home with Frances," Mrs. Braddocks put in.

"Poor chap, he looks awfully down," Braddocks said.

"I dare say he is," said Mrs. Braddocks.

"I have to shove off," I said. "Good night."

I said good night to Brett at the bar. The count was buying champagne. "Will you take a glass of wine with us, sir?" he asked.

"No. Thanks awfully. I have to go."

"Really going?" Brett asked.

"Yes," I said. "I've got a rotten headache."

"I'll see you to-morrow?"

"Come in at the office."

"Hardly."

"Well, where will I see you?"

"Anywhere around five o'clock."

"Make it the other side of town then."

"Good. I'll be at the Crillon at five."

"Try and be there," I said.

"Don't worry," Brett said. "I've never let you down, have I?"

"Heard from Mike?"

"Letter to-day."

"Good night, sir," said the count.

I went out onto the sidewalk and walked down toward the Boulevard St. Michel, passed the tables of the Rotonde, still crowded, looked across the street at the Dôme, its tables running out to the edge of the pavement. Some one waved at me from a table, I did not see who it was and went on. I wanted to get home. The Boulevard Montparnasse was deserted. Lavigne's was closed tight, and they were stacking the tables outside the Closerie des Lilas. I passed Ney's statue standing among the new-leaved chestnut-trees in the arc-light. There was a faded purple wreath leaning against the base. I stopped and read the inscription: from the Bonapartist Groups, some date; I forget. He looked very fine, Marshal Ney in his top-boots, gesturing with his sword among the green new horse-chestnut leaves. My flat was just across the street, a little way down the Boulevard St. Michel.

There was a light in the concierge's room and I knocked on the door and she gave me my mail. I wished her good night and went up-stairs. There were two letters and some papers. I looked at them under the gas-light in the dining-room. The letters were from the States. One was a bank statement. It showed a balance of $2432.60. I got out my check-book and deducted four checks drawn since the first of the month, and discovered I had a balance of $1832.60. I wrote this on the back of the statement. The other letter was a wedding announcement. Mr. and Mrs. Aloysius Kirby announce the marriage of their daughter Katherine—I knew neither the girl nor the man she was marrying. They must be cir-cularizing the town. It was a funny name. I felt sure I could remember anybody with a name like Aloysius. It was a good Catholic name. There was a crest on the announcement. Like Zizi the Greek duke. And that count. The count was funny. Brett had a title, too. Lady Ashley. To hell with Brett. To hell with you, Lady Ashley.

I lit the lamp beside the bed, turned off the gas, and opened the wide windows. The bed was far back from the windows, and I sat with the windows open and undressed by the bed. Outside a night train, running on the street-car tracks, went by carrying vegetables to the markets. They were noisy at night when you could not sleep. Undressing, I looked at myself in the mirror of the big armoire beside the bed. That was a typically French way to furnish a room. Practical, too, I suppose. Of all the ways to be wounded. I suppose it was funny. I put on my pajamas and got into bed. I had the two bull-fight papers, and I took their wrap-pers off. One was orange. The other yellow. They would both have the same news, so whichever I read first would spoil the other. *Le Toril* was the better paper, so I started to read it. I read it all the way through, including the Petite Correspondance and the Cornigrams. I blew out the lamp. Perhaps I would be able to sleep.

My head started to work. The old grievance. Well, it was a rotten way to be wounded and flying on a joke front like the Italian. In the Italian hospital we were going to form a society. It had a funny name in Italian. I wonder what became of the others, the Italians. That was in the Ospedale Maggiore in Milano, Padiglione Ponte. The next building was the Padiglione Zonda. There was a statue of Ponte, or maybe it was Zonda. That was where the liaison colonel came to visit me. That was funny. That was about the first funny thing. I was all bandaged up. But they had told him about it. Then he made that wonderful speech: "You, a foreigner, an Englishman" (any foreigner was an Englishman) "have given more than your life." What a speech! I would like to have it illuminated to hang in the office. He never laughed. He was putting himself in my place, I guess. "Che mala fortuna! Che mala fortuna!"

I never used to realize it, I guess. I try and play it along and just not make trouble for people. Probably I never would have had any trouble if I hadn't run into Brett when they shipped me to England. I suppose she only wanted what she couldn't have. Well, people were that way. To hell with people. The Catholic Church had an awfully good way of handling all that. Good advice, anyway. Not to think about it. Oh, it was swell advice. Try and take it sometime. Try and take it.

I lay awake thinking and my mind jumping around. Then I couldn't keep away from it, and I started to think about Brett and all the rest of it went away. I was thinking about Brett and my mind stopped jumping around and started to go in sort of smooth waves. Then all of a sudden I started to cry. Then after a while it was better and I lay in bed and listened to the heavy trams go by and way down the street, and then I went to sleep.

I woke up. There was a row going on outside. I listened and I thought I recognized a voice. I put on a dressing-gown and went to the door. The concierge was talking down-stairs. She was very angry. I heard my name and called down the stairs.

"Is that you, Monsieur Barnes?" the concierge called.

"Yes. It's me."

"There's a species of woman here who's waked the whole street up. What kind of a dirty business at this time of night! She says she must see you. I've told her you're asleep."

Then I heard Brett's voice. Half asleep I had been sure it was Georgette. I don't know why. She could not have known my address.

"Will you send her up, please?"

Brett came up the stairs. I saw she was quite drunk. "Silly thing to do," she said. "Make an awful row. I say, you weren't asleep, were you?"

"What did you think I was doing?"

"Don't know. What time is it?"

I looked at the clock. It was half-past four. "Had no idea what hour it was," Brett said. "I say, can a chap sit down? Don't be cross, darling. Just left the count. He brought me here."

"What's he like?" I was getting brandy and soda and glasses.

"Just a little," said Brett. "Don't try and make me drunk. The count? Oh, rather. He's quite one of us."

"Is he a count?"

"Here's how. I rather think so, you know. Deserves to be, anyhow. Knows hell's own amount about people. Don't know where he got it all. Owns a chain of sweetshops in the States."

She sipped at her glass.

"Think he called it a chain. Something like that. Linked them all up. Told me a little about it. Damned interesting. He's one of us, though. Oh, quite. No doubt. One can always tell."

She took another drink.

"How do I buck on about all this? You don't mind, do you? He's putting up for Zizi, you know."

"Is Zizi really a duke, too?"

"I shouldn't wonder. Greek, you know. Rotten painter. I rather liked the count."

"Where did you go with him?"

"Oh, everywhere. He just brought me here now. Offered me ten thousand dollars to go to Biarritz with him. How much is that in pounds?"

"Around two thousand."

"Lot of money. I told him I couldn't do it. He was awfully nice about it. Told him I knew too many people in Biarritz."

Brett laughed.

"I say, you are slow on the up-take," she said. I had only sipped my brandy and soda. I took a long drink.

"That's better. Very funny," Brett said. "Then he wanted me to go to Cannes with him. Told him I knew too many people in Cannes. Monte Carlo. Told him I knew too many people in Monte Carlo. Told him I knew too many people everywhere. Quite true, too. So I asked him to bring me here."

She looked at me, her hand on the table, her glass raised. "Don't look like that," she said. "Told him I was in love with you. True, too. Don't look like that. He was damn nice about it. Wants to drive us out to dinner to-morrow night. Like to go?"

"Why not?"

"I'd better go now."

"Why?"

"Just wanted to see you. Damned silly idea. Want to get dressed and come down? He's got the car just up the street."

"The count?"

"Himself. And a chauffeur in livery. Going to drive me around and have breakfast in the Bois. Hampers. Got it all at Zelli's. Dozen bottles of Mumm's. Tempt you?"

"I have to work in the morning," I said. "I'm too far behind you now to catch up and be any fun."

"Don't be an ass."

"Can't do it."

"Right. Send him a tender message?"

"Anything. Absolutely."

"Good night, darling."

"Don't be sentimental."

"You make me ill."

We kissed good night and Brett shivered. "I'd better go," she said. "Good night, darling."

"You don't have to go."

"Yes."

We kissed again on the stairs and as I called for the cordon the concierge muttered something behind her door. I went back upstairs and from the open window watched Brett walking up the street to the big limousine drawn up to the curb under the arc-light. She got in and it started off. I turned around. On the table was an empty glass and a glass half-full of brandy and soda. I took them both out to the kitchen and poured the half-full glass down the sink. I turned off the gas in the dining-room, kicked off my slippers sitting on the bed, and got into bed. This was Brett, that I had felt like crying about. Then I thought of her walking up the street and stepping into the car, as I had last seen her, and of course in a little while I felt like hell again. It is awfully easy to be hard-boiled about everything in the daytime, but at night it is another thing.

5

In the morning I walked down the Boulevard to the Rue Soufflot for coffee and brioche. It was a fine morning. The horse-chestnut trees in the Luxembourg gardens were in bloom. There was the pleasant early-morning feeling of a hot day. I read the papers with the coffee and then smoked a cigarette. The flower-women were coming up from the market and arranging their daily stock. Students went by going up to the law school, or down to the Sorbonne. The Boulevard was busy with trams and people going to work. I got on an S bus and rode down to the Madeleine, standing on the back platform. From the Madeleine I walked along the Boulevard des Capucines to the Opéra, and up to my office. I passed the man with the jumping frogs and the man with the boxer toys. I stepped aside to avoid walking into the thread with which his girl assistant manipulated the boxers. She was standing looking away, the thread in her folded hands. The man was urging two tourists to buy. Three more tourists had stopped and were watching. I walked on behind a man who was pushing a roller that printed the name CINZANO on the sidewalk in damp letters. All along people were going to work. It felt pleasant to be going to work. I walked across the avenue and turned in to my office.

Up-stairs in the office I read the French morning papers, smoked, and then sat at the typewriter and got off a good morning's work. At eleven o'clock I went over to the Quai d'Orsay in a taxi and went in and sat with about a dozen correspondents, while the foreign-office mouthpiece, a young Nouvelle Revue Française diplomat in horn-rimmed spectacles, talked and answered questions for half an hour. The President of the Council was in Lyon making a speech, or, rather he was on his way back. Several people asked questions to hear themselves talk and there were a couple of questions asked by news service men who wanted to know the answers. There was no news. I shared a taxi back from the Quai d'Orsay with Woolsey and Krum.

"What do you do nights, Jake?" asked Krum. "I never see you around."

"Oh, I'm over in the Quarter."

"I'm coming over some night. The Dingo. That's the great place, isn't it?"

"Yes. That, or this new dive, the Select."

"I've meant to get over," said Krum. "You know how it is, though, with a wife and kids."

"Playing any tennis?" Woolsey asked.

"Well, no," said Krum. "I can't say I've played any this year. I've tried to get away, but Sundays it's always rained, and the courts are so damned crowded."

"The Englishmen all have Saturday off," Woolsey said.

"Lucky beggars," said Krum. "Well, I'll tell you. Some day I'm not going to be working for an agency. Then I'll have plenty of time to get out in the country."

"That's the thing to do. Live out in the country and have a little car."

"I've been thinking some about getting a car next year."

I banged on the glass. The chauffeur stopped. "Here's my street," I said. "Come in and have a drink."

"Thanks, old man," Krum said. Woolsey shook his head. "I've got to file that line he got off this morning."

I put a two-franc piece in Krum's hand.

"You're crazy, Jake," he said. "This is on me."

"It's all on the office, anyway."

"Nope. I want to get it."

I waved good-bye. Krum put his head out. "See you at the lunch on Wednesday."

"You bet."

I went to the office in the elevator. Robert Cohn was waiting for me. "Hello, Jake," he said. "Going out to lunch?"

"Yes. Let me see if there is anything new."

"Where will we eat?"

"Anywhere."

I was looking over my desk. "Where do you want to eat?"

"How about Vetzel's? They've got good hors d'œuvres."

In the restaurant we ordered hors d'œuvres and beer. The sommelier brought the beer, tall, beaded on the outside of the steins, and cold. There were a dozen different dishes of hors d'œuvres.

"Have any fun last night?" I asked.

"No. I don't think so."

"How's the writing going?"

"Rotten. I can't get this second book going."

"That happens to everybody."

"Oh, I'm sure of that. It gets me worried, though."

"Thought any more about going to South America?"

"I mean that."

"Well, why don't you start off?"

"Frances."

"Well," I said, "take her with you."

"She wouldn't like it. That isn't the sort of thing she likes. She likes a lot of people around."

"Tell her to go to hell."

"I can't. I've got certain obligations to her."

He shoved the sliced cucumbers away and took a pickled herring.

"What do you know about Lady Brett Ashley, Jake?"

"Her name's Lady Ashley. Brett's her own name. She's a nice girl," I said. "She's getting a divorce and she's going to marry Mike Campbell. He's over in Scotland now. Why?"

"She's a remarkably attractive woman."

"Isn't she?"

"There's a certain quality about her, a certain fineness. She seems to be absolutely fine and straight."

"She's very nice."

"I don't know how to describe the quality," Cohn said. "I suppose it's breeding."

"You sound as though you liked her pretty well."

"I do. I shouldn't wonder if I were in love with her."

"She's a drunk," I said. "She's in love with Mike Campbell, and she's going to marry him. He's going to be rich as hell some day."

"I don't believe she'll ever marry him."

"Why not?"

"I don't know. I just don't believe it. Have you known her a long time?"

"Yes," I said. "She was a V. A. D. in a hospital I was in during the war."

"She must have been just a kid then."

"She's thirty-four now."

"When did she marry Ashley?"

"During the war. Her own true love had just kicked off with the dysentery."

"You talk sort of bitter."

"Sorry. I didn't mean to. I was just trying to give you the facts."

"I don't believe she would marry anybody she didn't love."

"Well," I said. "She's done it twice."

"I don't believe it."

"Well," I said, "don't ask me a lot of fool questions if you don't like the answers."

"I didn't ask you that."

"You asked me what I knew about Brett Ashley."

"I didn't ask you to insult her."

"Oh, go to hell."

He stood up from the table his face white, and stood there white and angry behind the little plates of hors d'œuvres.

"Sit down," I said. "Don't be a fool."

"You've got to take that back."

"Oh, cut out the prep-school stuff."

"Take it back."

"Sure. Anything. I never heard of Brett Ashley. How's that?"

"No. Not that. About me going to hell."

"Oh, don't go to hell," I said. "Stick around. We're just starting lunch."

Cohn smiled again and sat down. He seemed glad to sit down. What the hell would he have done if he hadn't sat down? "You say such damned insulting things, Jake."

"I'm sorry. I've got a nasty tongue. I never mean it when I say nasty things."

"I know it," Cohn said. "You're really about the best friend I have, Jake."

God help you, I thought. "Forget what I said," I said out loud. "I'm sorry."

"It's all right. It's fine. I was just sore for a minute."

"Good. Let's get something else to eat."

After we finished the lunch we walked up to the Café de la Paix and had coffee. I could feel Cohn wanted to bring up Brett again, but I held him off it. We talked about one thing and another, and I left him to come to the office.

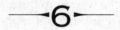

6

At five o'clock I was in the Hotel Crillon waiting for Brett. She was not there, so I sat down and wrote some letters. They were not very good letters but I hoped their being on Crillon stationery would help them. Brett did not turn up, so about quarter to six I went down to the bar and had a Jack Rose with George the barman. Brett had not been in the bar either, and so I looked for her up-stairs on my way out, and took a taxi to the Café Select. Crossing the Seine I saw a string of barges being towed empty down the current, riding high, the bargemen at the sweeps as they came toward the bridge. The river looked nice. It was always pleasant crossing bridges in Paris.

The taxi rounded the statue of the inventor of the semaphore engaged in doing same, and turned up the Boulevard Raspail, and I sat back to let that part of the ride pass. The Boulevard Raspail always made dull riding. It was like a certain stretch on the P.L.M. between Fontainebleau and Montereau that always made me feel bored and dead and dull until it was over. I suppose it is some association of ideas that makes those dead places in a journey. There are other streets in Paris as ugly as the Boulevard Raspail. It is a street I do not mind walking down at all. But I cannot stand to ride along it. Perhaps I had read something about it once. That was the way Robert Cohn was about all of Paris. I wondered where Cohn got that incapacity to enjoy Paris. Possibly from Mencken. Mencken hates Paris, I believe. So many young men get their likes and dislikes from Mencken.

The taxi stopped in front of the Rotonde. No matter what café in Montparnasse you ask a taxi-driver to bring you to from the right bank of the river, they always take you to the Rotonde. Ten years from now it will probably be the Dôme. It was near enough, anyway. I walked past the sad tables of the Rotonde to the Select. There were a few people inside at the bar, and outside, alone, sat Harvey Stone. He had a pile of saucers in front of him, and he needed a shave.

"Sit down," said Harvey, "I've been looking for you."

"What's the matter?"

"Nothing. Just looking for you."

"Been out to the races?"

"No. Not since Sunday."

"What do you hear from the States?"

"Nothing. Absolutely nothing."

"What's the matter?"

"I don't know. I'm through with them. I'm absolutely through with them."

He leaned forward and looked me in the eye.

"Do you want to know something, Jake?"

"Yes."

"I haven't had anything to eat for five days."

I figured rapidly back in my mind. It was three days ago that Harvey had won two hundred francs from me shaking poker dice in the New York Bar.

"What's the matter?"

"No money. Money hasn't come," he paused. "I tell you it's strange, Jake. When I'm like this I just want to be alone. I want to stay in my own room. I'm like a cat."

I felt in my pocket.

"Would a hundred help you any, Harvey?"

"Yes."

"Come on. Let's go and eat."

"There's no hurry. Have a drink."

"Better eat."

"No. When I get like this I don't care whether I eat or not."

We had a drink. Harvey added my saucer to his own pile.

"Do you know Mencken, Harvey?"

"Yes. Why?"

"What's he like?"

"He's all right. He says some pretty funny things. Last time I had dinner with him we talked about Hoffenheimer. 'The trouble is,' he said, 'he's a garter snapper.' That's not bad."

"That's not bad."

"He's through now," Harvey went on. "He's written about all the things he knows, and now he's on all the things he doesn't know."

"I guess he's all right," I said. "I just can't read him."

"Oh, nobody reads him now," Harvey said, "except the people that used to read the Alexander Hamilton Institute."

"Well," I said. "That was a good thing, too."

"Sure," said Harvey. So we sat and thought deeply for a while.

"Have another port?"

"All right," said Harvey.

"There comes Cohn," I said. Robert Cohn was crossing the street.

"That moron," said Harvey. Cohn came up to our table.

"Hello, you bums," he said.

"Hello, Robert," Harvey said. "I was just telling Jake here that you're a moron."

"What do you mean?"

"Tell us right off. Don't think. What would you rather do if you could do anything you wanted?"

Cohn started to consider.

"Don't think. Bring it right out."

"I don't know," Cohn said. "What's it all about, anyway?"

"I mean what would you rather do. What comes into your head first. No matter how silly it is."

"I don't know," Cohn said. "I think I'd rather play football again with what I know about handling myself, now."

"I misjudged you," Harvey said. "You're not a moron. You're only a case of arrested development."

"You're awfully funny, Harvey," Cohn said. "Some day somebody will push your face in."

Harvey Stone laughed. "You think so. They won't, though. Because it wouldn't make any difference to me. I'm not a fighter."

"It would make a difference to you if anybody did it."

"No, it wouldn't. That's where you make your big mistake. Because you're not intelligent."

"Cut it out about me."

"Sure," said Harvey. "It doesn't make any difference to me. You don't mean anything to me."

"Come on, Harvey," I said. "Have another porto."

"No," he said. "I'm going up the street and eat. See you later, Jake."

He walked out and up the street. I watched him crossing the street through the taxis, small, heavy, slowly sure of himself in the traffic.

"He always gets me sore," Cohn said. "I can't stand him."

"I like him," I said. "I'm fond of him. You don't want to get sore at him."

"I know it," Cohn said. "He just gets on my nerves."

"Write this afternoon?"

"No. I couldn't get it going. It's harder to do than my first book. I'm having a hard time handling it."

The sort of healthy conceit that he had when he returned from America early in the spring was gone. Then he had been sure of his work, only with these personal longings for adventure. Now the sureness was gone. Somehow I feel I have not shown Robert Cohn clearly. The reason is that until he fell in love with Brett, I never heard him make one remark that would, in any way, detach him from other people. He was nice to watch on the tennis-court, he had a good body, and he kept it in shape; he handled his cards well at bridge, and he had a funny sort of undergraduate quality about him. If he were in a crowd nothing he said stood out. He wore what used to be called polo shirts at school, and may be called that still, but he was not professionally youthful. I do not believe he thought about his clothes much. Externally he had been formed at Princeton. Internally he had been moulded by the two women who had trained him. He had a nice, boyish sort of cheerfulness that had never been trained out of him, and I probably have not brought it out. He loved to win at tennis. He probably loved to win as much as Lenglen, for instance. On the other hand, he was not angry at being beaten. When he fell in love with Brett his tennis game went all to pieces. People beat him who had never had a chance with him. He was very nice about it.

Anyhow, we were sitting on the terrace of the Café Select, and Harvey Stone had just crossed the street.

"Come on up to the Lilas," I said.

"I have a date."

"What time?"

"Frances is coming here at seven-fifteen."

"There she is."

Frances Clyne was coming toward us from across the street. She was a very tall girl who walked with a great deal of movement. She waved and smiled. We watched her cross the street.

"Hello," she said, "I'm so glad you're here, Jake. I've been wanting to talk to you."

"Hello, Frances," said Cohn. He smiled.

"Why, hello, Robert. Are you here?" She went on, talking rapidly. "I've had the darndest time. This one"—shaking her head at Cohn— "didn't come home for lunch."

"I wasn't supposed to."

"Oh, I know. But you didn't say anything about it to the cook. Then I had a date myself, and Paula wasn't at her office. I went to the Ritz and waited for her, and she never came, and of course I didn't have enough money to lunch at the Ritz——"

"What did you do?"

"Oh, went out, of course." She spoke in a sort of imitation joyful manner. "I always keep my appointments. No one keeps theirs, nowadays. I ought to know better. How are you, Jake, anyway?"

"Fine."

"That was a fine girl you had at the dance, and then went off with that Brett one."

"Don't you like her?" Cohn asked.

"I think she's perfectly charming. Don't you?"

Cohn said nothing.

"Look, Jake. I want to talk with you. Would you come over with me to the Dôme? You'll stay here, won't you, Robert? Come on, Jake."

We crossed the Boulevard Montparnasse and sat down at a table. A boy came up with the *Paris Times*, and I bought one and opened it.

"What's the matter, Frances?"

"Oh, nothing," she said, "except that he wants to leave me."

"How do you mean?"

"Oh, he told every one that we were going to be married, and I told my mother and every one, and now he doesn't want to do it."

"What's the matter?"

"He's decided he hasn't lived enough. I knew it would happen when he went to New York."

She looked up, very bright-eyed and trying to talk inconsequentially.

"I wouldn't marry him if he doesn't want to. Of course I wouldn't.

I wouldn't marry him now for anything. But it does seem to me to be a little late now, after we've waited three years, and I've just gotten my divorce."

I said nothing.

"We were going to celebrate so, and instead we've just had scenes. It's so childish. We have dreadful scenes, and he cries and begs me to be reasonable, but he says he just can't do it."

"It's rotten luck."

"I should say it is rotten luck. I've wasted two years and a half on him now. And I don't know now if any man will ever want to marry me. Two years ago I could have married anybody I wanted, down at Cannes. All the old ones that wanted to marry somebody chic and settle down were crazy about me. Now I don't think I could get anybody."

"Sure, you could marry anybody."

"No, I don't believe it. And I'm fond of him, too. And I'd like to have children. I always thought we'd have children."

She looked at me very brightly. "I never liked children much, but I don't want to think I'll never have them. I always thought I'd have them and then like them."

"He's got children."

"Oh, yes. He's got children, and he's got money, and he's got a rich mother, and he's written a book, and nobody will publish my stuff, nobody at all. It isn't bad, either. And I haven't got any money at all. I could have had alimony, but I got the divorce the quickest way."

She looked at me again very brightly.

"It isn't right. It's my own fault and it's not, too. I ought to have known better. And when I tell him he just cries and says he can't marry. Why can't he marry? I'd be a good wife. I'm easy to get along with. I leave him alone. It doesn't do any good."

"It's a rotten shame."

"Yes, it is a rotten shame. But there's no use talking about it, is there? Come on, let's go back to the café."

"And of course there isn't anything I can do."

"No. Just don't let him know I talked to you. I know what he wants." Now for the first time she dropped her bright, terribly cheerful manner. "He wants to go back to New York alone, and be there when his book comes out so when a lot of little chickens like it. That's what he wants."

"Maybe they won't like it. I don't think he's that way. Really."

"You don't know him like I do, Jake. That's what he wants to do. I know it. I know it. That's why he doesn't want to marry. He wants to have a big triumph this fall all by himself."

"Want to go back to the café?"

"Yes. Come on."

We got up from the table—they had never brought us a drink—and started across the street toward the Select, where Cohn sat smiling at us from behind the marble-topped table.

"Well, what are you smiling at?" Frances asked him. "Feel pretty happy?"

"I was smiling at you and Jake with your secrets."

"Oh, what I've told Jake isn't any secret. Everybody will know it soon enough. I only wanted to give Jake a decent version."

"What was it? About your going to England?"

"Yes, about my going to England. Oh, Jake! I forgot to tell you. I'm going to England."

"Isn't that fine!"

"Yes, that's the way it's done in the very best families. Robert's sending me. He's going to give me two hundred pounds and then I'm going to visit friends. Won't it be lovely? The friends don't know about it, yet."

She turned to Cohn and smiled at him. He was not smiling now.

"You were only going to give me a hundred pounds, weren't you, Robert? But I made him give me two hundred. He's really very generous. Aren't you, Robert?"

I do not know how people could say such terrible things to Robert Cohn. There are people to whom you could not say insulting things. They give you a feeling that the world would be destroyed, would actually be destroyed before your eyes, if you said certain things. But here was Cohn taking it all. Here it was, all going on right before me, and I did not even feel an impulse to try and stop it. And this was friendly joking to what went on later.

"How can you say such things, Frances?" Cohn interrupted.

"Listen to him. I'm going to England. I'm going to visit friends. Ever visit friends that didn't want you? Oh, they'll have to take me, all right. 'How do you do, my dear? Such a long time since we've seen you. And how is your dear mother?' Yes, how is my dear mother? She put all her money into French war bonds. Yes, she did. Probably the only person in the world that did. 'And what about Robert?' or else very careful talking around Robert. 'You must be most careful not to mention him, my dear.

Poor Frances has had a most unfortunate experience.' Won't it be fun, Robert? Don't you think it will be fun, Jake?"

She turned to me with that terribly bright smile. It was very satisfactory to her to have an audience for this.

"And where are you going to be, Robert? It's my own fault, all right. Perfectly my own fault. When I made you get rid of your little secretary on the magazine I ought to have known you'd get rid of me the same way. Jake doesn't know about that. Should I tell him?"

"Shut up, Frances, for God's sake."

"Yes, I'll tell him. Robert had a little secretary on the magazine. Just the sweetest little thing in the world, and he thought she was wonderful, and then I came along and he thought I was pretty wonderful, too. So I made him get rid of her, and he had brought her to Provincetown from Carmel when he moved the magazine, and he didn't even pay her fare back to the coast. All to please me. He thought I was pretty fine, then. Didn't you, Robert?

"You mustn't misunderstand, Jake, it was absolutely platonic with the secretary. Not even platonic. Nothing at all, really. It was just that she was so nice. And he did that just to please me. Well, I suppose that we that live by the sword shall perish by the sword. Isn't that literary, though? You want to remember that for your next book, Robert.

"You know Robert is going to get material for a new book. Aren't you, Robert? That's why he's leaving me. He's decided I don't film well. You see, he was so busy all the time that we were living together, writing on this book, that he doesn't remember anything about us. So now he's going out and get some new material. Well, I hope he gets something frightfully interesting.

"Listen, Robert, dear. Let me tell you something. You won't mind, will you? Don't have scenes with your young ladies. Try not to. Because you can't have scenes without crying, and then you pity yourself so much you can't remember what the other person's said. You'll never be able to remember any conversations that way. Just try and be calm. I know it's awfully hard. But remember, it's for literature. We all ought to make sacrifices for literature. Look at me. I'm going to England without a protest. All for literature. We must all help young writers. Don't you think so, Jake? But you're not a young writer. Are you, Robert? You're thirty-four. Still, I suppose that is young for a great writer. Look at Hardy. Look at Anatole France. He just died a little while ago. Robert doesn't think he's any good, though. Some of his French friends told him. He doesn't read French very well himself. He wasn't a good writer like you are, was he, Robert? Do you think he ever had to go and look for material? What do you suppose he said to his mistresses when he wouldn't marry them? I wonder if he cried, too? Oh, I've just thought of something." She put her gloved hand up to her lips. "I know the real reason why Robert won't marry me, Jake. It's just come to me. They've sent it to me in a vision in the Café Select. Isn't it mystic? Some day they'll put a tablet up. Like at Lourdes. Do you want to hear, Robert? I'll tell you. It's so simple. I wonder why I never thought about it. Why, you see, Robert's always wanted to have a mistress, and if he doesn't marry me, why, then he's had one. She was his mistress for over two years. See how it is? And if he marries me, like he's always promised he would, that would be the end of all the romance. Don't you think that's bright of me to figure that out? It's true, too. Look at him and see if it's not. Where are you going, Jake?"

"I've got to go in and see Harvey Stone a minute."

Cohn looked up as I went in. His face was white. Why did he sit there? Why did he keep on taking it like that?

As I stood against the bar looking out I could see them through the window. Frances was talking on to him, smiling brightly, looking into his face each time she asked: "Isn't it so, Robert?" Or maybe she did not ask that now. Perhaps she said something else. I told the barman I did not want anything to drink and went out through the side door. As I went out the door I looked back through the two thicknesses of glass and saw them sitting there. She was still talking to him. I went down a side street to the Boulevard Raspail. A taxi came along and I got in and gave the driver the address of my flat.

— 7 —

As I started up the stairs the concierge knocked on the glass of the door of her lodge, and as I stopped she came out. She had some letters and a telegram.

"Here is the post. And there was a lady here to see you."

"Did she leave a card?"

"No. She was with a gentleman. It was the one who was here last night. In the end I find she is very nice."

"Was she with a friend of mine?"

"I don't know. He was never here before. He was very large. Very, very large. She was very nice. Very, very nice. Last night she was, perhaps, a little—" She put her head on one hand and rocked it up and down. "I'll speak perfectly frankly, Monsieur Barnes. Last night I found her not so gentille. Last night I formed another idea of her. But listen to what I tell you. She is très, très gentille. She is of very good family. It is a thing you can see."

"They did not leave any word?"

"Yes. They said they would be back in an hour."

"Send them up when they come."

"Yes, Monsieur Barnes. And that lady, that lady there is some one. An eccentric, perhaps, but quelqu'un, quelqu'un!"

The concierge, before she became a concierge, had owned a drink-selling concession at the Paris race-courses. Her life-work lay in the pelouse, but she kept an eye on the people of the pesage, and she took great pride in telling me which of my guests were well brought up, which were of good family, who were sportsmen, a French word pronounced with the accent on the men. The only trouble was that people who did not fall into any of those three categories were very liable to be told there was no one home, chez Barnes. One of my friends, an extremely underfed-looking painter, who was obviously to Madame Duzinell neither well brought up, of good family, nor a sportsman, wrote me a letter asking if I could get him a pass to get by the concierge so he could come up and see me occasionally in the evenings.

I went up to the flat wondering what Brett had done to the concierge. The wire was a cable from Bill Gorton, saying he was arriving on the *France*. I put the mail on the table, went back to the bedroom, undressed and had a shower. I was rubbing down when I heard the door-bell pull. I put on a bathrobe and slippers and went to the door. It was Brett. Back of her was the count. He was holding a great bunch of roses.

"Hello, darling," said Brett. "Aren't you going to let us in?"

"Come on. I was just bathing."

"Aren't you the fortunate man. Bathing."

"Only a shower. Sit down, Count Mippipopolous. What will you drink?"

"I don't know whether you like flowers, sir," the count said, "but I took the liberty of just bringing these roses."

"Here, give them to me." Brett took them. "Get me some water in this, Jake." I filled the big earthenware jug with water in the kitchen, and Brett put the roses in it, and placed them in the centre of the dining-room table.

"I say. We have had a day."

"You don't remember anything about a date with me at the Crillon?"

"No. Did we have one? I must have been blind."

"You were quite drunk, my dear," said the count.

"Wasn't I, though? And the count's been a brick, absolutely."

"You've got hell's own drag with the concierge now."

"I ought to have. Gave her two hundred francs."

"Don't be a damned fool."

"His," she said, and nodded at the count.

"I thought we ought to give her a little something for last night. It was very late."

"He's wonderful," Brett said. "He remembers everything that's happened."

"So do you, my dear."

"Fancy," said Brett. "Who'd want to? I say, Jake, *do* we get a drink?"

"You get it while I go in and dress. You know where it is."

"Rather."

While I dressed I heard Brett put down glasses and then a siphon, and then heard them talking. I dressed slowly, sitting on the bed. I felt tired and pretty rotten. Brett came in the room, a glass in her hand, and sat on the bed.

"What's the matter, darling? Do you feel rocky?"

She kissed me coolly on the forehead.

"Oh, Brett, I love you so much."

"Darling," she said. Then: "Do you want me to send him away?"

"No. He's nice."

"I'll send him away."

"No, don't."

"Yes, I'll send him away."

"You can't just like that."

"Can't I, though? You stay here. He's mad about me, I tell you."

She was gone out of the room. I lay face down on the bed. I was having a bad time. I heard them talking but I did not listen. Brett came in and sat on the bed.

"Poor old darling." She stroked my head.

"What did you say to him?" I was lying with my face away from her. I did not want to see her.

"Sent him for champagne. He loves to go for champagne."

Then later: "Do you feel better, darling? Is the head any better?"

"It's better."

"Lie quiet. He's gone to the other side of town."

"Couldn't we live together, Brett? Couldn't we just live together?"

"I don't think so. I'd just *tromper* you with everybody. You couldn't stand it."

"I stand it now."

"That would be different. It's my fault, Jake. It's the way I'm made."

"Couldn't we go off in the country for a while?"

"It wouldn't be any good. I'll go if you like. But I couldn't live quietly in the country. Not with my own true love."

"I know."

"Isn't it rotten? There isn't any use my telling you I love you."

"You know I love you."

"Let's not talk. Talking's all bilge. I'm going away from you, and then Michael's coming back."

"Why are you going away?"

"Better for you. Better for me."

"When are you going?"

"Soon as I can."

"Where?"

"San Sebastian."

"Can't we go together?"

"No. That would be a hell of an idea after we'd just talked it out."

"We never agreed."

"Oh, you know as well as I do. Don't be obstinate, darling."

"Oh, sure," I said. "I know you're right. I'm just low, and when I'm low I talk like a fool."

I sat up, leaned over, found my shoes beside the bed and put them on. I stood up.

"Don't look like that, darling."

"How do you want me to look?"

"Oh, don't be a fool. I'm going away to-morrow."

"To-morrow?"

"Yes. Didn't I say so? I am."

"Let's have a drink, then. The count will be back."

"Yes. He should be back. You know he's extraordinary about buying champagne. It means any amount to him."

We went into the dining-room. I took up the brandy bottle and poured Brett a drink and one for myself. There was a ring at the bell-pull. I went to the door and there was the count. Behind him was the chauffeur carrying a basket of champagne.

"Where should I have him put it, sir?" asked the count.

"In the kitchen," Brett said.

"Put it in there, Henry," the count motioned. "Now go down and get the ice." He stood looking after the basket inside the kitchen door. "I think you'll find that's very good wine," he said. "I know we don't get much of a chance to judge good wine in the States now, but I got this from a friend of mine that's in the business."

"Oh, you always have some one in the trade," Brett said.

"This fellow raises the grapes. He's got thousands of acres of them."

"What's his name?" asked Brett. "Veuve Clicquot?"

"No," said the count. "Mumm. He's a baron."

"Isn't it wonderful," said Brett. "We all have titles. Why haven't you a title, Jake?"

"I assure you, sir," the count put his hand on my arm. "It never does a man any good. Most of the time it costs you money."

"Oh, I don't know. It's damned useful sometimes," Brett said.

"I've never known it to do me any good."

"You haven't used it properly. I've had hell's own amount of credit on mine."

"Do sit down, count," I said. "Let me take that stick."

The count was looking at Brett across the table under the gas-light. She was smoking a cigarette and flicking the ashes on the rug. She saw me notice it. "I say, Jake, I don't want to ruin your rugs. Can't you give a chap an ash-tray?"

I found some ash-trays and spread them around. The chauffeur came up with a bucket full of salted ice. "Put two bottles in it, Henry," the count called.

"Anything else, sir?"

"No. Wait down in the car." He turned to Brett and to me. "We'll want to ride out to the Bois for dinner?"

"If you like," Brett said. "I couldn't eat a thing."

"I always like a good meal," said the count.

"Should I bring the wine in, sir?" asked the chauffeur.

"Yes. Bring it in, Henry," said the count. He took out a heavy pigskin cigar-case and offered it to me. "Like to try a real American cigar?"

"Thanks," I said. "I'll finish the cigarette."

He cut off the end of his cigar with a gold cutter he wore on one end of his watch-chain.

"I like a cigar to really draw," said the count. "Half the cigars you smoke don't draw."

He lit the cigar, puffed at it, looking across the table at Brett. "And when you're divorced, Lady Ashley, then you won't have a title."

"No. What a pity."

"No," said the count. "You don't need a title. You got class all over you."

"Thanks. Awfully decent of you."

"I'm not joking you," the count blew a cloud of smoke. "You got the most class of anybody I ever seen. You got it. That's all."

"Nice of you," said Brett. "Mummy would be pleased. Couldn't you write it out, and I'll send it in a letter to her."

"I'd tell her, too," said the count. "I'm not joking you. I never joke people. Joke people and you make enemies. That's what I always say."

"You're right," Brett said. "You're terribly right. I always joke people and I haven't a friend in the world. Except Jake here."

"You don't joke him."

"That's it."

"Do you, now?" asked the count. "Do you joke him?"

Brett looked at me and wrinkled up the corners of her eyes.

"No," she said. "I wouldn't joke him."

"See," said the count. "You don't joke him."

"This is a hell of a dull talk," Brett said. "How about some of that champagne?"

The count reached down and twirled the bottles in the shiny bucket. "It isn't cold, yet. You're always drinking, my dear. Why don't you just talk?"

"I've talked too ruddy much. I've talked myself all out to Jake."

"I should like to hear you really talk, my dear. When you talk to me you never finish your sentences at all."

"Leave 'em for you to finish. Let any one finish them as they like."

"It is a very interesting system," the count reached down and gave the bottles a twirl. "Still I would like to hear you talk some time."

"Isn't he a fool?" Brett asked.

"Now," the count brought up a bottle. "I think this is cool."

I brought a towel and he wiped the bottle dry and held it up. "I like to drink champagne from magnums. The wine is better but it would have been too hard to cool." He held the bottle, looking at it. I put out the glasses.

"I say. You might open it," Brett suggested.

"Yes, my dear. Now I'll open it."

It was amazing champagne.

"I say that is wine," Brett held up her glass. "We ought to toast something. 'Here's to royalty.'"

"This wine is too good for toast-drinking, my dear. You don't want to mix emotions up with a wine like that. You lose the taste."

Brett's glass was empty.

"You ought to write a book on wines, count," I said.

"Mr. Barnes," answered the count, "all I want out of wines is to enjoy them."

"Let's enjoy a little more of this," Brett pushed her glass forward.

The count poured very carefully. "There, my dear. Now you enjoy that slowly, and then you can get drunk."

"Drunk? Drunk?"

"My dear, you are charming when you are drunk."

"Listen to the man."

"Mr. Barnes," the count poured my glass full. "She is the only lady I have ever known who was as charming when she was drunk as when she was sober."

"You haven't been around much, have you?"

"Yes, my dear. I have been around very much. I have been around a very great deal."

"Drink your wine," said Brett. "We've all been around. I dare say Jake here has seen as much as you have."

"My dear, I am sure Mr. Barnes has seen a lot. Don't think I don't think so, sir. I have seen a lot, too."

"Of course you have, my dear," Brett said. "I was only ragging."

"I have been in seven wars and four revolutions," the count said.

"Soldiering?" Brett asked.

"Sometimes, my dear. And I have got arrow wounds. Have you ever seen arrow wounds?"

"Let's have a look at them."

The count stood up, unbuttoned his vest, and opened his shirt. He pulled up the undershirt onto his chest and stood, his chest black, and big stomach muscles bulging under the light.

"You see them?"

Below the line where his ribs stopped were two raised white welts. "See on the back where they come out." Above the small of the back were the same two scars, raised as thick as a finger.

"I say. Those are something."

"Clean through."

The count was tucking in his shirt.

"Where did you get those?" I asked.

"In Abyssinia. When I was twenty-one years old."

"What were you doing?" asked Brett. "Were you in the army?"

"I was on a business trip, my dear."

"I told you he was one of us. Didn't I?" Brett turned to me. "I love you, count. You're a darling."

"You make me very happy, my dear. But it isn't true."

"Don't be an ass."

"You see, Mr. Barnes, it is because I have lived very much that now I can enjoy everything so well. Don't you find it like that?"

"Yes. Absolutely."

"I know," said the count. "That is the secret. You must get to know the values."

"Doesn't anything ever happen to your values?" Brett asked.

"No. Not any more."

"Never fall in love?"

"Always," said the count. "I am always in love."

"What does that do to your values?"

"That, too, has got a place in my values."

"You haven't any values. You're dead, that's all."

"No, my dear. You're not right. I'm not dead at all."

We drank three bottles of the champagne and the count left the basket in my kitchen. We dined at a restaurant in the Bois. It was a good dinner. Food had an excellent place in the count's values. So did wine. The count was in fine form during the meal. So was Brett. It was a good party.

"Where would you like to go?" asked the count after dinner. We were the only people left in the restaurant. The two waiters were standing over against the door. They wanted to go home.

"We might go up on the hill," Brett said. "Haven't we had a splendid party?"

The count was beaming. He was very happy.

"You are very nice people," he said. He was smoking a cigar again. "Why don't you get married, you two?"

"We want to lead our own lives," I said.

"We have our careers," Brett said. "Come on. Let's get out of this."

"Have another brandy," the count said.

"Get it on the hill."

"No. Have it here where it is quiet."

"You and your quiet," said Brett. "What is it men feel about quiet?"

"We like it," said the count. "Like you like noise, my dear."

"All right," said Brett. "Let's have one."

"Sommelier!" the count called.

"Yes, sir."

"What is the oldest brandy you have?"

"Eighteen eleven, sir."

"Bring us a bottle."

"I say. Don't be ostentatious. Call him off, Jake."

"Listen, my dear. I get more value for my money in old brandy than in any other antiquities."

"Got many antiquities?"

"I got a houseful."

Finally we went up to Montmartre. Inside Zelli's it was crowded, smoky, and noisy. The music hit you as you went in. Brett and I danced. It was so crowded we could barely move. The nigger drummer waved at Brett. We were caught in the jam, dancing in one place in front of him.

"Hahre you?"

"Great."

"Thaats good."

He was all teeth and lips.

"He's a great friend of mine," Brett said. "Damn good drummer."

The music stopped and we started toward the table where the count sat. Then the music started again and we danced. I looked at the count. He was sitting at the table smoking a cigar. The music stopped again.

"Let's go over."

Brett started toward the table. The music started and again we danced, tight in the crowd.

"You are a rotten dancer, Jake. Michael's the best dancer I know."

"He's splendid."

"He's got his points."

"I like him," I said. "I'm damned fond of him."

"I'm going to marry him," Brett said. "Funny. I haven't thought about him for a week."

"Don't you write him?"

"Not I. Never write letters."

"I'll bet he writes to you."

"Rather. Damned good letters, too."

"When are you going to get married?"

"How do I know? As soon as we can get the divorce. Michael's trying to get his mother to put up for it."

"Could I help you?"

"Don't be an ass. Michael's people have loads of money."

The music stopped. We walked over to the table. The count stood up.

"Very nice," he said. "You looked very, very nice."

"Don't you dance, count?" I asked.

"No. I'm too old."

"Oh, come off it," Brett said.

"My dear, I would do it if I would enjoy it. I enjoy to watch you dance."

"Splendid," Brett said. "I'll dance again for you some time. I say. What about your little friend, Zizi?"

"Let me tell you. I support that boy, but I don't want to have him around."

"He is rather hard."

"You know I think that boy's got a future. But personally I don't want him around."

"Jake's rather the same way."

"He gives me the willies."

"Well," the count shrugged his shoulders. "About his future you can't ever tell. Anyhow, his father was a great friend of my father."

"Come on. Let's dance," Brett said.

We danced. It was crowded and close.

"Oh, darling," Brett said, "I'm so miserable."

I had that feeling of going through something that has all happened before. "You were happy a minute ago."

The drummer shouted: "You can't two time——"

"It's all gone."

"What's the matter?"

"I don't know. I just feel terribly."

". . . . . ." the drummer chanted. Then turned to his sticks.

"Want to go?"

I had the feeling as in a nightmare of it all being something repeated, something I had been through and that now I must go through again.

". . . . . ." the drummer sang softly.

"Let's go," said Brett. "You don't mind."

". . . . . ." the drummer shouted and grinned at Brett.

"All right," I said. We got out from the crowd. Brett went to the dressing-room.

"Brett wants to go," I said to the count. He nodded. "Does she? That's fine. You take the car. I'm going to stay here for a while, Mr. Barnes."

We shook hands.

"It was a wonderful time," I said. "I wish you would let me get this." I took a note out of my pocket.

"Mr. Barnes, don't be ridiculous," the count said.

Brett came over with her wrap on. She kissed the count and put her hand on his shoulder to keep him from standing up. As we went out the door I looked back and there were three girls at his table. We got into the big car. Brett gave the chauffeur the address of her hotel.

"No, don't come up," she said at the hotel. She had rung and the door was unlatched.

"Really?"

"No. Please."

"Good night, Brett," I said. "I'm sorry you feel rotten."

"Good night, Jake. Good night, darling. I won't see you again." We kissed standing at the door. She pushed me away. We kissed again. "Oh, don't!" Brett said.

She turned quickly and went into the hotel. The chauffeur drove me around to my flat. I gave him twenty francs and he touched his cap and said: "Good night, sir," and drove off. I rang the bell. The door opened and I went up-stairs and went to bed.

BOOK TWO

— 8 —

I did not see Brett again until she came back from San Sebastian. One card came from her from there. It had a picture of the Concha, and said: "Darling. Very quiet and healthy. Love to all the chaps. BRETT."

Nor did I see Robert Cohn again. I heard Frances had left for England and I had a note from Cohn saying he was going out in the country for a couple of weeks, he did not know where, but that he wanted to hold me to the fishing-trip in Spain we had talked about last winter. I could reach him always, he wrote, through his bankers.

Brett was gone, I was not bothered by Cohn's troubles, I rather enjoyed not having to play tennis, there was plenty of work to do, I went often to the races, dined with friends, and put in some extra time at the office getting things ahead so I could leave it in charge of my secretary when Bill Gorton and I should shove off to Spain the end of June. Bill Gorton arrived, put up a couple of days at the flat and went off to Vienna. He was very cheerful and said the States were wonderful. New York was wonderful. There had been a grand theatrical season and a whole crop of great young light heavyweights. Any one of them was a good prospect to grow up, put on weight and trim Dempsey. Bill was very happy. He had made a lot of money on his last book, and was going to make a lot more. We had a good time while he was in Paris, and then he went off to Vienna. He was coming back in three weeks and we would leave for Spain to get in some fishing and go to the fiesta at Pamplona. He wrote that Vienna was wonderful. Then a card from Budapest: "Jake, Budapest is wonderful." Then I got a wire: "Back on Monday."

Monday evening he turned up at the flat. I heard his taxi stop and went to the window and called to him; he waved and started up-stairs carrying his bags. I met him on the stairs, and took one of the bags.

"Well," I said, "I hear you had a wonderful trip."

"Wonderful," he said. "Budapest is absolutely wonderful."

"How about Vienna?"

"Not so good, Jake. Not so good. It seemed better than it was."

"How do you mean?" I was getting glasses and a siphon.

"Tight, Jake. I was tight."

"That's strange. Better have a drink."

Bill rubbed his forehead. "Remarkable thing," he said. "Don't know how it happened. Suddenly it happened."

"Last long?"

"Four days, Jake. Lasted just four days."

"Where did you go?"

"Don't remember. Wrote you a post-card. Remember that perfectly."

"Do anything else?"

"Not so sure. Possible."

"Go on. Tell me about it."

"Can't remember. Tell you anything I could remember."

"Go on. Take that drink and remember."

"Might remember a little," Bill said. "Remember something about a prize-fight. Enormous Vienna prize-fight. Had a nigger in it. Remember the nigger perfectly."

"Go on."

"Wonderful nigger. Looked like Tiger Flowers, only four times as big. All of a sudden everybody started to throw things. Not me. Nigger'd just knocked local boy down. Nigger put up his glove. Wanted to make a speech. Awful noble-looking nigger. Started to make a speech. Then local white boy hit him. Then he knocked white boy cold. Then everybody commenced to throw chairs. Nigger went home with us in our car. Couldn't get his clothes. Wore my coat. Remember the whole thing now. Big sporting evening."

"What happened?"

"Loaned the nigger some clothes and went around with him to try and get his money. Claimed nigger owed them money on account of wrecking hall. Wonder who translated? Was it me?"

"Probably it wasn't you."

"You're right. Wasn't me at all. Was another fellow. Think we called him the local Harvard man. Remember him now. Studying music."

"How'd you come out?"

"Not so good, Jake. Injustice everywhere. Promoter claimed nigger promised let local boy stay. Claimed nigger violated contract. Can't knock out Vienna boy in Vienna. 'My God, Mister Gorton,' said nigger, 'I didn't do nothing in there for forty minutes but try and let him stay. That white boy musta ruptured himself swinging at me. I never did hit him.' "

"Did you get any money?"

"No money, Jake. All we could get was nigger's clothes. Somebody took his watch, too. Splendid nigger. Big mistake to have come to Vienna. Not so good, Jake. Not so good."

"What became of the nigger?"

"Went back to Cologne. Lives there. Married. Got a family. Going to write me a letter and send me the money I loaned him. Wonderful nigger. Hope I gave him the right address."

"You probably did."

"Well, anyway, let's eat," said Bill. "Unless you want me to tell you some more travel stories."

"Go on."

"Let's eat."

We went down-stairs and out onto the Boulevard St. Michel in the warm June evening.

"Where will we go?"

"Want to eat on the island?"

"Sure."

We walked down the Boulevard. At the juncture of the Rue Denfert-Rochereau with the Boulevard is a statue of two men in flowing robes.

"I know who they are." Bill eyed the monument. "Gentlemen who invented pharmacy. Don't try and fool me on Paris."

We went on.

"Here's a taxidermist's," Bill said. "Want to buy anything? Nice stuffed dog?"

"Come on," I said. "You're pie-eyed."

"Pretty nice stuffed dogs," Bill said. "Certainly brighten up your flat."

"Come on."

"Just one stuffed dog. I can take 'em or leave 'em alone. But listen, Jake. Just one stuffed dog."

"Come on."

"Mean everything in the world to you after you bought it. Simple exchange of values. You give them money. They give you a stuffed dog."

"We'll get one on the way back."

"All right. Have it your own way. Road to hell paved with unbought stuffed dogs. Not my fault."

We went on.

"How'd you feel that way about dogs so sudden?"

"Always felt that way about dogs. Always been a great lover of stuffed animals."

We stopped and had a drink.

"Certainly like to drink," Bill said. "You ought to try it some times, Jake."

"You're about a hundred and forty-four ahead of me."

"Ought not to daunt you. Never be daunted. Secret of my success. Never been daunted. Never been daunted in public."

"Where were you drinking?"

"Stopped at the Crillon. George made me a couple of Jack Roses. George's a great man. Know the secret of his success? Never been daunted."

"You'll be daunted after about three more pernods."

"Not in public. If I begin to feel daunted I'll go off by myself. I'm like a cat that way."

"When did you see Harvey Stone?"

"At the Crillon. Harvey was just a little daunted. Hadn't eaten for three days. Doesn't eat any more. Just goes off like a cat. Pretty sad."

"He's all right."

"Splendid. Wish he wouldn't keep going off like a cat, though. Makes me nervous."

"What'll we do to-night?"

"Doesn't make any difference. Only let's not get daunted. Suppose they got any hard-boiled eggs here? If they had hard-boiled eggs here we wouldn't have to go all the way down to the island to eat."

"Nix," I said. "We're going to have a regular meal."

"Just a suggestion," said Bill. "Want to start now?"

"Come on."

We started on again down the Boulevard. A horse-cab passed us. Bill looked at it.

"See that horse-cab? Going to have that horse-cab stuffed for you for Christmas. Going to give all my friends stuffed animals. I'm a nature-writer."

A taxi passed, some one in it waved, then banged for the driver to stop. The taxi backed up to the curb. In it was Brett.

"Beautiful lady," said Bill. "Going to kidnap us."

"Hullo!" Brett said. "Hullo!"

"This is Bill Gorton. Lady Ashley."

Brett smiled at Bill. "I say I'm just back. Haven't bathed even. Michael comes in to-night."

"Good. Come on and eat with us, and we'll all go to meet him."

"Must clean myself."

"Oh, rot! Come on."

"Must bathe. He doesn't get in till nine."

"Come and have a drink, then, before you bathe."

"Might do that. Now you're not talking rot."

We got in the taxi. The driver looked around.

"Stop at the nearest bistro," I said.

"We might as well go to the Closerie," Brett said. "I can't drink these rotten brandies."

"Closerie des Lilas."

Brett turned to Bill.

"Have you been in this pestilential city long?"

"Just got in to-day from Budapest."

"How was Budapest?"

"Wonderful. Budapest was wonderful."

"Ask him about Vienna."

"Vienna," said Bill, "is a strange city."

"Very much like Paris," Brett smiled at him, wrinkling the corners of her eyes.

"Exactly," Bill said. "Very much like Paris at this moment."

"You have a good start."

Sitting out on the terrace of the Lilas Brett ordered a whiskey and soda, I took one, too, and Bill took another pernod.

"How are you, Jake?"

"Great," I said. "I've had a good time."

Brett looked at me. "I was a fool to go away," she said. "One's an ass to leave Paris."

"Did you have a good time?"

"Oh, all right. Interesting. Not frightfully amusing."

"See anybody?"

"No, hardly anybody. I never went out."

"Didn't you swim?"

"No. Didn't do a thing."

"Sounds like Vienna," Bill said.

Brett wrinkled up the corners of her eyes at him.

"So that's the way it was in Vienna."

"It was like everything in Vienna."

Brett smiled at him again.

"You've a nice friend, Jake."

"He's all right," I said. "He's a taxidermist."

"That was in another country," Bill said. "And besides all the animals were dead."

"One more," Brett said, "and I must run. Do send the waiter for a taxi."

"There's a line of them. Right out in front."

"Good."

We had the drink and put Brett into her taxi.

"Mind you're at the Select around ten. Make him come. Michael will be there."

"We'll be there," Bill said. The taxi started and Brett waved.

"Quite a girl," Bill said. "She's damned nice. Who's Michael?"

"The man she's going to marry."

"Well, well," Bill said. "That's always just the stage I meet anybody. What'll I send them? Think they'd like a couple of stuffed race-horses?"

"We better eat."

"Is she really Lady something or other?" Bill asked in the taxi on our way down to the Ile Saint Louis.

"Oh, yes. In the stud-book and everything."

"Well, well."

We ate dinner at Madame Lecomte's restaurant on the far side of the island. It was crowded with Americans and we had to stand up and wait for a place. Some one had put it in the American Women's Club list as a quaint restaurant on the Paris quais as yet untouched by Americans, so we had to wait forty-five minutes for a table. Bill had eaten at the restaurant in 1918, and right after the armistice, and Madame Lecomte made a great fuss over seeing him.

"Doesn't get us a table, though," Bill said. "Grand woman, though."

We had a good meal, a roast chicken, new green beans, mashed potatoes, a salad, and some apple-pie and cheese.

"You've got the world here all right," Bill said to Madame Lecomte. She raised her hand. "Oh, my God!"

"You'll be rich."

"I hope so."

After the coffee and a *fine* we got the bill, chalked up the same as ever on a slate, that was doubtless one of the "quaint" features, paid it, shook hands, and went out.

"You never come here any more, Monsieur Barnes," Madame Lecomte said.

"Too many compatriots."

"Come at lunch-time. It's not crowded then."

"Good. I'll be down soon."

We walked along under the trees that grew out over the river on the Quai d'Orléans side of the island. Across the river were the broken walls of old houses that were being torn down.

"They're going to cut a street through."

"They would," Bill said.

We walked on and circled the island. The river was dark and a bateau mouche went by, all bright with lights, going fast and quiet up and out of sight under the bridge. Down the river was Notre Dame squatting against the night sky. We crossed to the left bank of the Seine by the wooden foot-bridge from the Quai de Béthune, and stopped on the bridge and looked down the river at Notre Dame. Standing on the bridge the island looked dark, the houses were high against the sky, and the trees were shadows.

"It's pretty grand," Bill said. "God, I love to get back."

We leaned on the wooden rail of the bridge and looked up the river to the lights of the big bridges. Below the water was smooth and black. It made no sound against the piles of the bridge. A man and a girl passed us. They were walking with their arms around each other.

We crossed the bridge and walked up the Rue du Cardinal Lemoine. It was steep walking, and we went all the way up to the Place de la Contrescarpe. The arc-light shone through the leaves of the trees in the square, and underneath the trees was an S bus ready to start. Music came out of the door of the Nègre Joyeux. Through the window of the Café des Amateurs I saw the long zinc bar. Outside on the terrace working people were drinking. In the open kitchen of the Amateurs a girl was cooking potato-chips in oil. There was an iron pot of stew. The girl ladled some onto a plate for an old man who stood holding a bottle of red wine in one hand.

"Want to have a drink?"

"No," said Bill. "I don't need it."

We turned to the right off the Place de la Contrescarpe, walking along smooth narrow streets with high old houses on both sides. Some of the houses jutted out toward the street. Others were cut back. We came onto the Rue du Pot de Fer and followed it along until it brought us to the rigid north and south of the Rue Saint Jacques and then walked south, past Val de Grâce, set back behind the courtyard and the iron fence, to the Boulevard de Port Royal.

"What do you want to do?" I asked. "Go up to the café and see Brett and Mike?"

"Why not?"

We walked along Port Royal until it became Montparnasse, and then on past the Lilas, Lavigne's, and all the little cafés, Damoy's, crossed the street to the Rotonde, past its lights and tables to the Select.

Michael came toward us from the tables. He was tanned and healthy-looking.

"Hel-lo, Jake," he said. "Hel-lo! Hel-lo! How are you, old lad?"

"You look very fit, Mike."

"Oh, I am. I'm frightfully fit. I've done nothing but walk. Walk all day long. One drink a day with my mother at tea."

Bill had gone into the bar. He was standing talking with Brett, who was sitting on a high stool, her legs crossed. She had no stockings on.

"It's good to see you, Jake," Michael said. "I'm a little tight you know. Amazing, isn't it? Did you see my nose?"

There was a patch of dried blood on the bridge of his nose.

"An old lady's bags did that," Mike said. "I reached up to help her with them and they fell on me."

Brett gestured at him from the bar with her cigarette-holder and wrinkled the corners of her eyes.

"An old lady," said Mike. "Her bags *fell* on me. Let's go in and see Brett. I say, she is a piece. You *are* a lovely lady, Brett. Where did you get that hat?"

"Chap bought it for me. Don't you like it?"

"It's a dreadful hat. Do get a good hat."

"Oh, we've so much money now," Brett said. "I say, haven't you met Bill yet? You *are* a lovely host, Jake."

She turned to Mike. "This is Bill Gorton. This drunkard is Mike Campbell. Mr. Campbell is an undischarged bankrupt."

"Aren't I, though? You know I met my ex-partner yesterday in London. Chap who did me in."

"What did he say?"

"Bought me a drink. I thought I might as well take it. I say, Brett, you *are* a lovely piece. Don't you think she's beautiful?"

"Beautiful. With this nose?"

"It's a lovely nose. Go on, point it at me. Isn't she a lovely piece?"

"Couldn't we have kept the man in Scotland?"

"I say, Brett, let's turn in early."

"Don't be indecent, Michael. Remember there are ladies at this bar."

"Isn't she a lovely piece? Don't you think so, Jake?"

"There's a fight to-night," Bill said. "Like to go?"

"Fight," said Mike. "Who's fighting?"

"Ledoux and somebody."

"He's very good, Ledoux," Mike said. "I'd like to see it, rather"—he was making an effort to pull himself together—"but I can't go. I had a date with this thing here. I say, Brett, do get a new hat."

Brett pulled the felt hat down far over one eye and smiled out from under it. "You two run along to the fight. I'll have to be taking Mr. Campbell home directly."

"I'm not tight," Mike said. "Perhaps just a little. I say, Brett, you are a lovely piece."

"Go on to the fight," Brett said. "Mr. Campbell's getting difficult. What are these outbursts of affection, Michael?"

"I say, you are a lovely piece."

We said good night. "I'm sorry I can't go," Mike said. Brett laughed. I looked back from the door. Mike had one hand on the bar and was leaning toward Brett, talking. Brett was looking at him quite coolly, but the corners of her eyes were smiling.

Outside on the pavement I said: "Do you want to go to the fight?"

"Sure," said Bill. "If we don't have to walk."

"Mike was pretty excited about his girl friend," I said in the taxi.

"Well," said Bill. "You can't blame him such a hell of a lot."

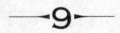

The Ledoux–Kid Francis fight was the night of the 20th of June. It was a good fight. The morning after the fight I had a letter from Robert Cohn, written from Hendaye. He was having a very quiet time, he said, bathing, playing some golf and much bridge. Hendaye had a splendid beach, but he was anxious to start on the fishing-trip. When would I be down? If I would buy him a double-tapered line he would pay me when I came down.

That same morning I wrote Cohn from the office that Bill and I would leave Paris on the 25th unless I wired him otherwise, and would meet him at Bayonne, where we could get a bus over the mountains to Pamplona. The same evening about seven o'clock I stopped in at the Select to see Michael and Brett. They were not there, and I went over to the Dingo. They were inside sitting at the bar.

"Hello, darling." Brett put out her hand.

"Hello, Jake," Mike said. "I understand I was tight last night."

"Weren't you, though," Brett said. "Disgraceful business."

"Look," said Mike, "when do you go down to Spain? Would you mind if we came down with you?"

"It would be grand."

"You wouldn't mind, really? I've been at Pamplona, you know. Brett's mad to go. You're sure we wouldn't just be a bloody nuisance?"

"Don't talk like a fool."

"I'm a little tight, you know. I wouldn't ask you like this if I weren't. You're sure you don't mind?"

"Oh, shut up, Michael," Brett said. "How can the man say he'd mind now? I'll ask him later."

"But you don't mind, do you?"

"Don't ask that again unless you want to make me sore. Bill and I go down on the morning of the 25th."

"By the way, where is Bill?" Brett asked.

"He's out at Chantilly dining with some people."

"He's a good chap."

"Splendid chap," said Mike. "He is, you know."

"You don't remember him," Brett said.

"I do. Remember him perfectly. Look, Jake, we'll come down the night of the 25th. Brett can't get up in the morning."

"Indeed not!"

"If our money comes and you're sure you don't mind."

"It will come, all right. I'll see to that."

"Tell me what tackle to send for."

"Get two or three rods with reels, and lines, and some flies."

"I won't fish," Brett put in.

"Get two rods, then, and Bill won't have to buy one."

"Right," said Mike. "I'll send a wire to the keeper."

"Won't it be splendid," Brett said. "Spain! We *will* have fun."

"The 25th. When is that?"

"Saturday."

"We *will* have to get ready."

"I say," said Mike, "I'm going to the barber's."

"I must bathe," said Brett. "Walk up to the hotel with me, Jake. Be a good chap."

"We *have* got the loveliest hotel," Mike said. "I think it's a brothel!"

"We left our bags here at the Dingo when we got in, and they asked us at this hotel if we wanted a room for the afternoon only. Seemed frightfully pleased we were going to stay all night."

"*I* believe it's a brothel," Mike said. "And *I* should know."

"Oh, shut it and go and get your hair cut."

Mike went out. Brett and I sat on at the bar.

"Have another?"

"Might."

"I needed that," Brett said.

We walked up the Rue Delambre.

"I haven't seen you since I've been back," Brett said.

"No."

"How *are* you, Jake?"

"Fine."

Brett looked at me. "I say," she said, "is Robert Cohn going on this trip?"

"Yes. Why?"

"Don't you think it will be a bit rough on him?"

"Why should it?"

"Who did you think I went down to San Sebastian with?"

"Congratulations," I said.

We walked along.

"What did you say that for?"

"I don't know. What would you like me to say?"

We walked along and turned a corner.

"He behaved rather well, too. He gets a little dull."

"Does he?"

"I rather thought it would be good for him."

"You might take up social service."

"Don't be nasty."

"I won't."

"Didn't you really know?"

"No," I said. "I guess I didn't think about it."

"Do you think it will be too rough on him?"

"That's up to him," I said. "Tell him you're coming. He can always not come."

"I'll write him and give him a chance to pull out of it."

I did not see Brett again until the night of the 24th of June.

"Did you hear from Cohn?"

"Rather. He's keen about it."

"My God!"

"I thought it was rather odd myself."

"Says he can't wait to see me."

"Does he think you're coming alone?"

"No. I told him we were all coming down together. Michael and all."

"He's wonderful."

"Isn't he?"

They expected their money the next day. We arranged to meet at

Pamplona. They would go directly to San Sebastian and take the train from there. We would all meet at the Montoya in Pamplona. If they did not turn up on Monday at the latest we would go on ahead up to Burguete in the mountains, to start fishing. There was a bus to Burguete. I wrote out an itinerary so they could follow us.

Bill and I took the morning train from the Gare d'Orsay. It was a lovely day, not too hot, and the country was beautiful from the start. We went back into the diner and had breakfast. Leaving the dining-car I asked the conductor for tickets for the first service.

"Nothing until the fifth."

"What's this?"

There were never more than two servings of lunch on that train, and always plenty of places for both of them.

"They're all reserved," the dining-car conductor said. "There will be a fifth service at three-thirty."

"This is serious," I said to Bill.

"Give him ten francs."

"Here," I said. "We want to eat in the first service."

The conductor put the ten francs in his pocket.

"Thank you," he said. "I would advise you gentlemen to get some sandwiches. All the places for the first four services were reserved at the office of the company."

"You'll go a long way, brother," Bill said to him in English. "I suppose if I'd given you five francs you would have advised us to jump off the train."

"*Comment?*"

"Go to hell!" said Bill. "Get the sandwiches made and a bottle of wine. You tell him, Jake."

"And send it up to the next car." I described where we were.

In our compartment were a man and his wife and their young son.

"I suppose you're Americans, aren't you?" the man asked. "Having a good trip?"

"Wonderful," said Bill.

"That's what you want to do. Travel while you're young. Mother and I always wanted to get over, but we had to wait a while."

"You could have come over ten years ago, if you'd wanted to," the wife said. "What you always said was: 'See America first!' I will say we've seen a good deal, take it one way and another."

"Say, there's plenty of Americans on this train," the husband said.

"They've got seven cars of them from Dayton, Ohio. They've been on a pilgrimage to Rome, and now they're going down to Biarritz and Lourdes."

"So, that's what they are. Pilgrims. Goddam Puritans," Bill said.

"What part of the States you boys from?"

"Kansas City," I said. "He's from Chicago."

"You both going to Biarritz?"

"No. We're going fishing in Spain."

"Well, I never cared for it, myself. There's plenty that do out where I come from, though. We got some of the best fishing in the State of Montana. I've been out with the boys, but I never cared for it any."

"Mighty little fishing you did on them trips," his wife said.

He winked at us.

"You know how the ladies are. If there's a jug goes along, or a case of beer, they think it's hell and damnation."

"That's the way men are," his wife said to us. She smoothed her comfortable lap. "I voted against prohibition to please him, and because I like a little beer in the house, and then he talks that way. It's a wonder they ever find any one to marry them."

"Say," said Bill, "do you know that gang of Pilgrim Fathers have cornered the dining-car until half past three this afternoon?"

"How do you mean? They can't do a thing like that."

"You try and get seats."

"Well, mother, it looks as though we better go back and get another breakfast."

She stood up and straightened her dress.

"Will you boys keep an eye on our things? Come on, Hubert."

They all three went up to the wagon restaurant. A little while after they were gone a steward went through announcing the first service, and pilgrims, with their priests, commenced filing down the corridor. Our friend and his family did not come back. A waiter passed in the corridor with our sandwiches and the bottle of Chablis, and we called him in.

"You're going to work to-day," I said.

He nodded his head. "They start now, at ten-thirty."

"When do we eat?"

"Huh! When do I eat?"

He left two glasses for the bottle, and we paid him for the sandwiches and tipped him.

"I'll get the plates," he said, "or bring them with you."

We ate the sandwiches and drank the Chablis and watched the country out of the window. The grain was just beginning to ripen and the fields were full of poppies. The pastureland was green, and there were fine trees, and sometimes big rivers and chateaux off in the trees.

At Tours we got off and bought another bottle of wine, and when we got back in the compartment the gentleman from Montana and his wife and his son, Hubert, were sitting comfortably.

"Is there good swimming in Biarritz?" asked Hubert.

"That boy's just crazy till he can get in the water," his mother said. "It's pretty hard on youngsters travelling."

"There's good swimming," I said. "But it's dangerous when it's rough."

"Did you get a meal?" Bill asked.

"We sure did. We set right there when they started to come in, and they must have just thought we were in the party. One of the waiters said something to us in French, and then they just sent three of them back."

"They thought we were snappers, all right," the man said. "It certainly shows you the power of the Catholic Church. It's a pity you boys ain't Catholics. You could get a meal, then, all right."

"I am," I said. "That's what makes me so sore."

Finally at a quarter past four we had lunch. Bill had been rather difficult at the last. He buttonholed a priest who was coming back with one of the returning streams of pilgrims.

"When do us Protestants get a chance to eat, father?"

"I don't know anything about it. Haven't you got tickets?"

"It's enough to make a man join the Klan," Bill said. The priest looked back at him.

Inside the dining-car the waiters served the fifth successive table d'hôte meal. The waiter who served us was soaked through. His white jacket was purple under the arms.

"He must drink a lot of wine."

"Or wear purple undershirts."

"Let's ask him."

"No. He's too tired."

The train stopped for half an hour at Bordeaux and we went out through the station for a little walk. There was not time to get in to the town. Afterward we passed through the Landes and watched the sun set. There were wide fire-gaps cut through the pines, and you could look up them like avenues and see wooded hills way off. About seven-thirty we had dinner and watched the country through the open window in the diner. It was all sandy pine country full of heather. There were little clearings with houses in them, and once in a while we passed a sawmill. It got dark and we could feel the country hot and sandy and dark outside of the window, and about nine o'clock we got into Bayonne. The man and his wife and Hubert all shook hands with us. They were going on to La Négresse to change for Biarritz.

"Well, I hope you have lots of luck," he said.

"Be careful about those bull-fights."

"Maybe we'll see you at Biarritz," Hubert said.

We got off with our bags and rod-cases and passed through the dark station and out to the lights and the line of cabs and hotel buses. There, standing with the hotel runners, was Robert Cohn. He did not see us at first. Then he started forward.

"Hello, Jake. Have a good trip?"

"Fine," I said. "This is Bill Gorton."

"How are you?"

"Come on," said Robert. "I've got a cab." He was a little near-sighted. I had never noticed it before. He was looking at Bill, trying to make him out. He was shy, too.

"We'll go up to my hotel. It's all right. It's quite nice."

We got into the cab, and the cabman put the bags up on the seat beside him and climbed up and cracked his whip, and we drove over the dark bridge and into the town.

"I'm awfully glad to meet you," Robert said to Bill. "I've heard so much about you from Jake and I've read your books. Did you get my line, Jake?"

The cab stopped in front of the hotel and we all got out and went in. It was a nice hotel, and the people at the desk were very cheerful, and we each had a good small room.

━1O━

In the morning it was bright, and they were sprinkling the streets of the town, and we all had breakfast in a café. Bayonne is a nice town. It is like a very clean Spanish town and it is on a big river. Already, so early in the morning, it was very hot on the bridge across the river. We walked out on the bridge and then took a walk through the town.

I was not at all sure Mike's rods would come from Scotland in time, so we hunted a tackle store and finally bought a rod for Bill up-stairs over a drygoods store. The man who sold the tackle was out, and we had to wait for him to come back. Finally he came in, and we bought a pretty good rod cheap, and two landing-nets.

We went out into the street again and took a look at the cathedral. Cohn made some remark about it being a very good example of something or other, I forget what. It seemed like a nice cathedral, nice and dim, like Spanish churches. Then we went up past the old fort and out to the local Syndicat d'Initiative office, where the bus was supposed to start from. There they told us the bus service did not start until the 1st of July. We found out at the tourist office what we ought to pay for a motor-car to Pamplona and hired one at a big garage just around the corner from the Municipal Theatre for four hundred francs. The car was to pick us up at the hotel in forty minutes, and we stopped at the café on the square where we had eaten breakfast, and had a beer. It was hot, but the town had a cool, fresh, early-morning smell and it was pleasant sitting in the café. A breeze started to blow, and you could feel that the air came from the sea. There were pigeons out in the square, and the houses were a yellow, sun-baked color, and I did not want to leave the café. But we had to go to the hotel to get our bags packed and pay the bill. We paid for the beers, we matched and I think Cohn paid, and went up to the hotel. It was only sixteen francs apiece for Bill and me, with ten per cent added for the service, and we had the bags sent down and waited for Robert Cohn. While we were waiting I saw a cockroach on the parquet floor that must have been at least three inches long. I pointed him out to Bill and then put my shoe on him. We agreed he must have just come in from the garden. It was really an awfully clean hotel.

Cohn came down, finally, and we all went out to the car. It was a big, closed car, with a driver in a white duster with blue collar and cuffs, and we had him put the back of the car down. He piled in the bags and we started off up the street and out of the town. We passed some lovely gardens and had a good look back at the town, and then we were out in the country, green and rolling, and the road climbing all the time. We passed lots of Basques with oxen, or cattle, hauling carts along the road, and nice farmhouses, low roofs, and all white-plastered. In the Basque country the land all looks very rich and green and the houses and villages look well-off and clean. Every village had a pelota court and on some of them kids were playing in the hot sun. There were signs on the walls of the churches saying it was forbidden to play pelota against them, and the houses in the villages had red tiled roofs, and then the road turned off and commenced to climb and we were going way up close along a hillside, with a valley below and hills stretched off back toward the sea. You couldn't see the sea. It was too far away. You could see only hills and more hills, and you knew where the sea was.

We crossed the Spanish frontier. There was a little stream and a bridge, and Spanish carabineers, with patent-leather Bonaparte hats, and short guns on their backs, on one side, and on the other fat Frenchmen in képis and mustaches. They only opened one bag and took the passports in and looked at them. There was a general store and inn on each side of the line. The chauffeur had to go in and fill out some papers about the car and we got out and went over to the stream to see if there were any trout. Bill tried to talk some Spanish to one of the carabineers, but it did not go very well. Robert Cohn asked, pointing with his finger, if there were any trout in the stream, and the carabineer said yes, but not many.

I asked him if he ever fished, and he said no, that he didn't care for it.

Just then an old man with long, sunburned hair and beard, and clothes that looked as though they were made of gunny-sacking, came striding up to the bridge. He was carrying a long staff, and he had a kid slung on his back, tied by the four legs, the head hanging down.

The carabineer waved him back with his sword. The man turned without saying anything, and started back up the white road into Spain.

"What's the matter with the old one?" I asked.

"He hasn't got any passport."

I offered the guard a cigarette. He took it and thanked me.

"What will he do?" I asked.

The guard spat in the dust.

"Oh, he'll just wade across the stream."

"Do you have much smuggling?"

"Oh," he said, "they go through."

The chauffeur came out, folding up the papers and putting them in the inside pocket of his coat. We all got in the car and it started up the white dusty road into Spain. For a while the country was much as it had been; then, climbing all the time, we crossed the top of a Col, the road winding back and forth on itself, and then it was really Spain. There were long brown mountains and a few pines and far-off forests of beech-trees on some of the mountainsides. The road went along the summit of the Col and then dropped down, and the driver had to honk, and slow up, and turn out to avoid running into two donkeys that were sleeping in the road. We came down out of the mountains and through an oak forest, and there were white cattle grazing in the forest. Down below there were grassy plains and clear streams, and then we crossed a stream and went through a gloomy little village, and started to climb again. We climbed up and up and crossed another high Col and turned along it, and the road ran down to the right, and we saw a whole new range of mountains off to the south, all brown and baked-looking and furrowed in strange shapes.

After a while we came out of the mountains, and there were trees along both sides of the road, and a stream and ripe fields of grain, and the road went on, very white and straight ahead, and then lifted to a little rise, and off on the left was a hill with an old castle, with buildings close around it and a field of grain going right up to the walls and shifting in the wind. I was up in front with the driver and I turned around. Robert Cohn was asleep, but Bill looked and nodded his head. Then we crossed a wide plain, and there was a big river off on the right shining in the sun from between the line of trees, and away off you could see the plateau of Pamplona rising out of the plain, and the walls of the city, and the great brown cathedral, and the broken skyline of the other churches. In back of the plateau were the mountains, and every way you looked there were other mountains, and ahead the road stretched out white across the plain going toward Pamplona.

We came into the town on the other side of the plateau, the road slanting up steeply and dustily with shade-trees on both sides, and then levelling out through the new part of town they are building up outside the old walls. We passed the bull-ring, high and white and concrete-looking in the sun, and then came into the big square by a side street and stopped in front of the Hotel Montoya.

The driver helped us down with the bags. There was a crowd of kids watching the car, and the square was hot, and the trees were green, and the flags hung on their staffs, and it was good to get out of the sun and under the shade of the arcade that runs all the way around the square. Montoya was glad to see us, and shook hands and gave us good rooms looking out on the square, and then we washed and cleaned up and went down-stairs in the dining-room for lunch. The driver stayed for lunch, too, and afterward we paid him and he started back to Bayonne.

There are two dining-rooms in the Montoya. One is up-stairs on the second floor and looks out on the square. The other is down one floor below the level of the square and has a door that opens on the back street that the bulls pass along when they run through the streets early in the morning on their way to the ring. It is always cool in the down-stairs dining-room and we had a very good lunch. The first meal in Spain was always a shock with the hors d'œuvres, an egg course, two meat courses, vegetables, salad, and dessert and fruit. You have to drink plenty of wine to get it all down. Robert Cohn tried to say he did not want any of the second meat course, but we would not interpret for him, and so the waitress brought him something else as a replacement, a plate of cold meats, I think. Cohn had been rather nervous ever since we had met at Bayonne. He did not know whether we knew Brett had been with him at San Sebastian, and it made him rather awkward.

"Well," I said, "Brett and Mike ought to get in to-night."

"I'm not sure they'll come," Cohn said.

"Why not?" Bill said. "Of course they'll come."

"They're always late," I said.

"I rather think they're not coming," Robert Cohn said.

He said it with an air of superior knowledge that irritated both of us.

"I'll bet you fifty pesetas they're here to-night," Bill said. He always bets when he is angered, and so he usually bets foolishly.

"I'll take it," Cohn said. "Good. You remember it, Jake. Fifty pesetas."

"I'll remember it myself," Bill said. I saw he was angry and wanted to smooth him down.

"It's a sure thing they'll come," I said. "But maybe not to-night."

"Want to call it off?" Cohn asked.

"No. Why should I? Make it a hundred if you like."

"All right. I'll take that."

"That's enough," I said. "Or you'll have to make a book and give me some of it."

"I'm satisfied," Cohn said. He smiled. "You'll probably win it back at bridge, anyway."

"You haven't got it yet," Bill said.

We went out to walk around under the arcade to the Café Iruña for coffee. Cohn said he was going over and get a shave.

"Say," Bill said to me, "have I got any chance on that bet?"

"You've got a rotten chance. They've never been on time anywhere. If their money doesn't come it's a cinch they won't get in tonight."

"I was sorry as soon as I opened my mouth. But I had to call him. He's all right, I guess, but where does he get this inside stuff? Mike and Brett fixed it up with us about coming down here."

I saw Cohn coming over across the square.

"Here he comes."

"Well, let him not get superior and Jewish."

"The barber shop's closed," Cohn said. "It's not open till four."

We had coffee at the Iruña, sitting in comfortable wicker chairs looking out from the cool of the arcade at the big square. After a while Bill went to write some letters and Cohn went over to the barber-shop. It was still closed, so he decided to go up to the hotel and get a bath, and I sat out in front of the café and then went for a walk in the town. It was very hot, but I kept on the shady side of the streets and went through the market and had a good time seeing the town again. I went to the Ayuntamiento and found the old gentleman who subscribes for the bull-fight tickets for me every year, and he had gotten the money I sent him from Paris and renewed my subscriptions, so that was all set. He was the archivist, and all the archives of the town were in his office. That has nothing to do with the story. Anyway, his office had a green baize door and a big wooden door, and when I went out I left him sitting among the archives that covered all the walls, and I shut both the doors, and as I went out of the building into the street the porter stopped me to brush off my coat.

"You must have been in a motor-car," he said.

The back of the collar and the upper part of the shoulders were gray with dust.

"From Bayonne."

"Well, well," he said. "I knew you were in a motor-car from the way the dust was." So I gave him two copper coins.

At the end of the street I saw the cathedral and walked up toward it. The first time I ever saw it I thought the facade was ugly but I liked it now. I went inside. It was dim and dark and the pillars went high up, and there were people praying, and it smelt of incense, and there were some wonderful big windows. I knelt and started to pray and prayed for everybody I thought of, Brett and Mike and Bill and Robert Cohn and myself, and all the bull-fighters, separately for the ones I liked, and lumping all the rest, then I prayed for myself again, and while I was praying for myself I found I was getting sleepy, so I prayed that the bull-fights would be good, and that it would be a fine fiesta, and that we would get some fishing. I wondered if there was anything else I might pray for, and I thought I would like to have some money, so I prayed that I would make a lot of money, and then I started to think how I would make it, and thinking of making money reminded me of the count, and I started wondering about where he was, and regretting I hadn't seen him since that night in Montmartre, and about something funny Brett told me about him, and as all the time I was kneeling with my forehead on the wood in front of me, and was thinking of myself as praying, I was a little ashamed, and regretted that I was such a rotten Catholic, but realized there was nothing I could do about it, at least for a while, and maybe never, but that anyway it was a grand religion, and I only wished I felt religious and maybe I would the next time; and then I was out in the hot sun on the steps of the cathedral, and the forefingers and the thumb of my right hand were still damp, and I felt them dry in the sun. The sunlight was hot and hard, and I crossed over beside some buildings, and walked back along side-streets to the hotel.

At dinner that night we found that Robert Cohn had taken a bath, had had a shave and a haircut and a shampoo, and something put on his hair afterward to make it stay down. He was nervous, and I did not try to help him any. The train was due in at nine o'clock from San Sebastian, and, if Brett and Mike were coming, they would be on it. At twenty minutes to nine we were not half through dinner. Robert Cohn got up from the table and said he would go to the station. I said I would go with him, just to devil him. Bill said he would be damned if he would leave his dinner. I said we would be right back.

We walked to the station. I was enjoying Cohn's nervousness. I hoped Brett would be on the train. At the station the train was late, and we sat on a baggage-truck and waited outside in the dark. I have never seen a man in civil life as nervous as Robert Cohn—nor as eager. I was enjoying it. It was lousy to enjoy it, but I felt lousy. Cohn had a wonderful quality of bringing out the worst in anybody.

After a while we heard the train-whistle way off below on the other side of the plateau, and then we saw the headlight coming up the hill. We went inside the station and stood with a crowd of people just back of the gates, and the train came in and stopped, and everybody started coming out through the gates.

They were not in the crowd. We waited till everybody had gone through and out of the station and gotten into buses, or taken cabs, or were walking with their friends or relatives through the dark into the town.

"I knew they wouldn't come," Robert said. We were going back to the hotel.

"I thought they might," I said.

Bill was eating fruit when we came in and finishing a bottle of wine.

"Didn't come, eh?"

"No."

"Do you mind if I give you that hundred pesetas in the morning, Cohn?" Bill asked. "I haven't changed any money here yet."

"Oh, forget about it," Robert Cohn said. "Let's bet on something else. Can you bet on bull-fights?"

"You could," Bill said, "but you don't need to."

"It would be like betting on the war," I said. "You don't need any economic interest."

"I'm very curious to see them," Robert said.

Montoya came up to our table. He had a telegram in his hand. "It's for you." He handed it to me.

It read: "Stopped night San Sebastian."

"It's from them," I said. I put it in my pocket. Ordinarily I should have handed it over.

"They've stopped over in San Sebastian," I said. "Send their regards to you."

Why I felt that impulse to devil him I do not know. Of course I do know. I was blind, unforgivingly jealous of what had happened to him. The fact that I took it as a matter of course did not alter that any. I certainly did hate him. I do not think I ever really hated him until he had that little spell of superiority at lunch—that and when he went through all that barbering. So I put the telegram in my pocket. The telegram came to me, anyway.

"Well," I said. "We ought to pull out on the noon bus for Burguete. They can follow us if they get in to-morrow night."

There were only two trains up from San Sebastian, an early morning train and the one we had just met.

"That sounds like a good idea," Cohn said.

"The sooner we get on the stream the better."

"It's all one to me when we start," Bill said. "The sooner the better."

We sat in the Iruña for a while and had coffee and then took a little walk out to the bull-ring and across the field and under the trees at the edge of the cliff and looked down at the river in the dark, and I turned in early. Bill and Cohn stayed out in the café quite late, I believe, because I was asleep when they came in.

In the morning I bought three tickets for the bus to Burguete. It was scheduled to leave at two o'clock. There was nothing earlier. I was sitting over at the Iruña reading the papers when I saw Robert Cohn coming across the square. He came up to the table and sat down in one of the wicker chairs.

"This is a comfortable café," he said. "Did you have a good night, Jake?"

"I slept like a log."

"I didn't sleep very well. Bill and I were out late, too."

"Where were you?"

"Here. And after it shut we went over to that other café. The old man there speaks German and English."

"The Café Suizo."

"That's it. He seems like a nice old fellow. I think it's a better café than this one."

"It's not so good in the daytime," I said. "Too hot. By the way, I got the bus tickets."

"I'm not going up to-day. You and Bill go on ahead."

"I've got your ticket."

"Give it to me. I'll get the money back."

"It's five pesetas."

Robert Cohn took out a silver five-peseta piece and gave it to me.

"I ought to stay," he said. "You see I'm afraid there's some sort of misunderstanding."

"Why," I said. "They may not come here for three or four days now if they start on parties at San Sebastian."

"That's just it," said Robert. "I'm afraid they expected to meet me at San Sebastian, and that's why they stopped over."

"What makes you think that?"

"Well, I wrote suggesting it to Brett."

"Why in hell didn't you stay there and meet them, then?" I started to say, but I stopped. I thought that idea would come to him by itself, but I do not believe it ever did.

He was being confidential now and it was giving him pleasure to be able to talk with the understanding that I knew there was something between him and Brett.

"Well, Bill and I will go up right after lunch," I said.

"I wish I could go. We've been looking forward to this fishing all winter." He was being sentimental about it. "But I ought to stay. I really ought. As soon as they come I'll bring them right up."

"Let's find Bill."

"I want to go over to the barber-shop."

"See you at lunch."

I found Bill up in his room. He was shaving.

"Oh, yes, he told me all about it last night," Bill said. "He's a great little confider. He said he had a date with Brett at San Sebastian."

"The lying bastard!"

"Oh, no," said Bill. "Don't get sore. Don't get sore at this stage of the trip. How did you ever happen to know this fellow anyway?"

"Don't rub it in."

Bill looked around, half-shaved, and then went on talking into the mirror while he lathered his face.

"Didn't you send him with a letter to me in New York last winter? Thank God, I'm a travelling man. Haven't you got some more Jewish friends you could bring along?" He rubbed his chin with his thumb, looked at it, and then started scraping again.

"You've got some fine ones yourself."

"Oh, yes. I've got some darbs. But not alongside of this Robert Cohn. The funny thing is he's nice, too. I like him. But he's just so awful."

"He can be damn nice."

"I know it. That's the terrible part."

I laughed.

"Yes. Go on and laugh," said Bill. "You weren't out with him last night until two o'clock."

"Was he very bad?"

"Awful. What's all this about him and Brett, anyway? Did she ever have anything to do with him?"

He raised his chin up and pulled it from side to side.

"Sure. She went down to San Sebastian with him."

"What a damn-fool thing to do. Why did she do that?"

"She wanted to get out of town and she can't go anywhere alone. She said she thought it would be good for him."

"What bloody-fool things people do. Why didn't she go off with some of her own people? Or you?"—he slurred that over—"or me? Why not me?" He looked at his face carefully in the glass, put a big dab of lather on each cheek-bone. "It's an honest face. It's a face any woman would be safe with."

"She'd never seen it."

"She should have. All women should see it. It's a face that ought to be thrown on every screen in the country. Every woman ought to be given a copy of this face as she leaves the altar. Mothers should tell their daughters about this face. My son"—he pointed the razor at me—"go west with this face and grow up with the country."

He ducked down to the bowl, rinsed his face with cold water, put on some alcohol, and then looked at himself carefully in the glass, pulling down his long upper lip.

"My God!" he said, "isn't it an awful face?"

He looked in the glass.

"And as for this Robert Cohn," Bill said, "he makes me sick, and he can go to hell, and I'm damn glad he's staying here so we won't have him fishing with us."

"You're damn right."

"We're going trout-fishing. We're going trout-fishing in the Irati River, and we're going to get tight now at lunch on the wine of the country, and then take a swell bus ride."

"Come on. Let's go over to the Iruña and start," I said.

—1 1—

It was baking hot in the square when we came out after lunch with our bags and the rod-case to go to Burguete. People were on top of the bus, and others were climbing up a ladder. Bill went up and Robert sat beside Bill to save a place for me, and I went back in the hotel to get a couple of bottles of wine to take with us. When I came out the bus was crowded. Men and women were sitting on all the baggage and boxes on top, and the women all had their fans going in the sun. It certainly was hot. Robert climbed down and I fitted into the place he had saved on the one wooden seat that ran across the top.

Robert Cohn stood in the shade of the arcade waiting for us to start. A Basque with a big leather wine-bag in his lap lay across the top of the bus in front of our seat, leaning back against our legs. He offered the wine-skin to Bill and to me, and when I tipped it up to drink he imitated the sound of a klaxon motor-horn so well and so suddenly that I spilled some of the wine, and everybody laughed. He apologized and made me take another drink. He made the klaxon again a little later, and it fooled me the second time. He was very good at it. The Basques liked it. The man next to Bill was talking to him in Spanish and Bill was not getting it, so he offered the man one of the bottles of wine. The man waved it away. He said it was too hot and he had drunk too much at lunch. When Bill offered the bottle the second time he took a long drink, and then the bottle went all over that part of the bus. Every one took a drink very politely, and then they made us cork it up and put it away. They all wanted us to drink from their leather wine-bottles. They were peasants going up into the hills.

Finally, after a couple more false klaxons, the bus started, and Robert Cohn waved good-bye to us, and all the Basques waved good-bye to him. As soon as we started out on the road outside of town it was cool. It felt nice riding high up and close under the trees. The bus went quite fast and made a good breeze, and as we went out along the road with the dust powdering the trees and down the hill, we had a fine view, back through the trees, of the town rising up from the bluff above the river. The Basque lying against my knees pointed out the view with the neck of the wine-bottle, and winked at us. He nodded his head.

"Pretty nice, eh?"

"These Basques are swell people," Bill said.

The Basque lying against my legs was tanned the color of saddle-leather. He wore a black smock like all the rest. There were wrinkles in his tanned neck. He turned around and offered his wine-bag to Bill. Bill handed him one of our bottles. The Basque wagged a forefinger at him and handed the bottle back, slapping in the cork with the palm of his hand. He shoved the wine-bag up.

"Arriba! Arriba!" he said. "Lift it up."

Bill raised the wine-skin and let the stream of wine spurt out and into his mouth, his head tipped back. When he stopped drinking and tipped the leather bottle down a few drops ran down his chin.

"No! No!" several Basques said. "Not like that." One snatched the bottle away from the owner, who was himself about to give a demonstration. He was a young fellow and he held the wine-bottle at full arms' length and raised it high up, squeezing the leather bag with his hand so the stream of wine hissed into his mouth. He held the bag out there, the wine making a flat, hard trajectory into his mouth, and he kept on swallowing smoothly and regularly.

"Hey!" the owner of the bottle shouted. "Whose wine is that?"

The drinker waggled his little finger at him and smiled at us with his eyes. Then he bit the stream off sharp, made a quick lift with the wine-bag and lowered it down to the owner. He winked at us. The owner shook the wine-skin sadly.

We passed through a town and stopped in front of the posada, and the driver took on several packages. Then we started on again, and outside the town the road commenced to mount. We were going through farming country with rocky hills that sloped down into the fields. The grain-fields went up the hillsides. Now as we went higher there was a wind blowing the grain. The road was white and dusty, and the dust rose under the wheels and hung in the air behind us. The road climbed up into the hills and left the rich grain-fields below. Now there were only patches of grain on the bare hillsides and on each side of the water-courses. We turned sharply out to the side of the road to give room to pass to a long string of six mules, following one after the other, hauling a high-hooded wagon loaded with freight. The wagon and the mules were covered with dust. Close behind was another string of mules and another wagon. This was loaded with lumber, and the arriero driving the mules leaned back and put on the thick wooden brakes as we passed. Up here the country was quite barren and the hills were rocky and hard-baked clay furrowed by the rain.

We came around a curve into a town, and on both sides opened out a sudden green valley. A stream went through the centre of the town and fields of grapes touched the houses.

The bus stopped in front of a posada and many of the passengers got down, and a lot of the baggage was unstrapped from the roof from under the big tarpaulins and lifted down. Bill and I got down and went into the posada. There was a low, dark room with saddles and harness, and hay-forks made of white wood, and clusters of canvas rope-soled shoes and hams and slabs of bacon and white garlics and long sausages hanging from the roof. It was cool and dusky, and we stood in front of a long wooden counter with two women behind it serving drinks. Behind them were shelves stacked with supplies and goods.

We each had an aguardiente and paid forty centimes for the two drinks. I gave the woman fifty centimes to make a tip, and she gave me back the copper piece, thinking I had misunderstood the price.

Two of our Basques came in and insisted on buying a drink. So they bought a drink and then we bought a drink, and then they slapped us on the back and bought another drink. Then we bought, and then we all went out into the sunlight and the heat, and climbed back on top of the bus. There was plenty of room now for every one to sit on the seat, and the Basque who had been lying on the tin roof now sat between us. The woman who had been serving drinks came out wiping her hands on her apron and talked to somebody inside the bus. Then the driver came out swinging two flat leather mail-pouches and climbed up, and everybody waving we started off.

The road left the green valley at once, and we were up in the hills again. Bill and the wine-bottle Basque were having a conversation. A man leaned over from the other side of the seat and asked in English: "You're Americans?"

"Sure."

"I been there," he said. "Forty years ago."

He was an old man, as brown as the others, with the stubble of a white beard.

"How was it?"

"What you say?"

"How was America?"

"Oh, I was in California. It was fine."

"Why did you leave?"

"What you say?"

"Why did you come back here?"

"Oh! I come back to get married. I was going to go back but my wife she don't like to travel. Where you from?"

"Kansas City."

"I been there," he said. "I been in Chicago, St. Louis, Kansas City, Denver, Los Angeles, Salt Lake City."

He named them carefully.

"How long were you over?"

"Fifteen years. Then I come back and got married."

"Have a drink?"

"All right," he said. "You can't get this in America, eh?"

"There's plenty if you can pay for it."

"What you come over here for?"

"We're going to the fiesta at Pamplona."

"You like the bull-fights?"

"Sure. Don't you?"

"Yes," he said. "I guess I like them."

Then after a little:

"Where you go now?"

"Up to Burguete to fish."

"Well," he said, "I hope you catch something."

He shook hands and turned around to the back seat again. The other Basques had been impressed. He sat back comfortably and smiled at me when I turned around to look at the country. But the effort of talking American seemed to have tired him. He did not say anything after that.

The bus climbed steadily up the road. The country was barren and rocks stuck up through the clay. There was no grass beside the road. Looking back we could see the country spread out below. Far back the fields were squares of green and brown on the hillsides. Making the horizon were the brown mountains. They were strangely shaped. As we climbed higher the horizon kept changing. As the bus ground slowly up the road we could see other mountains coming up in the south. Then the road came over the crest, flattened out, and went into a forest. It was a forest of cork oaks, and the sun came through the trees in patches, and there were cattle grazing back in the trees. We went through the forest and the road came out and turned along a rise of land, and out ahead of us was a rolling green plain, with dark mountains beyond it. These were not like the brown, heat-baked mountains we had left behind. These were wooded and there were clouds coming down from them. The green plain stretched off. It was cut by fences and the white of the road showed through the trunks of a double line of trees that crossed the plain toward the north. As we came to the edge of the rise we saw the red roofs and white houses of Burguete ahead strung out on the plain, and away off on the shoulder of the first dark mountain was the gray metal-sheathed roof of the monastery of Roncesvalles.

"There's Roncevaux," I said.

"Where?"

"Way off there where the mountain starts."

"It's cold up here," Bill said.

"It's high," I said. "It must be twelve hundred metres."

"It's awful cold," Bill said.

The bus levelled down onto the straight line of road that ran to Burguete. We passed a crossroads and crossed a bridge over a stream. The houses of Burguete were along both sides of the road. There were no side-streets. We passed the church and the school-yard, and the bus stopped. We got down and the driver handed down our bags and the rod-case. A carabineer in his cocked hat and yellow leather cross-straps came up.

"What's in there?" he pointed to the rod-case.

I opened it and showed him. He asked to see our fishing permits and I got them out. He looked at the date and then waved us on.

"Is that all right?" I asked.

"Yes. Of course."

We went up the street, past the whitewashed stone houses, families sitting in their doorways watching us, to the inn.

The fat woman who ran the inn came out from the kitchen and shook hands with us. She took off her spectacles, wiped them, and put them on again. It was cold in the inn and the wind was starting to blow outside. The woman sent a girl up-stairs with us to show the room. There were two beds, a washstand, a clothes-chest, and a big, framed steel-engraving of Nuestra Señora de Roncesvalles. The wind was blowing against the shutters. The room was on the north side of the inn. We washed, put on sweaters, and came down-stairs into the dining-room. It had a stone floor, low ceiling, and was oak-panelled. The shutters were all up and it was so cold you could see your breath.

"My God!" said Bill. "It can't be this cold to-morrow. I'm not going to wade a stream in this weather."

There was an upright piano in the far corner of the room beyond the wooden tables and Bill went over and started to play.

"I got to keep warm," he said.

I went out to find the woman and ask her how much the room and board was. She put her hands under her apron and looked away from me.

"Twelve pesetas."

"Why, we only paid that in Pamplona."

She did not say anything, just took off her glasses and wiped them on her apron.

"That's too much," I said. "We didn't pay more than that at a big hotel."

"We've put in a bathroom."

"Haven't you got anything cheaper?"

"Not in the summer. Now is the big season."

We were the only people in the inn. Well, I thought, it's only a few days.

"Is the wine included?"

"Oh, yes."

"Well," I said. "It's all right."

I went back to Bill. He blew his breath at me to show how cold it was, and went on playing. I sat at one of the tables and looked at the pictures on the wall. There was one panel of rabbits, dead, one of pheasants, also dead, and one panel of dead ducks. The panels were all dark and smoky-looking. There was a cupboard full of liqueur bottles. I looked at them all. Bill was still playing. "How about a hot rum punch?" he said. "This isn't going to keep me warm permanently."

I went out and told the woman what a rum punch was and how to make it. In a few minutes a girl brought a stone pitcher, steaming, into the room. Bill came over from the piano and we drank the hot punch and listened to the wind.

"There isn't too much rum in that."

I went over to the cupboard and brought the rum bottle and poured a half-tumblerful into the pitcher.

"Direct action," said Bill. "It beats legislation."

The girl came in and laid the table for supper.

"It blows like hell up here," Bill said.

The girl brought in a big bowl of hot vegetable soup and the wine. We had fried trout afterward and some sort of a stew and a big bowl full of wild strawberries. We did not lose money on the wine, and the girl was shy but nice about bringing it. The old woman looked in once and counted the empty bottles.

After supper we went up-stairs and smoked and read in bed to keep warm. Once in the night I woke and heard the wind blowing. It felt good to be warm and in bed.

—12—

When I woke in the morning I went to the window and looked out. It had cleared and there were no clouds on the mountains. Outside under the window were some carts and an old diligence, the wood of the roof cracked and split by the weather. It must have been left from the days before the motor-buses. A goat hopped up on one of the carts and then to the roof of the diligence. He jerked his head at the other goats below and when I waved at him he bounded down.

Bill was still sleeping, so I dressed, put on my shoes outside in the hall, and went down-stairs. No one was stirring down-stairs, so I unbolted the door and went out. It was cool outside in the early morning and the sun had not yet dried the dew that had come when the wind died down. I hunted around in the shed behind the inn and found a sort of mattock, and went down toward the stream to try and dig some worms for bait. The stream was clear and shallow but it did not look trouty. On the grassy bank where it was damp I drove the mattock into the earth and loosened a chunk of sod. There were worms underneath. They slid out of sight as I lifted the sod and I dug carefully and got a good many. Digging at the edge of the damp ground I filled two empty tobacco-tins with worms and sifted dirt onto them. The goats watched me dig.

When I went back into the inn the woman was down in the kitchen, and I asked her to get coffee for us, and that we wanted a lunch. Bill was awake and sitting on the edge of the bed.

"I saw you out of the window," he said. "Didn't want to interrupt you. What were you doing? Burying your money?"

"You lazy bum!"

"Been working for the common good? Splendid. I want you to do that every morning."

"Come on," I said. "Get up."

"What? Get up? I never get up."

He climbed into bed and pulled the sheet up to his chin.

"Try and argue me into getting up."

I went on looking for the tackle and putting it all together in the tackle-bag.

"Aren't you interested?" Bill asked.

"I'm going down and eat."

"Eat? Why didn't you say eat? I thought you just wanted me to get up for fun. Eat? Fine. Now you're reasonable. You go out and dig some more worms and I'll be right down."

"Oh, go to hell!"

"Work for the good of all." Bill stepped into his underclothes. "Show irony and pity."

I started out of the room with the tackle-bag, the nets, and the rod-case.

"Hey! come back!"

I put my head in the door.

"Aren't you going to show a little irony and pity?"

I thumbed my nose.

"That's not irony."

As I went down-stairs I heard Bill singing, "Irony and Pity. When you're feeling . . . Oh, Give them Irony and Give them Pity. Oh, give them Irony. When they're feeling . . . Just a little irony. Just a little pity . . ." He kept on singing until he came down-stairs. The tune was: "The Bells are Ringing for Me and my Gal." I was reading a week-old Spanish paper.

"What's all this irony and pity?"

"What? Don't you know about Irony and Pity?"

"No. Who got it up?"

"Everybody. They're mad about it in New York. It's just like the Fratellinis used to be."

The girl came in with the coffee and buttered toast. Or, rather, it was bread toasted and buttered.

"Ask her if she's got any jam," Bill said. "Be ironical with her."

"Have you got any jam?"

"That's not ironical. I wish I could talk Spanish."

The coffee was good and we drank it out of big bowls. The girl brought in a glass dish of raspberry jam.

"Thank you."

"Hey! that's not the way," Bill said. "Say something ironical. Make some crack about Primo de Rivera."

"I could ask her what kind of a jam they think they've gotten into in the Riff."

"Poor," said Bill. "Very poor. You can't do it. That's all. You don't understand irony. You have no pity. Say something pitiful."

"Robert Cohn."

"Not so bad. That's better. Now why is Cohn pitiful? Be ironic."

He took a big gulp of coffee.

"Aw, hell!" I said. "It's too early in the morning."

"There you go. And you claim you want to be a writer, too. You're only a newspaper man. An expatriated newspaper man. You ought to be ironical the minute you get out of bed. You ought to wake up with your mouth full of pity."

"Go on," I said. "Who did you get this stuff from?"

"Everybody. Don't you read? Don't you ever see anybody? You know what you are? You're an expatriate. Why don't you live in New York? Then you'd know these things. What do you want me to do? Come over here and tell you every year?"

"Take some more coffee," I said.

"Good. Coffee is good for you. It's the caffeine in it. Caffeine, we are here. Caffeine puts a man on her horse and a woman in his grave. You know what's the trouble with you? You're an expatriate. One of the worst type. Haven't you heard that? Nobody that ever left their own country ever wrote anything worth printing. Not even in the newspapers."

He drank the coffee.

"You're an expatriate. You've lost touch with the soil. You get precious. Fake European standards have ruined you. You drink yourself to death. You become obsessed by sex. You spend all your time talking, not working. You are an expatriate, see? You hang around cafés."

"It sounds like a swell life," I said. "When do I work?"

"You don't work. One group claims women support you. Another group claims you're impotent."

"No," I said. "I just had an accident."

"Never mention that," Bill said. "That's the sort of thing that can't be spoken of. That's what you ought to work up into a mystery. Like Henry's bicycle."

He had been going splendidly, but he stopped. I was afraid he thought he had hurt me with that crack about being impotent. I wanted to start him again.

"It wasn't a bicycle," I said. "He was riding horseback."

"I heard it was a tricycle."

"Well," I said. "A plane is sort of like a tricycle. The joystick works the same way."

"But you don't pedal it."

"No," I said, "I guess you don't pedal it."

"Let's lay off that," Bill said.

"All right. I was just standing up for the tricycle."

"I think he's a good writer, too," Bill said. "And you're a hell of a good guy. Anybody ever tell you were a good guy?"

"I'm not a good guy."

"Listen. You're a hell of a good guy, and I'm fonder of you than anybody on earth. I couldn't tell you that in New York. It'd mean I was a faggot. That was what the Civil War was about. Abraham Lincoln was a faggot. He was in love with General Grant. So was Jefferson Davis. Lincoln just freed the slaves on a bet. The Dred Scott case was framed by the Anti-Saloon League. Sex explains it all. The Colonel's Lady and Judy O'Grady are Lesbians under their skin."

He stopped.

"Want to hear some more?"

"Shoot," I said.

"I don't know any more. Tell you some more at lunch."

"Old Bill," I said.

"You bum!"

We packed the lunch and two bottles of wine in the rucksack, and Bill put it on. I carried the rod-case and the landing-nets slung over my back. We started up the road and then went across a meadow and found a path that crossed the fields and went toward the woods on the slope of the first hill. We walked across the fields on the sandy path. The fields were rolling and grassy and the grass was short from the sheep grazing. The cattle were up in the hills. We heard their bells in the woods.

The path crossed a stream on a foot-log. The log was surfaced off, and there was a sapling bent across for a rail. In the flat pool beside the stream tadpoles spotted the sand. We went up a steep bank and across the rolling fields. Looking back we saw Burguete, white houses and red roofs, and the white road with a truck going along it and the dust rising.

Beyond the fields we crossed another faster-flowing stream. A sandy road led down to the ford and beyond into the woods. The path crossed the stream on another foot-log below the ford, and joined the road, and we went into the woods.

It was a beech wood and the trees were very old. Their roots bulked above the ground and the branches were twisted. We walked on the road between the thick trunks of the old beeches and the sunlight came through the leaves in light patches on the grass. The trees were big, and the foliage was thick but it was not gloomy. There was no undergrowth, only the smooth grass, very green and fresh, and the big gray trees well spaced as though it were a park.

"This is country," Bill said.

The road went up a hill and we got into thick woods, and the road kept on climbing. Sometimes it dipped down but rose again steeply. All the time we heard the cattle in the woods. Finally, the road came out on the top of the hills. We were on the top of the height of land that was the highest part of the range of wooded hills we had seen from Burguete. There were wild strawberries growing on the sunny side of the ridge in a little clearing in the trees.

Ahead the road came out of the forest and went along the shoulder of the ridge of hills. The hills ahead were not wooded, and there were great fields of yellow gorse. Way off we saw the steep bluffs, dark with trees and jutting with gray stone, that marked the course of the Irati River.

"We have to follow this road along the ridge, cross these hills, go through the woods on the far hills, and come down to the Irati valley," I pointed out to Bill.

"That's a hell of a hike."

"It's too far to go and fish and come back the same day, comfortably."

"Comfortably. That's a nice word. We'll have to go like hell to get there and back and have any fishing at all."

It was a long walk and the country was very fine, but we were tired when we came down the steep road that led out of the wooded hills into the valley of the Río de la Fábrica.

The road came out from the shadow of the woods into the hot sun. Ahead was a river-valley. Beyond the river was a steep hill. There was a field of buckwheat on the hill. We saw a white house under some trees on the hillside. It was very hot and we stopped under some trees beside a dam that crossed the river.

Bill put the pack against one of the trees and we jointed up the rods, put on the reels, tied on leaders, and got ready to fish.

"You're sure this thing has trout in it?" Bill asked.

"It's full of them."

"I'm going to fish a fly. You got any McGintys?"

"There's some in there."

"You going to fish bait?"

"Yeah. I'm going to fish the dam here."

"Well, I'll take the fly-book, then." He tied on a fly. "Where'd I better go? Up or down?"

"Down is the best. They're plenty up above, too."

Bill went down the bank.

"Take a worm can."

"No, I don't want one. If they won't take a fly I'll just flick it around."

Bill was down below watching the stream.

"Say," he called up against the noise of the dam. "How about putting the wine in that spring up the road?"

"All right," I shouted. Bill waved his hand and started down the stream. I found the two wine-bottles in the pack, and carried them up the road to where the water of a spring flowed out of an iron pipe. There was a board over the spring and I lifted it and, knocking the corks firmly into the bottles, lowered them down into the water. It was so cold my hand and wrist felt numbed. I put back the slab of wood, and hoped nobody would find the wine.

I got my rod that was leaning against the tree, took the bait-can and landing-net, and walked out onto the dam. It was built to provide a head of water for driving logs. The gate was up, and I sat on one of the squared timbers and watched the smooth apron of water before the river tumbled into the falls. In the white water at the foot of the dam it was deep. As I baited up, a trout shot up out of the white water into the falls and was carried down. Before I could finish baiting, another trout jumped at the falls, making the same lovely arc and disappearing into the water that was thundering down. I put on a good-sized sinker and dropped into the white water close to the edge of the timbers of the dam.

I did not feel the first trout strike. When I started to pull up I felt that I had one and brought him, fighting and bending the rod almost double, out of the boiling water at the foot of the falls, and swung him up and onto the dam. He was a good trout, and I banged his head against the timber so that he quivered out straight, and then slipped him into my bag.

While I had him on, several trout had jumped at the falls. As soon as I baited up and dropped in again I hooked another and brought him in the same way. In a little while I had six. They were all about the same size. I laid them out, side by side, all their heads pointing the same way, and looked at them. They were beautifully colored and firm and hard from the cold water. It was a hot day, so I slit them all and shucked out the insides, gills and all, and tossed them over across the river. I took the trout ashore, washed them in the cold, smoothly heavy water above the dam, and then picked some ferns and packed them all in the bag, three trout on a layer of ferns, then another layer of ferns, then three more trout, and then covered them with ferns. They looked nice in the ferns, and now the bag was bulky, and I put it in the shade of the tree.

It was very hot on the dam, so I put my worm-can in the shade with the bag, and got a book out of the pack and settled down under the tree to read until Bill should come up for lunch.

It was a little past noon and there was not much shade, but I sat against the trunk of two of the trees that grew together, and read. The book was something by A. E. W. Mason, and I was reading a wonderful story about a man who had been frozen in the Alps and then fallen into a glacier and disappeared, and his bride was going to wait twenty-four years exactly for his body to come out on the moraine, while her true love waited too, and they were still waiting when Bill came up.

"Get any?" he asked. He had his rod and his bag and his net all in one hand, and he was sweating. I hadn't heard him come up, because of the noise from the dam.

"Six. What did you get?"

Bill sat down, opened up his bag, laid a big trout on the grass. He took out three more, each one a little bigger than the last, and laid them side by side in the shade from the tree. His face was sweaty and happy.

"How are yours?"

"Smaller."

"Let's see them."

"They're packed."

"How big are they really?"

"They're all about the size of your smallest."

"You're not holding out on me?"

"I wish I were."

"Get them all on worms?"

"Yes."

"You lazy bum!"

Bill put the trout in the bag and started for the river, swinging the open bag. He was wet from the waist down and I knew he must have been wading the stream.

I walked up the road and got out the two bottles of wine. They were cold. Moisture beaded on the bottles as I walked back to the trees. I spread the lunch on a newspaper, and uncorked one of the bottles and leaned the other against a tree. Bill came up drying his hands, his bag plump with ferns.

"Let's see that bottle," he said. He pulled the cork, and tipped up the bottle and drank. "Whew! That makes my eyes ache."

"Let's try it."

The wine was icy cold and tasted faintly rusty.

"That's not such filthy wine," Bill said.

"The cold helps it," I said.

We unwrapped the little parcels of lunch.

"Chicken."

"There's hard-boiled eggs."

"Find any salt?"

"First the egg," said Bill. "Then the chicken. Even Bryan could see that."

"He's dead. I read it in the paper yesterday."

"No. Not really?"

"Yes. Bryan's dead."

Bill laid down the egg he was peeling.

"Gentlemen," he said, and unwrapped a drumstick from a piece of newspaper. "I reverse the order. For Bryan's sake. As a tribute to the Great Commoner. First the chicken; then the egg."

"Wonder what day God created the chicken?"

"Oh," said Bill, sucking the drumstick, "how should we know? We should not question. Our stay on earth is not for long. Let us rejoice and believe and give thanks."

"Eat an egg."

Bill gestured with the drumstick in one hand and the bottle of wine in the other.

"Let us rejoice in our blessings. Let us utilize the fowls of the air. Let us utilize the product of the vine. Will you utilize a little, brother?"

"After you, brother."

Bill took a long drink.

"Utilize a little, brother," he handed me the bottle. "Let us not doubt, brother. Let us not pry into the holy mysteries of the hen-coop with simian fingers. Let us accept on faith and simply say—I want you to join with me in saying—What shall we say, brother?" He pointed the drumstick at me and went on. "Let me tell you. We will say, and I for one am proud to say—and I want you to say with me, on your knees, brother. Let no man be ashamed to kneel here in the great out-of-doors. Remember the woods were God's first temples. Let us kneel and say: 'Don't eat that, Lady—that's Mencken.' "

"Here," I said. "Utilize a little of this."

We uncorked the other bottle.

"What's the matter?" I said. "Didn't you like Bryan?"

"I loved Bryan," said Bill. "We were like brothers."

"Where did you know him?"

"He and Mencken and I all went to Holy Cross together."

"And Frankie Frisch."

"It's a lie. Frankie Frisch went to Fordham."

"Well," I said, "I went to Loyola with Bishop Manning."

"It's a lie," Bill said. "I went to Loyola with Bishop Manning myself."

"You're cock-eyed," I said.

"On wine?"

"Why not?"

"It's the humidity," Bill said. "They ought to take this damn humidity away."

"Have another shot."

"Is this all we've got?"

"Only the two bottles."

"Do you know what you are?" Bill looked at the bottle affectionately.

"No," I said.

"You're in the pay of the Anti-Saloon League."

"I went to Notre Dame with Wayne B. Wheeler."

"It's a lie," said Bill. "I went to Austin Business College with Wayne B. Wheeler. He was class president."

"Well," I said, "the saloon must go."

"You're right there, old classmate," Bill said. "The saloon must go, and I will take it with me."

"You're cock-eyed."

"On wine?"

"On wine."

"Well, maybe I am."

"Want to take a nap?"

"All right."

We lay with our heads in the shade and looked up into the trees.

"You asleep?"

"No," Bill said. "I was thinking."

I shut my eyes. It felt good lying on the ground.

"Say," Bill said, "what about this Brett business?"

"What about it?"

"Were you ever in love with her?"

"Sure."

"For how long?"

"Off and on for a hell of a long time."

"Oh, hell!" Bill said. "I'm sorry, fella."

"It's all right," I said. "I don't give a damn any more."

"Really?"

"Really. Only I'd a hell of a lot rather not talk about it."

"You aren't sore I asked you?"

"Why the hell should I be?"

"I'm going to sleep," Bill said. He put a newspaper over his face.

"Listen, Jake," he said, "are you really a Catholic?"

"Technically."

"What does that mean?"

"I don't know."

"All right, I'll go to sleep now," he said. "Don't keep me awake by talking so much."

I went to sleep, too. When I woke up Bill was packing the rucksack. It was late in the afternoon and the shadow from the trees was long and went out over the dam. I was stiff from sleeping on the ground.

"What did you do? Wake up?" Bill asked. "Why didn't you spend the night?" I stretched and rubbed my eyes.

"I had a lovely dream," Bill said. "I don't remember what it was about, but it was a lovely dream."

"I don't think I dreamt."

"You ought to dream," Bill said. "All our biggest business men have been dreamers. Look at Ford. Look at President Coolidge. Look at Rockefeller. Look at Jo Davidson."

I disjointed my rod and Bill's and packed them in the rod-case. I put the reels in the tackle-bag. Bill had packed the rucksack and we put one of the trout-bags in. I carried the other.

"Well," said Bill, "have we got everything?"

"The worms."

"Your worms. Put them in there."

He had the pack on his back and I put the worm-cans in one of the outside flap pockets.

"You got everything now?"

I looked around on the grass at the foot of the elm-trees.

"Yes."

We started up the road into the woods. It was a long walk home to Burguete, and it was dark when we came down across the fields to the road, and along the road between the houses of the town, their windows lighted, to the inn.

We stayed five days at Burguete and had good fishing. The nights were cold and the days were hot, and there was always a breeze even in the heat of the day. It was hot enough so that it felt good to wade in a cold stream, and the sun dried you when you came out and sat on the bank. We found a stream with a pool deep enough to swim in. In the evenings we played three-handed bridge with an Englishman named Harris, who had walked over from Saint Jean Pied de Port and was stopping at the inn for the fishing. He was very pleasant and went with us twice to the Irati River. There was no word from Robert Cohn nor from Brett and Mike.

One morning I went down to breakfast and the Englishman, Harris, was already at the table. He was reading the paper through spectacles. He looked up and smiled.

"Good morning," he said. "Letter for you. I stopped at the post and they gave it me with mine."

The letter was at my place at the table, leaning against a coffee-cup. Harris was reading the paper again. I opened the letter. It had been forwarded from Pamplona. It was dated San Sebastian, Sunday:

> Dear Jake,
> We got here Friday, Brett passed out on the train, so brought her here for 3 days rest with old friends of ours. We go to Montoya Hotel Pamplona Tuesday, arriving at I don't know what hour. Will you send a note by the bus to tell us what to do to rejoin you all on Wednesday. All our love and sorry to be late, but Brett was really done in and will be quite all right by Tues. and is practically so now. I know her so well and try to look after her but it's not so easy. Love to all the chaps,
>
> Michael.

"What day of the week is it?" I asked Harris.

"Wednesday, I think. Yes, quite. Wednesday. Wonderful how one loses track of the days up here in the mountains."

"Yes. We've been here nearly a week."

"I hope you're not thinking of leaving?"

"Yes. We'll go in on the afternoon bus, I'm afraid."

"What a rotten business. I had hoped we'd all have another go at the Irati together."

"We have to go in to Pamplona. We're meeting people there."

"What rotten luck for me. We've had a jolly time here at Burguete."

"Come on in to Pamplona. We can play some bridge there, and there's going to be a damned fine fiesta."

"I'd like to. Awfully nice of you to ask me. I'd best stop on here, though. I've not much more time to fish."

"You want those big ones in the Irati."

"I say, I do, you know. They're enormous trout there."

"I'd like to try them once more."

"Do. Stop over another day. Be a good chap."

"We really have to get into town," I said.

"What a pity."

After breakfast Bill and I were sitting warming in the sun on a bench out in front of the inn and talking it over. I saw a girl coming up the road from the centre of the town. She stopped in front of us and took a telegram out of the leather wallet that hung against her skirt.

"Para ustedes?"

I looked at it. The address was: "Barnes, Burguete."

"Yes. It's for us."

She brought out a book for me to sign, and I gave her a couple of coppers. The telegram was in Spanish:

VENGO JUEVES COHN

I handed it to Bill.

"What does the word Cohn mean?" he asked.

"What a lousy telegram!" I said. "He could send ten words for the same price. 'I come Thursday.' That gives you a lot of dope, doesn't it?"

"It gives you all the dope that's of interest to Cohn."

"We're going in, anyway," I said. "There's no use trying to move Brett and Mike out here and back before the fiesta. Should we answer it?"

"We might as well," said Bill. "There's no need for us to be snooty."

We walked up to the post-office and asked for a telegraph blank.

"What will we say?" Bill asked.

" 'Arriving to-night.' That's enough."

We paid for the message and walked back to the inn. Harris was there and the three of us walked up to Roncesvalles. We went through the monastery.

"It's remarkable place," Harris said, when we came out. "But you know I'm not much on those sort of places."

"Me either," Bill said.

"It's a remarkable place, though," Harris said. "I wouldn't not have seen it. I'd been intending coming up each day."

"It isn't the same as fishing, though, is it?" Bill asked. He liked Harris.

"I say not."

We were standing in front of the old chapel of the monastery.

"Isn't that a pub across the way?" Harris asked. "Or do my eyes deceive me?"

"It has the look of a pub," Bill said.

"It looks to me like a pub," I said.

"I say," said Harris, "let's utilize it." He had taken up utilizing from Bill.

We had a bottle of wine apiece. Harris would not let us pay.

He talked Spanish quite well, and the innkeeper would not take our money.

"I say. You don't know what it's meant to me to have you chaps up here."

"We've had a grand time, Harris."

Harris was a little tight.

"I say. Really you don't know how much it means. I've not had much fun since the war."

"We'll fish together again, some time. Don't you forget it, Harris."

"We must. We *have* had such a jolly good time."

"How about another bottle around?"

"Jolly good idea," said Harris.

"This is mine," said Bill. "Or we don't drink it."

"I wish you'd let me pay for it. It *does* give me pleasure, you know."

"This is going to give me pleasure," Bill said.

The innkeeper brought in the fourth bottle. We had kept the same glasses. Harris lifted his glass.

"I say. You know this does utilize well."

Bill slapped him on the back.

"Good old Harris."

"I say. You know my name isn't really Harris. It's Wilson Harris. All one name. With a hyphen, you know."

"Good old Wilson-Harris," Bill said. "We call you Harris because we're so fond of you."

"I say, Barnes. You don't know what this all means to me."

"Come on and utilize another glass," I said.

"Barnes. Really, Barnes, you can't know. That's all."

"Drink up, Harris."

We walked back down the road from Roncesvalles with Harris between us. We had lunch at the inn and Harris went with us to the bus. He gave us his card, with his address in London and his club and his business address, and as we got on the bus he handed us each an envelope. I opened mine and there were a dozen flies in it. Harris had tied them himself. He tied all his own flies.

"I say, Harris—" I began.

"No, no!" he said. He was climbing down from the bus. "They're not first-rate flies at all. I only thought if you fished them some time it might remind you of what a good time we had."

The bus started. Harris stood in front of the post-office. He waved. As we started along the road he turned and walked back toward the inn.

"Say, wasn't that Harris nice?" Bill said.

"I think he really did have a good time."

"Harris? You bet he did."

"I wish he'd come into Pamplona."

"He wanted to fish."

"Yes. You couldn't tell how English would mix with each other, anyway."

"I suppose not."

We got into Pamplona late in the afternoon and the bus stopped in front of the Hotel Montoya. Out in the plaza they were stringing electric-light wires to light the plaza for the fiesta. A few kids came up when the bus stopped, and a customs officer for the town made all the people getting down from the bus open their bundles on the sidewalk. We went into the hotel and on the stairs I met Montoya. He shook hands with us, smiling in his embarrassed way.

"Your friends are here," he said.

"Mr. Campbell?"

"Yes. Mr. Cohn and Mr. Campbell and Lady Ashley."

He smiled as though there were something I would hear about.

"When did they get in?"

"Yesterday. I've saved you the rooms you had."

"That's fine. Did you give Mr. Campbell the room on the plaza?"

"Yes. All the rooms we looked at."

"Where are our friends now?"

"I think they went to the pelota."

"And how about the bulls?"

Montoya smiled. "To-night," he said. "To-night at seven o'clock they bring in the Villar bulls, and to-morrow come the Miuras. Do you all go down?"

"Oh, yes. They've never seen a desencajonada."

Montoya put his hand on my shoulder.

"I'll see you there."

He smiled again. He always smiled as though bull-fighting were a very special secret between the two of us; a rather shocking but really very deep secret that we knew about. He always smiled as though there were something lewd about the secret to outsiders, but that it was something that we understood. It would not do to expose it to people who would not understand.

"Your friend, is he aficionado, too?" Montoya smiled at Bill.

"Yes. He came all the way from New York to see the San Fermines."

"Yes?" Montoya politely disbelieved. "But he's not aficionado like you."

He put his hand on my shoulder again embarrassedly.

"Yes," I said. "He's a real aficionado."

"But he's not aficionado like you are."

Afición means passion. An aficionado is one who is passionate about the bull-fights. All the good bull-fighters stayed at Montoya's hotel; that is, those with afición stayed there. The commercial bull-fighters stayed once, perhaps, and then did not come back. The good ones came each year. In Montoya's room were their photographs. The photographs were dedicated to Juanito Montoya or to his sister. The photographs of bull-fighters Montoya had really believed in were framed. Photographs of bull-fighters who had been without afición Montoya kept in a drawer of his desk. They often had the most flattering inscriptions. But they did not mean anything. One day Montoya took them all out and dropped them in the waste-basket. He did not want them around.

We often talked about bulls and bull-fighters. I had stopped at the

Montoya for several years. We never talked for very long at a time. It was simply the pleasure of discovering what we each felt. Men would come in from distant towns and before they left Pamplona stop and talk for a few minutes with Montoya about bulls. These men were aficionados. Those who were aficionados could always get rooms even when the hotel was full. Montoya introduced me to some of them. They were always very polite at first, and it amused them very much that I should be an American. Somehow it was taken for granted that an American could not have afición. He might simulate it or confuse it with excitement, but he could not really have it. When they saw that I had afición, and there was no password, no set questions that could bring it out, rather it was a sort of oral spiritual examination with the questions always a little on the defensive and never apparent, there was this same embarrassed putting the hand on the shoulder, or a "Buen hombre." But nearly always there was the actual touching. It seemed as though they wanted to touch you to make it certain.

Montoya could forgive anything of a bull-fighter who had afición. He could forgive attacks of nerves, panic, bad unexplainable actions, all sorts of lapses. For one who had afición he could forgive anything. At once he forgave me all my friends. Without his ever saying anything they were simply a little something shameful between us, like the spilling open of the horses in bull-fighting.

Bill had gone up-stairs as we came in, and I found him washing and changing in his room.

"Well," he said, "talk a lot of Spanish?"

"He was telling me about the bulls coming in tonight."

"Let's find the gang and go down."

"All right. They'll probably be at the café."

"Have you got tickets?"

"Yes. I got them for all the unloadings."

"What's it like?" He was pulling his cheek before the glass, looking to see if there were unshaved patches under the line of the jaw.

"It's pretty good," I said. "They let the bulls out of the cages one at a time, and they have steers in the corral to receive them and keep them from fighting, and the bulls tear in at the steers and the steers run around like old maids trying to quiet them down."

"Do they ever gore the steers?"

"Sure. Sometimes they go right after them and kill them."

"Can't the steers do anything?"

"No. They're trying to make friends."

"What do they have them in for?"

"To quiet down the bulls and keep them from breaking their horns against the stone walls, or goring each other."

"Must be swell being a steer."

We went down the stairs and out of the door and walked across the square toward the café Iruña. There were two lonely looking ticket-houses standing in the square. Their windows, marked SOL, SOL Y SOM-BRA, and SOMBRA, were shut. They would not open until the day before the fiesta.

Across the square the white wicker tables and chairs of the Iruña extended out beyond the Arcade to the edge of the street. I looked for Brett and Mike at the tables. There they were. Brett and Mike and Robert Cohn. Brett was wearing a Basque beret. So was Mike. Robert Cohn was bare-headed and wearing his spectacles. Brett saw us coming and waved. Her eyes crinkled up as we came up to the table.

"Hello, you chaps!" she called.

Brett was happy. Mike had a way of getting an intensity of feeling into shaking hands. Robert Cohn shook hands because we were back.

"Where the hell have you been?" I asked.

"I brought them up here," Cohn said.

"What rot," Brett said. "We'd have gotten here earlier if you hadn't come."

"You'd never have gotten here."

"What rot! You chaps are brown. Look at Bill."

"Did you get good fishing?" Mike asked. "We wanted to join you."

"It wasn't bad. We missed you."

"I wanted to come," Cohn said, "but I thought I ought to bring them."

"You bring us. What rot."

"Was it really good?" Mike asked. "Did you take many?"

"Some days we took a dozen apiece. There was an Englishman up there."

"Named Harris," Bill said. "Ever know him, Mike? He was in the war, too."

"Fortunate fellow," Mike said. "What times we had. How I wish those dear days were back."

"Don't be an ass."

"Were you in the war, Mike?" Cohn asked.

"Was I not."

"He was a very distinguished soldier," Brett said. "Tell them about the time your horse bolted down Piccadilly."

"I'll not. I've told that four times."

"You never told me," Robert Cohn said.

"I'll not tell that story. It reflects discredit on me."

"Tell them about your medals."

"I'll not. That story reflects great discredit on me."

"What story's that?"

"Brett will tell you. She tells all the stories that reflect discredit on me."

"Go on. Tell it, Brett."

"Should I?"

"I'll tell it myself."

"What medals have you got, Mike?"

"I haven't got any medals."

"You must have some."

"I suppose I've the usual medals. But I never sent in for them. One time there was this whopping big dinner and the Prince of Wales was to be there, and the cards said medals will be worn. So naturally I had no medals, and I stopped at my tailor's and he was impressed by the invitation, and I thought that's a good piece of business, and I said to him: 'You've got to fix me up with some medals.' He said: 'What medals, sir?' And I said: 'Oh, any medals. Just give me a few medals.' So he said: 'What medals *have* you, sir?' And I said: 'How should I know?' Did he think I spent all my time reading the bloody gazette? 'Just give me a good lot. Pick them out yourself.' So he got me some medals, you know, miniature medals, and handed me the box, and I put it in my pocket and forgot it. Well, I went to the dinner, and it was the night they'd shot Henry Wilson, so the Prince didn't come and the King didn't come, and no one wore any medals, and all these coves were busy taking off their medals, and I had mine in my pocket."

He stopped for us to laugh.

"Is that all?"

"That's all. Perhaps I didn't tell it right."

"You didn't," said Brett. "But no matter."

We were all laughing.

"Ah, yes," said Mike. "I know now. It was a damn dull dinner, and I couldn't stick it, so I left. Later on in the evening I found the box in my pocket. What's this? I said. Medals? Bloody military medals? So I cut them all off their backing—you know, they put them on a strip—and gave them all around. Gave one to each girl. Form of souvenir. They thought I was hell's own shakes of a soldier. Give away medals in a night club. Dashing fellow."

"Tell the rest," Brett said.

"Don't you think that was funny?" Mike asked. We were all laughing. "It was. I swear it was. Any rate, my tailor wrote me and wanted the medals back. Sent a man around. Kept on writing for months. Seems some chap had left them to be cleaned. Frightfully military cove. Set hell's own store by them." Mike paused. "Rotten luck for the tailor," he said.

"You don't mean it," Bill said. "I should think it would have been grand for the tailor."

"Frightfully good tailor. Never believe it to see me now," Mike said. "I used to pay him a hundred pounds a year just to keep him quiet. So he wouldn't send me any bills. Frightful blow to him when I went bankrupt. It was right after the medals. Gave his letters rather a bitter tone."

"How did you go bankrupt?" Bill asked.

"Two ways," Mike said. "Gradually and then suddenly."

"What brought it on?"

"Friends," said Mike. "I had a lot of friends. False friends. Then I had creditors, too. Probably had more creditors than anybody in England."

"Tell them about in the court," Brett said.

"I don't remember," Mike said. "I was just a little tight."

"Tight!" Brett exclaimed. "You were blind!"

"Extraordinary thing," Mike said. "Met my former partner the other day. Offered to buy me a drink."

"Tell them about your learned counsel," Brett said.

"I will not," Mike said. "My learned counsel was blind, too. I say this is a gloomy subject. Are we going down and see these bulls unloaded or not?"

"Let's go down."

We called the waiter, paid, and started to walk through the town. I started off walking with Brett, but Robert Cohn came up and joined her on the other side. The three of us walked along, past the Ayuntamiento with the banners hung from the balcony, down past the market and down past the steep street that led to the bridge across the Arga. There were many people walking to go and see the bulls, and carriages drove down the hill and across the bridge, the drivers, the horses, and the whips rising above the walking people in the street. Across the bridge we turned up a road to the corrals. We passed a wine-shop with a sign in the window: Good Wine 30 Céntimos A Liter.

"That's where we'll go when funds get low," Brett said.

The woman standing in the door of the wine-shop looked at us as we passed. She called to some one in the house and three girls came to the window and stared. They were staring at Brett.

At the gate of the corrals two men took tickets from the people that went in. We went in through the gate. There were trees inside and a low, stone house. At the far end was the stone wall of the corrals, with apertures in the stone that were like loopholes running all along the face of each corral. A ladder led up to the top of the wall, and people were climbing up the ladder and spreading down to stand on the walls that separated the two corrals. As we came up to the ladder, walking across the grass under the trees, we passed the big, gray painted cages with the bulls in them. There was one bull in each travelling-box. They had come by train from a bull-breeding ranch in Castile, and had been unloaded off flat-cars at the station and brought up here to be let out of their cages into the corrals. Each cage was stencilled with the name and the brand of the bull-breeder.

We climbed up and found a place on the wall looking down into the corral. The stone walls were whitewashed, and there was straw on the ground and wooden feed-boxes and water-troughs set against the wall.

"Look up there," I said.

Beyond the river rose the plateau of the town. All along the old walls and ramparts people were standing. The three lines of fortifications made three black lines of people. Above the walls there were heads in the windows of the houses. At the far end of the plateau boys had climbed into the trees.

"They must think something is going to happen," Brett said.

"They want to see the bulls."

Mike and Bill were on the other wall across the pit of the corral. They waved to us. People who had come late were standing behind us, pressing against us when other people crowded them.

"Why don't they start?" Robert Cohn asked.

A single mule was hitched to one of the cages and dragged it up against the gate in the corral wall. The men shoved and lifted it with crowbars into position against the gate. Men were standing on the wall ready to pull up the gate of the corral and then the gate of the cage. At the other end of the corral a gate opened and two steers came in, swaying their heads and trotting, their lean flanks swinging. They stood together at the far end, their heads toward the gate where the bull would enter.

"They don't look happy," Brett said.

The men on top of the wall leaned back and pulled up the door of the corral. Then they pulled up the door of the cage.

I leaned way over the wall and tried to see into the cage. It was dark. Some one rapped on the cage with an iron bar. Inside something seemed to explode. The bull, striking into the wood from side to side with his horns, made a great noise. Then I saw a dark muzzle and the shadow of horns, and then, with a clattering on the wood in the hollow box, the bull charged and came out into the corral, skidding with his forefeet in the straw as he stopped, his head up, the great hump of muscle on his neck swollen tight, his body muscles quivering as he looked up at the crowd on the stone walls. The two steers backed away against the wall, their heads sunken, their eyes watching the bull.

The bull saw them and charged. A man shouted from behind one of the boxes and slapped his hat against the planks, and the bull, before he reached the steer, turned, gathered himself and charged where the man had been, trying to reach him behind the planks with a half-dozen quick, searching drives with the right horn.

"My God, isn't he beautiful?" Brett said. We were looking right down on him.

"Look how he knows how to use his horns," I said. "He's got a left and a right just like a boxer."

"Not really?"

"You watch."

"It goes too fast."

"Wait. There'll be another one in a minute."

They had backed up another cage into the entrance. In the far corner a man, from behind one of the plank shelters, attracted the bull, and while the bull was facing away the gate was pulled up and a second bull came out into the corral.

He charged straight for the steers and two men ran out from behind the planks and shouted, to turn him. He did not change his direction and the men shouted: "Hah! Hah! Toro!" and waved their arms; the two steers turned sideways to take the shock, and the bull drove into one of the steers.

"Don't look," I said to Brett. She was watching, fascinated.

"Fine," I said. "If it doesn't buck you."

"I saw it," she said. "I saw him shift from his left to his right horn."

"Damn good!"

The steer was down now, his neck stretched out, his head twisted, he lay the way he had fallen. Suddenly the bull left off and made for the other steer which had been standing at the far end, his head swinging, watching it all. The steer ran awkwardly and the bull caught him, hooked him lightly in the flank, and then turned away and looked up at the crowd on the walls, his crest of muscle rising. The steer came up to him and made as though to nose at him and the bull hooked perfunctorily. The next time he nosed at the steer and then the two of them trotted over to the other bull.

When the next bull came out, all three, the two bulls and the steer, stood together, their heads side by side, their horns against the new-comer. In a few minutes the steer picked the new bull up, quieted him down, and made him one of the herd. When the last two bulls had been unloaded the herd were all together.

The steer who had been gored had gotten to his feet and stood against the stone wall. None of the bulls came near him, and he did not attempt to join the herd.

We climbed down from the wall with the crowd, and had a last look at the bulls through the loopholes in the wall of the corral. They were all quiet now, their heads down. We got a carriage outside and rode up to the café. Mike and Bill came in half an hour later. They had stopped on the way for several drinks.

We were sitting in the café.

"That's an extraordinary business," Brett said.

"Will those last ones fight as well as the first?" Robert Cohn asked. "They seemed to quiet down awfully fast."

"They all know each other," I said. "They're only dangerous when they're alone, or only two or three of them together."

"What do you mean, dangerous?" Bill said. "They all looked dangerous to me."

"They only want to kill when they're alone. Of course, if you went in there you'd probably detach one of them from the herd, and he'd be dangerous."

"That's too complicated," Bill said. "Don't you ever detach me from the herd, Mike."

"I say," Mike said, "they *were* fine bulls, weren't they? Did you see their horns?"

"Did I not," said Brett. "I had no idea what they were like."

"Did you see the one hit that steer?" Mike asked. "That was extraordinary."

"It's no life being a steer," Robert Cohn said.

"Don't you think so?" Mike said. "I would have thought you'd loved being a steer, Robert."

"What do you mean, Mike?"

"They lead such a quiet life. They never say anything and they're always hanging about so."

We were embarrassed. Bill laughed. Robert Cohn was angry. Mike went on talking.

"I should think you'd love it. You'd never have to say a word. Come on, Robert. Do say something. Don't just sit there."

"I said something, Mike. Don't you remember? About the steers."

"Oh, say something more. Say something funny. Can't you see we're all having a good time here?"

"Come off it, Michael. You're drunk," Brett said.

"I'm not drunk. I'm quite serious. *Is* Robert Cohn going to follow Brett around like a steer all the time?"

"Shut up, Michael. Try and show a little breeding."

"Breeding be damned. Who has any breeding, anyway, except the bulls? Aren't the bulls lovely? Don't you like them, Bill? Why don't you say something, Robert? Don't sit there looking like a bloody funeral. What if Brett did sleep with you? She's slept with lots of better people than you."

"Shut up," Cohn said. He stood up. "Shut up, Mike."

"Oh, don't stand up and act as though you were going to hit me. That won't make any difference to me. Tell me, Robert. Why do you follow Brett around like a poor bloody steer? Don't you know you're not wanted? I know when I'm not wanted. Why don't you know when you're not wanted? You came down to San Sebastian where you weren't wanted, and followed Brett around like a bloody steer. Do you think that's right?"

"Shut up. You're drunk."

"Perhaps I am drunk. Why aren't you drunk? Why don't you ever get drunk, Robert? You know you didn't have a good time at San Sebastian because none of our friends would invite you on any of the parties.

You can't blame them hardly. Can you? I asked them to. They wouldn't do it. You can't blame them, now. Can you? Now, answer me. Can you blame them?"

"Go to hell, Mike."

"I can't blame them. Can you blame them? Why do you follow Brett around? Haven't you any manners? How do you think it makes *me* feel?"

"You're a splendid one to talk about manners," Brett said. "You've such lovely manners."

"Come on, Robert," Bill said.

"What do you follow her around for?"

Bill stood up and took hold of Cohn.

"Don't go," Mike said. "Robert Cohn's going to buy a drink."

Bill went off with Cohn. Cohn's face was sallow. Mike went on talking. I sat and listened for a while. Brett looked disgusted.

"I say, Michael, you might not be such a bloody ass," she interrupted. "I'm not saying he's not right, you know." She turned to me.

The emotion left Mike's voice. We were all friends together.

"I'm not so damn drunk as I sounded," he said.

"I know you're not," Brett said.

"We're none of us sober," I said.

"I didn't say anything I didn't mean."

"But you put it so badly," Brett laughed.

"He was an ass, though. He came down to San Sebastian where he damn well wasn't wanted. He hung around Brett and just *looked* at her. It made me damned well sick."

"He did behave very badly," Brett said.

"Mark you. Brett's had affairs with men before. She tells me all about everything. She gave me this chap Cohn's letters to read. I wouldn't read them."

"Damned noble of you."

"No, listen, Jake. Brett's gone off with men. But they weren't ever Jews, and they didn't come and hang about afterward."

"Damned good chaps," Brett said. "It's all rot to talk about it. Michael and I understand each other."

"She gave me Robert Cohn's letters. I wouldn't read them."

"You wouldn't read any letters, darling. You wouldn't read mine."

"I can't read letters," Mike said. "Funny, isn't it?"

"You can't read anything."

"No. You're wrong there. I read quite a bit. I read when I'm at home."

"You'll be writing next," Brett said. "Come on, Michael. Do buck up. You've got to go through with this thing now. He's here. Don't spoil the fiesta."

"Well, let him behave, then."

"He'll behave. I'll tell him."

"You tell him, Jake. Tell him either he must behave or get out."

"Yes," I said, "it would be nice for me to tell him."

"Look, Brett. Tell Jake what Robert calls you. That *is* perfect, you know."

"Oh, no. I can't."

"Go on. We're all friends. Aren't we all friends, Jake?"

"I can't tell him. It's too ridiculous."

"I'll tell him."

"You won't, Michael. Don't be an ass."

"He calls her Circe," Mike said. "He claims she turns men into swine. Damn good. I wish I were one of these literary chaps."

"He'd be good, you know," Brett said. "He writes a good letter."

"I know," I said. "He wrote me from San Sebastian."

"That was nothing," Brett said. "He can write a damned amusing letter."

"She made me write that. She was supposed to be ill."

"I damned well was, too."

"Come on," I said, "we must go in and eat."

"How should I meet Cohn?" Mike said.

"Just act as though nothing had happened."

"It's quite all right with me," Mike said. "I'm not embarrassed."

"If he says anything, just say you were tight."

"Quite. And the funny thing is I think I was tight."

"Come on," Brett said. "Are these poisonous things paid for? I must bathe before dinner."

We walked across the square. It was dark and all around the square were the lights from the cafés under the arcades. We walked across the gravel under the trees to the hotel.

They went up-stairs and I stopped to speak with Montoya.

"Well, how did you like the bulls?" he asked.

"Good. They were nice bulls."

"They're all right"—Montoya shook his head—"but they're not too good."

"What didn't you like about them?"

"I don't know. They just didn't give me the feeling that they were so good."

"I know what you mean."

"They're all right."

"Yes. They're all right."

"How did your friends like them?"

"Fine."

"Good," Montoya said.

I went up-stairs. Bill was in his room standing on the balcony looking out at the square. I stood beside him.

"Where's Cohn?"

"Up-stairs in his room."

"How does he feel?"

"Like hell, naturally. Mike was awful. He's terrible when he's tight."

"He wasn't so tight."

"The hell he wasn't. I know what we had before we came to the café."

"He sobered up afterward."

"Good. He was terrible. I don't like Cohn, God knows, and I think it was a silly trick for him to go down to San Sebastian, but nobody has any business to talk like Mike."

"How'd you like the bulls?"

"Grand. It's grand the way they bring them out."

"To-morrow come the Miuras."

"When does the fiesta start?"

"Day after to-morrow."

"We've got to keep Mike from getting so tight. That kind of stuff is terrible."

"We'd better get cleaned up for supper."

"Yes. That will be a pleasant meal."

"Won't it?"

As a matter of fact, supper was a pleasant meal. Brett wore a black, sleeveless evening dress. She looked quite beautiful. Mike acted as though nothing had happened. I had to go up and bring Robert Cohn down. He was reserved and formal, and his face was still taut and sallow, but he cheered up finally. He could not stop looking at Brett. It seemed to make him happy. It must have been pleasant for him to see her looking so lovely, and know he had been away with her and that every one knew it. They could not take that away from him. Bill was very funny. So was Michael. They were good together.

It was like certain dinners I remember from the war. There was much wine, an ignored tension, and a feeling of things coming that you could not prevent happening. Under the wine I lost the disgusted feeling and was happy. It seemed they were all such nice people.

— 14 —

I do not know what time I got to bed. I remember undressing, putting on a bathrobe, and standing out on the balcony. I knew I was quite drunk, and when I came in I put on the light over the head of the bed and started to read. I was reading a book by Turgenieff. Probably I read the same two pages over several times. It was one of the stories in "A Sportsman's Sketches." I had read it before, but it seemed quite new. The country became very clear and the feeling of pressure in my head seemed to loosen. I was very drunk and I did not want to shut my eyes because the room would go round and round. If I kept on reading that feeling would pass.

I heard Brett and Robert Cohn come up the stairs. Cohn said good night outside the door and went on up to his room. I heard Brett go into the room next door. Mike was already in bed. He had come in with me an hour before. He woke as she came in, and they talked together. I heard them laugh. I turned off the light and tried to go to sleep. It was not necessary to read any more. I could shut my eyes without getting the wheeling sensation. But I could not sleep. There is no reason why because it is dark you should look at things differently from when it is light. The hell there isn't!

I figured that all out once, and for six months I never slept with the electric light off. That was another bright idea. To hell with women, anyway. To hell with you, Brett Ashley.

Women made such swell friends. Awfully swell. In the first place, you had to be in love with a woman to have a basis of friendship. I had been having Brett for a friend. I had not been thinking about her side of it. I had been getting something for nothing. That only delayed the presentation of the bill. The bill always came. That was one of the swell things you could count on.

I thought I had paid for everything. Not like the woman pays and pays and pays. No idea of retribution or punishment. Just exchange of values. You gave up something and got something else. Or you worked for something. You paid some way for everything that was any good. I paid my way into enough things that I liked, so that I had a good time. Either you paid by learning about them, or by experience, or by taking chances, or by money. Enjoying living was learning to get your money's worth and knowing when you had it. You could get your money's worth. The world was a good place to buy in. It seemed like a fine philosophy. In five years, I thought, it will seem just as silly as all the other fine philosophies I've had.

Perhaps that wasn't true, though. Perhaps as you went along you did learn something. I did not care what it was all about. All I wanted to know was how to live in it. Maybe if you found out how to live in it you learned from that what it was all about.

I wished Mike would not behave so terribly to Cohn, though. Mike was a bad drunk. Brett was a good drunk. Bill was a good drunk. Cohn was never drunk. Mike was unpleasant after he passed a certain point. I liked to see him hurt Cohn. I wished he would not do it, though, because afterward it made me disgusted at myself. That was morality; things that made you disgusted afterward. No, that must be immorality. That was a large statement. What a lot of bilge I could think up at night. What rot, I could hear Brett say it. What rot! When you were with the English you got into the habit of using English expressions in your thinking. The English spoken language—the upper classes, anyway—must have fewer words than the Eskimo. Of course I didn't know anything about the Eskimo. Maybe the Eskimo was a fine language. Say the Cherokee. I didn't know anything about the Cherokee, either. The English talked with inflected phrases. One phrase to mean everything. I liked them, though. I liked the way they talked. Take Harris. Still Harris was not the upper classes.

I turned on the light again and read. I read the Turgenieff. I knew that now, reading it in the oversensitized state of my mind after much too much brandy, I would remember it somewhere, and afterward it would seem as though it had really happened to me. I would always have it. That was another good thing you paid for and then had. Some time along toward daylight I went to sleep.

The next two days in Pamplona were quiet, and there were no more rows. The town was getting ready for the fiesta. Workmen put up the gate-posts that were to shut off the side streets when the bulls were released from the corrals and came running through the streets in the morning on their way to the ring. The workmen dug holes and fitted in the timbers, each timber numbered for its regular place. Out on the plateau beyond the town employees of the bull-ring exercised picador horses, galloping them stiff-legged on the hard, sun-baked fields behind the bull-ring. The big gate of the bull-ring was open, and inside the amphitheatre was being swept. The ring was rolled and sprinkled, and carpenters replaced weakened or cracked planks in the barrera. Standing at the edge of the smooth rolled sand you could look up in the empty stands and see old women sweeping out the boxes.

Outside, the fence that led from the last street of the town to the entrance of the bull-ring was already in place and made a long pen; the crowd would come running down with the bulls behind them on the morning of the day of the first bull-fight. Out across the plain, where the horse and cattle fair would be, some gypsies had camped under the trees. The wine and aguardiente sellers were putting up their booths. One booth advertised ANIS DEL TORO. The cloth sign hung against the planks in the hot sun. In the big square that was the centre of the town there was no change yet. We sat in the white wicker chairs on the terrasse of the café and watched the motor-buses come in and unload peasants from the country coming in to the market, and we watched the buses fill up and start out with peasants sitting with their saddle-bags full of the things they had bought in the town. The tall gray motor-buses were the only life of the square except for the pigeons and the man with a hose who sprinkled the gravelled square and watered the streets.

In the evening was the paseo. For an hour after dinner every one, all the good-looking girls, the officers from the garrison, all the fashionable people of the town, walked in the street on one side of the square while the café tables filled with the regular after-dinner crowd.

During the morning I usually sat in the café and read the Madrid papers and then walked in the town or out into the country. Sometimes Bill went along. Sometimes he wrote in his room. Robert Cohn spent the mornings studying Spanish or trying to get a shave at the barber-shop. Brett and Mike never got up until noon. We all had a vermouth at the café. It was a quiet life and no one was drunk. I went to church a couple of times, once with Brett. She said she wanted to hear me go to confession, but I told her that not only was it impossible but it was not as interesting as it sounded, and, besides, it would be in a language she did not know. We met Cohn as we came out of church, and although it was obvious he had followed us, yet he was very pleasant and nice, and we all three went for a walk out to the gypsy camp, and Brett had her fortune told.

It was a good morning, there were high white clouds above the mountains. It had rained a little in the night and it was fresh and cool on the plateau, and there was a wonderful view. We all felt good and we felt healthy, and I felt quite friendly to Cohn. You could not be upset about anything on a day like that.

That was the last day before the fiesta.

─•15•─

At noon of Sunday, the 6th of July, the fiesta exploded. There is no other way to describe it. People had been coming in all day from the country, but they were assimilated in the town and you did not notice them. The square was as quiet in the hot sun as on any other day. The peasants were in the outlying wine-shops. There they were drinking, getting ready for the fiesta. They had come in so recently from the plains and the hills that it was necessary that they make their shifting in values gradually. They could not start in paying café prices. They got their money's worth in the wine-shops. Money still had a definite value in hours worked and bushels of grain sold. Late in the fiesta it would not matter what they paid, nor where they bought.

Now on the day of the starting of the fiesta of San Fermin they had been in the wine-shops of the narrow streets of the town since early morning. Going down the streets in the morning on the way to mass in the cathedral, I heard them singing through the open doors of the shops. They were warming up. There were many people at the eleven o'clock mass. San Fermin is also a religious festival.

I walked down the hill from the cathedral and up the street to the café on the square. It was a little before noon. Robert Cohn and Bill were sitting at one of the tables. The marble-topped tables and the white wicker chairs were gone. They were replaced by cast-iron tables and severe folding chairs. The café was like a battleship stripped for action.

Today the waiters did not leave you alone all morning to read without asking if you wanted to order something. A waiter came up as soon as I sat down.

"What are you drinking?" I asked Bill and Robert.

"Sherry," Cohn said.

"Jerez," I said to the waiter.

Before the waiter brought the sherry the rocket that announced the fiesta went up in the square. It burst and there was a gray ball of smoke high up above the Theatre Gayarre, across on the other side of the plaza. The ball of smoke hung in the sky like a shrapnel burst, and as I watched, another rocket came up to it, trickling smoke in the bright sunlight. I saw the bright flash as it burst and another little cloud of smoke appeared. By the time the second rocket had burst there were so many people in the arcade, that had been empty a minute before, that the waiter, holding the bottle high up over his head, could hardly get through the crowd to our table. People were coming into the square from all sides, and down the street we heard the pipes and the fifes and the drums coming. They were playing the *riau-riau* music, the pipes shrill and the drums pounding, and behind them came the men and boys dancing. When the fifers stopped they all crouched down in the street, and when the reed-pipes and the fifes shrilled, and the flat, dry, hollow drums tapped it out again, they all went up in the air dancing. In the crowd you saw only the heads and shoulders of the dancers going up and down.

In the square a man, bent over, was playing on a reed-pipe, and a crowd of children were following him shouting, and pulling at his clothes. He came out of the square, the children following him, and piped them past the café and down a side street. We saw his blank pock-marked face as he went by, piping, the children close behind him shouting and pulling at him.

"He must be the village idiot," Bill said. "My God! look at that!"

Down the street came dancers. The street was solid with dancers, all men. They were all dancing in time behind their own fifers and drummers. They were a club of some sort, and all wore workmen's blue smocks, and red handkerchiefs around their necks, and carried a great banner on two poles. The banner danced up and down with them as they came down surrounded by the crowd.

"Hurray for Wine! Hurray for the Foreigners!" was painted on the banner.

"Where are the foreigners?" Robert Cohn asked.

"We're the foreigners," Bill said.

All the time rockets were going up. The café tables were all full now. The square was emptying of people and the crowd was filling the cafés.

"Where's Brett and Mike?" Bill asked.

"I'll go and get them," Cohn said.

"Bring them here."

The fiesta was really started. It kept up day and night for seven days. The dancing kept up, the drinking kept up, the noise went on. The things that happened could only have happened during a fiesta. Everything became quite unreal finally and it seemed as though nothing could have any consequences. It seemed out of place to think of consequences during the fiesta. All during the fiesta you had the feeling, even when it was quiet, that you had to shout any remark to make it heard. It was the same feeling about any action. It was a fiesta and it went on for seven days.

That afternoon was the big religious procession. San Fermin was translated from one church to another. In the procession were all the dignitaries, civil and religious. We could not see them because the crowd was too great. Ahead of the formal procession and behind it danced the *riau-riau* dancers. There was one mass of yellow shirts dancing up and down in the crowd. All we could see of the procession through the closely pressed people that crowded all the side streets and curbs were the great giants, cigar-store Indians, thirty feet high, Moors, a King and Queen, whirling and waltzing solemnly to the *riau-riau*.

They were all standing outside the chapel where San Fermin and the dignitaries had passed in, leaving a guard of soldiers, the giants, with the men who danced in them standing beside their resting frames, and the dwarfs moving with their whacking bladders through the crowd. We started inside and there was a smell of incense and people filing back into the church, but Brett was stopped just inside the door because she had no hat, so we went out again and along the street that ran back from the chapel into town. The street was lined on both sides with people keeping their place at the curb for the return of the procession. Some dancers formed a circle around Brett and started to dance. They wore big wreaths of white garlics around their necks. They took Bill and me by the arms and put us in the circle. Bill started to dance, too. They were all chanting. Brett wanted to dance but they did not want her to. They wanted her as an image to dance around. When the song ended with the sharp *riau-riau!* they rushed us into a wine-shop.

We stood at the counter. They had Brett seated on a wine-cask. It was dark in the wine-shop and full of men singing, hard-voiced singing. Back of the counter they drew the wine from casks. I put down money for the wine, but one of the men picked it up and put it back in my pocket.

"I want a leather wine-bottle," Bill said.

"There's a place down the street," I said. "I'll go get a couple."

The dancers did not want me to go out. Three of them were sitting on the high wine-cask beside Brett, teaching her to drink out of the wine-skins. They had hung a wreath of garlics around her neck. Some one insisted on giving her a glass. Somebody was teaching Bill a song. Singing it into his ear. Beating time on Bill's back.

I explained to them that I would be back. Outside in the street I went down the street looking for the shop that made leather wine-bottles. The crowd was packed on the sidewalks and many of the shops were shuttered, and I could not find it. I walked as far as the church, looking on both sides of the street. Then I asked a man and he took me by the arm and led me to it. The shutters were up but the door was open.

Inside it smelled of fresh tanned leather and hot tar. A man was stencilling completed wine-skins. They hung from the roof in bunches. He took one down, blew it up, screwed the nozzle tight, and then jumped on it.

"See! It doesn't leak."

"I want another one, too. A big one."

He took down a big one that would hold a gallon or more, from the roof. He blew it up, his cheeks puffing ahead of the wine-skin, and stood on the bota holding on to a chair.

"What are you going to do? Sell them in Bayonne?"

"No. Drink out of them."

He slapped me on the back.

"Good man. Eight pesetas for the two. The lowest price."

The man who was stencilling the new ones and tossing them into a pile stopped.

"It's true," he said. "Eight pesetas is cheap."

I paid and went out and along the street back to the wine-shop. It was darker than ever inside and very crowded. I did not see Brett and Bill, and some one said they were in the back room. At the counter the girl filled the two wine-skins for me. One held two litres. The other held five litres. Filling them both cost three pesetas sixty céntimos. Some one at the counter, that I had never seen before, tried to pay for the wine, but I finally paid for it myself. The man who had wanted to pay then bought me a drink. He would not let me buy one in return, but said he would take a rinse of the mouth from the new wine-bag. He tipped the big five-litre bag up and squeezed it so the wine hissed against the back of his throat.

"All right," he said, and handed back the bag.

In the back room Brett and Bill were sitting on barrels surrounded by the dancers. Everybody had his arms on everybody else's shoulders, and they were all singing. Mike was sitting at a table with several men in their shirt-sleeves, eating from a bowl of tuna fish, chopped onions and vinegar. They were all drinking wine and mopping up the oil and vinegar with pieces of bread.

"Hello, Jake. Hello!" Mike called. "Come here. I want you to meet my friends. We're all having an hors d'œuvre."

I was introduced to the people at the table. They supplied their names to Mike and sent for a fork for me.

"Stop eating their dinner, Michael," Brett shouted from the wine-barrels.

"I don't want to eat up your meal," I said when some one handed me a fork.

"Eat," he said. "What do you think it's here for?"

I unscrewed the nozzle of the big wine-bottle and handed it around. Every one took a drink, tipping the wine-skin at arm's length.

Outside, above the singing, we could hear the music of the procession going by.

"Isn't that the procession?" Mike asked.

"Nada," some one said. "It's nothing. Drink up. Lift the bottle."

"Where did they find you?" I asked Mike.

"Some one brought me here," Mike said. "They said you were here."

"Where's Cohn?"

"He's passed out," Brett called. "They've put him away somewhere."

"Where is he?"

"I don't know."

"How should we know," Bill said. "I think he's dead."

"He's not dead," Mike said. "I know he's not dead. He's just passed out on Anís del Mono."

As he said Anís del Mono one of the men at the table looked up, brought out a bottle from inside his smock, and handed it to me.

"No," I said. "No, thanks!"

"Yes. Yes. Arriba! Up with the bottle!"

I took a drink. It tasted of licorice and warmed all the way. I could feel it warming in my stomach.

"Where the hell is Cohn?"

"I don't know," Mike said. "I'll ask. Where is the drunken comrade?" he asked in Spanish.

"You want to see him?"

"Yes," I said.

"Not me," said Mike. "This gent."

The Anís del Mono man wiped his mouth and stood up.

"Come on."

In a back room Robert Cohn was sleeping quietly on some wine-casks. It was almost too dark to see his face. They had covered him with a coat and another coat was folded under his head. Around his neck and on his chest was a big wreath of twisted garlics.

"Let him sleep," the man whispered. "He's all right."

Two hours later Cohn appeared. He came into the front room still with the wreath of garlics around his neck. The Spaniards shouted when he came in. Cohn wiped his eyes and grinned.

"I must have been sleeping," he said.

"Oh, not at all," Brett said.

"You were only dead," Bill said.

"Aren't we going to go and have some supper?" Cohn asked.

"Do you want to eat?"

"Yes. Why not? I'm hungry."

"Eat those garlics, Robert," Mike said. "I say. Do eat those garlics."

Cohn stood there. His sleep had made him quite all right.

"Do let's go and eat," Brett said. "I must get a bath."

"Come on," Bill said. "Let's translate Brett to the hotel."

We said good-bye to many people and shook hands with many people and went out. Outside it was dark.

"What time is it do you suppose?" Cohn asked.

"It's to-morrow," Mike said. "You've been asleep two days."

"No," said Cohn, "what time is it?"

"It's ten o'clock."

"What a lot we've drunk."

"You mean what a lot *we've* drunk. You went to sleep."

Going down the dark streets to the hotel we saw the sky-rockets going up in the square. Down the side streets that led to the square we saw the square solid with people, those in the centre all dancing.

It was a big meal at the hotel. It was the first meal of the prices being doubled for the fiesta, and there were several new courses. After the dinner we were out in the town. I remember resolving that I would stay up all night to watch the bulls go through the streets at six o'clock in the morning, and being so sleepy that I went to bed around four o'clock. The others stayed up.

My own room was locked and I could not find the key, so I went up-stairs and slept on one of the beds in Cohn's room. The fiesta was going on outside in the night, but I was too sleepy for it to keep me awake. When I woke it was the sound of the rocket exploding that announced the release of the bulls from the corrals at the edge of town. They would race through the streets and out to the bull-ring. I had been sleeping heavily and I woke feeling I was too late. I put on a coat of Cohn's and went out on the balcony. Down below the narrow street was empty. All the balconies were crowded with people. Suddenly a crowd came down the street. They were all running, packed close together. They passed along and up the street toward the bull-ring and behind them came more men running faster, and then some stragglers who were really running. Behind them was a little bare space, and then the bulls galloping, tossing their heads up and down. It all went out of sight around the corner. One man fell, rolled to the gutter, and lay quiet. But the bulls went right on and did not notice him. They were all running together.

After they went out of sight a great roar came from the bull-ring. It kept on. Then finally the pop of the rocket that meant the bulls had gotten through the people in the ring and into the corrals. I went back in the room and got into bed. I had been standing on the stone balcony in bare feet. I knew our crowd must have all been out at the bull-ring. Back in bed, I went to sleep.

Cohn woke me when he came in. He started to undress and went over and closed the window because the people on the balcony of the house just across the street were looking in.

"Did you see the show?" I asked.

"Yes. We were all there."

"Anybody get hurt?"

"One of the bulls got into the crowd in the ring and tossed six or eight people."

"How did Brett like it?"

"It was all so sudden there wasn't any time for it to bother anybody."

"I wish I'd been up."

"We didn't know where you were. We went to your room but it was locked."

"Where did you stay up?"

"We danced at some club."

"I got sleepy," I said.

"My gosh! I'm sleepy now," Cohn said. "Doesn't this thing ever stop?"

"Not for a week."

Bill opened the door and put his head in.

"Where were you, Jake?"

"I saw them go through from the balcony. How was it?"

"Grand."

"Where you going?"

"To sleep."

No one was up before noon. We ate at tables set out under the arcade. The town was full of people. We had to wait for a table. After lunch we went over to the Iruña. It had filled up, and as the time for the bull-fight came it got fuller, and the tables were crowded closer. There was a close, crowded hum that came every day before the bull-fight. The café did not make this same noise at any other time, no matter how crowded it was. This hum went on, and we were in it and a part of it.

I had taken six seats for all the fights. Three of them were barreras, the first row at the ring-side, and three were sobrepuertas, seats with wooden backs, half-way up the amphitheatre. Mike thought Brett had best sit high up for her first time, and Cohn wanted to sit with them. Bill and I were going to sit in the barreras, and I gave the extra ticket to a waiter to sell. Bill said something to Cohn about what to do and how to look so he would not mind the horses. Bill had seen one season of bull-fights.

"I'm not worried about how I'll stand it. I'm only afraid I may be bored," Cohn said.

"You think so?"

"Don't look at the horses, after the bull hits them," I said to Brett. "Watch the charge and see the picador try and keep the bull off, but then don't look again until the horse is dead if it's been hit."

"I'm a little nervy about it," Brett said. "I'm worried whether I'll be able to go through with it all right."

"You'll be all right. There's nothing but that horse part that will bother you, and they're only in for a few minutes with each bull. Just don't watch when it's bad."

"She'll be all right," Mike said. "I'll look after her."

"I don't think you'll be bored," Bill said.

"I'm going over to the hotel to get the glasses and the wine-skin," I said. "See you back here. Don't get cock-eyed."

"I'll come along," Bill said. Brett smiled at us.

We walked around through the arcade to avoid the heat of the square.

"That Cohn gets me," Bill said. "He's got this Jewish superiority so strong that he thinks the only emotion he'll get out of the fight will be being bored."

"We'll watch him with the glasses," I said.

"Oh, to hell with him!"

"He spends a lot of time there."

"I want him to stay there."

In the hotel on the stairs we met Montoya.

"Come on," said Montoya. "Do you want to meet Pedro Romero?"

"Fine," said Bill. "Let's go see him."

We followed Montoya up a flight and down the corridor.

"He's in room number eight," Montoya explained. "He's getting dressed for the bull-fight."

Montoya knocked on the door and opened it. It was a gloomy room with a little light coming in from the window on the narrow street. There were two beds separated by a monastic partition. The electric light was on. The boy stood very straight and unsmiling in his bull-fighting clothes. His jacket hung over the back of a chair. They were just finishing winding his sash. His black hair shone under the electric light. He wore a white linen shirt and the sword-handler finished his sash and stood up and stepped back. Pedro Romero nodded, seeming very far away and dignified when we shook hands. Montoya said something about what great aficionados we were, and that we wanted to wish him luck. Romero listened very seriously. Then he turned to me. He was the best-looking boy I have ever seen.

"You go to the bull-fight," he said in English.

"You know English," I said, feeling like an idiot.

"No," he answered, and smiled.

One of three men who had been sitting on the beds came up and asked us if we spoke French. "Would you like me to interpret for you? Is there anything you would like to ask Pedro Romero?"

We thanked him. What was there that you would like to ask? The boy was nineteen years old, alone except for his sword-handler, and the three hangers-on, and the bull-fight was to commence in twenty minutes. We wished him "Mucha suerte," shook hands, and went out. He was standing, straight and handsome and altogether by himself, alone in the room with the hangers-on as we shut the door.

"He's a fine boy, don't you think so?" Montoya asked.

"He's a good-looking kid," I said.

"He looks like a torero," Montoya said. "He has the type."

"He's a fine boy."

"We'll see how he is in the ring," Montoya said.

We found the big leather wine-bottle leaning against the wall in my room, took it and the field-glasses, locked the door, and went downstairs.

It was a good bull-fight. Bill and I were very excited about Pedro Romero. Montoya was sitting about ten places away. After Romero had killed his first bull Montoya caught my eye and nodded his head. This was a real one. There had not been a real one for a long time. Of the other two matadors, one was very fair and the other was passable. But there was no comparison with Romero, although neither of his bulls was much.

Several times during the bull-fight I looked up at Mike and Brett and Cohn, with the glasses. They seemed to be all right. Brett did not look upset. All three were leaning forward on the concrete railing in front of them.

"Let me take the glasses," Bill said.

"Does Cohn look bored?" I asked.

"That kike!"

Outside the ring, after the bull-fight was over, you could not move in the crowd. We could not make our way through but had to be moved with the whole thing, slowly, as a glacier, back to town. We had that disturbed emotional feeling that always comes after a bull-fight, and the feeling of elation that comes after a good bull-fight. The fiesta was going on. The drums pounded and the pipe music was shrill, and everywhere the flow of the crowd was broken by patches of dancers. The dancers were in a crowd, so you did not see the intricate play of the feet. All you saw was the heads and shoulders going up and down, up and down.

Finally, we got out of the crowd and made for the café. The waiter saved chairs for the others, and we each ordered an absinthe and watched the crowd in the square and the dancers.

"What do you suppose that dance is?" Bill asked.

"It's a sort of jota."

"They're not all the same," Bill said. "They dance differently to all the different tunes."

"It's swell dancing."

In front of us on a clear part of the street a company of boys were dancing. The steps were very intricate and their faces were intent and concentrated. They all looked down while they danced. Their rope-soled shoes tapped and spatted on the pavement. The toes touched. The heels touched. The balls of the feet touched. Then the music broke wildly and the step was finished and they were all dancing on up the street.

"Here come the gentry," Bill said.

They were crossing the street.

"Hello, men," I said.

"Hello, gents!" said Brett. "You saved us seats? How nice."

"I say," Mike said, "that Romero what'shisname is somebody. Am I wrong?"

"Oh, isn't he lovely," Brett said. "And those green trousers."

"Brett never took her eyes off them."

"I say, I must borrow your glasses to-morrow."

"How did it go?"

"Wonderfully! Simply perfect. I say, it is a spectacle!"

"How about the horses?"

"I couldn't help looking at them."

"She couldn't take her eyes off them," Mike said. "She's an extraordinary wench."

"They do have some rather awful things happen to them," Brett said. "I couldn't look away, though."

"Did you feel all right?"

"I didn't feel badly at all."

"Robert Cohn did," Mike put in. "You were quite green, Robert."

"The first horse did bother me," Cohn said.

"You weren't bored, were you?" asked Bill.

Cohn laughed.

"No. I wasn't bored. I wish you'd forgive me that."

"It's all right," Bill said, "so long as you weren't bored."

"He didn't look bored," Mike said. "I thought he was going to be sick."

"I never felt that bad. It was just for a minute."

"*I* thought he was going to be sick. You weren't bored, were you, Robert?"

"Let up on that, Mike. I said I was sorry I said it."

"He was, you know. He was positively green."

"Oh, shove it along, Michael."

"You mustn't ever get bored at your first bull-fight, Robert," Mike said. "It might make such a mess."

"Oh, shove it along, Michael," Brett said.

"He said Brett was a sadist," Mike said. "Brett's not a sadist. She's just a lovely, healthy wench."

"Are you a sadist, Brett?" I asked.

"Hope not."

"He said Brett was a sadist just because she has a good, healthy stomach."

"Won't be healthy long."

Bill got Mike started on something else than Cohn. The waiter brought the absinthe glasses.

"Did you really like it?" Bill asked Cohn.

"No, I can't say I liked it. I think it's a wonderful show."

"Gad, yes! What a spectacle!" Brett said.

"I wish they didn't have the horse part," Cohn said.

"They're not important," Bill said. "After a while you never notice anything disgusting."

"It is a bit strong just at the start," Brett said. "There's a dreadful moment for me just when the bull starts for the horse."

"The bulls were fine," Cohn said.

"They were very good," Mike said.

"I want to sit down below, next time." Brett drank from her glass of absinthe.

"She wants to see the bull-fighters close by," Mike said.

"They are something," Brett said. "That Romero lad is just a child."

"He's a damned good-looking boy," I said. "When we were up in his room I never saw a better-looking kid."

"How old do you suppose he is?"

"Nineteen or twenty."

"Just imagine it."

The bull-fight on the second day was much better than on the first. Brett sat between Mike and me at the barrera, and Bill and Cohn went up above. Romero was the whole show. I do not think Brett saw any other bull-fighter. No one else did either, except the hard-shelled technicians. It was all Romero. There were two other matadors, but they did not count. I sat beside Brett and explained to Brett what it was all about. I told her about watching the bull, not the horse, when the bulls charged the picadors, and got her to watching the picador place the point of his pic so that she saw what it was all about, so that it became more something that was going on with a definite end, and less of a spectacle with unexplained horrors. I had her watch how Romero took the bull away from a fallen horse with his cape, and how he held him with the cape and turned him, smoothly and suavely, never wasting the bull. She saw how Romero avoided every brusque movement and saved his bulls for the last when he wanted them, not winded and discomposed but smoothly worn down. She saw how close Romero always worked to the bull, and I pointed out to her the tricks the other bull-fighters used to make it look as though they were working closely. She saw why she liked Romero's cape-work and why she did not like the others.

Romero never made any contortions, always it was straight and pure and natural in line. The others twisted themselves like cork-screws, their elbows raised, and leaned against the flanks of the bull after his horns had passed, to give a faked look of danger. Afterward, all that was faked turned bad and gave an unpleasant feeling. Romero's bull-fighting gave real emotion, because he kept the absolute purity of line in his movements and always quietly and calmly let the horns pass him close each time. He did not have to emphasize their closeness. Brett saw how something that was beautiful done close to the bull was ridiculous if it were done a little way off. I told her how since the death of Joselito all the bull-fighters had been developing a technique that simulated this appearance of danger in order to give a fake emotional feeling, while the bull-fighter was really safe. Romero had the old thing, the holding of his purity of line through the maximum of exposure, while he dominated the bull by making him realize he was unattainable, while he prepared him for the killing.

"I've never seen him do an awkward thing," Brett said.

"You won't until he gets frightened," I said.

"He'll never be frightened," Mike said. "He knows too damned much."

"He knew everything when he started. The others can't ever learn what he was born with."

"And God, what looks," Brett said.

"I believe, you know, that she's falling in love with this bull-fighter chap," Mike said.

"I wouldn't be surprised."

"Be a good chap, Jake. Don't tell her anything more about him. Tell her how they beat their old mothers."

"Tell me what drunks they are."

"Oh, frightful," Mike said. "Drunk all day and spend all their time beating their poor old mothers."

"He looks that way," Brett said.

"Doesn't he?" I said.

They had hitched the mules to the dead bull and then the whips cracked, the men ran, and the mules, straining forward, their legs pushing, broke into a gallop, and the bull, one horn up, his head on its side, swept a swath smoothly across the sand and out the red gate.

"This next is the last one."

"Not really," Brett said. She leaned forward on the barrera. Romero waved his picadors to their places, then stood, his cape against his chest, looking across the ring to where the bull would come out.

After it was over we went out and were pressed tight in the crowd.

"These bull-fights are hell on one," Brett said. "I'm limp as a rag."

"Oh, you'll get a drink," Mike said.

The next day Pedro Romero did not fight. It was Miura bulls, and a very bad bull-fight. The next day there was no bull-fight scheduled. But all day and all night the fiesta kept on.

16

In the morning it was raining. A fog had come over the mountains from the sea. You could not see the tops of the mountains. The plateau was dull and gloomy, and the shapes of the trees and the houses were changed. I walked out beyond the town to look at the weather. The bad weather was coming over the mountains from the sea.

The flags in the square hung wet from the white poles and the banners were wet and hung damp against the front of the houses, and in between the steady drizzle the rain came down and drove every one under the arcades and made pools of water in the square, and the streets wet and dark and deserted; yet the fiesta kept up without any pause. It was only driven under cover.

The covered seats of the bull-ring had been crowded with people sitting out of the rain watching the concourse of Basque and Navarrais dancers and singers, and afterward the Val Carlos dancers in their costumes danced down the street in the rain, the drums sounding hollow and damp, and the chiefs of the bands riding ahead on their big, heavy-footed horses, their costumes wet, the horses' coats wet in the rain. The crowd was in the cafés and the dancers came in, too, and sat, their tight-wound white legs under the tables, shaking the water from their belled caps, and spreading their red and purple jackets over the chairs to dry. It was raining hard outside.

I left the crowd in the café and went over to the hotel to get shaved for dinner. I was shaving in my room when there was a knock on the door.

"Come in," I called.

Montoya walked in.

"How are you?" he said.

"Fine," I said.

"No bulls to-day."

"No," I said, "nothing but rain."

"Where are your friends?"

"Over at the Iruña."

Montoya smiled his embarrassed smile.

"Look," he said. "Do you know the American ambassador?"

"Yes," I said. "Everybody knows the American ambassador."

"He's here in town, now."

"Yes," I said. "Everybody's seen them."

"I've seen them, too," Montoya said. He didn't say anything. I went on shaving.

"Sit down," I said. "Let me send for a drink."

"No, I have to go."

I finished shaving and put my face down into the bowl and washed it with cold water. Montoya was standing there looking more embarrassed.

"Look," he said. "I've just had a message from them at the Grand Hotel that they want Pedro Romero and Marcial Lalanda to come over for coffee to-night after dinner."

"Well," I said, "it can't hurt Marcial any."

"Marcial has been in San Sebastian all day. He drove over in a car this morning with Márquez. I don't think they'll be back to-night."

Montoya stood embarrassed. He wanted me to say something.

"Don't give Romero the message," I said.

"You think so?"

"Absolutely."

Montoya was very pleased.

"I wanted to ask you because you were an American," he said.

"That's what I'd do."

"Look," said Montoya. "People take a boy like that. They don't know what he's worth. They don't know what he means. Any foreigner can flatter him. They start this Grand Hotel business, and in one year they're through."

"Like Algabeño," I said.

"Yes, like Algabeño."

"They're a fine lot," I said. "There's one American woman down here now that collects bull-fighters."

"I know. They only want the young ones."

"Yes," I said. "The old ones get fat."

"Or crazy like Gallo."

"Well," I said, "it's easy. All you have to do is not give him the message."

"He's such a fine boy," said Montoya. "He ought to stay with his own people. He shouldn't mix in that stuff."

"Won't you have a drink?" I asked.

"No," said Montoya, "I have to go." He went out.

I went down-stairs and out the door and took a walk around through the arcades around the square. It was still raining. I looked in at the Iruña for the gang and they were not there, so I walked on around the square and back to the hotel. They were eating dinner in the down-stairs dining-room.

They were well ahead of me and it was no use trying to catch them. Bill was buying shoe-shines for Mike. Bootblacks opened the street door and each one Bill called over and started to work on Mike.

"This is the eleventh time my boots have been polished," Mike said. "I say, Bill is an ass."

The bootblacks had evidently spread the report. Another came in.

"Limpia botas?" he said to Bill.

"No," said Bill. "For this Señor."

The bootblack knelt down beside the one at work and started on Mike's free shoe that shone already in the electric light.

"Bill's a yell of laughter," Mike said.

I was drinking red wine, and so far behind them that I felt a little uncomfortable about all this shoe-shining. I looked around the room. At the next table was Pedro Romero. He stood up when I nodded, and asked me to come over and meet a friend. His table was beside ours, almost touching. I met the friend, a Madrid bull-fight critic, a little man with a drawn face. I told Romero how much I liked his work, and he was very pleased. We talked Spanish and the critic knew a little French. I reached to our table for my wine-bottle, but the critic took my arm. Romero laughed.

"Drink here," he said in English.

He was very bashful about his English, but he was really very pleased with it, and as we went on talking he brought out words he was not sure of, and asked me about them. He was anxious to know the English for *corrida de toros,* the exact translation. Bull-fight he was suspicious of. I explained that bull-fight in Spanish was the *lidia* of a *toro.* The Spanish word *corrida* means in English the running of bulls—the French translation is *course des taureaux.* The critic put that in. There is no Spanish word for bull-fight.

Pedro Romero said he had learned a little English in Gibraltar. He was born in Ronda. That is not far above Gibraltar. He started bull-fighting in Málaga in the bull-fighting school there. He had only been at it three years. The bull-fight critic joked him about the number of *Malagueño* expressions he used. He was nineteen years old, he said. His older brother was with him as a banderillero, but he did not live in this hotel. He lived in a smaller hotel with the other people who worked for Romero. He asked me how many times I had seen him in the ring. I told him only three. It was really only two, but I did not want to explain after I had made the mistake.

"Where did you see me the other time? In Madrid?"

"Yes," I lied. I had read the accounts of his two appearances in Madrid in the bull-fight papers, so I was all right.

"The first or the second time?"

"The first."

"I was very bad," he said. "The second time I was better. You remember?" He turned to the critic.

He was not at all embarrassed. He talked of his work as something altogether apart from himself. There was nothing conceited or braggartly about him.

"I like it very much that you like my work," he said. "But you haven't seen it yet. To-morrow, if I get a good bull, I will try and show it to you."

When he said this he smiled, anxious that neither the bull-fight critic nor I would think he was boasting.

"I am anxious to see it," the critic said. "I would like to be convinced."

"He doesn't like my work much." Romero turned to me. He was serious.

The critic explained that he liked it very much, but that so far it had been incomplete.

"Wait till to-morrow, if a good one comes out."

"Have you seen the bulls for to-morrow?" the critic asked me.

"Yes. I saw them unloaded."

Pedro Romero leaned forward.

"What did you think of them?"

"Very nice," I said. "About twenty-six arrobas. Very short horns. Haven't you seen them?"

"Oh, yes," said Romero.

"They won't weigh twenty-six arrobas," said the critic.

"No," said Romero.

"They've got bananas for horns," the critic said.

"You call them bananas?" asked Romero. He turned to me and smiled. "*You* wouldn't call them bananas?"

"No," I said. "They're horns all right."

"They're very short," said Pedro Romero. "Very, very short. Still, they aren't bananas."

"I say, Jake," Brett called from the next table, "you *have* deserted us."

"Just temporarily," I said. "We're talking bulls."

"You *are* superior."

"Tell him that bulls have no balls," Mike shouted. He was drunk.

Romero looked at me inquiringly.

"Drunk," I said. "Borracho! Muy borracho!"

"You might introduce your friends," Brett said. She had not stopped looking at Pedro Romero. I asked them if they would like to have coffee with us. They both stood up. Romero's face was very brown. He had very nice manners.

I introduced them all around and they started to sit down, but there was not enough room, so we all moved over to the big table by the wall to have coffee. Mike ordered a bottle of Fundador and glasses for everybody. There was a lot of drunken talking.

"Tell him I think writing is lousy," Bill said. "Go on, tell him. Tell him I'm ashamed of being a writer."

Pedro Romero was sitting beside Brett and listening to her.

"Go on. Tell him!" Bill said.

Romero looked up smiling.

"This gentleman," I said, "is a writer."

Romero was impressed. "This other one, too," I said, pointing at Cohn.

"He looks like Villalta," Romero said, looking at Bill. "Rafael, doesn't he look like Villalta?"

"I can't see it," the critic said.

"Really," Romero said in Spanish. "He looks a lot like Villalta. What does the drunken one do?"

"Nothing."

"Is that why he drinks?"

"No. He's waiting to marry this lady."

"Tell him bulls have no balls!" Mike shouted, very drunk, from the other end of the table.

"What does he say?"

"He's drunk."

"Jake," Mike called. "Tell him bulls have no balls!"

"You understand?" I said.

"Yes."

I was sure he didn't, so it was all right.

"Tell him Brett wants to see him put on those green pants."

"Pipe down, Mike."

"Tell him Brett is dying to know how he can get into those pants."

"Pipe down."

During this Romero was fingering his glass and talking with Brett. Brett was talking French and he was talking Spanish and a little English, and laughing.

Bill was filling the glasses.

"Tell him Brett wants to come into——"

"Oh, pipe down, Mike, for Christ's sake!"

Romero looked up smiling. "Pipe down! I know that," he said.

Just then Montoya came into the room. He started to smile at me, then he saw Pedro Romero with a big glass of cognac in his hand, sitting laughing between me and a woman with bare shoulders, at a table full of drunks. He did not even nod.

Montoya went out of the room. Mike was on his feet proposing a toast. "Let's all drink to——" he began. "Pedro Romero," I said. Everybody stood up. Romero took it very seriously, and we touched glasses and drank it down, I rushing it a little because Mike was trying to make it clear that that was not at all what he was going to drink to. But it went off all right, and Pedro Romero shook hands with every one and he and the critic went out together.

"My God! he's a lovely boy," Brett said. "And how I would love to see him get into those clothes. He must use a shoe-horn."

"I started to tell him," Mike began. "And Jake kept interrupting me.

Why do you interrupt me? Do you think you talk Spanish better than I do?"

"Oh, shut up, Mike! Nobody interrupted you."

"No, I'd like to get this settled." He turned away from me. "Do you think you amount to something, Cohn? Do you think you belong here among us? People who are out to have a good time? For God's sake don't be so noisy, Cohn!"

"Oh, cut it out, Mike," Cohn said.

"Do you think Brett wants you here? Do you think you add to the party? Why don't you say something?"

"I said all I had to say the other night, Mike."

"I'm not one of you literary chaps." Mike stood shakily and leaned against the table. "I'm not clever. But I do know when I'm not wanted. Why don't you see when you're not wanted, Cohn? Go away. Go away, for God's sake. Take that sad Jewish face away. Don't you think I'm right?"

He looked at us.

"Sure," I said. "Let's all go over to the Iruña."

"No. Don't you think I'm right? I love that woman."

"Oh, don't start that again. Do shove it along, Michael," Brett said.

"Don't you think I'm right, Jake?"

Cohn still sat at the table. His face had the sallow, yellow look it got when he was insulted, but somehow he seemed to be enjoying it. The childish, drunken heroics of it. It was his affair with a lady of title.

"Jake," Mike said. He was almost crying. "You know I'm right. Listen, you!" He turned to Cohn: "Go away! Go away now!"

"But I won't go, Mike," said Cohn.

"Then I'll make you!" Mike started toward him around the table. Cohn stood up and took off his glasses. He stood waiting, his face sallow, his hands fairly low, proudly and firmly waiting for the assault, ready to do battle for his lady love.

I grabbed Mike. "Come on to the café," I said. "You can't hit him here in the hotel."

"Good!" said Mike. "Good idea!"

We started off. I looked back as Mike stumbled up the stairs and saw Cohn putting his glasses on again. Bill was sitting at the table pouring another glass of Fundador. Brett was sitting looking straight ahead at nothing.

Outside on the square it had stopped raining and the moon was trying to get through the clouds. There was a wind blowing. The military band was playing and the crowd was massed on the far side of the square where the fireworks specialist and his son were trying to send up fire balloons. A balloon would start up jerkily, on a great bias, and be torn by the wind or blown against the houses of the square. Some fell into the crowd. The magnesium flared and the fireworks exploded and chased about in the crowd. There was no one dancing in the square. The gravel was too wet.

Brett came out with Bill and joined us. We stood in the crowd and watched Don Manuel Orquito, the fireworks king, standing on a little platform, carefully starting the balloons with sticks, standing above the heads of the crowd to launch the balloons off into the wind. The wind brought them all down, and Don Manuel Orquito's face was sweaty in the light of his complicated fireworks that fell into the crowd and charged and chased, sputtering and cracking, between the legs of the people. The people shouted as each new luminous paper bubble careened, caught fire, and fell.

"They're razzing Don Manuel," Bill said.

"How do you know he's Don Manuel?" Brett said.

"His name's on the programme. Don Manuel Orquito, the pirotécnico of esta ciudad."

"Globos iluminados," Mike said. "A collection of globos iluminados. That's what the paper said."

The wind blew the band music away.

"I say, I wish one would go up," Brett said. "That Don Manuel chap is furious."

"He's probably worked for weeks fixing them to go off, spelling out 'Hail to San Fermin,' " Bill said.

"Globos iluminados," Mike said. "A bunch of bloody globos iluminados."

"Come on," said Brett. "We can't stand here."

"Her ladyship wants a drink," Mike said.

"How you know things," Brett said.

Inside, the café was crowded and very noisy. No one noticed us come in. We could not find a table. There was a great noise going on.

"Come on, let's get out of here," Bill said.

Outside the paseo was going on under the arcade. There were some English and Americans from Biarritz in sport clothes scattered at the tables. Some of the women stared at the people going by with lorgnons.

We had acquired, at some time, a friend of Bill's from Biarritz. She was staying with another girl at the Grand Hotel. The other girl had a headache and had gone to bed.

"Here's the pub," Mike said. It was the Bar Milano, a small, tough bar where you could get food and where they danced in the back room. We all sat down at a table and ordered a bottle of Fundador. The bar was not full. There was nothing going on.

"This is a hell of a place," Bill said.

"It's too early."

"Let's take the bottle and come back later," Bill said. "I don't want to sit here on a night like this."

"Let's go and look at the English," Mike said. "I love to look at the English."

"They're awful," Bill said. "Where did they all come from?"

"They come from Biarritz," Mike said. "They come to see the last day of the quaint little Spanish fiesta."

"I'll festa them," Bill said.

"You're an extraordinarily beautiful girl." Mike turned to Bill's friend. "When did you come here?"

"Come off it, Michael."

"I say, she *is* a lovely girl. Where have I been? Where have I been looking all this while? You're a lovely thing. *Have* we met? Come along with me and Bill. We're going to festa the English."

"I'll festa them," Bill said. "What the hell are they doing at this fiesta?"

"Come on," Mike said. "Just us three. We're going to festa the bloody English. I hope you're not English? I'm Scotch. I hate the English. I'm going to festa them. Come on, Bill."

Through the window we saw them, all three arm in arm, going toward the café. Rockets were going up in the square.

"I'm going to sit here," Brett said.

"I'll stay with you," Cohn said.

"Oh, don't!" Brett said. "For God's sake, go off somewhere. Can't you see Jake and I want to talk?"

"I didn't," Cohn said. "I thought I'd sit here because I felt a little tight."

"What a hell of a reason for sitting with any one. If you're tight, go to bed. Go on to bed."

"Was I rude enough to him?" Brett asked. Cohn was gone. "My God! I'm so sick of him!"

"He doesn't add much to the gaiety."

"He depresses me so."

"He's behaved very badly."

"Damned badly. He had a chance to behave so well."

"He's probably waiting just outside the door now."

"Yes. He would. You know I do know how he feels. He can't believe it didn't mean anything."

"I know."

"Nobody else would behave as badly. Oh, I'm so sick of the whole thing. And Michael. Michael's been lovely, too."

"It's been damned hard on Mike."

"Yes. But he didn't need to be a swine."

"Everybody behaves badly," I said. "Give them the proper chance."

"You wouldn't behave badly." Brett looked at me.

"I'd be as big an ass as Cohn," I said.

"Darling, don't let's talk a lot of rot."

"All right. Talk about anything you like."

"Don't be difficult. You're the only person I've got, and I feel rather awful to-night."

"You've got Mike."

"Yes, Mike. Hasn't he been pretty?"

"Well," I said, "it's been damned hard on Mike, having Cohn around and seeing him with you."

"Don't I know it, darling? Please don't make me feel any worse than I do."

Brett was nervous as I had never seen her before. She kept looking away from me and looking ahead at the wall.

"Want to go for a walk?"

"Yes. Come on."

I corked up the Fundador bottle and gave it to the bartender.

"Let's have one more drink of that," Brett said. "My nerves are rotten."

We each drank a glass of the smooth amontillado brandy.

"Come on," said Brett.

As we came out the door I saw Cohn walk out from under the arcade.

"He *was* there," Brett said.

"He can't be away from you."

"Poor devil!"

"I'm not sorry for him. I hate him, myself."

"I hate him, too," she shivered. "I hate his damned suffering."

We walked arm in arm down the side street away from the crowd and the lights of the square. The street was dark and wet, and we walked along it to the fortifications at the edge of town. We passed wine-shops with light coming out from their doors onto the black, wet street, and sudden bursts of music.

"Want to go in?"

"No."

We walked out across the wet grass and onto the stone wall of the fortifications. I spread a newspaper on the stone and Brett sat down. Across the plain it was dark, and we could see the mountains. The wind was high up and took the clouds across the moon. Below us were the dark pits of the fortifications. Behind were the trees and the shadow of the cathedral, and the town silhouetted against the moon.

"Don't feel bad," I said.

"I feel like hell," Brett said. "Don't let's talk."

We looked out at the plain. The long lines of trees were dark in the moonlight. There were the lights of a car on the road climbing the mountain. Up on the top of the mountain we saw the lights of the fort. Below to the left was the river. It was high from the rain, and black and smooth. Trees were dark along the banks. We sat and looked out. Brett stared straight ahead. Suddenly she shivered.

"It's cold."

"Want to walk back?"

"Through the park."

We climbed down. It was clouding over again. In the park it was dark under the trees.

"Do you still love me, Jake?"

"Yes," I said.

"Because I'm a goner," Brett said.

"How?"

"I'm a goner. I'm mad about the Romero boy. I'm in love with him, I think."

"I wouldn't be if I were you."

"I can't help it. I'm a goner. It's tearing me all up inside."

"Don't do it."

"I can't help it. I've never been able to help anything."

"You ought to stop it."

"How can I stop it? I can't stop things. Feel that?"

Her hand was trembling.

"I'm like that all through."

"You oughtn't to do it."

"I can't help it. I'm a goner now, anyway. Don't you see the difference?"

"No."

"I've got to do something. I've got to do something I really want to do. I've lost my self-respect."

"You don't have to do that."

"Oh, darling, don't be difficult. What do you think it's meant to have that damned Jew about, and Mike the way he's acted?"

"Sure."

"I can't just stay tight all the time."

"No."

"Oh, darling, please stay by me. Please stay by me and see me through this."

"Sure."

"I don't say it's right. It is right though for me. God knows, I've never felt such a bitch."

"What do you want me to do?"

"Come on," Brett said. "Let's go and find him."

Together we walked down the gravel path in the park in the dark, under the trees and then out from under the trees and past the gate into the street that led into town.

Pedro Romero was in the café. He was at a table with other bull-fighters and bull-fight critics. They were smoking cigars. When we came in they looked up. Romero smiled and bowed. We sat down at a table half-way down the room.

"Ask him to come over and have a drink."

"Not yet. He'll come over."

"I can't look at him."

"He's nice to look at," I said.

"I've always done just what I wanted."

"I know."

"I do feel such a bitch."

"Well," I said.

"My God!" said Brett, "the things a woman goes through."

"Yes?"

"Oh, I do feel such a bitch."

I looked across at the table. Pedro Romero smiled. He said something to the other people at his table, and stood up. He came over to our table. I stood up and we shook hands.

"Won't you have a drink?"

"You must have a drink with me," he said. He seated himself, asking Brett's permission without saying anything. He had very nice manners. But he kept on smoking his cigar. It went well with his face.

"You like cigars?" I asked.

"Oh, yes. I always smoke cigars."

It was part of his system of authority. It made him seem older. I noticed his skin. It was clear and smooth and very brown. There was a triangular scar on his cheek-bone. I saw he was watching Brett. He felt there was something between them. He must have felt it when Brett gave him her hand. He was being very careful. I think he was sure, but he did not want to make any mistake.

"You fight to-morrow?" I said.

"Yes," he said. "Algabeño was hurt to-day in Madrid. Did you hear?"

"No," I said. "Badly?"

He shook his head.

"Nothing. Here," he showed his hand. Brett reached out and spread the fingers apart.

"Oh!" he said in English, "you tell fortunes?"

"Sometimes. Do you mind?"

"No. I like it." He spread his hand flat on the table. "Tell me I live for always, and be a millionaire."

He was still very polite, but he was surer of himself. "Look," he said, "do you see any bulls in my hand?"

He laughed. His hand was very fine and the wrist was small.

"There are thousands of bulls," Brett said. She was not at all nervous now. She looked lovely.

"Good," Romero laughed. "At a thousand duros apiece," he said to me in Spanish. "Tell me some more."

"It's a good hand," Brett said. "I think he'll live a long time."

"Say it to me. Not to your friend."

"I said you'd live a long time."

"I know it," Romero said. "I'm never going to die."

I tapped with my finger-tips on the table. Romero saw it. He shook his head.

"No. Don't do that. The bulls are my best friends."

I translated to Brett.

"You kill your friends?" she asked.

"Always," he said in English, and laughed. "So they don't kill me." He looked at her across the table.

"You know English well."

"Yes," he said. "Pretty well, sometimes. But I must not let anybody know. It would be very bad, a torero who speaks English."

"Why?" asked Brett.

"It would be bad. The people would not like it. Not yet."

"Why not?"

"They would not like it. Bull-fighters are not like that."

"What are bull-fighters like?"

He laughed and tipped his hat down over his eyes and changed the angle of his cigar and the expression of his face.

"Like at the table," he said. I glanced over. He had mimicked exactly the expression of Nacional. He smiled, his face natural again. "No. I must forget English."

"Don't forget it, yet," Brett said.

"No?"

"No."

"All right."

He laughed again.

"I would like a hat like that," Brett said.

"Good. I'll get you one."

"Right. See that you do."

"I will. I'll get you one to-night."

I stood up. Romero rose, too.

"Sit down," I said. "I must go and find our friends and bring them here."

He looked at me. It was a final look to ask if it were understood. It was understood all right.

"Sit down," Brett said to him. "You must teach me Spanish."

He sat down and looked at her across the table. I went out. The hard-eyed people at the bull-fighter table watched me go. It was not pleasant. When I came back and looked in the café, twenty minutes later, Brett and Pedro Romero were gone. The coffee-glasses and our three empty cognac-glasses were on the table. A waiter came with a cloth and picked up the glasses and mopped off the table.

17

Outside the Bar Milano I found Bill and Mike and Edna. Edna was the girl's name.

"We've been thrown out," Edna said.

"By the police," said Mike. "There's some people in there that don't like me."

"I've kept them out of four fights," Edna said. "You've got to help me."

Bill's face was red.

"Come back in, Edna," he said. "Go on in there and dance with Mike."

"It's silly," Edna said. "There'll just be another row."

"Damned Biarritz swine," Bill said.

"Come on," Mike said. "After all, it's a pub. They can't occupy a whole pub."

"Good old Mike," Bill said. "Damned English swine come here and insult Mike and try and spoil the fiesta."

"They're so bloody," Mike said. "I hate the English."

"They can't insult Mike," Bill said. "Mike is a swell fellow. They can't insult Mike. I won't stand it. Who cares if he is a damn bankrupt?" His voice broke.

"Who cares?" Mike said. "I don't care. Jake doesn't care. Do *you* care?"

"No," Edna said. "Are you a bankrupt?"

"Of course I am. You don't care, do you, Bill?"

Bill put his arm around Mike's shoulder.

"I wish to hell I was a bankrupt. I'd show those bastards."

"They're just English," Mike said. "It never makes any difference what the English say."

"The dirty swine," Bill said. "I'm going to clean them out."

"Bill," Edna looked at me. "Please don't go in again, Bill. They're so stupid."

"That's it," said Mike. "They're stupid. I knew that was what it was."

"They can't say things like that about Mike," Bill said.

"Do you know them?" I asked Mike.

"No. I never saw them. They say they know me."

"I won't stand it," Bill said.

"Come on. Let's go over to the Suizo," I said.

"They're a bunch of Edna's friends from Biarritz," Bill said.

"They're simply stupid," Edna said.

"One of them's Charley Blackman, from Chicago," Bill said.

"I was never in Chicago," Mike said.

Edna started to laugh and could not stop.

"Take me away from here," she said, "you bankrupts."

"What kind of a row was it?" I asked Edna. We were walking across the square to the Suizo. Bill was gone.

"I don't know what happened, but some one had the police called to keep Mike out of the back room. There were some people that had known Mike at Cannes. What's the matter with Mike?"

"Probably he owes them money," I said. "That's what people usually get bitter about."

In front of the ticket-booths out in the square there were two lines of people waiting. They were sitting on chairs or crouched on the ground with blankets and newspapers around them. They were waiting for the wickets to open in the morning to buy tickets for the bull-fight. The night was clearing and the moon was out. Some of the people in the line were sleeping.

At the Café Suizo we had just sat down and ordered Fundador when Robert Cohn came up.

"Where's Brett?" he asked.

"I don't know."

"She was with you."

"She must have gone to bed."

"She's not."

"I don't know where she is."

His face was sallow under the light. He was standing up.

"Tell me where she is."

"Sit down," I said. "I don't know where she is."

"The hell you don't!"

"You can shut your face."

"Tell me where Brett is."

"I'll not tell you a damn thing."

"You know where she is."

"If I did I wouldn't tell you."

"Oh, go to hell, Cohn," Mike called from the table. "Brett's gone off with the bull-fighter chap. They're on their honeymoon."

"You shut up."

"Oh, go to hell!" Mike said languidly.

"Is that where she is?" Cohn turned to me.

"Go to hell!"

"She was with you. Is that where she is?"

"Go to hell!"

"I'll make you tell me"—he stepped forward—"you damned pimp."

I swung at him and he ducked. I saw his face duck sideways in the light. He hit me and I sat down on the pavement. As I started to get on my feet he hit me twice. I went down backward under a table. I tried to get up and felt I did not have any legs. I felt I must get on my feet and try and hit him. Mike helped me up. Some one poured a carafe of water on my head. Mike had an arm around me, and I found I was sitting on a chair. Mike was pulling at my ears.

"I say, you were cold," Mike said.

"Where the hell were you?"

"Oh, I was around."

"You didn't want to mix in it?"

"He knocked Mike down, too," Edna said.

"He didn't knock me out," Mike said. "I just lay there."

"Does this happen every night at your fiestas?" Edna asked. "Wasn't that Mr. Cohn?"

"I'm all right," I said. "My head's a little wobbly."

There were several waiters and a crowd of people standing around.

"Vaya!" said Mike. "Get away. Go on."

The waiters moved the people away.

"It was quite a thing to watch," Edna said. "He must be a boxer."

"He is."

"I wish Bill had been here," Edna said. "I'd like to have seen Bill knocked down, too. I've always wanted to see Bill knocked down. He's so big."

"I was hoping he would knock down a waiter," Mike said, "and get arrested. I'd like to see Mr. Robert Cohn in jail."

"No," I said.

"Oh, no," said Edna. "You don't mean that."

"I do, though," Mike said. "I'm not one of these chaps likes being knocked about. I never play games, even."

Mike took a drink.

"I never liked to hunt, you know. There was always the danger of having a horse fall on you. How do you feel, Jake?"

"All right."

"You're nice," Edna said to Mike. "Are you really a bankrupt?"

"I'm a tremendous bankrupt," Mike said. "I owe money to everybody. Don't you owe any money?"

"Tons."

"I owe everybody money," Mike said. "I borrowed a hundred pesetas from Montoya to-night."

"The hell you did," I said.

"I'll pay it back," Mike said. "I always pay everything back."

"That's why you're a bankrupt, isn't it?" Edna said.

I stood up. I had heard them talking from a long way away. It all seemed like some bad play.

"I'm going over to the hotel," I said. Then I heard them talking about me.

"Is he all right?" Edna asked.

"We'd better walk with him."

"I'm all right," I said. "Don't come. I'll see you all later."

I walked away from the café. They were sitting at the table. I looked back at them and at the empty tables. There was a waiter sitting at one of the tables with his head in his hands.

Walking across the square to the hotel everything looked new and changed. I had never seen the trees before. I had never seen the flagpoles before, nor the front of the theatre. It was all different. I felt as I felt once coming home from an out-of-town football game. I was carrying a suit-case with my football things in it, and I walked up the street from the station in the town I had lived in all my life and it was all new. They were raking the lawns and burning leaves in the road, and I stopped for a long time and watched. It was all strange. Then I went on, and my feet seemed to be a long way off, and everything seemed to come from a long way off, and I could hear my feet walking a great distance away. I had been kicked in the head early in the game. It was like that crossing the square. It was like that going up the stairs in the hotel. Going up the stairs took a long time, and I had the feeling that I was carrying my suitcase. There was a light in the room. Bill came out and met me in the hall.

"Say," he said, "go up and see Cohn. He's been in a jam, and he's asking for you."

"The hell with him."

"Go on. Go on up and see him."

I did not want to climb another flight of stairs.

"What are you looking at me that way for?"

"I'm not looking at you. Go on up and see Cohn. He's in bad shape."

"You were drunk a little while ago," I said.

"I'm drunk now," Bill said. "But you go up and see Cohn. He wants to see you."

"All right," I said. It was just a matter of climbing more stairs. I went on up the stairs carrying my phantom suitcase. I walked down the hall to Cohn's room. The door was shut and I knocked.

"Who is it?"

"Barnes."

"Come in, Jake."

I opened the door and went in, and set down my suitcase. There was no light in the room. Cohn was lying, face down, on the bed in the dark.

"Hello, Jake."

"Don't call me Jake."

I stood by the door. It was just like this that I had come home. Now it was a hot bath that I needed. A deep, hot bath, to lie back in.

"Where's the bathroom?" I asked.

Cohn was crying. There he was, face down on the bed, crying.

He had on a white polo shirt, the kind he'd worn at Princeton.

"I'm sorry, Jake. Please forgive me."

"Forgive you, hell."

"Please forgive me, Jake."

I did not say anything. I stood there by the door.

"I was crazy. You must see how it was."

"Oh, that's all right."

"I couldn't stand it about Brett."

"You called me a pimp."

I did not care. I wanted a hot bath. I wanted a hot bath in deep water.

"I know. Please don't remember it. I was crazy."

"That's all right."

He was crying. His voice was funny. He lay there in his white shirt on the bed in the dark. His polo shirt.

"I'm going away in the morning."

He was crying without making any noise.

"I just couldn't stand it about Brett. I've been through hell, Jake. It's been simply hell. When I met her down here Brett treated me as though I were a perfect stranger. I just couldn't stand it. We lived together at San Sebastian. I suppose you know it. I can't stand it any more."

He lay there on the bed.

"Well," I said, "I'm going to take a bath."

"You were the only friend I had, and I loved Brett so."

"Well," I said, "so long."

"I guess it isn't any use," he said. "I guess it isn't any damn use."

"What?"

"Everything. Please say you forgive me, Jake."

"Sure," I said. "It's all right."

"I felt so terribly. I've been through such hell, Jake. Now everything's gone. Everything."

"Well," I said, "so long. I've got to go."

He rolled over, sat on the edge of the bed, and then stood up.

"So long, Jake," he said. "You'll shake hands, won't you?"

"Sure. Why not?"

We shook hands. In the dark I could not see his face very well.

"Well," I said, "see you in the morning."

"I'm going away in the morning."

"Oh, yes," I said.

I went out. Cohn was standing in the door of the room.

"Are you all right, Jake?" he asked.

"Oh, yes," I said. "I'm all right."

I could not find the bathroom. After a while I found it. There was a deep stone tub. I turned on the taps and the water would not run. I sat down on the edge of the bath-tub. When I got up to go I found I had taken off my shoes. I hunted for them and found them and carried them down-stairs. I found my room and went inside and undressed and got into bed.

I woke with a headache and the noise of the bands going by in the street. I remembered I had promised to take Bill's friend Edna to see the bulls go through the street and into the ring. I dressed and went down-stairs and out into the cold early morning. People were crossing the square, hurrying toward the bull-ring. Across the square were the two lines of men in front of the ticket-booths. They were still waiting for the tickets to go on sale at seven o'clock. I hurried across the street to the café. The waiter told me that my friends had been there and gone.

"How many were they?"

"Two gentlemen and a lady."

That was all right. Bill and Mike were with Edna. She had been afraid last night they would pass out. That was why I was to be sure to take her. I drank the coffee and hurried with the other people toward the bull-ring. I was not groggy now. There was only a bad headache. Everything looked sharp and clear, and the town smelt of the early morning.

The stretch of ground from the edge of the town to the bull-ring was muddy. There was a crowd all along the fence that led to the ring, and the outside balconies and the top of the bull-ring were solid with people. I heard the rocket and I knew I could not get into the ring in time to see the bulls come in, so I shoved through the crowd to the fence. I was pushed close against the planks of the fence. Between the two fences of the runway the police were clearing the crowd along. They walked or trotted on into the bull-ring. Then people commenced to come running. A drunk slipped and fell. Two policemen grabbed him and rushed him over to the fence. The crowd were running fast now. There was a great shout from the crowd, and putting my head through between the boards I saw the bulls just coming out of the street into the long running pen. They were going fast and gaining on the crowd. Just then another drunk started out from the fence with a blouse in his hands. He wanted to do capework with the bulls. The two policemen tore out, collared him, one hit him with a club, and they dragged him against the fence and stood flattened out against the fence as the last of the crowd and the bulls went by. There were so many people running ahead of the bulls that the mass thickened and slowed up going through the gate into the ring, and as the bulls passed, galloping together, heavy, muddy-sided, horns swinging, one shot ahead, caught a man in the running crowd in the back and lifted him in the air. Both the man's arms were by his sides, his head went back as the horn went in, and the bull lifted him and then dropped him. The bull picked another man running in front, but the man disappeared into the crowd, and the crowd was through the gate and into the ring with the bulls behind them. The red door of the ring went shut, the crowd on the outside balconies of the bull-ring were pressing through to the inside, there was a shout, then another shout.

The man who had been gored lay face down in the trampled mud. People climbed over the fence, and I could not see the man because the crowd was so thick around him. From inside the ring came the shouts. Each shout meant a charge by some bull into the crowd. You could tell by the degree of intensity in the shout how bad a thing it was that was happening. Then the rocket went up that meant the steers had gotten the bulls out of the ring and into the corrals. I left the fence and started back toward the town.

Back in the town I went to the café to have a second coffee and some buttered toast. The waiters were sweeping out the café and mopping off the tables. One came over and took my order.

"Anything happen at the encierro?"

"I didn't see it all. One man was badly cogido."

"Where?"

"Here." I put one hand on the small of my back and the other on my chest, where it looked as though the horn must have come through. The waiter nodded his head and swept the crumbs from the table with his cloth.

"Badly cogido," he said. "All for sport. All for pleasure."

He went away and came back with the long-handled coffee and milk pots. He poured the milk and coffee. It came out of the long spouts in two streams into the big cup. The waiter nodded his head.

"Badly cogido through the back," he said. He put the pots down on the table and sat down in the chair at the table. "A big horn wound. All for fun. Just for fun. What do you think of that?"

"I don't know."

"That's it. All for fun. Fun, you understand."

"You're not an aficionado?"

"Me? What are bulls? Animals. Brute animals." He stood up and put his hand on the small of his back. "Right through the back. A cornada right through the back. For fun—you understand."

He shook his head and walked away, carrying the coffee-pots. Two men were going by in the street. The waiter shouted to them. They were grave-looking. One shook his head. "Muerto!" he called.

The waiter nodded his head. The two men went on. They were on some errand. The waiter came over to my table.

"You hear? Muerto. Dead. He's dead. With a horn through him. All for morning fun. Es muy flamenco."

"It's bad."

"Not for me," the waiter said. "No fun in that for me."

Later in the day we learned that the man who was killed was named Vicente Gironés, and came from near Tafalla. The next day in the paper we read that he was twenty-eight years old, and had a farm, a wife, and two children. He had continued to come to the fiesta each year after he was married. The next day his wife came in from Tafalla to be with the body, and the day after there was a service in the chapel of San Fermin, and the coffin was carried to the railway-station by members of the dancing and drinking society of Tafalla. The drums marched ahead, and there was music on the fifes, and behind the men who carried the coffin walked the wife and two children. . . . Behind them marched all the members of the dancing and drinking societies of Pamplona, Estella, Tafalla, and Sangüesa who could stay over for the funeral. The coffin was loaded into the baggage-car of the train, and the widow and the two children rode, sitting, all three together, in an open third-class railway-carriage. The train started with a jerk, and then ran smoothly, going down grade around the edge of the plateau and out into the fields of grain that blew in the wind on the plain on the way to Tafalla.

The bull who killed Vicente Gironés was named Bocanegra, was Number 118 of the bull-breeding establishment of Sanchez Taberno, and was killed by Pedro Romero as the third bull of that same afternoon. His ear was cut by popular acclamation and given to Pedro Romero, who, in turn, gave it to Brett, who wrapped it in a handkerchief belonging to myself, and left both ear and handkerchief, along with a number of Muratti cigarette-stubs, shoved far back in the drawer of the bed-table that stood beside her bed in the Hotel Montoya, in Pamplona.

• • •

Back in the hotel, the night watchman was sitting on a bench inside the door. He had been there all night and was very sleepy. He stood up as I came in. Three of the waitresses came in at the same time. They had been to the morning show at the bull-ring. They went up-stairs laughing. I followed them up-stairs and went into my room. I took off my shoes and lay down on the bed. The window was open onto the balcony and the sunlight was bright in the room. I did not feel sleepy. It must have been half past three o'clock when I had gone to bed and the bands had waked me at six. My jaw was sore on both sides. I felt it with my thumb and fingers. That damn Cohn. He should have hit somebody the first time he was insulted, and then gone away. He was so sure that Brett loved him. He was going to stay, and true love would conquer all. Some one knocked on the door.

"Come in."

It was Bill and Mike. They sat down on the bed.

"Some encierro," Bill said. "Some encierro."

"I say, weren't you there?" Mike asked. "Ring for some beer, Bill."

"What a morning!" Bill said. He mopped off his face. "My God! what a morning! And here's old Jake. Old Jake, the human punching-bag."

"What happened inside?"

"Good God!" Bill said, "what happened, Mike?"

"There were these bulls coming in," Mike said. "Just ahead of them was the crowd, and some chap tripped and brought the whole lot of them down."

"And the bulls all came in right over them," Bill said.

"I heard them yell."

"That was Edna," Bill said.

"Chaps kept coming out and waving their shirts."

"One bull went along the barrera and hooked everybody over."

"They took about twenty chaps to the infirmary," Mike said.

"What a morning!" Bill said. "The damn police kept arresting chaps that wanted to go and commit suicide with the bulls."

"The steers took them in, in the end," Mike said.

"It took about an hour."

"It was really about a quarter of an hour," Mike objected.

"Oh, go to hell," Bill said. "You've been in the war. It was two hours and a half for me."

"Where's that beer?" Mike asked.

"What did you do with the lovely Edna?"

"We took her home just now. She's gone to bed."

"How did she like it?"

"Fine. We told her it was just like that every morning."

"She was impressed," Mike said.

"She wanted us to go down in the ring, too," Bill said. "She likes action."

"I said it wouldn't be fair to my creditors," Mike said.

"What a morning," Bill said. "And what a night!"

"How's your jaw, Jake?" Mike asked.

"Sore," I said.

Bill laughed.

"Why didn't you hit him with a chair?"

"You can talk," Mike said. "He'd have knocked you out, too. I never saw him hit me. I rather think I saw him just before, and then quite suddenly I was sitting down in the street, and Jake was lying under a table."

"Where did he go afterward?" I asked.

"Here she is," Mike said. "Here's the beautiful lady with the beer."

The chambermaid put the tray with the beer-bottles and glasses down on the table.

"Now bring up three more bottles," Mike said.

"Where did Cohn go after he hit me?" I asked Bill.

"Don't you know about that?" Mike was opening a beer-bottle. He poured the beer into one of the glasses, holding the glass close to the bottle.

"Really?" Bill asked.

"Why he went in and found Brett and the bull-fighter chap in the bull-fighter's room, and then he massacred the poor, bloody bull-fighter."

"No."

"Yes."

"What a night!" Bill said.

"He nearly killed the poor, bloody bull-fighter. Then Cohn wanted to take Brett away. Wanted to make an honest woman of her, I imagine. Damned touching scene."

He took a long drink of the beer.

"He is an ass."

"What happened?"

"Brett gave him what for. She told him off. I think she was rather good."

"I'll bet she was," Bill said.

"Then Cohn broke down and cried, and wanted to shake hands with the bull-fighter fellow. He wanted to shake hands with Brett, too."

"I know. He shook hands with me."

"Did he? Well, they weren't having any of it. The bull-fighter fellow was rather good. He didn't say much, but he kept getting up and getting knocked down again. Cohn couldn't knock him out. It must have been damned funny."

"Where did you hear all this?"

"Brett. I saw her this morning."

"What happened finally?"

"It seems the bull-fighter fellow was sitting on the bed. He'd been knocked down about fifteen times, and he wanted to fight some more. Brett held him and wouldn't let him get up. He was weak, but Brett couldn't hold him, and he got up. Then Cohn said he wouldn't hit him again. Said he couldn't do it. Said it would be wicked. So the bull-fighter chap sort of rather staggered over to him. Cohn went back against the wall.

" 'So you won't hit me?'

" 'No,' said Cohn. 'I'd be ashamed to.'

"So the bull-fighter fellow hit him just as hard as he could in the face, and then sat down on the floor. He couldn't get up, Brett said. Cohn wanted to pick him up and carry him to the bed. He said if Cohn helped him he'd kill him, and he'd kill him anyway this morning if Cohn wasn't out of town. Cohn was crying, and Brett had told him off, and he wanted to shake hands. I've told you that before."

"Tell the rest," Bill said.

"It seems the bull-fighter chap was sitting on the floor. He was waiting to get strength enough to get up and hit Cohn again. Brett wasn't having any shaking hands, and Cohn was crying and telling her how much he loved her, and she was telling him not to be a ruddy ass. Then Cohn leaned down to shake hands with the bull-fighter fellow. No hard feelings, you know. All for forgiveness. And the bull-fighter chap hit him in the face again."

"That's quite a kid," Bill said.

"He ruined Cohn," Mike said. "You know I don't think Cohn will ever want to knock people about again."

"When did you see Brett?"

"This morning. She came in to get some things. She's looking after this Romero lad."

He poured out another bottle of beer.

"Brett's rather cut up. But she loves looking after people. That's how we came to go off together. She was looking after me."

"I know," I said.

"I'm rather drunk," Mike said. "I think I'll *stay* rather drunk. This is all awfully amusing, but it's not too pleasant. It's not too pleasant for me."

He drank off the beer.

"I gave Brett what for, you know. I said if she would go about with Jews and bull-fighters and such people, she must expect trouble." He leaned forward. "I say, Jake, do you mind if I drink that bottle of yours? She'll bring you another one."

"Please," I said. "I wasn't drinking it, anyway."

Mike started to open the bottle. "Would you mind opening it?" I pressed up the wire fastener and poured it for him.

"You know," Mike went on, "Brett was rather good. She's always rather good. I gave her a fearful hiding about Jews and bull-fighters, and all those sort of people, and do you know what she said: 'Yes. I've had such a hell of a happy life with the British aristocracy!' "

He took a drink.

"That was rather good. Ashley, chap she got the title from, was a sailor, you know. Ninth baronet. When he came home he wouldn't sleep in a bed. Always made Brett sleep on the floor. Finally, when he got really bad, he used to tell her he'd kill her. Always slept with a loaded service revolver. Brett used to take the shells out when he'd gone to sleep. She hasn't had an absolutely happy life, Brett. Damned shame, too. She enjoys things so."

He stood up. His hand was shaky.

"I'm going in the room. Try and get a little sleep."

He smiled.

"We go too long without sleep in these fiestas. I'm going to start now and get plenty of sleep. Damn bad thing not to get sleep. Makes you frightfully nervy."

"We'll see you at noon at the Iruña," Bill said.

Mike went out the door. We heard him in the next room.

He rang the bell and the chambermaid came and knocked at the door.

"Bring up half a dozen bottles of beer and a bottle of Fundador," Mike told her.

"Sí, Señorito."

"I'm going to bed," Bill said. "Poor old Mike. I had a hell of a row about him last night."

"Where? At that Milano place?"

"Yes. There was a fellow there that had helped pay Brett and Mike out of Cannes, once. He was damned nasty."

"I know the story."

"I didn't. Nobody ought to have a right to say things about Mike."

"That's what makes it bad."

"They oughtn't to have any right. I wish to hell they didn't have any right. I'm going to bed."

"Was anybody killed in the ring?"

"I don't think so. Just badly hurt."

"A man was killed outside in the runway."

"Was there?" said Bill.

—18—

At noon we were all at the café. It was crowded. We were eating shrimps and drinking beer. The town was crowded. Every street was full. Big motor-cars from Biarritz and San Sebastian kept driving up and parking around the square. They brought people for the bull-fight. Sight-seeing cars came up, too. There was one with twenty-five Englishwomen in it. They sat in the big, white car and looked through their glasses at the fiesta. The dancers were all quite drunk. It was the last day of the fiesta.

The fiesta was solid and unbroken, but the motor-cars and tourist-cars made little islands of onlookers. When the cars emptied, the onlookers were absorbed into the crowd. You did not see them again except as sport clothes, odd-looking at a table among the closely packed peasants in black smocks. The fiesta absorbed even the Biarritz English so that you did not see them unless you passed close to a table. All the time there was music in the street. The drums kept on pounding and the pipes were going. Inside the cafés men with their hands gripping the table, or on each other's shoulders, were singing the hard-voiced singing.

"Here comes Brett," Bill said.

I looked and saw her coming through the crowd in the square, walking, her head up, as though the fiesta were being staged in her honor, and she found it pleasant and amusing.

"Hello, you chaps!" she said. "I say, I *have* a thirst."

"Get another big beer," Bill said to the waiter.

"Shrimps?"

"Is Cohn gone?" Brett asked.

"Yes," Bill said. "He hired a car."

The beer came. Brett started to lift the glass mug and her hand shook. She saw it and smiled, and leaned forward and took a long sip.

"Good beer."

"Very good," I said. I was nervous about Mike. I did not think he had slept. He must have been drinking all the time, but he seemed to be under control.

"I heard Cohn had hurt you, Jake," Brett said.

"No. Knocked me out. That was all."

"I say, he did hurt Pedro Romero," Brett said. "He hurt him most badly."

"How is he?"

"He'll be all right. He won't go out of the room."

"Does he look badly?"

"Very. He was really hurt. I told him I wanted to pop out and see you chaps for a minute."

"Is he going to fight?"

"Rather. I'm going with you, if you don't mind."

"How's your boy friend?" Mike asked. He had not listened to anything that Brett had said.

"Brett's got a bull-fighter," he said. "She had a Jew named Cohn, but he turned out badly."

Brett stood up.

"I am not going to listen to that sort of rot from you, Michael."

"How's your boy friend?"

"Damned well," Brett said. "Watch him this afternoon."

"Brett's got a bull-fighter," Mike said. "A beautiful, bloody bull-fighter."

"Would you mind walking over with me? I want to talk to you, Jake."

"Tell him all about your bull-fighter," Mike said. "Oh, to hell with your bull-fighter!" He tipped the table so that all the beers and the dish of shrimps went over in a crash.

"Come on," Brett said. "Let's get out of this."

In the crowd crossing the square I said: "How is it?"

"I'm not going to see him after lunch until the fight. His people come in and dress him. They're very angry about me, he says."

Brett was radiant. She was happy. The sun was out and the day was bright.

"I feel altogether changed," Brett said. "You've no idea, Jake."

"Anything you want me to do?"

"No, just go to the fight with me."

"We'll see you at lunch?"

"No. I'm eating with him."

We were standing under the arcade at the door of the hotel. They were carrying tables out and setting them up under the arcade.

"Want to take a turn out to the park?" Brett asked. "I don't want to go up yet. I fancy he's sleeping."

We walked along past the theatre and out of the square and along through the barracks of the fair, moving with the crowd between the lines of booths. We came out on a cross-street that led to the Paseo de Sarasate. We could see the crowd walking there, all the fashionably dressed people. They were making the turn at the upper end of the park.

"Don't let's go there," Brett said. "I don't want staring at just now."

We stood in the sunlight. It was hot and good after the rain and the clouds from the sea.

"I hope the wind goes down," Brett said. "It's very bad for him."

"So do I."

"He says the bulls are all right."

"They're good."

"Is that San Fermin's?"

Brett looked at the yellow wall of the chapel.

"Yes. Where the show started on Sunday."

"Let's go in. Do you mind? I'd rather like to pray a little for him or something."

We went in through the heavy leather door that moved very lightly. It was dark inside. Many people were praying. You saw them as your eyes adjusted themselves to the half-light. We knelt at one of the long wooden benches. After a little I felt Brett stiffen beside me, and saw she was looking straight ahead.

"Come on," she whispered throatily. "Let's get out of here. Makes me damned nervous."

Outside in the hot brightness of the street Brett looked up at the tree-tops in the wind. The praying had not been much of a success.

"Don't know why I get so nervy in church," Brett said. "Never does me any good."

We walked along.

"I'm damned bad for a religious atmosphere," Brett said. "I've the wrong type of face.

"You know," Brett said, "I'm not worried about him at all. I just feel happy about him."

"Good."

"I wish the wind would drop, though."

"It's liable to go down by five o'clock."

"Let's hope."

"You might pray," I laughed.

"Never does me any good. I've never gotten anything I prayed for. Have you?"

"Oh, yes."

"Oh, rot," said Brett. "Maybe it works for some people, though you don't look very religious, Jake."

"I'm pretty religious."

"Oh, rot," said Brett. "Don't start proselyting to-day. To-day's going to be bad enough as it is."

It was the first time I had seen her in the old happy, careless way since before she went off with Cohn. We were back again in front of the hotel. All the tables were set now, and already several were filled with people eating.

"Do look after Mike," Brett said. "Don't let him get too bad."

"Your frients haff gone up-stairs," the German maître d'hôtel said in English. He was a continual eavesdropper. Brett turned to him:

"Thank you, so much. Have you anything else to say?"

"No, *ma'am*."

"Good," said Brett.

"Save us a table for three," I said to the German. He smiled his dirty little pink-and-white smile.

"Iss madam eating here?"

"No," Brett said.

"Den I think a tabul for two will be enuff."

"Don't talk to him," Brett said. "Mike must have been in bad shape," she said on the stairs. We passed Montoya on the stairs. He bowed and did not smile.

"I'll see you at the café," Brett said. "Thank you, so much, Jake."

We had stopped at the floor our rooms were on. She went straight down the hall and into Romero's room. She did not knock. She simply opened the door, went in, and closed it behind her.

I stood in front of the door of Mike's room and knocked. There was no answer. I tried the knob and it opened. Inside the room was in great disorder. All the bags were opened and clothing was strewn around. There were empty bottles beside the bed. Mike lay on the bed looking like a death mask of himself. He opened his eyes and looked at me.

"Hello, Jake," he said very slowly. "I'm getting a lit tle sleep. I've want ed a lit tle sleep for a long time."

"Let me cover you over."

"No. I'm quite warm."

"Don't go. I have n't got ten to sleep yet."

"You'll sleep, Mike. Don't worry, boy."

"Brett's got a bull-fighter," Mike said. "But her Jew has gone away."

He turned his head and looked at me.

"Damned good thing, what?"

"Yes. Now go to sleep, Mike. You ought to get some sleep."

"I'm just start ing. I'm go ing to get a lit tle sleep."

He shut his eyes. I went out of the room and turned the door to quietly. Bill was in my room reading the paper.

"See Mike?"

"Yes."

"Let's go and eat."

"I won't eat down-stairs with that German head waiter. He was damned snotty when I was getting Mike up-stairs."

"He was snotty to us, too."

"Let's go out and eat in the town."

We went down the stairs. On the stairs we passed a girl coming up with a covered tray.

"There goes Brett's lunch," Bill said.

"And the kid's," I said.

Outside on the terrace under the arcade the German head waiter came up. His red cheeks were shiny. He was being polite.

"I haff a tabul for two for you gentlemen," he said.

"Go sit at it," Bill said. We went on out across the street.

We ate at a restaurant in a side street off the square. They were all men eating in the restaurant. It was full of smoke and drinking and singing. The food was good and so was the wine. We did not talk much.

Afterward we went to the café and watched the fiesta come to the boiling-point. Brett came over soon after lunch. She said she had looked in the room and that Mike was asleep.

When the fiesta boiled over and toward the bull-ring we went with the crowd. Brett sat at the ringside between Bill and me. Directly below us was the callejon, the passageway between the stands and the red fence of the barrera. Behind us the concrete stands filled solidly. Out in front, beyond the red fence, the sand of the ring was smooth-rolled and yellow. It looked a little heavy from the rain, but it was dry in the sun and firm and smooth. The sword-handlers and bull-ring servants came down the callejon carrying on their shoulders the wicker baskets of fighting capes and muletas. They were bloodstained and compactly folded and packed in the baskets. The sword-handlers opened the heavy leather sword-cases so the red wrapped hilts of the sheaf of swords showed as the leather case leaned against the fence. They unfolded the dark-stained red flannel of the muletas and fixed batons in them to spread the stuff and give the matador something to hold. Brett watched it all. She was absorbed in the professional details.

"He's his name stencilled on all the capes and muletas," she said. "Why do they call them muletas?"

"I don't know."

"I wonder if they ever launder them."

"I don't think so. It might spoil the color."

"The blood must stiffen them," Bill said.

"Funny," Brett said. "How one doesn't mind the blood."

Below in the narrow passage of the callejon the sword-handlers arranged everything. All the seats were full. Above, all the boxes were full. There was not an empty seat except in the President's box. When he came in the fight would start. Across the smooth sand, in the high doorway that led into the corrals, the bull-fighters were standing, their arms furled in their capes, talking, waiting for the signal to march in across the arena. Brett was watching them with the glasses.

"Here, would you like to look?"

I looked through the glasses and saw the three matadors. Romero was in the centre, Belmonte on his left, Marcial on his right. Back of them were their people, and behind the banderilleros, back in the passageway and in the open space of the corral, I saw the picadors. Romero was wearing a black suit. His tricornered hat was low down over his eyes. I could not see his face clearly under the hat, but it looked badly

marked. He was looking straight ahead. Marcial was smoking a cigarette guardedly, holding it in his hand. Belmonte looked ahead, his face
wan and yellow, his long wolf jaw out. He was looking at nothing. Neither he nor Romero seemed to have anything in common with the others. They were all alone. The President came in; there was handclapping
above us in the grand stand, and I handed the glasses to Brett. There was
applause. The music started. Brett looked through the glasses.

"Here, take them," she said.

Through the glasses I saw Belmonte speak to Romero. Marcial
straightened up and dropped his cigarette, and, looking straight ahead,
their heads back, their free arms swinging, the three matadors walked
out. Behind them came all the procession, opening out, all striding in
step, all the capes furled, everybody with free arms swinging, and behind
rode the picadors, their pics rising like lances. Behind all came the two
trains of mules and the bull-ring servants. The matadors bowed, holding
their hats on, before the President's box, and then came over to the barrera below us. Pedro Romero took off his heavy gold-brocaded cape and
handed it over the fence to his sword-handler. He said something to the
sword-handler. Close below us we saw Romero's lips were puffed, both
eyes were discolored. His face was discolored and swollen. The
sword-handler took the cape, looked up at Brett, and came over to us
and handed up the cape.

"Spread it out in front of you," I said.

Brett leaned forward. The cape was heavy and smoothly stiff with
gold. The sword-handler looked back, shook his head, and said something. A man beside me leaned over toward Brett.

"He doesn't want you to spread it," he said. "You should fold it and
keep it in your lap."

Brett folded the heavy cape.

Romero did not look up at us. He was speaking to Belmonte. Belmonte had sent his formal cape over to some friends. He looked across
at them and smiled, his wolf smile that was only with the mouth. Romero
leaned over the barrera and asked for the water-jug. The sword-handler
brought it and Romero poured water over the percale of his fighting-
cape, and then scuffed the lower folds in the sand with his slippered
foot.

"What's that for?" Brett asked.

"To give it weight in the wind."

"His face looks bad," Bill said.

"He feels very badly," Brett said. "He should be in bed."

The first bull was Belmonte's. Belmonte was very good. But because he got thirty thousand pesetas and people had stayed in line all night to buy tickets to see him, the crowd demanded that he should be more than very good. Belmonte's great attraction is working close to the bull. In bull-fighting they speak of the terrain of the bull and the terrain of the bull-fighter. As long as a bull-fighter stays in his own terrain he is comparatively safe. Each time he enters into the terrain of the bull he is in great danger. Belmonte, in his best days, worked always in the terrain of the bull. This way he gave the sensation of coming tragedy. People went to the corrida to see Belmonte, to be given tragic sensations, and perhaps to see the death of Belmonte. Fifteen years ago they said if you wanted to see Belmonte you should go quickly, while he was still alive. Since then he has killed more than a thousand bulls. When he retired the legend grew up about how his bull-fighting had been, and when he came out of retirement the public were disappointed because no real man could work as close to the bulls as Belmonte was supposed to have done, not, of course, even Belmonte.

Also Belmonte imposed conditions and insisted that his bulls should not be too large, nor too dangerously armed with horns, and so the element that was necessary to give the sensation of tragedy was not there, and the public, who wanted three times as much from Belmonte, who was sick with a fistula, as Belmonte had ever been able to give, felt defrauded and cheated, and Belmonte's jaw came further out in contempt, and his face turned yellower, and he moved with greater difficulty as his pain increased, and finally the crowd were actively against him, and he was utterly contemptuous and indifferent. He had meant to have a great afternoon, and instead it was an afternoon of sneers, shouted insults, and finally a volley of cushions and pieces of bread and vegetables, thrown down at him in the plaza where he had had his greatest triumphs. His jaw only went further out. Sometimes he turned to smile that toothed, long-jawed, lipless smile when he was called something particularly insulting, and always the pain that any movement produced grew stronger and stronger, until finally his yellow face was parchment color, and after his second bull was dead and the throwing of bread and cushions was over, after he had saluted the President with the same wolf-jawed smile and contemptuous eyes, and handed his sword over the barrera to be wiped, and put back in its case, he passed through into the callejón and leaned on the barrera below us, his head on his arms, not seeing, not hearing anything, only going through his pain. When he looked up, finally, he asked for a drink of water. He swallowed a little, rinsed his mouth, spat the water, took his cape, and went back into the ring.

Because they were against Belmonte the public were for Romero. From the moment he left the barrera and went toward the bull they applauded him. Belmonte watched Romero, too, watched him always without seeming to. He paid no attention to Marcial. Marcial was the sort of thing he knew all about. He had come out of retirement to compete with Marcial, knowing it was a competition gained in advance. He had expected to compete with Marcial and the other stars of the decadence of bull-fighting, and he knew that the sincerity of his own bull-fighting would be so set off by the false aesthetics of the bull-fighters of the decadent period that he would only have to be in the ring. His return from retirement had been spoiled by Romero. Romero did always, smoothly, calmly, and beautifully, what he, Belmonte, could only bring himself to do now sometimes. The crowd felt it, even the people from Biarritz, even the American ambassador saw it, finally. It was a competition that Belmonte would not enter because it would lead only to a bad horn wound or death. Belmonte was no longer well enough. He no longer had his greatest moments in the bull-ring. He was not sure that there were any great moments. Things were not the same and now life only came in flashes. He had flashes of the old greatness with his bulls, but they were not of value because he had discounted them in advance when he had picked the bulls out for their safety, getting out of a motor and leaning on a fence, looking over at the herd on the ranch of his friend the bull-breeder. So he had two small, manageable bulls without much horns, and when he felt the greatness again coming, just a little of it through the pain that was always with him, it had been discounted and sold in advance, and it did not give him a good feeling. It was the greatness, but it did not make bull-fighting wonderful to him any more.

Pedro Romero had the greatness. He loved bull-fighting, and I think he loved the bulls, and I think he loved Brett. Everything of which he could control the locality he did in front of her all that afternoon. Never once did he look up. He made it stronger that way, and did it for himself, too, as well as for her. Because he did not look up to ask if it pleased he did it all for himself inside, and it strengthened him, and yet he did it for her, too. But he did not do it for her at any loss to himself. He gained by it all through the afternoon.

His first "quite" was directly below us. The three matadors take the bull in turn after each charge he makes at a picador. Belmonte was the first. Marcial was the second. Then came Romero. The three of them were standing at the left of the horse. The picador, his hat down over his eyes, the shaft of his pic angling sharply toward the bull, kicked in the spurs and held them and with the reins in his left hand walked the horse forward toward the bull. The bull was watching. Seemingly he watched the white horse, but really he watched the triangular steel point of the pic. Romero, watching, saw the bull start to turn his head. He did not want to charge. Romero flicked his cape so the color caught the bull's eye. The bull charged with the reflex, charged, and found not the flash of color but a white horse, and a man leaned far over the horse, shot the steel point of the long hickory shaft into the hump of muscle on the bull's shoulder, and pulled his horse sideways as he pivoted on the pic, making a wound, enforcing the iron into the bull's shoulder, making him bleed for Belmonte.

The bull did not insist under the iron. He did not really want to get at the horse. He turned and the group broke apart and Romero was taking him out with his cape. He took him out softly and smoothly, and then stopped and, standing squarely in front of the bull, offered him the cape. The bull's tail went up and he charged, and Romero moved his arms ahead of the bull, wheeling, his feet firmed. The dampened, mud-weighted cape swung open and full as a sail fills, and Romero pivoted with it just ahead of the bull. At the end of the pass they were facing each other again. Romero smiled. The bull wanted it again, and Romero's cape filled again, this time on the other side. Each time he let the bull pass so close that the man and the bull and the cape that filled and pivoted ahead of the bull were all one sharply etched mass. It was all so slow and so controlled. It was as though he were rocking the bull to sleep. He made four veronicas like that, and finished with a half-veronica that turned his back on the bull and came away toward the applause, his hand on his hip, his cape on his arm, and the bull watching his back going away.

In his own bulls he was perfect. His first bull did not see well. After the first two passes with the cape Romero knew exactly how bad the vision was impaired. He worked accordingly. It was not brilliant bull-fighting. It was only perfect bull-fighting. The crowd wanted the bull changed. They made a great row. Nothing very fine could happen with a bull that could not see the lures, but the President would not order him replaced.

"Why don't they change him?" Brett asked.

"They've paid for him. They don't want to lose their money."

"It's hardly fair to Romero."

"Watch how he handles a bull that can't see the color."

"It's the sort of thing I don't like to see."

It was not nice to watch if you cared anything about the person who was doing it. With the bull who could not see the colors of the capes, or the scarlet flannel of the muleta, Romero had to make the bull consent with his body. He had to get so close that the bull saw his body, and would start for it, and then shift the bull's charge to the flannel and finish out the pass in the classic manner. The Biarritz crowd did not like it. They thought Romero was afraid, and that was why he gave that little sidestep each time as he transferred the bull's charge from his own body to the flannel. They preferred Belmonte's imitation of himself or Marcial's imitation of Belmonte. There were three of them in the row behind us.

"What's he afraid of the bull for? The bull's so dumb he only goes after the cloth."

"He's just a young bull-fighter. He hasn't learned it yet."

"But I thought he was fine with the cape before."

"Probably he's nervous now."

Out in the centre of the ring, all alone, Romero was going on with the same thing, getting so close that the bull could see him plainly, offering the body, offering it again a little closer, the bull watching dully, then so close that the bull thought he had him, offering again and finally drawing the charge and then, just before the horns came, giving the bull the red cloth to follow with that little, almost imperceptible, jerk that so offended the critical judgment of the Biarritz bull-fight experts.

"He's going to kill now," I said to Brett. "The bull's still strong. He wouldn't wear himself out."

Out in the centre of the ring Romero profiled in front of the bull, drew the sword out from the folds of the muleta, rose on his toes, and sighted along the blade. The bull charged as Romero charged. Romero's left hand dropped the muleta over the bull's muzzle to blind him, his left shoulder went forward between the horns as the sword went in, and for just an instant he and the bull were one, Romero way out over the bull, the right arm extended high up to where the hilt of the sword had gone in between the bull's shoulders. Then the figure was broken. There was a little jolt as Romero came clear, and then he was standing, one hand up, facing the bull, his shirt ripped out from under his sleeve, the white blowing in the wind, and the bull, the red sword hilt tight between his shoulders, his head going down and his legs settling.

"There he goes," Bill said.

Romero was close enough so the bull could see him. His hand still up, he spoke to the bull. The bull gathered himself, then his head went forward and he went over slowly, then all over, suddenly, four feet in the air.

They handed the sword to Romero, and carrying it blade down, the muleta in his other hand, he walked over to in front of the President's box, bowed, straightened, and came over to the barrera and handed over the sword and muleta.

"Bad one," said the sword-handler.

"He made me sweat," said Romero. He wiped off his face. The sword-handler handed him the water-jug. Romero wiped his lips. It hurt him to drink out of the jug. He did not look up at us.

Marcial had a big day. They were still applauding him when Romero's last bull came in. It was the bull that had sprinted out and killed the man in the morning running.

During Romero's first bull his hurt face had been very noticeable. Everything he did showed it. All the concentration of the awkwardly delicate working with the bull that could not see well brought it out. The fight with Cohn had not touched his spirit but his face had been smashed and his body hurt. He was wiping all that out now. Each thing that he did with this bull wiped that out a little cleaner. It was a good bull, a big bull, and with horns, and it turned and recharged easily and surely. He was what Romero wanted in bulls.

When he had finished his work with the muleta and was ready to kill, the crowd made him go on. They did not want the bull killed yet, they did not want it to be over. Romero went on. It was like a course in bull-fighting. All the passes he linked up, all completed, all slow, templed and smooth. There were no tricks and no mystifications. There was no brusqueness. And each pass as it reached the summit gave you a sudden ache inside. The crowd did not want it ever to be finished.

The bull was squared on all four feet to be killed, and Romero killed directly below us. He killed not as he had been forced to by the last bull, but as he wanted to. He profiled directly in front of the bull, drew the sword out of the folds of the muleta and sighted along the blade. The bull watched him. Romero spoke to the bull and tapped one of his feet.

The bull charged and Romero waited for the charge, the muleta held
low, sighting along the blade, his feet firm. Then without taking a step
forward, he became one with the bull, the sword was in high between
the shoulders, the bull had followed the low-swung flannel, that disappeared as Romero lurched clear to the left, and it was over. The bull tried
to go forward, his legs commenced to settle, he swung from side to side,
hesitated, then went down on his knees, and Romero's older brother
leaned forward behind him and drove a short knife into the bull's neck
at the base of the horns. The first time he missed. He drove the knife in
again, and the bull went over, twitching and rigid. Romero's brother,
holding the bull's horn in one hand, the knife in the other, looked up at
the President's box. Handkerchiefs were waving all over the bull-ring.
The President looked down from the box and waved his handkerchief.
The brother cut the notched black ear from the dead bull and trotted
over with it to Romero. The bull lay heavy and black on the sand, his
tongue out. Boys were running toward him from all parts of the arena,
making a little circle around him. They were starting to dance around
the bull.

Romero took the ear from his brother and held it up toward the
President. The President bowed and Romero, running to get ahead of
the crowd, came toward us. He leaned up against the barrera and gave
the ear to Brett. He nodded his head and smiled. The crowd were all
about him. Brett held down the cape.

"You liked it?" Romero called.

Brett did not say anything. They looked at each other and smiled.
Brett had the ear in her hand.

"Don't get bloody," Romero said, and grinned. The crowd wanted
him. Several boys shouted at Brett. The crowd was the boys, the dancers,
and the drunks. Romero turned and tried to get through the crowd.
They were all around him trying to lift him and put him on their shoulders. He fought and twisted away, and started running, in the midst of
them, toward the exit. He did not want to be carried on people's shoulders. But they held him and lifted him. It was uncomfortable and his legs
were spraddled and his body was very sore. They were lifting him and
all running toward the gate. He had his hand on somebody's shoulder.
He looked around at us apologetically. The crowd, running, went out
the gate with him.

We all three went back to the hotel. Brett went upstairs. Bill and I
sat in the down-stairs dining-room and ate some hard-boiled eggs and

drank several bottles of beer. Belmonte came down in his street clothes with his manager and two other men. They sat at the next table and ate. Belmonte ate very little. They were leaving on the seven o'clock train for Barcelona. Belmonte wore a blue-striped shirt and a dark suit, and ate soft-boiled eggs. The others ate a big meal. Belmonte did not talk. He only answered questions.

Bill was tired after the bull-fight. So was I. We both took a bull-fight very hard. We sat and ate the eggs and I watched Belmonte and the people at his table. The men with him were tough-looking and businesslike.

"Come on over to the café," Bill said. "I want an absinthe."

It was the last day of the fiesta. Outside it was beginning to be cloudy again. The square was full of people and the fireworks experts were making up their set pieces for the night and covering them over with beech branches. Boys were watching. We passed stands of rockets with long bamboo stems. Outside the café there was a great crowd. The music and the dancing were going on. The giants and the dwarfs were passing.

"Where's Edna?" I asked Bill.

"I don't know."

We watched the beginning of the evening of the last night of the fiesta. The absinthe made everything seem better. I drank it without sugar in the dripping glass, and it was pleasantly bitter.

"I feel sorry about Cohn," Bill said. "He had an awful time."

"Oh, to hell with Cohn," I said.

"Where do you suppose he went?"

"Up to Paris."

"What do you suppose he'll do?"

"Oh, to hell with him."

"What do you suppose he'll do?"

"Pick up with his old girl, probably."

"Who was his old girl?"

"Somebody named Frances."

We had another absinthe.

"When do you go back?" I asked.

"To-morrow."

After a little while Bill said: "Well, it was a swell fiesta."

"Yes," I said; "something doing all the time."

"You wouldn't believe it. It's like a wonderful nightmare."

"Sure," I said. "I'd believe anything. Including nightmares."

"What's the matter? Feel low?"

"Low as hell."

"Have another absinthe. Here, waiter! Another absinthe for this señor."

"I feel like hell," I said.

"Drink that," said Bill. "Drink it slow."

It was beginning to get dark. The fiesta was going on. I began to feel drunk but I did not feel any better.

"How do you feel?"

"I feel like hell."

"Have another?"

"It won't do any good."

"Try it. You can't tell; maybe this is the one that gets it. Hey, waiter! Another absinthe for this señor!"

I poured the water directly into it and stirred it instead of letting it drip. Bill put in a lump of ice. I stirred the ice around with a spoon in the brownish, cloudy mixture.

"How is it?"

"Fine."

"Don't drink it fast that way. It will make you sick."

I set down the glass. I had not meant to drink it fast.

"I feel tight."

"You ought to."

"That's what you wanted, wasn't it?"

"Sure. Get tight. Get over your damn depression."

"Well, I'm tight. Is that what you want?"

"Sit down."

"I won't sit down," I said. "I'm going over to the hotel."

I was very drunk. I was drunker than I ever remembered having been. At the hotel I went up-stairs. Brett's door was open. I put my head in the room. Mike was sitting on the bed. He waved a bottle.

"Jake," he said. "Come in, Jake."

I went in and sat down. The room was unstable unless I looked at some fixed point.

"Brett, you know. She's gone off with the bull-fighter chap."

"No."

"Yes. She looked for you to say good-bye. They went on the seven o'clock train."

"Did they?"

"Bad thing to do," Mike said. "She shouldn't have done it."

"No."

"Have a drink? Wait while I ring for some beer."

"I'm drunk," I said. "I'm going in and lie down."

"Are you blind? I was blind myself."

"Yes," I said, "I'm blind."

"Well, bung-o," Mike said. "Get some sleep, old Jake."

I went out the door and into my own room and lay on the bed. The bed went sailing off and I sat up in bed and looked at the wall to make it stop. Outside in the square the fiesta was going on. It did not mean anything. Later Bill and Mike came in to get me to go down and eat with them. I pretended to be asleep.

"He's asleep. Better let him alone."

"He's blind as a tick," Mike said. They went out.

I got up and went to the balcony and looked out at the dancing in the square. The world was not wheeling any more. It was just very clear and bright, and inclined to blur at the edges. I washed, brushed my hair. I looked strange to myself in the glass, and went down-stairs to the dining-room.

"Here he is!" said Bill. "Good old Jake! I knew you wouldn't pass out."

"Hello, you old drunk," Mike said.

"I got hungry and woke up."

"Eat some soup," Bill said.

The three of us sat at the table, and it seemed as though about six people were missing.

BOOK THREE

—19—

In the morning it was all over. The fiesta was finished. I woke about nine o'clock, had a bath, dressed, and went down-stairs. The square was empty and there were no people on the streets. A few children were picking up rocket-sticks in the square. The cafés were just opening and the waiters were carrying out the comfortable white wicker chairs and arranging them around the marble-topped tables in the shade of the arcade. They were sweeping the streets and sprinkling them with a hose.

I sat in one of the wicker chairs and leaned back comfortably. The waiter was in no hurry to come. The white-paper announcements of the unloading of the bulls and the big schedules of special trains were still up on the pillars of the arcade. A waiter wearing a blue apron came out with a bucket of water and a cloth, and commenced to tear down the notices, pulling the paper off in strips and washing and rubbing away the paper that stuck to the stone. The fiesta was over.

I drank a coffee and after a while Bill came over. I watched him come walking across the square. He sat down at the table and ordered a coffee.

"Well," he said, "it's all over."

"Yes," I said. "When do you go?"

"I don't know. We better get a car, I think. Aren't you going back to Paris?"

"No. I can stay away another week. I think I'll go to San Sebastian."

"I want to get back."

"What's Mike going to do?"

"He's going to Saint Jean de Luz."

"Let's get a car and all go as far as Bayonne. You can get the train up from there to-night."

"Good. Let's go after lunch."

"All right. I'll get the car."

We had lunch and paid the bill. Montoya did not come near us. One of the maids brought the bill. The car was outside. The chauffeur piled and strapped the bags on top of the car and put them in beside him in the front seat and we got in. The car went out of the square, along through the side streets, out under the trees and down the hill and away from Pamplona. It did not seem like a very long ride. Mike had a bottle of Fundador. I only took a couple of drinks. We came over the mountains and out of Spain and down the white roads and through the overfoliaged, wet, green, Basque country, and finally into Bayonne. We left Bill's baggage at the station, and he bought a ticket to Paris. His train left at seven-ten. We came out of the station. The car was standing out in front.

"What shall we do about the car?" Bill asked.

"Oh, bother the car," Mike said. "Let's just keep the car with us."

"All right," Bill said. "Where shall we go?"

"Let's go to Biarritz and have a drink."

"Old Mike the spender," Bill said.

We drove in to Biarritz and left the car outside a very Ritz place. We went into the bar and sat on high stools and drank a whiskey and soda.

"That drink's mine," Mike said.

"Let's roll for it."

So we rolled poker dice out of a deep leather dice-cup. Bill was out first roll. Mike lost to me and handed the bartender a hundred-franc note. The whiskeys were twelve francs apiece. We had another round and Mike lost again. Each time he gave the bartender a good tip. In a room off the bar there was a good jazz band playing. It was a pleasant bar. We had another round. I went out on the first roll with four kings. Bill and Mike rolled. Mike won the first roll with four jacks. Bill won the second. On the final roll Mike had three kings and let them stay. He handed the dice-cup to Bill. Bill rattled them and rolled, and there were three kings, an ace, and a queen.

"It's yours, Mike," Bill said. "Old Mike, the gambler."

"I'm so sorry," Mike said. "I can't get it."

"What's the matter?"

"I've no money," Mike said. "I'm stony. I've just twenty francs. Here, take twenty francs."

Bill's face sort of changed.

"I just had enough to pay Montoya. Damned lucky to have it, too."

"I'll cash you a check," Bill said.

"That's damned nice of you, but you see I can't write checks."

"What are you going to do for money?"

"Oh, some will come through. I've two weeks allowance should be here. I can live on tick at this pub in Saint Jean."

"What do you want to do about the car?" Bill asked me. "Do you want to keep it on?"

"It doesn't make any difference. Seems sort of idiotic."

"Come on, let's have another drink," Mike said.

"Fine. This one is on me," Bill said. "Has Brett any money?" He turned to Mike.

"I shouldn't think so. She put up most of what I gave to old Montoya."

"She hasn't any money with her?" I asked.

"I shouldn't think so. She never has any money. She gets five hundred quid a year and pays three hundred and fifty of it in interest to Jews."

"I suppose they get it at the source," said Bill.

"Quite. They're not really Jews. We just call them Jews. They're Scotsmen, I believe."

"Hasn't she any at all with her?" I asked.

"I hardly think so. She gave it all to me when she left."

"Well," Bill said, "we might as well have another drink."

"Damned good idea," Mike said. "One never gets anywhere by discussing finances."

"No," said Bill. Bill and I rolled for the next two rounds. Bill lost and paid. We went out to the car.

"Anywhere you'd like to go, Mike?" Bill asked.

"Let's take a drive. It might do my credit good. Let's drive about a little."

"Fine. I'd like to see the coast. Let's drive down toward Hendaye."

"I haven't any credit along the coast."

"You can't ever tell," said Bill.

We drove out along the coast road. There was the green of the headlands, the white, red-roofed villas, patches of forest, and the ocean very blue with the tide out and the water curling far out along the beach. We drove through Saint Jean de Luz and passed through villages farther down the coast. Back of the rolling country we were going through we saw the mountains we had come over from Pamplona. The road went on ahead. Bill looked at his watch. It was time for us to go back. He knocked on the glass and told the driver to turn around. The driver backed the car out into the grass to turn it. In back of us were the woods, below a stretch of meadow, then the sea.

At the hotel where Mike was going to stay in Saint Jean we stopped the car and he got out. The chauffeur carried in his bags. Mike stood by the side of the car.

"Good-bye, you chaps," Mike said. "It was a damned fine fiesta."

"So long, Mike," Bill said.

"I'll see you around," I said.

"Don't worry about money," Mike said. "You can pay for the car, Jake, and I'll send you my share."

"So long, Mike."

"So long, you chaps. You've been damned nice."

We all shook hands. We waved from the car to Mike. He stood in the road watching. We got to Bayonne just before the train left. A porter carried Bill's bags in from the consigne. I went as far as the inner gate to the tracks.

"So long, fella," Bill said.

"So long, kid!"

"It was swell. I've had a swell time."

"Will you be in Paris?"

"No, I have to sail on the 17th. So long, fella!"

"So long, old kid!"

He went in through the gate to the train. The porter went ahead with the bags. I watched the train pull out. Bill was at one of the windows. The window passed, the rest of the train passed, and the tracks were empty. I went outside to the car.

"How much do we owe you?" I asked the driver. The price to Bayonne had been fixed at a hundred and fifty pesetas.

"Two hundred pesetas."

"How much more will it be if you drive me to San Sebastian on your way back?"

"Fifty pesetas."

"Don't kid me."

"Thirty-five pesetas."

"It's not worth it," I said. "Drive me to the Hotel Panier Fleuri."

At the hotel I paid the driver and gave him a tip. The car was powdered with dust. I rubbed the rod-case through the dust. It seemed the last thing that connected me with Spain and the fiesta. The driver put the car in gear and went down the street. I watched it turn off to take the road to Spain. I went into the hotel and they gave me a room. It was the same room I had slept in when Bill and Cohn and I were in Bayonne. That seemed a very long time ago. I washed, changed my shirt, and went out in the town.

At a newspaper kiosque I bought a copy of the New York *Herald* and sat in a café to read it. It felt strange to be in France again. There was a safe, suburban feeling. I wished I had gone up to Paris with Bill, except that Paris would have meant more fiesta-ing. I was through with fiestas for a while. It would be quiet in San Sebastian. The season does not open there until August. I could get a good hotel room and read and swim. There was a fine beach there. There were wonderful trees along the promenade above the beach, and there were many children sent down with their nurses before the season opened. In the evening there would be band concerts under the trees across from the Café Marinas. I could sit in the Marinas and listen.

"How does one eat inside?" I asked the waiter. Inside the café was a restaurant.

"Well. Very well. One eats very well."

"Good."

I went in and ate dinner. It was a big meal for France but it seemed very carefully apportioned after Spain. I drank a bottle of wine for company. It was a Château Margaux. It was pleasant to be drinking slowly and to be tasting the wine and to be drinking alone. A bottle of wine was good company. Afterward I had coffee. The waiter recommended a Basque liqueur called Izarra. He brought in the bottle and poured a liqueur-glass full. He said Izarra was made of the flowers of the Pyrenees. The veritable flowers of the Pyrenees. It looked like hair-oil and smelled like Italian *strega*. I told him to take the flowers of the Pyrenees away and bring me a *vieux marc*. The *marc* was good. I had a second *marc* after the coffee.

The waiter seemed a little offended about the flowers of the Pyrenees, so I overtipped him. That made him happy. It felt comfortable to be in a country where it is so simple to make people happy. You can never tell whether a Spanish waiter will thank you. Everything is on such a clear financial basis in France. It is the simplest country to live in. No one makes things complicated by becoming your friend for any obscure reason. If you want people to like you you have only to spend a little money. I spent a little money and the waiter liked me. He appreciated my valuable qualities. He would be glad to see me back. I would dine there again some time and he would be glad to see me, and would want me at his table. It would be a sincere liking because it would have a sound basis. I was back in France.

Next morning I tipped every one a little too much at the hotel to make more friends, and left on the morning train for San Sebastian. At the station I did not tip the porter more than I should because I did not think I would ever see him again. I only wanted a few good French friends in Bayonne to make me welcome in case I should come back there again. I knew that if they remembered me their friendship would be loyal.

At Irún we had to change trains and show passports. I hated to leave France. Life was so simple in France. I felt I was a fool to be going back into Spain. In Spain you could not tell about anything. I felt like a fool to be going back into it, but I stood in line with my passport, opened my bags for the customs, bought a ticket, went through a gate, climbed onto the train, and after forty minutes and eight tunnels I was at San Sebastian.

Even on a hot day San Sebastian has a certain early-morning quality. The trees seem as though their leaves were never quite dry. The streets feel as though they had just been sprinkled. It is always cool and shady on certain streets on the hottest day. I went to a hotel in the town where I had stopped before, and they gave me a room with a balcony that opened out above the roofs of the town. There was a green mountain-side beyond the roofs.

I unpacked my bags and stacked my books on the table beside the head of the bed, put out my shaving things, hung up some clothes in the big armoire, and made up a bundle for the laundry. Then I took a shower in the bathroom and went down to lunch. Spain had not changed to summer-time, so I was early. I set my watch again. I had recovered an hour by coming to San Sebastian.

As I went into the dining-room the concierge brought me a police bulletin to fill out. I signed it and asked him for two telegraph forms, and wrote a message to the Hotel Montoya, telling them to forward all mail and telegrams for me to this address. I calculated how many days

I would be in San Sebastian and then wrote out a wire to the office asking them to hold mail, but forward all wires for me to San Sebastian for six days. Then I went in and had lunch.

After lunch I went up to my room, read a while, and went to sleep. When I woke it was half past four. I found my swimming-suit, wrapped it with a comb in a towel, and went down-stairs and walked up the street to the Concha. The tide was about half-way out. The beach was smooth and firm, and the sand yellow. I went into a bathing-cabin, undressed, put on my suit, and walked across the smooth sand to the sea. The sand was warm under bare feet. There were quite a few people in the water and on the beach. Out beyond where the headlands of the Concha almost met to form the harbor there was a white line of breakers and the open sea. Although the tide was going out, there were a few slow rollers. They came in like undulations in the water, gathered weight of water, and then broke smoothly on the warm sand. I waded out. The water was cold. As a roller came I dove, swam out under water, and came to the surface with all the chill gone. I swam out to the raft, pulled myself up, and lay on the hot planks. A boy and girl were at the other end. The girl had undone the top strap of her bathing-suit and was browning her back. The boy lay face downward on the raft and talked to her. She laughed at things he said, and turned her brown back in the sun. I lay on the raft in the sun until I was dry. Then I tried several dives. I dove deep once, swimming down to the bottom. I swam with my eyes open and it was green and dark. The raft made a dark shadow. I came out of the water beside the raft, pulled up, dove once more, holding it for length, and then swam ashore. I lay on the beach until I was dry, then went into the bathing-cabin, took off my suit, sloshed myself with fresh water, and rubbed dry.

I walked around the harbor under the trees to the casino, and then up one of the cool streets to the Café Marinas. There was an orchestra playing inside the café and I sat out on the terrace and enjoyed the fresh coolness in the hot day, and had a glass of lemon-juice and shaved ice and then a long whiskey and soda. I sat in front of the Marinas for a long time and read and watched the people, and listened to the music.

Later when it began to get dark, I walked around the harbor and out along the promenade, and finally back to the hotel for supper. There was a bicycle-race on, the Tour du Pays Basque, and the riders were stopping that night in San Sebastian. In the dining-room, at one side, there was a long table of bicycle-riders, eating with their trainers and managers. They were all French and Belgians, and paid close attention to their meal, but they were having a good time. At the head of the table were two good-looking French girls, with much Rue du Faubourg Montmartre chic. I could not make out whom they belonged to. They all spoke in slang at the long table and there were many private jokes and some jokes at the far end that were not repeated when the girls asked to hear them. The next morning at five o'clock the race resumed with the last lap, San Sebastian–Bilbao. The bicycle-riders drank much wine, and were burned and browned by the sun. They did not take the race seriously except among themselves. They had raced among themselves so often that it did not make much difference who won. Especially in a foreign country. The money could be arranged.

The man who had a matter of two minutes lead in the race had an attack of boils, which were very painful. He sat on the small of his back. His neck was very red and the blond hairs were sunburned. The other riders joked him about his boils. He tapped on the table with his fork.

"Listen," he said, "to-morrow my nose is so tight on the handle-bars that the only thing touches those boils is a lovely breeze."

One of the girls looked at him down the table, and he grinned and turned red. The Spaniards, they said, did not know how to pedal.

I had coffee out on the terrasse with the team manager of one of the big bicycle manufacturers. He said it had been a very pleasant race, and would have been worth watching if Bottechia had not abandoned it at Pamplona. The dust had been bad, but in Spain the roads were better than in France. Bicycle road-racing was the only sport in the world, he said. Had I ever followed the Tour de France? Only in the papers. The Tour de France was the greatest sporting event in the world. Following and organizing the road races had made him know France. Few people know France. All spring and all summer and all fall he spent on the road with bicycle road-racers. Look at the number of motor-cars now that followed the riders from town to town in a road race. It was a rich country and more *sportif* every year. It would be the most *sportif* country in the world. It was bicycle road-racing did it. That and football. He knew France. *La France Sportive.* He knew road-racing. We had a cognac. After all, though, it wasn't bad to get back to Paris. There is only one Paname. In all the world, that is. Paris is the town the most *sportif* in the world. Did I know the *Chope de Negre*? Did I not. I would see him there some time. I certainly would. We would drink another *fine* together. We certainly would. They started at six o'clock less a quarter in the morning. Would I be up for the depart? I would certainly try to. Would I like him to call me? It was very interesting. I would leave a call at the desk. He would not mind calling me. I could not let him take the trouble. I would leave a call at the desk. We said good-bye until the next morning.

In the morning when I awoke the bicycle-riders and their following cars had been on the road for three hours. I had coffee and the papers in bed and then dressed and took my bathing-suit down to the beach. Everything was fresh and cool and damp in the early morning. Nurses in uniform and in peasant costume walked under the trees with children. The Spanish children were beautiful. Some bootblacks sat together under a tree talking to a soldier. The soldier had only one arm. The tide was in and there was a good breeze and a surf on the beach.

I undressed in one of the bath-cabins, crossed the narrow line of beach and went into the water. I swam out, trying to swim through the rollers, but having to dive sometimes. Then in the quiet water I turned and floated. Floating I saw only the sky, and felt the drop and lift of the swells. I swam back to the surf and coasted in, face down, on a big roller, then turned and swam, trying to keep in the trough and not have a wave break over me. It made me tired, swimming in the trough, and I turned and swam out to the raft. The water was buoyant and cold. It felt as though you could never sink. I swam slowly, it seemed like a long swim with the high tide, and then pulled up on the raft and sat, dripping, on the boards that were becoming hot in the sun. I looked around at the bay, the old town, the casino, the line of trees along the promenade, and the big hotels with their white porches and gold-lettered names. Off on the right, almost closing the harbor, was a green hill with a castle. The raft rocked with the motion of the water. On the other side of the narrow gap that led into the open sea was another high headland. I thought I would like to swim across the bay but I was afraid of cramp.

I sat in the sun and watched the bathers on the beach. They looked very small. After a while I stood up, gripped with my toes on the edge of the raft as it tipped with my weight, and dove cleanly and deeply, to come up through the lightening water, blew the salt water out of my head, and swam slowly and steadily in to shore.

After I was dressed and had paid for the bath-cabin, I walked back to the hotel. The bicycle-racers had left several copies of *L'Auto* around, and I gathered them up in the reading-room and took them out and sat in an easy chair in the sun to read about and catch up on French sporting life. While I was sitting there the concierge came out with a blue envelope in his hand.

"A telegram for you, sir."

I poked my finger along under the fold that was fastened down, spread it open, and read it. It had been forwarded from Paris:

COULD YOU COME HOTEL MONTANA MADRID AM
RATHER IN TROUBLE BRETT.

I tipped the concierge and read the message again. A postman was coming along the sidewalk. He turned into the hotel. He had a big moustache and looked very military. He came out of the hotel again. The concierge was just behind him.

"Here's another telegram for you, sir."

"Thank you," I said.

I opened it. It was forwarded from Pamplona.

COULD YOU COME HOTEL MONTANA MADRID AM
RATHER IN TROUBLE BRETT.

The concierge stood there waiting for another tip, probably.

"What time is there a train for Madrid?"

"It left at nine this morning. There is a slow train at eleven, and the Sud Express at ten to-night."

"Get me a berth on the Sud Express. Do you want the money now?"

"Just as you wish," he said. "I will have it put on the bill."

"Do that."

Well, that meant San Sebastian all shot to hell. I suppose, vaguely, I had expected something of the sort. I saw the concierge standing in the doorway.

"Bring me a telegram form, please."

He brought it and I took out my fountain-pen and printed:

LADY ASHLEY HOTEL MONTANA MADRID ARRIVING
SUD EXPRESS TOMORROW LOVE JAKE.

That seemed to handle it. That was it. Send a girl off with one man. Introduce her to another to go off with him. Now go and bring her back. And sign the wire with love. That was it all right. I went in to lunch.

I did not sleep much that night on the Sud Express. In the morning I had breakfast in the dining-car and watched the rock and pine country between Avila and Escorial. I saw the Escorial out of the window, gray and long and cold in the sun, and did not give a damn about it. I saw Madrid come up over the plain, a compact white sky-line on the top of a little cliff away off across the sun-hardened country.

The Norte station in Madrid is the end of the line. All trains finish there. They don't go on anywhere. Outside were cabs and taxis and a line of hotel runners. It was like a country town. I took a taxi and we climbed up through the gardens, by the empty palace and the unfinished church on the edge of the cliff, and on up until we were in the high, hot, modern town. The taxi coasted down a smooth street to the Puerta del Sol, and then through the traffic and out into the Carrera San Jerónimo. All the shops had their awnings down against the heat. The windows on the sunny side of the street were shuttered. The taxi stopped at the curb. I saw the sign HOTEL MONTANA on the second floor. The taxi-driver carried the bags in and left them by the elevator. I could not make the elevator work, so I walked up. On the second floor up was a cut brass sign: HOTEL MONTANA. I rang and no one came to the door. I rang again and a maid with a sullen face opened the door.

"Is Lady Ashley here?" I asked.

She looked at me dully.

"Is an Englishwoman here?"

She turned and called some one inside. A very fat woman came to the door. Her hair was gray and stiffly oiled in scallops around her face. She was short and commanding.

"Muy buenas," I said. "Is there an Englishwoman here? I would like to see this English lady."

"Muy buenas. Yes, there is a female English. Certainly you can see her if she wishes to see you."

"She wishes to see me."

"The chica will ask her."

"It is very hot."

"It is very hot in the summer in Madrid."

"And how cold in winter."

"Yes, it is very cold in winter."

Did I want to stay myself in person in the Hotel Montana?

Of that as yet I was undecided, but it would give me pleasure if my bags were brought up from the ground floor in order that they might not be stolen. Nothing was ever stolen in the Hotel Montana. In other fondas, yes. Not here. No. The personages of this establishment were rigidly selectioned. I was happy to hear it. Nevertheless I would welcome the upbringal of my bags.

The maid came in and said that the female English wanted to see the male English now, at once.

"Good," I said. "You see. It is as I said."

"Clearly."

I followed the maid's back down a long, dark corridor. At the end she knocked on a door.

"Hello," said Brett. "Is it you, Jake?"

"It's me."

"Come in. Come in."

I opened the door. The maid closed it after me. Brett was in bed. She had just been brushing her hair and held the brush in her hand. The room was in that disorder produced only by those who have always had servants.

"Darling!" Brett said.

I went over to the bed and put my arms around her. She kissed me, and while she kissed me I could feel she was thinking of something else. She was trembling in my arms. She felt very small.

"Darling! I've had such a hell of a time."

"Tell me about it."

"Nothing to tell. He only left yesterday. I made him go."

"Why didn't you keep him?"

"I don't know. It isn't the sort of thing one does. I don't think I hurt him any."

"You were probably damn good for him."

"He shouldn't be living with any one. I realized that right away."

"No."

"Oh, hell!" she said, "let's not talk about it. Let's never talk about it."

"All right."

"It was rather a knock his being ashamed of me. He was ashamed of me for a while, you know."

"No."

"Oh, yes. They ragged him about me at the café, I guess. He wanted me to grow my hair out. Me, with long hair. I'd look so like hell."

"It's funny."

"He said it would make me more womanly. I'd look a fright."

"What happened?"

"Oh, he got over that. He wasn't ashamed of me long."

"What was it about being in trouble?"

"I didn't know whether I could make him go, and I didn't have a sou to go away and leave him. He tried to give me a lot of money, you know. I told him I had scads of it. He knew that was a lie. I couldn't take his money, you know."

"No."

"Oh, let's not talk about it. There were some funny things, though. Do give me a cigarette."

I lit the cigarette.

"He learned his English as a waiter in Gib."

"Yes."

"He wanted to marry me, finally."

"Really?"

"Of course. I can't even marry Mike."

"Maybe he thought that would make him Lord Ashley."

"No. It wasn't that. He really wanted to marry me. So I couldn't go away from him, he said. He wanted to make it sure I could never go away from him. After I'd gotten more womanly, of course."

"You ought to feel set up."

"I do. I'm all right again. He's wiped out that damned Cohn."

"Good."

"You know I'd have lived with him if I hadn't seen it was bad for him. We got along damned well."

"Outside of your personal appearance."

"Oh, he'd have gotten used to that."

She put out the cigarette.

"I'm thirty-four, you know. I'm not going to be one of these bitches that ruins children."

"No."

"I'm not going to be that way. I feel rather good, you know. I feel rather set up."

"Good."

She looked away. I thought she was looking for another cigarette. Then I saw she was crying. I could feel her crying. Shaking and crying. She wouldn't look up. I put my arms around her.

"Don't let's ever talk about it. Please don't let's ever talk about it."

"Dear Brett."

"I'm going back to Mike." I could feel her crying as I held her close. "He's so damned nice and he's so awful. He's my sort of thing."

She would not look up. I stroked her hair. I could feel her shaking.

"I won't be one of those bitches," she said. "But, oh, Jake, please let's never talk about it."

We left the Hotel Montana. The woman who ran the hotel would not let me pay the bill. The bill had been paid.

"Oh, well. Let it go," Brett said. "It doesn't matter now."

We rode in a taxi down to the Palace Hotel, left the bags, arranged for berths on the Sud Express for the night, and went into the bar of the hotel for a cocktail. We sat on high stools at the bar while the barman shook the Martinis in a large nickelled shaker.

"It's funny what a wonderful gentility you get in the bar of a big hotel," I said.

"Barmen and jockeys are the only people who are polite any more."

"No matter how vulgar a hotel is, the bar is always nice."

"It's odd."

"Bartenders have always been fine."

"You know," Brett said, "it's quite true. He is only nineteen. Isn't it amazing?"

We touched the two glasses as they stood side by side on the bar. They were coldly beaded. Outside the curtained window was the summer heat of Madrid.

"I like an olive in a Martini," I said to the barman.

"Right you are, sir. There you are."

"Thanks."

"I should have asked, you know."

The barman went far enough up the bar so that he would not hear our conversation. Brett had sipped from the Martini as it stood, on the wood. Then she picked it up. Her hand was steady enough to lift it after that first sip.

"It's good. Isn't it a nice bar?"

"They're all nice bars."

"You know I didn't believe it at first. He was born in 1905. I was in school in Paris, then. Think of that."

"Anything you want me to think about it?"

"Don't be an ass. *Would* you buy a lady a drink?"

"We'll have two more Martinis."

"As they were before, sir?"

"They were very good." Brett smiled at him.

"Thank you, ma'am."

"Well, bung-o," Brett said.

"Bung-o!"

"You know," Brett said, "he'd only been with two women before. He never cared about anything but bull-fighting."

"He's got plenty of time."

"I don't know. He thinks it was me. Not the show in general."

"Well, it was you."

"Yes. It was me."

"I thought you weren't going to ever talk about it."

"How can I help it?"

"You'll lose it if you talk about it."

"I just talk around it. You know I feel rather damned good, Jake."

"You should."

"You know it makes one feel rather good deciding not to be a bitch."

"Yes."

"It's sort of what we have instead of God."

"Some people have God," I said. "Quite a lot."

"He never worked very well with me."

"Should we have another Martini?"

The barman shook up two more Martinis and poured them out into fresh glasses.

"Where will we have lunch?" I asked Brett. The bar was cool. You could feel the heat outside through the window.

"Here?" asked Brett.

"It's rotten here in the hotel. Do you know a place called Botín's?" I asked the barman.

"Yes, sir. Would you like to have me write out the address?"

"Thank you."

We lunched up-stairs at Botín's. It is one of the best restaurants in the world. We had roast young suckling pig and drank *rioja alta*. Brett did not eat much. She never ate much. I ate a very big meal and drank three bottles of *rioja alta*.

"How do you feel, Jake?" Brett asked. "My God! what a meal you've eaten."

"I feel fine. Do you want a dessert?"

"Lord, no."

Brett was smoking.

"You like to eat, don't you?" she said.

"Yes," I said. "I like to do a lot of things."

"What do you like to do?"

"Oh," I said, "I like to do a lot of things. Don't you want a dessert?"

"You asked me that once," Brett said.

"Yes," I said. "So I did. Let's have another bottle of *rioja alta.*"

"It's very good."

"You haven't drunk much of it," I said.

"I have. You haven't seen."

"Let's get two bottles," I said. The bottles came. I poured a little in my glass, then a glass for Brett, then filled my glass. We touched glasses.

"Bung-o!" Brett said. I drank my glass and poured out another. Brett put her hand on my arm.

"Don't get drunk, Jake," she said. "You don't have to."

"How do you know?"

"Don't," she said. "You'll be all right."

"I'm not getting drunk," I said. "I'm just drinking a little wine. I like to drink wine."

"Don't get drunk," she said. "Jake, don't get drunk."

"Want to go for a ride?" I said. "Want to ride through the town?"

"Right," Brett said. "I haven't seen Madrid. I should see Madrid."

"I'll finish this," I said.

Down-stairs we came out through the first-floor dining-room to the street. A waiter went for a taxi. It was hot and bright. Up the street was a little square with trees and grass where there were taxis parked. A taxi came up the street, the waiter hanging out at the side. I tipped him and told the driver where to drive, and got in beside Brett. The driver started up the street. I settled back. Brett moved close to me. We sat close against each other. I put my arm around her and she rested against me comfortably. It was very hot and bright, and the houses looked sharply white. We turned out onto the Gran Vía.

"Oh, Jake," Brett said, "we could have had such a damned good time together."

Ahead was a mounted policeman in khaki directing traffic. He raised his baton. The car slowed suddenly pressing Brett against me.

"Yes," I said. "Isn't it pretty to think so?"

THE END

Appendix I

Pamplona, July 1923

The following essay first appeared in *The Toronto Star Weekly* on October 27, 1923, under the title "World's Series of Bull Fighting a Mad, Whirling Carnival."

In Pamplona, a white-walled, sun baked town high up in the hills of Navarre, is held in the first two weeks of July each year the World's Series of bull fighting.

Bull fight fans from all Spain jam into the little town. Hotels double their prices and fill every room. The cafés under the wide arcades that run around the Plaza de la Constitución have every table crowded, the tall Pilgrim Father sombreros of Andalusia siting over the same table with straw hats from Madrid and the flat blue Basque caps of Navarre and the Basque country.

Really beautiful girls, gorgeous, bright shawls over their shoulders, dark, dark-eyed, black-lace mantillas over their hair, walk with their escorts in the crowds that pass from morning until night along the narrow walk that runs between inner and outer belts of café tables under the shade of the arcade out of the white glare of the Plaza de la Constitución. All day and all night there is dancing in the streets. Bands of blue-shirted peasants whirl and lift and swing behind a drum, fife and reed instruments in the ancient Basque Riau Riau dances. And at night there is the throb of the big drums and the military band as the whole town dances in the great open square of the Plaza.

We landed at Pamplona at night. The streets were solid with people dancing. Music was pounding and throbbing. Fireworks were being set off from the big public square. All the carnivals I had ever seen paled down in comparison. A rocket exploded over our heads with a blinding burst and the stick came whirling and whishing down. Dancers, snapping their fingers and whirling in perfect time through the crowd, bumped into us before we could get our bags down from the top of the station bus. Finally I got the bags through the crowd to the hotel.

We had wired and written for rooms two weeks ahead. Nothing had been saved. We were offered a single room with a single bed opening on to the kitchen ventilator shaft for seven dollars a day apiece. There was a big row with the landlady, who stood in front of her desk with her hands on her hips, and her broad Indian face perfectly placid, and told us in a few words of French and much Basque Spanish that she had to make all her money for the whole year in the next ten days. That people would come and that people would have to pay what she asked. She could show us a better room for ten dollars apiece. We said it would be preferable to sleep in the street with the pigs. The landlady agreed that might be possible. We said we preferred it to such a hotel. All perfectly amicable. The landlady considered. We stood our ground. Mrs. Hemingway sat down on our rucksacks.

"I can get you a room in a house in the town. You can eat here," said the landlady.

"How much?"

"Five dollars."

We started off through the dark, narrow, carnival mad streets with a boy carrying our rucksacks. It was a lovely big room in an old Spanish house with walls thick as a fortress. A cool, pleasant room, with a red tile floor and two big, comfortable beds set back in an alcove. A window opened on to an iron grilled porch out over the street. We were very comfortable.

All night long the wild music kept up in the street below. Several times in the night there was a wild roll of drumming, and I got out of bed and across the tiled floor to the balcony. But it was always the same. Men, blue-shirted, bareheaded, whirling and floating in a wild fantastic dance down the streets behind the rolling drums and shrill fifes.

Just at daylight there was a crash of music in the street below. Real military music. Herself was up, dressed, at the window.

"Come on," she said. "They're all going somewhere." Down below the street was full of people. It was five o'clock in the morning. They were all going in one direction. I dressed in a hurry and we started after them.

Figure 1. Ernest Hemingway, Duff Twysden, Harold Loeb, Hadley Richardson Hemingway, Donald Ogden Stewart, and Patrick Guthrie at a sidewalk café in Pamplona during the 1925 San Fermín festival. Ernest Hemingway Collection, John F. Kennedy Presidential Library and Museum, Boston.

Figure 2. Jules Pascin, *Hemingway at the Café du Dôme* (*ca.* 1922 or 1925), pen and ink, pastel and wash; 8¼" x 11⅝", signed and stamped with the Atelier mark. Collection of James Moody, Ithaca, NY. Reproduced with the permission of Mr. James Moody.

Figure 3. Ernest Hemingway's ticket stub for the bullfights at Pamplona on July 7, 1923.   Ernest Hemingway Personal Papers, Other Materials, Bullfights: Ticket Stubs, 1923, John F. Kennedy Presidential Library and Museum, Boston.

Figure 4. Ernest Hemingway's ticket stub for the bullfights at Pamplona on July 9, 1924.   Ernest Hemingway Personal Papers, Other Materials, Bullfights: Ticket Stubs, 1924–25, John F. Kennedy Presidential Library and Museum, Boston.

Figure 5. Ernest Hemingway trying his hand at bullfighting in Pamplona, 1924. He can be seen right of center, in white pants and dark sweater, facing a charging bull. Ernest Hemingway Collection, John F. Kennedy Presidential Library and Museum, Boston.

Bull Gores 2 Yanks Acting as Toreadores

[Chicago Tribune Foreign News Service.]
[Copyright: 1924: By The Chicago Tribune.]

MADRID, July 28.—MacDonald Ogden Stewart and Ernest Hemingway of Oak Park, Ill., two American writers, were gored today by a bull in the bull ring at Pamplona, Spain, where they went to attend a fiesta. Stewart had two ribs broken and Hemingway was bruised. Both their lives were saved.

Stewart, Hemingway, John Dos Passos, and Robert McAlmon, all American writers resident of Paris, went to Pamplona to take part in an old fashioned celebration there which is noted all over Spain. It is the custom to barricade the side streets of the town and drive the bulls for the day's fighting from the station to the arena, the larger part of the populace flying before them. Afterwards a bull with bandaged horns is sent to the arena, where the toreadors play leap frog and tag with the animal.

ERNEST M. HEMINGWAY.
[Geno-Fish Photo.]

Tossed Into Air.

Part of the initiation of young manhood in Pamplona consists of being thrown by the bandaged bull. Stewart and Hemingway participated in the event successfully the first day. But on the second day Stewart was thrown. He had said he could leap on the bull's back, blow smoke in his eyes, and then beat him down.

The chief toreador presented Stewart with a scarlet cloak, which the American could not refuse. Then during the handshaking the bull rushed for Stewart, lifted him on his horns, tossed him over, threw him into the air, and later tried to gore him. Hemingway rushed to rescue his comrade and was also gored. He was saved from death only because the bull's horns were bandaged.

Figure 7. Program from the annual festival and bullfights in Pamplona, 1924. Ernest Hemingway Personal Papers, Other Materials, Bullfights: Programs from Pamplona, John F. Kennedy Presidential Library and Museum, Boston.

Figure 6. A news clipping belonging to Ernest Hemingway from *The Chicago Tribune*, July 28, 1924, with the headline "Bull Gores 2 Yanks Acting as Toreadores." Ernest Hemingway Collection, John F. Kennedy Presidential Library and Museum, Boston.

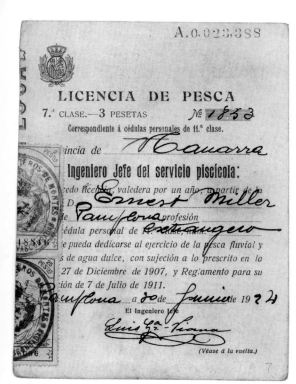

Figure 8. Ernest Hemingway's fishing license for the Navarre region to fish the Irati River in 1924.   Ernest Hemingway Collection, John F. Kennedy Presidential Library and Museum, Boston.

Figure 9. Ernest Hemingway in the Basque countryside, 1924 or 1925. Ernest Hemingway Collection, John F. Kennedy Presidential Library and Museum, Boston.

Figure 10. Postcard picture of Ernest Hemingway at the beach at Hendaye in August 1926.   Ernest Hemingway Collection, John F. Kennedy Presidential Library and Museum, Boston.

Figure 11. Ernest, Hadley, and John Hadley Nicanor "Jack" Hemingway in Schruns, 1926. Ernest Hemingway Collection, John F. Kennedy Presidential Library and Museum, Boston.

Figure 12. The "dangerous summer" of 1926: Gerald and Sarah Murphy, Pauline Pfeiffer, Ernest and Hadley Hemingway, and bootblacks in Pamplona.

Ernest Hemingway Collection, John F. Kennedy Presidential Library and Museum, Boston.

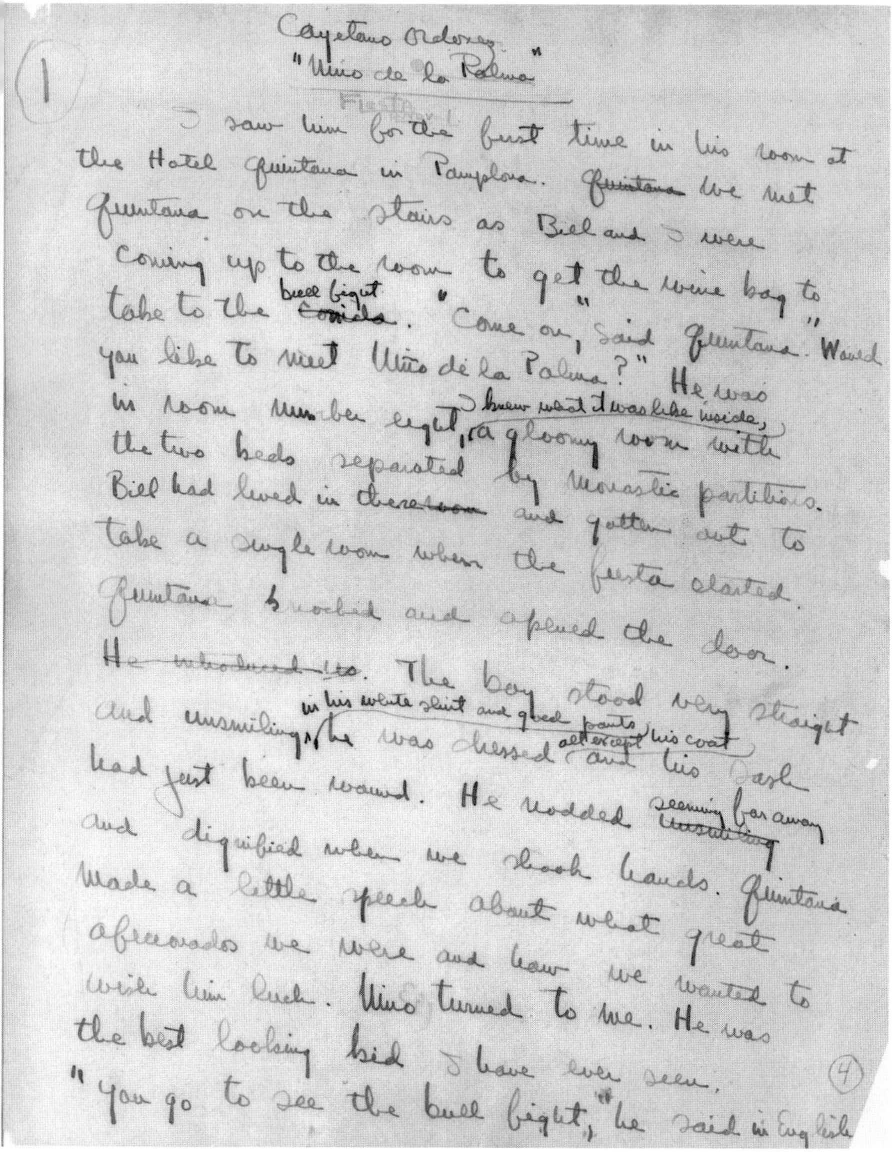

Cayetano Ordoñez
"Niño de la Palma"

I saw him for the first time in his room at the Hotel Quintana in Pamplona. Quintana We met Quintana on the stairs as Bill and I were coming up to the room to get the wine bag to take to the bull fight. "Come on, said Quintana. Would you like to meet Niño de la Palma?" He was in room number eight, I knew what it was like inside, a gloomy room with the two beds separated by monastic partitions. Bill had lived in there and gotten out to take a single room when the fiesta started. Quintana knocked and opened the door. He introduced us. The boy stood very straight and unsmiling in his white shirt and black pants he was dressed all except his coat and his dark had just been wound. He nodded seeming far away and dignified when we shook hands. Quintana made a little speech about what great aficionados we were and how we wanted to wish him luck. Niño turned to me. He was the best looking kid I have ever seen. "You go to see the bull fight," he said in English

Figure 13. Handwritten first page of the earliest draft of *The Sun Also Rises*, written on a loose sheet.   Ernest Hemingway Collection, Manuscripts, *The Sun Also Rises*, Item 193, page 1, John F. Kennedy Presidential Library and Museum, Boston.

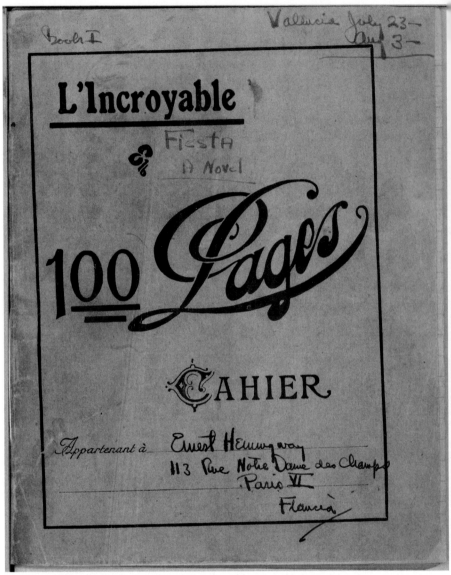

Figure 14. Cover of the first of seven notebooks in which Hemingway wrote most of the first draft of *The Sun Also Rises*, provisionally titled *Fiesta: A Novel*. This notebook is labeled Book I and dated Valencia, July 23–August 3 [1925]. It continues from the thirty-one loose sheets, which begin with the page illustrated in Figure 13.   Ernest Hemingway Collection, Manuscripts, *The Sun Also Rises*, Item 194, folder 1, page 1, John F. Kennedy Presidential Library and Museum, Boston.

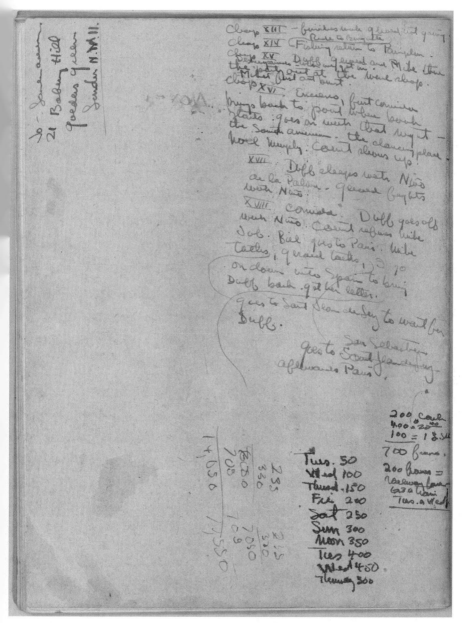

Figure 15. Hemingway's projected outline for *The Sun Also Rises* from chapter thirteen of the first draft. It is written on the inside back cover of the third notebook, together with accounts and an address.   Ernest Hemingway Collection, Manuscripts, *The Sun Also Rises*, Item 194, folder 3, page 53, John F. Kennedy Presidential Library and Museum, Boston.

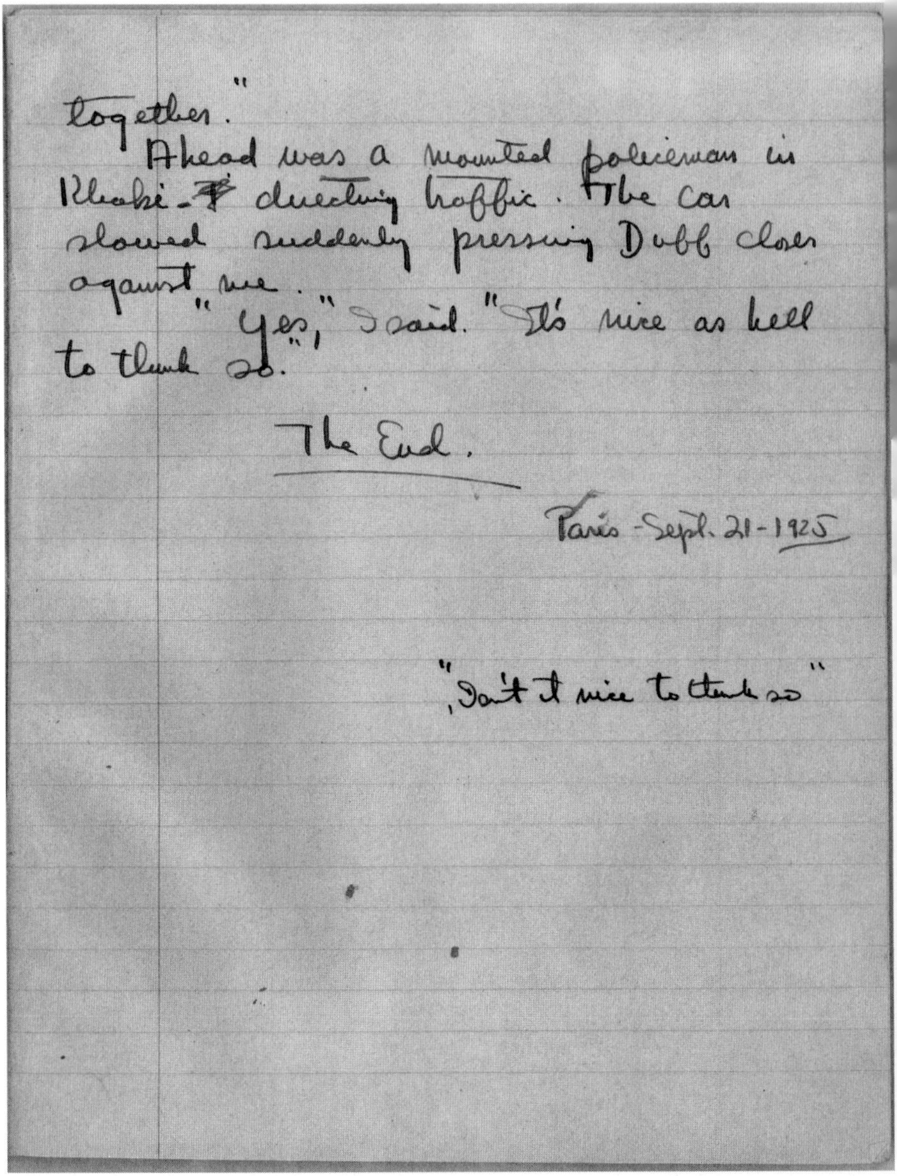

together."

"Ahead was a mounted policeman in Khaki. directing traffic. The car slowed suddenly pressing Dubb closer against me.

"Yes," I said. "It's nice as hell to think so."

The End.

Paris - Sept. 21 - 1925

"Isn't it nice to think so"

Figure 16. Last page of the first draft of *The Sun Also Rises* from notebook seven. The page is dated Paris, September 21, 1925. Ernest Hemingway Collection, Manuscripts, *The Sun Also Rises*, Item 194, folder 6, page 56, John F. Kennedy Presidential Library and Museum, Boston.

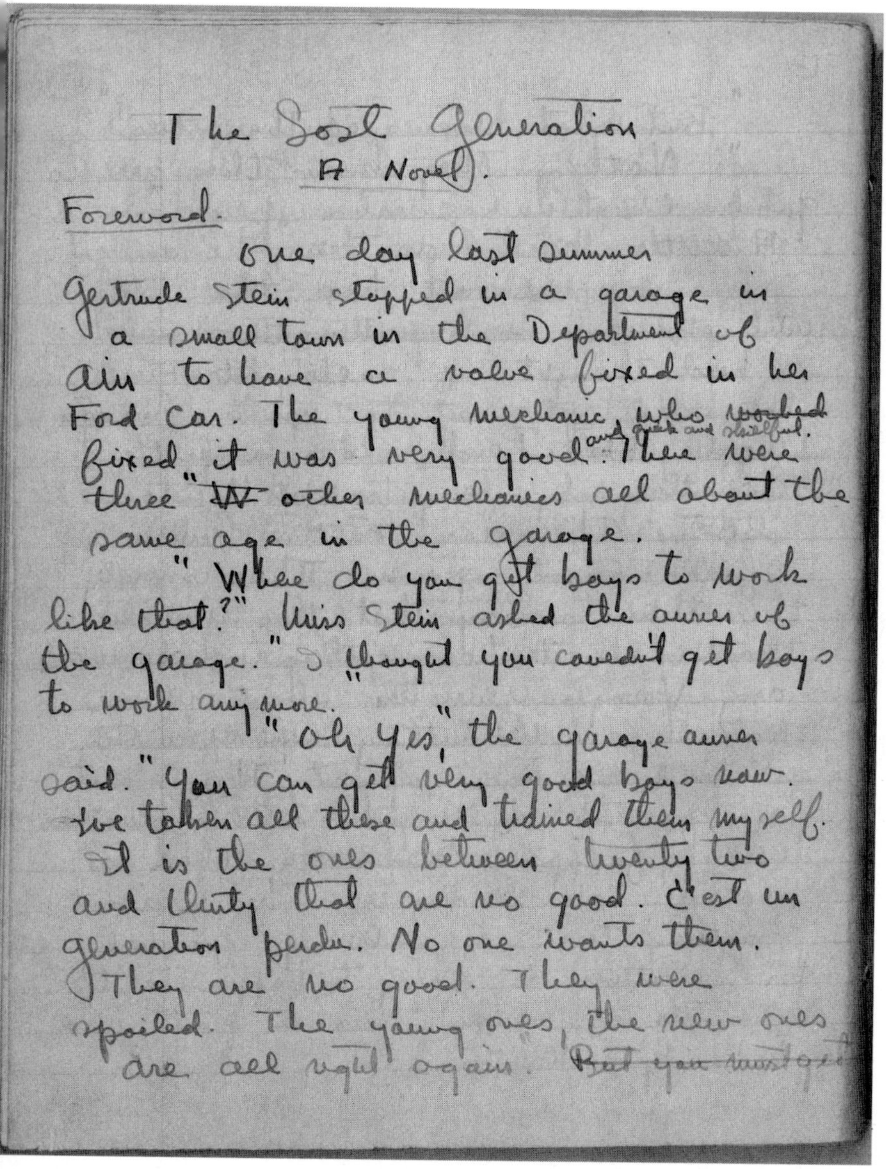

The Lost Generation
A Novel.

Foreword.

One day last summer Gertrude Stein stopped in a garage in a small town in the Department of Ain to have a valve fixed in her Ford Car. The young mechanic, who ~~worked~~ quick and skilful. fixed it was very good. ~~"~~ There were three ~~It~~ ~~other~~ mechanics all about the same age in the garage.

"Where do you get boys to work like that?" Miss Stein asked the owner of the garage. "I thought you couldn't get boys to work any more."

"Oh yes," the garage owner said. "You can get very good boys now. I've taken all these and trained them myself. It is the ones between twenty two and thirty that are no good. C'est un generation perdu. No one wants them. They are no good. They were spoiled. The young ones, the new ones are all right again. ~~But you must get~~

Figure 17. First page of the unpublished Foreword written in an eighth notebook labeled "Chartres, September 27, 1925." The title at this time was *The Lost Generation: A Novel.* Ernest Hemingway Collection, Manuscripts, *The Sun Also Rises*, Item 202c, page 1, John F. Kennedy Presidential Library and Museum, Boston.

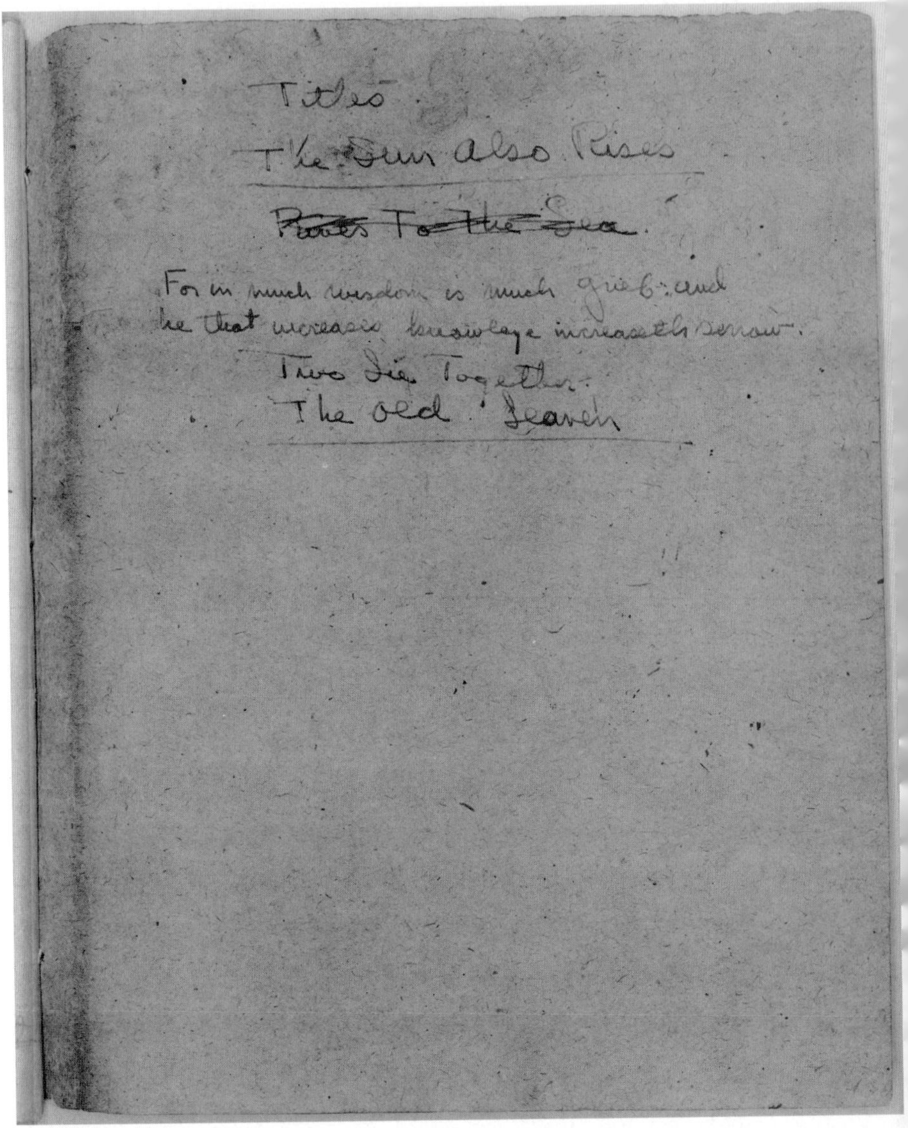

Figure 18. List of possible titles for *The Sun Also Rises*, written opposite the first page of the unpublished Foreword in the eighth notebook.   Ernest Hemingway Collection, Manuscripts, *The Sun Also Rises*, Item 202c, page 1, John F. Kennedy Presidential Library and Museum, Boston.

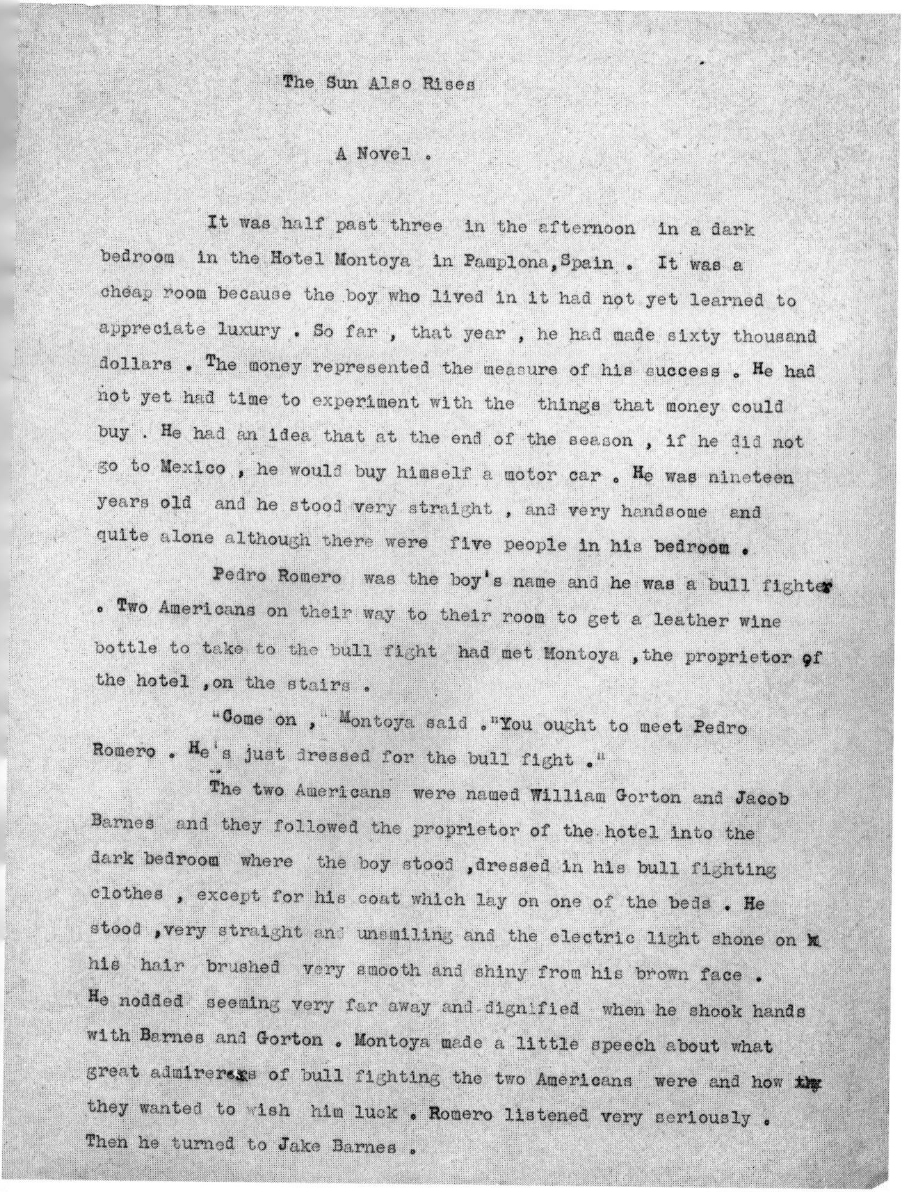

The Sun Also Rises

A Novel .

It was half past three in the afternoon in a dark bedroom in the Hotel Montoya in Pamplona, Spain . It was a cheap room because the boy who lived in it had not yet learned to appreciate luxury . So far , that year , he had made sixty thousand dollars . The money represented the measure of his success . He had not yet had time to experiment with the things that money could buy . He had an idea that at the end of the season , if he did not go to Mexico , he would buy himself a motor car . He was nineteen years old and he stood very straight , and very handsome and quite alone although there were five people in his bedroom .

Pedro Romero was the boy's name and he was a bull fighter . Two Americans on their way to their room to get a leather wine bottle to take to the bull fight had met Montoya , the proprietor of the hotel , on the stairs .

"Come on , " Montoya said . "You ought to meet Pedro Romero . He's just dressed for the bull fight ."

The two Americans were named William Gorton and Jacob Barnes and they followed the proprietor of the hotel into the dark bedroom where the boy stood , dressed in his bull fighting clothes , except for his coat which lay on one of the beds . He stood , very straight and unsmiling and the electric light shone on his hair brushed very smooth and shiny from his brown face . He nodded seeming very far away and dignified when he shook hands with Barnes and Gorton . Montoya made a little speech about what great admirerss of bull fighting the two Americans were and how they wanted to wish him luck . Romero listened very seriously . Then he turned to Jake Barnes .

Figure 19. One of Hemingway's attempts at switching the novel to third-person narration.   Ernest Hemingway Collection, Manuscripts, *The Sun Also Rises*, Item 197a, page 1, John F. Kennedy Presidential Library and Museum, Boston.

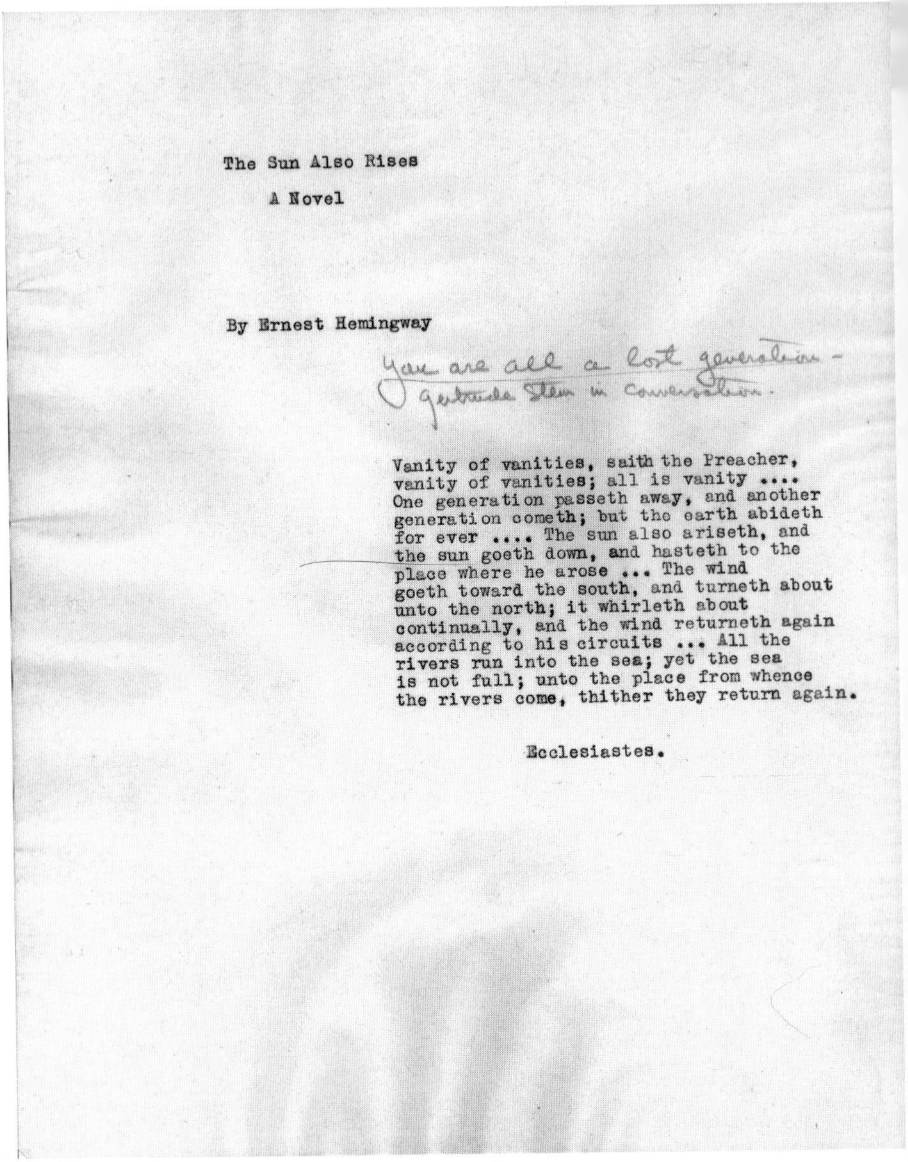

The Sun Also Rises

A Novel

By Ernest Hemingway

You are all a lost generation -
Gertrude Stein in conversation.

Vanity of vanities, saith the Preacher,
vanity of vanities; all is vanity ....
One generation passeth away, and another
generation cometh; but the earth abideth
for ever .... The sun also ariseth, and
the sun goeth down, and hasteth to the
place where he arose ... The wind
goeth toward the south, and turneth about
unto the north; it whirleth about
continually, and the wind returneth again
according to his circuits ... All the
rivers run into the sea; yet the sea
is not full; unto the place from whence
the rivers come, thither they return again.

Ecclesiastes.

Figure 20. Typescript title page of *The Sun Also Rises* with Hemingway's handwritten pencil addition of Gertrude Stein's remark, "You are all a lost generation," to balance the epigraph from Ecclesiastes.   Ernest Hemingway Collection, Manuscripts, *The Sun Also Rises*, Item 200, John F. Kennedy Presidential Library and Museum, Boston.

The crowd was all going toward the great public square. People were pouring into it from every street and moving out of it toward the open country we could see through the narrow gaps in the high walls.

"Let's get some coffee," said Herself.

"Do you think we've got time? Hey, what's going to happen?" I asked a newsboy.

"Encierro," he said scornfully. "The encierro commences at six o'clock."

"What's the encierro?" I asked him.

"Oh, ask me tomorrow," he said, and started to run. The entire crowd was running now.

"I've got to have my coffee. No matter what it is," Herself said.

The waiter poured two streams of coffee and milk into the glass out of his big kettles. The crowd was still running, coming from all the streets that fed into the Plaza.

"What is the encierro anyway?" Herself asked, gulping the coffee.

"All I know is that they let the bulls out into the streets."

We started out after the crowd. Out of a narrow gate into a great yellow open space of country with the new concrete bull ring standing high and white and black with people. The yellow and red Spanish flag blowing in the early morning breeze. Across the open and once inside the bull ring, we mounted to the top looking toward the town. It cost a peseta to go up to the top. All the other levels were free. There were easily twenty thousand people there. Everyone jammed on the outside of the big concrete amphitheater, looking toward the yellow town with the bright red roofs, where a long wooden pen ran from the entrance to the city gate, across the open bare ground to the bull ring.

It was really a double wooden fence, making a long entryway from the main street of the town into the bull ring itself. It made a runway about two hundred and fifty yards long. People were jammed solid on each side of it. Looking up it toward the main street.

Then far away there was a dull report.

"They're off," everybody shouted.

"What is it?" I asked the man next to me who was leaning far out over the concrete rail.

"The bulls! They have released them from the corrals on the far side of the city. They are racing through the city."

"Whew," said Herself. "What do they do that for?"

Then down the narrow fenced runway came a crowd of men and

boys running. Running as hard as they could go. The gate feeding into the bull ring was opened and they all ran pell mell under the entrance levels into the ring. Then there came another crowd. Running even harder. Straight up the long pen from town.

"Where are the bulls?" asked Herself.

Then they came in sight. Eight bulls galloping along, full tilt, heavy set, black, glistening, sinister, their horns bare, tossing their heads. And running with them three steers with bells on their necks. They ran in a solid mass, and ahead of them sprinted, tore, ran and bolted the rear guard of men and boys of Pamplona who had allowed themselves to be chased through the streets for a morning's pleasure.

A boy in his blue shirt, red sash, white canvas shoes with the inevitable leather wine bottle hung from his shoulders, stumbled as he sprinted down the straightaway. The first bull lowered his head and made a jerky, sideways toss. The boy crashed up against the fence and lay there limp, the herd running solidly together passed him up. The crowd roared.

Everybody made a dash for the inside of the ring, and we got into a box just in time to see the bulls come into the ring filled with men. The men ran in a panic to each side. The bulls, still bunched solidly together, ran straight with the steers across the ring and into the entrance that led to the pens.

That was the entry. Every morning during the bull fighting festival of San Fermín at Pamplona the bulls that are to fight in the afternoon are released from their corrals at six o'clock in the morning and race through the main street of the town for a mile and a half to the pen. The men who run ahead of them do it for the fun of the thing. It has been going on each year since a couple of hundred years before Columbus had his historic interview with Queen Isabella in the camp outside of Granada.

There are two things in favor of there being no accidents. First, that fighting bulls are not aroused and vicious when they are together. Second, that the steers are relied upon to keep them moving.

Sometimes things go wrong, a bull will be detached from the herd as they pile through into the pen and with his crest up, a ton of speed and viciousness, his needle sharp horns lowered, will charge again and again into the packed mass of men and boys in the bull ring. There is no place for the men to get out of the ring. It is too jammed for them to climb out of the barrera or red fence that rims the field. They have to stay in and take it. Eventually the steers get the bull out of the ring and into the pen. He may wound or kill thirty men before they get him out. No armed men are allowed to oppose him. That is the chance the Pamplona bull fight fans take every morning during the Feria. It is the Pamplona tradition of giving the bulls a final shot at everyone in town before they enter the pens. They will not leave until they come out into the glare of the arena to die in the afternoon.

Consequently Pamplona is the toughest bull fight town in the world. The amateur fight that comes immediately after the bulls have entered the pens proves that. Every seat in the great amphitheater is packed. About three hundred men with capes, odd pieces of cloth, old shirts, anything that will imitate a bull fighter's cape, are singing and dancing in the arena. There is a shout, and the bull pen opens. Out comes a young bull just about as fast as he can come. On his horns are leather knobs to prevent his goring anyone. He charges and hits a man. Tosses him high in the air and the crowd roars. The man comes down on the ground, and the bull goes for him, bumping him with his head. Worrying him with his horns. Several amateur bull fighters are flopping their capes in his face to make the bull charge and leave the man on the ground. Then the bull charges and bags another man. The crowd roars with delight.

Then the bull will turn like a cat and get somebody who has been acting very brave about ten feet behind him. Then he will toss a man over the fence. Then he picks out one man and follows him in a wild twisting charge through the entire crowd until he bags him. The barrera is packed with men and boys sitting along the top, and the bull decides to clear them all off. He goes along, hooking carefully with his horn and dropping them off with a toss of his horns like a man pitching hay.

Each time the bull bags someone the crowd roars with joy. Most of it is home talent stuff. The braver the man has been or the more elegant pass he has attempted with his cape before the bull gets him the more the crowd roars. No one is armed. No one hurts or plagues the bull in any way. A man who grabbed the bull by the tail and tried to hang on was hissed and booed by the crowd and the next time he tried it was knocked down by another man in the bull ring. No one enjoys it all more than the bull.

As soon as he shows signs of tiring from his charges, the two old steers, one brown and the other looking like a big Holstein, come trotting in and alongside the young bull who falls in behind them like a dog and follows them meekly on a tour of the arena and then out.

Another comes right in, and the charging and tossing, the ineffectual cape waving, and wonderful music are repeated right over again. But always different. Some of the animals in this morning amateur fight are steers. Fighting bulls from the best strain who had some imperfection or other in build so they could never command the high prices paid for combat animals, $2000 to $3000 apiece. But there is nothing lacking in their fighting spirit.

The show comes off every morning. Everybody in town turns out at five thirty when the military bands go through the streets. Many of them stay up all night for it. We didn't miss one, and it is quelque sporting event that will get us both up at five thirty o'clock in the morning for six days running.

As far as I know we were the only English speaking people in Pamplona during the Feria of last year [July].

There were three minor earthquakes while we were there. Terrific cloud bursts in the mountains and the Ebro River flooded out Zaragossa. For two days the bull ring was under water and the Corrida had to be suspended for the first time in over a hundred years. That was during the middle of the fair. Everyone was desperate. On the third day it looked gloomier than ever, poured rain all morning, and then at noon the clouds rolled away up across the valley, the sun came out bright and hot and baking and that afternoon there was perhaps the greatest bull fight I will ever see.

There were rockets going up into the air and the arena was nearly full when we got into one of the regular seats. The sun was hot and baking. Over on the other side we could see the bull fighters standing ready to come in. All wearing their oldest clothes because of the heavy, muddy going in the arena. We picked out the three matadors of the afternoon with our glasses. Only one of them was new. Olmos, a chubby faced, jolly looking man, something like Tris Speaker. The others we had seen often before. Maera, dark, spare and deadly looking, one of the very greatest toreros of all time. The third, young Algabeño, the son of a famous bull fighter, a slim young Andalusian with a charming Indian looking face. All were wearing the suits they had probably started bull fighting with, too tight, old fashioned, outmoded.

There was the procession of entrance. The wild bull fight music played, the preliminaries were quickly over, the picadors retired along the red fence with their horses, the heralds sounded their trumpets and the door of the bull pen swung open. The bull came out in a rush, saw a man standing near the barrera and charged him. The man vaulted near over the fence and the bull charged the barrera. He crashed into the fence in full charge and ripped a two by eight plank solidly out in a splintering smash. He broke his horn doing it and the crowd called for a new bull. The trained steers trotted in, the bull fell meekly behind them, and the three of them trotted out of the arena.

The next bull came in with the same rush. He was Maera's bull and after perfect cape play Maera planted the banderillos. Maera is Herself's favorite bull fighter. And if you want to keep any conception of yourself as a brave, hard, perfectly balanced, thoroughly competent man in your wife's mind never take her to a real bull fight. I used to go into the amateur fights in the mornings to try and win back a small amount of her esteem but the more I discovered that bull fighting required a very great quantity of a certain type of courage of which I had an almost complete lack the more it became apparent that any admiration she might ever redevelop for me would have to be simply an antidote to the real admiration for Maera and Villalta. You cannot compete with bull fighters on their own ground. If anywhere. The only way most husbands are able to keep any drag with their wives at all is that, first there are only a limited number of bull fighters, second there are only a limited number of wives who have ever seen bull fights.

Maera planted his first pair of banderillos sitting down on the edge of the little step that runs around the barrera. He snarled at the bull and as the animal charged leaned back tight against the fence and as the horns struck on either side of him, swung forward over the brute's head and planted the two darts in his hump. He planted the next pair the same way, so near to us we could have leaned over and touched him. Then he went out to kill the bull and after he had made absolutely unbelievable passes with the little red cloth of the muleta drew up his sword and as the bull charged Maera thrust. The sword shot out of his hand and the bull caught him. He went up in the air on the horns of the bull and then came down. Young Algabeño flopped his cape in the bull's face. The bull charged him and Maera staggered to his feet. But his wrist was sprained.

With his wrist sprained, so that every time he raised it to sight for a thrust it brought beads of sweat out on his face, Maera tried again and again to make his death thrust. He lost his sword again and again, picked it up with his left hand from the mud floor of the arena and transferred it to the right for the thrust. Finally, he made it and the bull went over. The bull nearly got him twenty times. As he came in to stand up under us at the barrera side his wrist was swollen to twice normal size. I thought of prize fighters I had seen quit because they had hurt their hands.

There was almost no pause while the mules galloped in and hitched on to the first bull and dragged him out and the second came in with a rush. The picadors took the first shock of him with their bull lances. There was the snort and charge, the shock and mass against the sky, the wonderful defense by the picador with his lance that held off the bull, and then Rosario Olmos stepped out with his cape.

Once he flopped the cape at the bull and floated it around in an easy graceful swing. Then he tried the same swing, the classic "Veronica" and the bull caught him at the end of it. Instead of stopping at the finish the bull charged on in. He caught Olmos squarely with his horn, hoisted him high in the air. He fell heavily and the bull was on top of him, driving his horns again and again into him. Olmos lay on the sand, his head on his arms. One of his teammates was flopping his cape madly in the bull's face. The bull lifted his head for an instant and charged and got his man. Just one terrific toss. Then he whirled and chased a man just in back of him toward the barrera. The man was running full tilt and as he put his hand on the fence to vault it the bull had him and caught him with his horn, shooting him way up into the crowd. He rushed toward the fallen man he had tossed who was getting to his feet and all alone Algabeño grabbed him by the tail. He hung on until I thought he or the bull would break. The wounded man got to his feet and started away.

The bull turned like a cat and charged Algabeño and Algabeño met him with the cape. Once, twice, three times he made the perfect, floating, slow swing with the cape, perfectly, graceful, debonair, back on his heels, baffling the bull. And he had command of the situation. There never was such a scene at any world's series game.

There are no substitute matadors allowed. Maera was finished. His wrist could not lift a sword for weeks. Olmos had been gored badly through the body. It was Algabeño's bull. This one and the next five.

He handled them all. Did it all. Cape play easy, graceful, confident. Beautiful work with the muleta. And serious, deadly killing. Five bulls he killed, one after the other, and each one was a separate problem to be worked out with death. At the end there was nothing debonair about him. It was only a question if he would last through or if the bulls would get him. They were all very wonderful bulls.

"He is a very great kid," said Herself. "He is only twenty."

"I wish we knew him," I said.

"Maybe we will some day," she said. She considered a moment. "He will probably be spoiled by then."

They make twenty thousand a year.

That was just three months ago. It seems in a different century now, working in an office. It is a very long way from the sun baked town of Pamplona, where the men race through the streets in the mornings ahead of the bulls to the morning ride to work on a Bay-Caledonia car. But it is only fourteen days by water to Spain and there is no need for a castle. There is always that room at 5 Calle de Eslava, and a son, if he is to redeem the family reputation as a bull fighter, must start very early.

Appendix II

Early Drafts

The following fourteen passages are early drafts of the novel. As discussed in the Introduction, the beginning of the novel was changed dramatically, but before giving up on it, Hemingway tried several different approaches, which are included here. Other passages were extensively reworked or cut. The passages are arranged generally according to their original relation to the book. The item numbers refer to the cataloguing system of the Hemingway Collection at the John F. Kennedy Presidential Library and Museum in Boston.

1. Item 193. Early handwritten ink draft of the initial beginning of the novel, with an epigraph on the first page and a typed list of the characters of the book. After these thirty-one handwritten pages, Hemingway wrote the rest of the first draft in seven notebooks.

First Page:
Facing Page One of Chapter One
The grave's a fine and secret place
But none I think do there embrace . . .
Marvell

Second Page:
Original name
Neil
Elizabeth Brett Murray

Names for Duff—
Married Lord Robert Ashley
Name generally used Brett Ashley

Other characters
Bill Gorton
Gerald Cohn
Mike Campbell
Jake Barnes
Harvey Stone

Cayetano Ordoñez
"Niño de la Palma"

I saw him for the first time in his room at the Hotel Quintana in Pamplona. We met Quintana on the stairs as Bill and I were coming up to the room to get the wine bag to take to the bull fight.

"Come on," said Quintana. "Would you like to meet Niño de la Palma?"

He was in his room number eight. I knew what it was like inside, a gloomy room with the two beds separated by monastic partitions. Bill had lived in there and gotten out to take a single room when the fiesta started. Quintana knocked and opened the door. The boy stood very straight and unsmiling in his white shirt and good pants. He was dressed all except his coat and his sash had just been wound. He nodded seeming far away and dignified when we shook hands. Quintana made a little speech about what great aficionados we were and how we wanted to wish him luck. Niño turned to me. He was the best looking kid I have ever seen.

"You go to see the bull fight," he said in English.

"You know English," I said feeling like an idiot as I said it.

"No," he said and smiled.

A Spanish newspaper man from San Sebastian came up and asked us if we spoke French.

"Would you like me to interpret for you? Is there anything you would like to ask?" he said.

We thanked him. What was there that you would like to ask. The boy was nineteen years old, alone except for his sword handler and this newspaper man and the bull fight was to commence in twenty minutes.

We wished Niño, "Mucha Suerte," shook hands and went out of the dark room. He was standing, straight and handsome, looking the essence of torero, alone in the room with the two hangers on as we went out into the corridor.

"He's a fine boy, don't you think so?" Quintana said.

"He's a good looking kid," I said.

"We'll see in the Plaza," Quintana said.

We found the big leather wine bag leaning against the wall in the room, took it and the field glasses, locked the door and went down stairs. Across the square at the café we found the others, drinking Fundador cognac, drank a quick one and got them up from the tables and started across the square for the corrida. It was very crowded and as we passed the Quintana the bull fighters were getting into the bus. We saw Niño and I forget whether we waved to him or not. Probably not. I rather think not.

He was very fine that day in the bull ring but had poor bulls to work with. All the same his cape work was beautiful. I had never seen such suave, slow, perfectly timed and artistic cape work. With the muleta he was merely intelligent and he killed quickly and well. But he was a hell of a fine bull fighter. He did it all so easily, simply and unhurried.

That night Quintana and I had a long talk about him. We agreed he was the best torero we had seen, the finest and purest style and the most authority in the ring. We were both very happy about it. Bull fighters like that are as rare as [Enrico] Caruso's or Adelina Pattis. There are always plenty of tenors and no lack of sopranos just as there are lots of acceptable bull fighters. But when a great one comes along you know the difference. The crowd that day had been excited over a young bull fighter named Aquero from Bilbao. He was flashy, tricky and vulgar and his kills gave the results of a great swordsman. They were really tricks though. He went in to kill so fast that the eye was deceived. Really he killed in as absolute safety as any of the bad stickers. All he had was a good eye and a strong wrist. I had been disgusted by him. He was cheap and left a bad taste in my mouth. We talked about him too and then I went down to supper, the drinking, the fireworks in the square and dancing and the cafés until bed at three o'clock in the morning.

At six our door was banged open and three men came in carrying a fourth, his legs hanging. I woke as the door opened and my first thought was that I must have overslept and missed the morning amateur fight and someone was being brought in wounded. Then one of the men said,

"It's not here," and they went out. As they turned I couldn't quite see the face of the man they were carrying. But it looked like Niño. Anyway they put him in number eight.

I did not see him again until the evening before the fight in which Algabeño was to alternate with Belmonte.

In the meantime our Ambassador got into town. He came in a big Rolls Royce and it stopped in the square in front of the café and nobody came out to greet him and there wasn't any sort of a reception. He stood looking big and solid and rather cunningly stupid evidently expecting someone to make a fuss over him and no one came. There were two women with him one tall one in blue, perfectly dressed shanty Irish looking, sort of a White House hostess and the other a cute little short one, the kind that does it so well you cannot tell whether her hair is a lovely sunburnt color or whether she dyes it. You know the kind, perfectly done for what she is and capable of taking any man away after he has passed a certain age.

Well they stood out there on the sidewalk and a crowd gathered to look at the car and everybody in the café had taken a good look at them and was back to drinking again. All except us that is.

Duff said, "I say. That's a shabby way to treat an Ambassador."

Don said, "But he's only an American Ambassador."

Bill said, "They don't know that here though."

"Go on Hem," Duff said. "You know him. Go out and say something to him."

"Give him the keys of the city," Pat said.

"Give him the key to my room," Don said.

"Go on Hem. You really ought," Duff said.

I did not want to go out. Still after all he was our Ambassador.

"Go on," Hadley said. "Tell them to come and have a drink."

So I went out and shook hands with him and met the White House hostess one and the little lively one and explained to a policeman that this was the American Ambassador and he did not have to pay any tax on his car and sent another policeman for the Alcalde and took his card up to the other hotel to reserve two rooms for a lady friend who was coming and then we talked. That is the short lively one talked. She happened to be married to a friend of mine, a painter named Carleton, and I'd heard the story and knew the original Mrs. Carleton and so it was interesting if not pleasant to see her.

She had been to thirty-four bull fights and this was her first time in

Spain. They were all going back to St. Sebastian tonight after the bull fight and come up the next day to spend the night and see the Belmonte fight. I told her Belmonte was going to stop at our hotel. She just worshiped Belmonte—and Marcial Salanda! I told her Marcial Salanda was at our hotel now.

"What hotel is it? The Grand?"

"No," I said, "the Quintana."

"Do tell Marcial I'm in town."

"Surely," I said. "I'm going over and see him now get dressed for the fight."

"And do tell me," she said. "Have you seen Niño de la Palma? I think he's absolutely the most divine boy. Is he at your hotel too?"

"Yes. Do you want me to tell him you're in town?"

She had been turning all this ~~thing that she takes the husbands away from their wives with~~ sex appeal on me all the time we were talking and of course you are never immune at the time and it had a warming effect but when I said that about Niño she chilled it off sharp. She was afraid she was being kidded.

"Oh no," she said, "I've never met him. I've just seen him in the ring."

"Where, at Madrid?"

"No, at Seville."

We talked a little more and the Alcalde came up wearing a brown slouch felt hat with cigarette ashes on his vest and looking rather embarrassed. So I said we would see them and they said the usual sort of thing and all the warmed up feeling from when the short one was talking to me had died out and I wanted to say something or other to bother her so I said, "Tell me. Do you really want me to tell Marcial you're in town?"

She took it as a compliment and pursed her lips and turned on all this stuff again and said, "Really. I don't know. Yes, tell him I'm in town and I'm angry at him because he didn't come out to Tovar's that last time."

So we shook hands and I went back to the table where they had all been trying to ruin my social position by trying to buy the chauffeur a drink. But the chauffeur had been very haughty and refused. So they tried to buy the uniformed equerry or A.D.T. delivery boy or whatever he was a drink. But he was even haughtier.

So we all went to the bull fight and I didn't stop and see Marcial

Salanda in his room because I had seen him and talked with him on the stairs as he was going upstairs and he was nervous enough fighting Miura bulls as it was and worried because the picadors couldn't get big enough horses and it was no day to go butting in on him with a lot of farewell wishes. So we went out to the bull fight and it was rotten, almost the worst I've ever seen. You don't know anything about bull fights so I won't tell about it except that it could not have been worse. The bulls were Miuras and enormous and they would not charge and ~~finally everybody was scared~~ the bull fighters could not do anything with them and nobody gained anything by the day. It took about three hours to kill the six of them and there was plenty of trouble and no glory.

The Ambassador and the two ladies sat in a box with the Alcalde and I looked at them once with the glasses. The uniformed messenger boy was there too and the short one with the sex appeal was leaning forward very intent and earnest. The White House hostess in the blue dress watched the fight too but I don't believe she saw much of it. The Ambassador was smoking a cigar so I suppose he was happy. The Alcalde looked miserable. The one in uniform looked very English and superior to it all.

It made me feel sick looking at them and I wished I had not gone out to speak to them but I had wished that the minute I went out and ever since. It is funny how people like that can ruin anything. They could not ruin the bull fight though because that was done by Don Eduardo Miura who sent the collection of so called bulls. They were splendid looking and acting too when they were unloaded from their cages into the corrales, enormous red ones, cathedrals the paper called them. So maybe it was not Don Eduardo. He must have known how they would act though. Anyway it was rotten.

The next day there was no bull fight. It was a Friday and they had scheduled it as a day of rest so the last two bull fights would come on Saturday and Sunday. It rained and we went to a concert in the morning and an artistic representation in the bull ring in the afternoon. It drizzled all through the artistic representation and when we got to the café we found the rest of the gang there already and drinking absinthe. They had not been able to last it out. All the time we were sitting at the café the big motor cars kept coming into the square. All kinds of cars—all with chauffeurs—bringing the haute monde from Biarritz and San Sebastian to see Belmonte the next day. They were a terrible looking lot. The men all wore golf clothes—loud tweeds and looking pink and white as though they had all had facial massages and the women had veils. Belmonte drew them because he has been fashionable. His portrait has been painted by Zuloaga and they know he gets 30,000 pesetas for a fight and it is very smart to see him. "You know I detest bull fighting but Belmonte is simply divine."

Poor Belmonte has made millions but he has not got them now, only friends, big social friends, and so he is back at the business. He has hemorrhoids ~~terribly~~ so he can hardly move and this is always spoken of as his mysterious sickness. He looks sick and he is sick and he can not take time off to be operated on because he has so many contracts signed and he cannot bear to give up any of the 30,000 pesetas. So society people go to see him whenever he fights and he reserves the right to choose the bulls and fights with the bulls about the size they teach kids on in the bull fight school at Malaga. Well none of that has anything to do with the story and I suppose you think there isn't any story anyway but it sort of moves along in time and anyway there is a lot of dope about high society in it and that is always interesting.

Well that night a friend of Don's got in and she had a couple of drinks with us too at the café and she had a girl friend with her too but the girl friend did not appear and when we saw her later we were glad enough. We all went over to the Quintana pretty tight and while the others went into the downstairs dining room I said I wanted to go upstairs and wash my hands. Upstairs at the desk I met Quintana. He looked worried.

"Well," he said, "how about it?"

Just then Marcial Salanda came upstairs and stopped and shook hands with us. He had spent the day in San Sebastian. He went on up climbing the stairs.

"He looks tired," I said.

"Yes," said Quintana. "Look do you know the American Ambassador?"

"I've met him."

"What is he like?"

I tried to be both brief and just. Then I told him about the short Mrs. Carleton and her message to Marcial and that I had not given it and would not.

Quintana put his lips together and blew his cheeks full of air.

"What kind of woman is she?"

"She took the husband she's got now away from his wife and now she's sent him off to Burgos and she's here because she likes young bull fighters."

"Listen," Quintana said. "A messenger just came over from the Grand Hotel to say the American Ambassador would expect Marcial Salanda and Niño de la Palma at ten o'clock. What would you do about it?"

"Well they can't hurt Marcial anymore except keep him up late but they've no damn right to start a kid like Niño."

"What would you do? I just won't deliver the message. Is that right?" He looked at me.

He started talking in French. It was stuff he did not know how to say in English. I said a lot too. We would both have gone big in a Y.M.C.A. lecture. I was a little tight and Quintana was impassioned. As a matter of fact, I was impassioned too. We both love bull fighting and when once in twenty years a kid comes along with everything in the world and people would wreck him to make a nymphomaniac's holiday and start him away from being a bull fighter and living like a bull fighter and in on this Grand Hotel business that he ought not to touch until he is safely arrived, and then it's poison, well we got pretty well worked up and shook hands and felt we'd each met someone who knew life and other drunk feelings. Only Quintana wasn't drunk. It was only me who was drunk.

So I went down to supper and already the crowd had gotten way ahead of me. They were way out ahead and it was no use trying to catch them. I forget what they were started on but it was funny and Don kept punctuating it by buying shoe shines for Pat. Boot blacks kept coming through the door that opened on the street and every one Don started in to work on Pat.

"This is the eleventh time my boots have been polished," Pat said. "I say Don is an ass."

Just then another boot black came in.

"Limpia botas?" he said to Don.

"No. For esta Señor," Don said. The boot black knelt down beside the one at work and started on Pat's free shoe that was already shining in the electric light.

"He's a yell of laughter," Pat said.

I was drinking red wine and far enough behind them so I felt embarrassed, no not embarrassed but a little uncomfortable, by all this shoe shining.

I looked ~~away from the table and~~ around the room and at the next table was Niño. He stood up when I nodded and asked me to come over and meet a friend. His table was right beside ours, almost touching. I met the friend, a Madrid bull fight critic, a little man with a nice face, they asked me to sit down and we started to talk bulls. I told Niño how much I liked his work and he was very pleased. We talked Spanish and the critic knew a little French. I reached to our table for my wine bottle but the critic took my arm.

Niño laughed. "Drink here," he said in English.

That was the way his English was. He knew how to say most things but he claimed not to know any English at all. He was really very pleased with what he knew and as we went on talking he brought out words he was not sure of and asked about them. He was anxious to know the English for Corrida de Toros, the exact translation. Bull fight he was suspicious of. I explained that bull fight was lidia of a toro. The Spanish expression Corrida means the running of bulls—the French translation is Course des taureaux. The critic put that in. There is no Spanish word for bull fight.

Niño said he had picked up a little English in Gibraltar. He was born in Ronda. That is not far from Gibraltar. He started in bull fighting in Malaga in the bull fight school there. He had only been at it three years. The bull fight critic joked him about the number of Malaguena expressions he used. He was nineteen years old. His older brother was with him as a banderillero but he did not live in this hotel. He lived in a smaller hotel with the other banderilleros and the picadors. I wanted to ask him about that, but I did not. He asked me how many times I had seen him in the ring. I told him only three. It was really only two but I did not want to explain after I had made the mistake. I said I had not yet seen him do a complete job with the muleta, faena it is called.

But his cape work and his intelligence I admired very much.

"Where did you see me the other time," he asked, "in Madrid?"

"Yes," I lied. I had read the accounts of his two appearances there so I was all right.

"The first or the second time?"

"The first," I said.

"It was very bad," he said. "The second time it was better. You remember?" he asked the critic.

He was not at all embarrassed. He talked of his work as something altogether apart from himself. There was nothing conceited or braggardly about him.

"I like it very much that you like my work," he said. "But you haven't seen it yet. Day after tomorrow if I get a good bull I will show it to you."

When he said this he smiled anxious that neither the bull fight critic nor I would think he was boasting.

"I am anxious to see it," the critic said. "I want to be convinced."

"He doesn't like my work much," Niño said to me.

The critic explained that he liked it very much but he had not yet seen it complete.

"Wait till Sunday. If a good one comes out."

"I say Hem you have deserted us," Duff said from the big table.

"Just temporarily," I said. "We're talking bulls."

"You are superior."

"Tell him that bulls have no balls," Patrick blurted out.

Niño looked at me enquiringly.

"Drunk," I said. "Borracho. Muy borracho. How do you say it in Spanish?"

"Yes," said Niño. "Drunk. Sauced. Pickled. Stewed. Piped." He gave half a dozen Spanish equivalents. The critic gave three more.

"There are more ways to say that than anything," Niño said.

"With us too."

"You might introduce your friends," Duff said. She had not stopped looking at Niño. I asked them if they would like to have coffee with us. They both stood up.

So I introduced them all around and they started to sit down but there wasn't really enough room so we all moved over to the big table by the wall to have coffee. Pat ordered a bottle of Fundador and glasses for everybody and there was a lot of drunken talking.

"Tell him I think writing is lousy," Don said. "Go on tell him. Tell him I'm ashamed to be a writer."

Niño was listening to Duff trying to talk Spanish.

"Go on tell him," Don said.

Niño looked up smiling.

"This gentleman," I said, "is a writer."

Niño was impressed. "This other one too," I said pointing at Loeb.

"He looks like Villalta," Niño said looking at Don. "Rafael. Doesn't he look like Villalta?"

"I don't see it," the critic said.

"Really," Niño said. "He looks a lot like Villalta. What does the drunken one do?"

"Nothing," I said.

"Is that why he drinks?"

"No. He's waiting to marry this lady."

"It's better to do something in the meantime."

"Tell him bulls have no balls," said Pat very drunk at the other end of the table.

"What does he say?"

"He's drunk."

"Ernest," Pat called. "Tell him bulls have no balls."

"You understand?" I said.

"Yes."

I knew he didn't so it was all right.

"Tell him Duff wants to see him put on those green pants."

"Pipe down Pat."

"Tell him Duff is dying to know how he can get into those pants."

"Pipe down."

During this Niño was fingering his glass and holding a conversation with Hadley and Duff. They were talking French and he was talking Spanish and a little English and laughing.

Don was filling the glasses.

"Tell him Duff wants to come into—"

"Oh pipe down Pat for Christ's sake."

Niño looked up smiling. "Pipe down. I know that," he said.

Just then Quintana came into the room. You ought to have seen his face. He started to smile at me then he saw Niño with a big glass of cognac in his hand, sitting laughing between me and two women one with bare shoulders and a table full of drunks. He did not even nod. All of a sudden I realized how funny it was.

Quintana went out of the room and I was nervous about Pat and he was getting on his feet to give a toast. "Let's all drink to—" he began.

"To Niño de la Palma," I butted in and everybody stood up and Niño took it very seriously and we touched glasses and drank it down. I rushed it a little because Pat was trying to make it clear that that wasn't at all what he was going to drink to. But it went off all right and Niño shook hands with everyone and said how much he had enjoyed it and he and the critic went out together.

"My God he's a lovely boy," Duff said, "and how I would love to see him get into those clothes. He must use a shoe horn."

"I started to tell him," Pat began. "And Ernest kept interrupting me. Why do you interrupt me? Do you think you talk Spanish better than I do?"

"Oh shut up Pat."

"No. I'd like to get this settled." He turned away from me. "Do you think you amount to something Harold? Do you think you belong here among us? People who are out to have a good time. For God's sake don't be so noisy Harold."

"Oh cut it out Pat," Harold answered. He was in love with Duff and she had slept with him while Pat was away in Scotland and told Pat about it and it had not seemed to make any difference but now whenever he got drunk he kept coming back to it. She had slept with other men before but they had not been of Harold's lover and had not come on parties afterwards. Harold thought that true love would conquer all. He used to explain it. He never moved away from Duff all during the fiesta. It annoyed her and it made Pat crazy.

"Do you think Duff wants you here? Do you think you add to the party? Why don't you say something?"

"I said all I had to say the other night Pat."

There had been one of these barnyard scenes until two o'clock in the morning three nights before.

"I'm not one of you literary chaps." Pat stood wobbly. "I'm not clever. But I do know when I'm not wanted. Why don't you see you're not wanted, Loeb. Go away . . . Go away for God's sake. ~~Take that sad Jewish face away.~~ Don't you think I'm right?"

He looked at us.

"Sure," I said. "Let's all go over to the café."

"No." Not joking. "Don't you think I'm right? I love that woman."

"Oh ~~stop the~~ don't start that again. Do shut up Patrick," Duff said.

"Don't you think I'm right Ernest?"

Loeb just sat there. He never had enough sense to go away. He seemed to enjoy it. Someway it was pleasant, all a form of connecting him up with Duff. He sat there looking through his spectacles, taking it all seriously. His affair with a lady of title.

"Ernest," Pat said. He was almost crying. "You know I'm right. Listen you," he turned to Loeb, "go away. Go away now."

"But I won't go Pat," said Loeb.

"Then I'll make you." Pat started toward him and Loeb stepped back to take off his glasses. "I'm just like the bulls," Pat said. "I can stand just so much."

Loeb had his glasses off and stood proudly and firmly ready for the assault, ready to do battle for his lady love.

I grabbed Pat. "Come to the café," I said. "Don't hit him here in the hotel."

"Good," said Pat. "Good idea."

We started off. I looked back as Pat stumbled on the stairs and saw Harold putting his glasses back on. Hadley and Duff followed us. They were talking, I believe, about their mothers.

2. Item 194, 1-1 to 1-20. After writing the first chapter on loose sheets, Hemingway switched to notebooks. He wrote the rest of the first draft of the novel in seven notebooks, each with unnumbered pages and bearing his name and Paris address: 113 Rue Notre Dame des Champs, Paris VI, France. His working title for the book, *Fiesta: A Novel*, is written on the cover of each notebook, all of which are dated with varying degrees of precision:

Book I. Valencia July 23–Aug 3

Book II. Valencia Aug 3—Madrid Aug 5–6 San Sebastian Aug 8–9, Hendaye Aug 10–11–12 Aout 1925.

Book III. Hendaye Aug 12–13–14–15–16–17 Paris Aug 19–20 Aout 1925.

Book IV. Paris Aug 20–21–22–23–24–25–26–27–28–29 Aout 1925.

Book V. Finished Sept 9 Paris.

Book VI. Sept 9—Paris.

Book VII. [Dated within at end of manuscript "Paris Sept 21, 1925."]

The following is the original chapters II and III of the first draft. Much of this was cut from the book. It includes the earliest preserved draft of the scene that Hemingway wrote about Braddocks (a pun on Ford Madox Ford) cutting Hilaire Beloc. Upon the advice of F. Scott Fitzgerald, Hemingway cut the reworked passage from the galleys of *The Sun Also Rises*. When Hemingway rediscovered this early manuscript in a trunk in the Ritz Hotel in Paris, this passage was one of the inspirations for *A Moveable Feast*, in which he wrote a revised version of it as one of the sketches of his early days in Paris.

p. 38 Niño de la Palma. Continued from loose sheets.

CHAPTER II

That was the kind of crowd we were, a fine lot. Bill was the best of the lot and he was on a hilarious drunk and thought everybody else was and became angry if they were not. Duff ~~had been somebody once~~ had something once, she still had a certain wonderful vitality and her looks, and she still had a title which she had been trying to get rid of for two years and the strain of waiting for the divorce and living like an outcast had her drinking until she was the typical Montparnasse drunk, doing absolutely nothing else except occasionally posing for people who flattered her by ~~wanting~~ begging to paint her. She always became bored with the pictures before they were finished and none of the artists even got that quality that they wanted to paint her for. Maybe it was not there. Maybe it only showed when she was drunk and as she could only command her will enough to make her pose in the early hours of the afternoon when she first got up from bed—but that is all getting poetic and speculative. Probably the best reason for her posing was that it flattered her to be asked and it gave her some shadow of something to do. She only posed for bad third rate salon painters. A Greek Duke, with a coronet on his walking sticks and little sweaty Levantine hands and face, who eventually tried to borrow money, and no one ever knew whether he was a Duke or not, a rich American who was learning to be a portrait painter and who sent his car around for her, he later became an interior decorator, and a whole group of what one called Fairies, both English and American. It is true the first rate painters had all painted her long ago. She was thirty-four years old.

She had divorced one husband for something or other, mutual consent I believe, and not until after he had put a notice in the papers that after this date he would not be responsible for any debts etc. He was a Scotchman and valued his money and found Duff quite too expensive for what he got, which wasn't much as she had married him ~~to end his pleading~~ to get rid of him bothering and to get away from home. Then she had ~~divorced her second hus~~ gotten a separation from her second husband, who had the title, because he was a dipsomaniac. He having been a sailor and learned it in the North Sea commanding a destroyer and when he found that Duff didn't love him he tried to kill her and between times slept on the floor and was never sober ~~and the~~ and ~~the~~

~~crisis came~~ had great spells of crying. They had a son and he wouldn't divorce and wouldn't give grounds for divorce ~~and in~~ but there was a separation and Duff went off with Pat one afternoon to the continent, she having offered to at lunch because Pat was lonely and sick and as she said, "One of us, obviously a good chap."

They did the whole thing before the ~~train left Dover train left~~ Boulogne train left at 9:30. ~~and~~ They ~~stayed in Paris a year~~ came to Paris on their way to Saint Jean de Guy and they stayed the night in a hotel which had only one room free and that with a double bed. "We'd no idea of anything of that sort," Duff said. "Pat said we'd go find another hotel but I said 'No why not. What's the odds.' "

Pat at that time was sick, it was all he had brought back with him from the two years he had spent in Spain in some sort of importing business except the elaborately ~~printed~~ engraved shares of the company which represented all of the ten thousand pounds he had come into from his father's estate after the war. He was also an undischarged bankrupt, which is ~~a very serious~~ quite a serious thing in England and had various habits that Duff felt sorry for and did not think a man should have and cured him by ~~the~~ constant watchfulness and the exercise of her then very strong will. Pat was a charming companion, one of the very most charming, and he was nice and he was weak but he had a certain very hard gentleness that could not be touched and that never disappeared until the liquor absolutely dissolved him entire.

Pat sober was nice, Pat a little drunk was even nicer, Pat quite drunk began to be objectionable and Pat very drunk was embarrassing. I don't know just when it was Duff became definitely a drunk, a drunk that is as she was in Montparnasse. Whether it was the boredom and the uncertainty of their position. ~~and by now she and Pat were one.~~ They spent their time in sleeping as long as possible and then drinking, that is stating a complicated process very simply, and waiting for Pat's weekly allowance which was always late and therefore always spent and borrowed into a week or more in advance. There was nothing to do but drink. Understand the drinking was not done alone in their rooms. It was all at the cafés and "parties." And each day became a replica of the day before, there were very few differences, you had been to bed late or gone to bed early, you felt ~~topping~~ good or you felt bad, you felt like eating something or you ~~felt~~ couldn't face the thought of food, it had been a good party the night before or it had been a bore, Patrick had behaved abominably or Patrick had been a model of admirable behavior, but usually it had been a good party because alcohol, either brandy and soda or whiskey and soda had a tendency to make everything much better and for a time quite all right. If Patrick had behaved well it was probably a good party and Patrick of whom I am very fond, almost as fond as I am of Duff and of whom I have given a very bad picture had a strong tendency, as I say, to behave well.

In fact you could always count on him to behave absolutely as one should until this alcoholic process had taken place which always seemed like that old experiment we did in grammar school physiology of dissolving a bone in vinegar to prove it had something or other in it. Anyway the vinegar quite changed the bone and made it very unlike its-self and you could bend it back and forth and if it was a long enough bone and you had used enough vinegar you could tie it into a knot.

Duff with drinking was quite different than Pat. She drank much more but she never lost her form, form being used in the tennis or golf sense. She was always clean bred, generous and her lines were always as sharp. It did not dissolve her in any way. But when she had been drunk she always spoke of it as having been blind, "My God, weren't we blind last night?" Short for blind drunk and the curious part was that that was just what she became. Drinking, and I mean drinking, not just the odd drink or two, or three or four cocktails, with wine at the meal, but real drinking, whiskey's and sodas from four in the afternoon until two in the morning, that kind of drinking that gets the good people because it is only the good people who can do it affected Duff in three successive stages. First she lost her power of speech and just sat and listened, then she lost her sight and saw nothing that went on, and finally she ceased to hear. And all the time anyone coming in would never know that she had been drinking.

Anyone coming in and greeting her she would ~~rouse~~ automatically respond, be pleasant to them, "Hullo: Where have you been?" but in in reality she neither heard nor saw anything.

I do not know why I have put all this down. It may mix up the story but I wanted to show you what a fine crowd we were; what a good crowd for a nineteen year old kid to get in with. ~~There were two others~~ I remember when I was ~~very~~ quite young and my parents were ~~in the~~ going through a period of great religious fervor that there were ~~many~~ several things my mother said she would rather see me in my grave than do. They were quite unimportant things such as smoking cigarettes, gambling, and drinking and the last two were quite unthought of ~~sins~~

and far off sins. Gambling I believe ~~I~~ had existed in the form of betting on the then invincible giants of the high school football team. Drinking was ~~supposed~~ coupled with gambling as a sin which my mother would rather see me in my grave than do for especial reasons as both vices were supposed to run in my mother's family and to have caused the disgrace or extinction of various uncles who contributed much to the Romance of boyhood. I attended the funeral of one of these uncles who had succumbed to a combination of ~~all~~ these vices with several others which were too terrible even to be warned against and being very young, coming late and being seated in the front row I did not perceive the uncle for a long time. There had been much talking and references to the departed brother and I, who remembered this uncle very fondly because of his notable gifts at Christmas time and because he was the first man in town to own an automobile and one of the notable patrons of the horse show and an organizer of sinister things known as French Fêtes on his grounds for the benefit of the local hospital and in other ways a source of great pride to me and not a little income looked vainly for him all through the talking and the singing. There was a soloist who sang to one side of the great mass of flowers directly in front of us, my mother and I and other black-clothed people with handkerchiefs in the front row. And as I watched the ~~pulsing and~~ prominent vocal cords of the soloist, she wore a high collar~~, and~~ made of some sort of netting, and wondered what held it up under her chin and what they had done with Uncle ~~Rafael Ernest~~ Jacob, after whom I had been named. I suddenly saw in the midst of the mass of flowers the high, gallant, hooked purple nose of Uncle ~~Rafael~~ Jacob. I had been nearly touching him all the time. I was frozen with an absolutely new sensation all through the rest of the funeral, afraid to look—and unable to look away from that majestic, cold purple nose and even afterward when my mother told me of things she would rather see me in my grave than do the words in my grave brought back Uncle ~~Rafael~~ Jacob and I thought of myself lying a ~~majestic cold purple~~ nose rising from the banks of flowers.

It seemed strange though that anything I could do would make her wish to see me in that condition and it ~~warped me~~ prejudiced me against all her views and moral values. So I will not judge the gang who were at Pamplona and I will not say that it would be better for Niño de la Palma to be in his grave than to train with a crowd like that because if he did train with them he would be in his grave soon enough and no matter how attractive a grave may seem to old people ~~or as~~ or to heroes or as an alternative to sin to religious mothers it is no place for a nineteen year old kid.

Probably any amount of this does not seem to have anything to do with the story and perhaps it has not. I am sick of these ones with their clear restrained writing and I am going to try to get in the whole business and to do that there has to be things that seem as though they ~~did~~ had nothing to do with it just as in life. In life people are not conscious of these special moments that novelists build their whole structures on. That is most people are not. That surely has nothing to do with the story but you can not tell until you finish it because none of the significant things are going to have any literary signs marking them. You have to figure them out by yourself.

Now when my friends read this they will say it is awful. ~~It is not what they had hoped or expected from me.~~ Gertrude Stein once told me that remarks are not literature. All right, let it go at that. Only this time all the remarks are going in and if it is not literature who claimed it was anyway.

~~To understand this situation in Pamplona you have to understand Paris. Not the Paris of Victor Hugo, or Murger or of 1914-1919 or the Paris of France but the section of Paris consisting of bounded at one end by the Closerie des Lilas, which is quite outside the limits, and on the other end by the so we had better make the boundaries at that end Lavigne's restaurant—the Negre de Toulouse, and at the other end by the Café Select. That is its east and west boundaries and the north boundary is the Ciqoque and the south the Dingo and the Strix and the Hotel Istria. Inside the limits is the Café du Dome, which hardly figures and the Café Rotunde which might as well be in China. There is a sort of neutral corridor leaching from this Paris to Montmartre which consists of Zelli's, Kelly's, now Shanley's and several nigger joints. This Paris is a very sad and dull place, and has few permanent inhabitants. It seems as though the lily like English and American youths and not so young who Fairies lived there permanently but this is a mistake because they take flight like the birds and go off to Brussels or London or the Basque coast to return again even more like the birds. I know they go away because I have observed the phenomenon myself and have even been questioned by certain very arrogant or extremely apologetic friends as to whether just over from England or Kansas City of Khartoum as to whether I had seen them. It is interesting that they go away and quite pleasant but the pleasure is diminished by the fact that one cannot count on it and many~~

~~times they are gone for several days and one does not notice it and so cannot enjoy it. Once I remember they were all gone to Brussels for a week and were back before I had noticed that they were gone away and a weeks enjoyment of their absence was lost.~~

~~There are other fairly permanent inhabitants.~~

CHAP III

To understand what happened in Pamplona you must understand the Quarter in Paris. ~~This is probably too much to ask of any reader. There has been so much written about the Quarter that it needs defining.~~ There is nothing romantic about the Quarter and very little that is beautiful. Roughly it is a section of Paris along the Boulevard Montparnasse and the streets just off the Boulevard. It is really more a state of mind than a geographical area. ~~For instance there is a sort of neutral corridor runs from it up to Montmartre at night.~~ This state of mind is principally contempt. Those who work have the greatest contempt for those who don't. With the loafers it is bad form to mention work. There is a woman painter who has had seven abortions in the last year and she has great contempt, concealed in pity of course, for the wife of another painter who has had five miscarriages in an attempt to have a baby. There are old painters who have contempt for young painters who feel contempt for the old painters. There are contemptuous critics and contemptuous writers. Everybody in the Quarter loathes almost everybody else and the Quarter itself. They live on because there are so many people of their own kind and because no matter how low in their minds they may feel there is some one who can be sneered at.

The only jolly people are the drunks and they eventually get depressed. The Germans too seem happy, but that perhaps is because they can only get two week visas to visit Paris and so they make a party of it. The fairies, who seem to be always present, but who really leave in periodical flights for Brussels, Berlin or the Basque Coast, to return again like the birds, even more like the birds, are not gay. The most regular residents perhaps are the ~~groups of~~ Scandinavians. They are not gay either. The Quarter characters are not happy except for the girl who can always be depended upon to shout obscenities and whose complexion, appetite and ability to get blind drunk night after night and be as cheerful as a young calf remains the same although she is getting to weigh well over two hundred pounds make her the heroine of the Quarter. It is too sad and cruel a place to write about. I have to put it in because Gerald had spent two years in it. That accounts for a great many things. During this time he had lived with a woman who lived on gossip and so he had lived in an atmosphere of abortions, doubts and incidents confirming these doubts as to the sex of different friends, dirty rumors, dirtier reports, still dirtier suspicions, and a constant fear and dread by his companion that he was going with other women and was now at the point of leaving her. Somehow during this time he wrote a novel, a first and last novel. ~~It was about his early life but.~~ He was the hero of it, but it was skillfully and neatly done and it made a nice novel. At that time he had only two friends, an English writer named ~~Bradox~~ Braddocks and myself. He gave the novel to Braddocks to read and Braddocks, who was very busy on something of his own and who, as the years went on found it increasingly difficult to read the works of writers other than himself did not read the novel but returned it to Gerald with the remark that this was excellent stuff, some excellent stuff, but there was a part, just a small part he wanted to talk over with Gerald sometime.

Gerald asked Braddocks what the part was and Braddocks replied that it was a matter of organization, a slight matter of organization.

Gerald, eager to learn and with the racial-willingness to accept useful criticism pressed to know what it was.

"I'm much too busy now to go into it Cohn. Come around some time next week and we'll talk it over."

That night after dinner, Braddocks came over to our flat. "I say," he said. "Do me a favor, that's a good chap. Read this thing of Cohn's and tell me if it's any good. Mind you I don't think that it can be any good. But read it and just let me know what it's all about."

At that time, a fellow named Dos Passos was in town and we were accustomed to go and drink in the cool of the evenings at a place called the Closerie des Lilas which is quite outside of the Quarter and where we knew a waiter who would give us two whiskeys for the price of one whiskey owing to a dislike he had for his boss.

This waiter raised potatoes in a garden outside of Paris beyond Montrouge and as we were sitting watching it get dark and the few local tarts go by in the dusk on the sidewalk and the great slow horses go by on the Boulevard streets and the people going home from work and the chauffeurs drinking in the bistro next door and talking with the waiter about his potato crop, from which he expected great things if it would rain, who should come along but Braddocks.

Braddocks came along breathing heavily and wearing a wide black hat.

"Whose that?" said Dos.

"Braddocks," said I. "The writer."

"Good God," said Dos.

"Hullo. May I join you," said Braddocks.

"Have a drink."

"What's that you chaps are drinking?"

"Whiskey," I said.

"You must be rich."

"Dos Passos," I said, "is a famous author. He wrote a book called The Holy Grail. It's about the war. He got half a million for the movie rights."

"Don't pull my leg," said Braddocks. "I know all about Dos Passos."

He settled ~~back breathing~~ heavily into his chair, breathing with difficulty.

We looked out on the Boulevard. The waiter came and went. Braddocks was haughty with him speaking literary French through his bad teeth and his mustache. Along the sidewalk came a rather tall, gray, lantern jawed man walking with a tall woman wearing an Italian infantry officer's blue cape. They looked at the table as they went past, saw no one they knew and went on. Evidently, they were looking for someone.

Braddocks clapped me on the knee.

"I say did you see me cut him? Did you see me cut him? Can't I cut people tho!"

"Who is he?"

"Belloc. Hasn't a friend in the world. I say did you see me cut him."

"Hilaire Belloc?"

"Belloc. Of course. He's absolutely done for. Absolutely through."

"What did you row with him about?"

"There was no row. Simply a matter of religious intolerance. Not a review in England will touch him, I tell you."

Dos and I left soon after. I will never forget Braddocks' face, his large red face with the walrus mustache as it gloated over the cutting. I was very impressed. I did not know that the literary life could become so intense, also I was possessed of a valuable piece of gossip.

The next afternoon I was sitting at the Café du Dôme at a table with several people. The distinguished looking lantern jawed man with the woman wearing the blue infantry cape came out of the café and past our table.

"There's Hilaire Belloc," I said to the people at the table. "He hasn't a friend in the world."

"Where?" said several people eagerly.

"There," I said, "standing with the woman in the blue cape."

"You mean that man in the gray suit?"

"Yes," I said. "There's not a review in England will publish him."

"Hell. That's not Belloc." My friend said. "That's Allister Crowley."

So I have never felt the same about Braddocks since. I would avoid, if it were possible, putting him in this story except that he was a great friend of Cohn and Cohn is the hero.

Gerald Cohn was middleweight boxing champion of Princeton: He cared nothing for boxing, in fact he disliked it, but he learned it painfully and thoroly ~~is~~ to counter-act the feeling of inferiority and shyness he had ~~felt~~ first felt on being treated as a jew at Princeton. There was a certain comfort in knowing he could knock ~~out~~ down anybody who was snotty to him altho, being very shy and a thoroly nice boy he never fought except in the gym. He was Spider Kelly's star pupil, the only complete fighter Spider ever turned out of all the young gentlemen he taught boxing to. He was so good that Spider promptly over-matched him and got his nose permanently flattened. This increased Gerald's distaste for boxing but gave him a certain sense of satisfaction and it really improved the nose ~~a~~ very much. In his last year at Princeton he read too much and took to wearing spectacles. I never met any one in his class who remembered him. They did not even remember that he was middleweight boxing champion. ~~Maybe he~~ I was always inclined to think perhaps he was not. ~~I am inclined to think he was and~~ But last year I verified it from Spider Kelly.

"Gee," said Spider. "How that kike hated to fight and what a sweet scrapper he was."

I mistrust all frank and simple people especially when their stories hold together and I had always thought that perhaps a horse had stepped on Gerald's face or that maybe his mother had been frightened or seen something or bumped into something but Spider Kelly verified the story. He was very interested to know what had become of Gerald.

Gerald Cohn was a member through his father of one of the ~~oldest~~ richest Jewish families in the east and through his mother of one of the oldest. At ~~his prep~~ the military school where he prepped for Princeton and where he had played a good end on the football team no one had made him ~~race conscious~~ conscious of his race. No one had ever made him at all race conscious until he went to Princeton. He was a nice boy, a friendly boy, and ~~a~~ very shy and it made him bitter. He took it out in boxing and he came out of Princeton with an exaggerated self consciousness and the flattened nose and was married by the first girl who was nice to him. He stayed married five years, had three children, lost the fifty thousand dollars his father left him, the balance of the estate went to his mother, hardened into a rather unattractive mold under domestic unhappiness, and just when he had made up his mind to leave his wife she left him and went off with a miniature painter. As he had been thinking for months about leaving his wife and had not done it because he felt it would be too cruel to deprive her of himself her departure was a very healthful shock.

The divorce was arranged and Gerald ~~came to Europe. He fell among literary people and was induced to back one of the first and longest lived of the many reviews to be printed in English on the continent for sale in America. It was a nice idea and they put out nearly a years the review for nearly a year before the last five thousand~~ went out to the coast. In California he fell among literary people and as he still had a little of the fifty thousand left was ~~induced~~ wheedled into backing a review of the arts. The review commenced publication in Carmel, California and finished in Provincetown Mass. By that time Gerald, who had been regarded as an angel and whose name only appeared on the Editorial page as a member of the advisory board, had become the sole editor—it was his money and he liked the power of editing. He was sorry when the magazine became too expensive and he had to give it up. By that time though he had other things to worry about. He had been taken in hand by a lady ~~with~~ who hoped to rise with the magazine. She was very forceful and he never had a chance. Also he was sure that he loved her. She saw to that. And when she saw that the magazine was not going to rise she became a little disgusted with Gerald and decided that she might as well get what there was to get while there was still something ~~to get~~ there so she urged that they go to Europe. They came to Europe, where the lady had been educated, and stayed three years. During those three years Gerald had two friends as I have said, Braddocks and myself. The lady who had him found toward the end of the second year that her looks were going and her attitude toward Gerald changed from one of careless possession and exploitation to absolute determination that he ~~would~~ should marry her. ~~I forgot to~~ During this time Gerald's mother had married again and settled a comfortable allowance on him, about three hundred dollars a month. During these two years and a half I do not believe that Gerald looked at another woman. He was fairly happy, except that he would rather have been in America, and he discovered writing. He wrote the novel and it was not a bad novel. He read a great deal, played bridge, played tennis and boxed at a local gymnasium.

I first became aware of his lady's attitude toward him one night after we had dined together. We had dined at ~~the~~ l'Avenue's restaurant and afterward had coffee at the Café de Versailles. We had several cognacs after the coffees and then I said I must go. I wanted to take a walk and then get to work. Cohn had been talking about himself and I going off on a week end trip and doing some walking. I suggested we fly to Strasbourg and walk up to Saint Odile or through some of that country.

"I know a girl in Strasbourg who can show us the town," I said.

Somebody kicked me under the table. I thought it was accidental and went on. "She's been there two years and she knows it like a book. She's a swell girl."

I was kicked again under the table and looking saw Frances, Gerald's lady, her chin lifting ~~her chin~~ and her face hardening.

"Hell," I said. "Why go to Strasbourg. We could go to Dole or up in the Ardennes."

Gerald look relieved. I was not kicked again. I said good night and went out. Gerald said he was going to buy a paper and followed me out the door of the Café.

"For God's sake," he said. "What did you say that about that girl in Strasbourg for? Didn't you see Frances?"

"No," I said. "Why should I? She's a damned nice girl who's taking her doctorate there. She's engaged to a friend of mine."

"It doesn't make any difference," Cohn said. "Any girl. I couldn't go that would be all."

"Don't be silly."

"You don't know Frances," he said. "Any girl. Didn't you see the way she looked."

"Oh well," I said. "Let's go to Senlis."

"Don't be sore."

"I'm not sore. Senlis is a nice town and we can take a little walk in the woods and then come home."

"Good," Gerald said. "That will be fine."

"Well I'll see you tomorrow at the ~~tennis~~ courts," I said. "It was a nice dinner."

"Good night," he said and started back to the Café.

"Hey," I said. "You forgot to get your paper."

"That's so," he said and walked with me up to the kiosque at the corner.

"You're not sore are you Jake?" he said as he turned with the paper in his hand.

"No," I said. "Why should I be?"

"That's fine," he said and I watched him walking back to the Café holding his paper.

I rather liked him and evidently she led him a hell of a life.

3. Item 194, 2-27 to 2-29. The following passage from the first handwritten draft of the novel is the first scene between Brett and Jake, which takes place at his apartment while the count is out getting champagne. Hemingway reworked the passage considerably in the final version, tightening the dialogue and cutting many of Brett and Jake's statements about being in love.

While I dressed I heard Duff put down glasses and then a siphon and then them talking. I dressed slowly, sitting on the bed. Somehow I felt tired. Duff came in the room, a glass in her hand, and sat on the bed.

"What's the matter Darling? Do you feel rocky?"

She kissed me on the forehead. ~~I felt ashamed that my forehead was hot from dressing.~~

"Oh Duff, I love you so much."

"Darling," she said. "Then, do you want me to send him away?"

"No. He's nice."

"I'll send him away."

"No. Don't."

"Yes. I'll send him away."

"You can't just like that."

"Can't I though."

"You stay here. He's mad about me I tell you."

She was gone out of the room. I lay back on the bed. I was having a bad time. ~~Sometimes they came like that.~~ I heard them talking but I did not listen. Duff came in and sat on the bed.

"Poor old Darling ~~Jake~~," she stroked my head.

"What did you say to him?" I was lying with my head away from her.

"Sent him for champagne. He loves to go for champagne."

Then later. "Do you feel better, Darling? Did I help you any?"

"Oh Duff."

"Lie quiet. He's gone to the other side of town."

"Couldn't we live together, Duff? Couldn't we just live together?"

"I don't think so. I'd just ~~betray~~ trompé you with everybody. You couldn't stand it."

"I stand it now."

"That would be different. It's my fault Jake. It's the way I'm made."

"Couldn't we go off in the country for a while."

"It wouldn't be any good. I'll go if you like. But I couldn't live quietly, not with my own true love."

"I know."

"Isn't it rotten. You know I feel rather quiet and ~~good~~ cool today. It's good to talk it out now when we're quiet. Isn't any use my telling you I love you."

"You know I love you."

"I love you and I'll love you always. I never told any man that."

"I love you and I'll love you always."

"It's terrible loving when you've loved so many times that you know what it is."

"I don't know. I've never loved a lot of people."

"Yes, you have."

"Not the same way."

"Oh, let's not talk. Talking's all bilge. I'm going away from you and then ~~Mike's~~ Michael's coming back."

"Why are you going away?"

"Better for you. Better for me."

"When are you going?"

"Soon as I can."

"Where?"

"San Sebastian."

"Can't we go together?"

"No. That would be a hell of a thing to do after we've just talked it out."

"We never agreed."

"Oh you know as well as I do. Don't be obstinate ~~Jake~~ Darling."

"All right," I said, "you're right."

I sat up, found my shoes at the side of the bed, put them on and stood up.

"Don't look like that, Darling."

"How do you want me to look?"

"Oh don't be a fool. I'm going away tomorrow."

"Tomorrow?"

"Yes, didn't I say so? Well I am."

"Let's have a drink then. The count will be back."

"Yes, he should be back. You know he's extraordinary about buying champagne. It means any amount to him."

4. Item 194, 3-53. Hemingway's brief outline of the chapter-by-chapter progression of the novel, handwritten on the back of the third notebook. This is the only existing outline that he wrote.

Chap XIII—finishes with Gerald not going

Chap XIV Ride to Burguete Fishing return to Pamplona.

Chap XV Duff Gerald and Mike there Desencajonada—which we get in. the party out at the wine shop. Mike's first out burst.

Chap XVI Encierro, first corrida brings back to point where book starts. Goes on with that night—the South American. the dancing place. Noel Murphy. Count shows up.

XVII Duff sleeps with Niño de la Palma. Gerald fights with Niño.

XVIII Corrida. Duff goes off with Niño. Count refuses Mike job. Bill goes to Paris. Mike talks, goes to Saint Jean de Luz to wait for Duff. Gerald talks, goes to Saint Jean de Luz San Sebastian. afterwards Paris. I go on down into Spain to bring Duff back. get her letter.

5. Item 194, 4-7, 4-11 to 4-14. The following passages from the first handwritten draft of the novel relate two stories about a man frozen in a glacier in the Alps, which Hemingway cut down to a brief mention when Jake Barnes and Bill Gorton are fishing on the Irati River in chapter XII. The first story, by A. E. W.

Mason, is titled "The Crystal Trench" and is quoted extensively, while the second story was conceived by Hemingway.

It was around noon and there was not much shade but I sat against the trunks of two of the trees that grew together and read. The book was something by A. E. W. Mason and I was reading a wonderful story about a man who had been frozen in the Alps and then fallen into a glacier and disappeared and his bride was going to wait 24 years exactly for his body to come out on the Moraine while her true love waited too and they were still waiting when Bill came up. . . . [Item 194, 4-7]

Afterwards Bill lay down to sleep ~~with his head on his arm~~ and I went back to A. E. W. Mason. Bill was sleeping, his head on his arm. I took a paper out of the pack and spread it over his face to keep the flies ~~away~~ off. He stirred but went on sleeping. In the story I was reading they were both grown old. Twenty-four years had passed. She was no longer a bright English school girl bride. She was a middle aged woman and together they were going back to keep their rendezvous with the glacier. I lit a cigarette. It was a splendid story you could see what was going to happen. I wished it was not so short. It was the last story in the book I had not read. I went on reading. He found the body all right.

Under the ice Mark Frobisher lay quietly, like a youth asleep. The twenty-four years had cut not a line about his mouth, not a wrinkle about his eyes. The years had taken no toll of him. He was as young, his features were as clear and handsome, as on the day when he had set out upon his tragic expedition. And over him bent his wife, a woman worn, lined, and old.

You could feel it coming.

He gently raised Stella Frobisher to her feet.

"Will you stand aside for a little?" he said. "I will call you."

She moved obediently a few yards away, and Challoner summoned the porters. Very carefully they cut the ice away. They waved like the ad for the mausoleum where the workmen laid every stone with reverent fingers.

Then he called aloud:

"Stella!" And she returned.

There was no sheet of ice between them now; the young man and the worn woman who had spent a couple of months of their youth together met thus at last. But the meeting was as brief as a spark.

The airs of heaven beat upon Mark Frobisher, and suddenly his face seemed to quiver and his features to be obscured. Stella uttered a scream of terror, and covered her face with her hands.

Just as you thought. But there was something else. While he crumbled a small trifle tinkled on the ice with a metallic sound.

I read on about the trifle. The trifle was the point of the whole story. I was sorry that it was the last story. I shut the book and wondered if I could get any more A. E. W. Mason's at the railway library in Pamplona. Maybe there would be a Stanley Weyman, maybe there would be a Sax Rolmer. It was funny about the glacier. Why did not some one write some good mountain stories. ~~Lots of writers went there. It was full of them. I thought of a~~ Once I was on the Todenfeldt glacier, the snow was blowing and the ice was blown clear of snow. Blue ice humped out in the sunlight. It clouded over and the glacier was dark and you could not see the ice for the snow blowing. We brought down a dead German with a rope around him. His wife was down in the club hut waiting for everyone to come down to supper. The avalanche had not treated him like Mark Frobisher. When we dug him out, he was doubled back like a folding ruler ~~all broken~~. He had been facing it and it bent him back the wrong way. We ski-ied down with him. Sometimes we hauled him and sometimes we let him slide on ahead. Down below was the hut with snow blowing around it. When we came in sight of the hut I went ahead to get a blanket. At the end toward the wind the shutters were up. As I came around the corner I saw his wife inside through the window. She was sitting beside the stove mending his socks. I put the skis against the wall of the hut and opened the door and went in. The caretaker was cutting wood in the entryway. I opened the main door and went in.

His wife looked up. I saw she was disappointed it was me.

"Heil," she said.

I went on into the Mathassen lager to get a blanket. She was sitting there by the stove mending his socks. He was a doctor from Frankfurt. I ~~couldn't~~ went out with the blanket. I had it rolled up and I hoped she wouldn't notice it.

"What? You're going out," she said.

"Just to see Ignatz."

Ignatz was the caretaker. I gave him the blanket and told him about it and he put on his skis and started out. I got down my own skis and put them on ~~again and started out~~. I went in the opposite direction from where they were coming down with him and stayed away for an hour.

Finally it was dark and I had to come back to the hut. You could write a story about that.

"Say," said Bill from under the paper. "What do you say we start back?"

"Through sleeping?"

"I've been awake for half an hour."

His head came out from under the newspaper and he sat up.

"You go to sleep?"

"No I was thinking."

"What about?"

"In the winter up in the mountains."

"In the winter time when the willowy wind—" ~~in the wood shed on the window pane in the woodshed." and the women folks ride velocepedes~~

"That's it." [Item 194, 4-11 to 4-14]

6. Item 195a. Handwritten four-page first draft of the scene between Jake and the waiter about the goring of Vicente Gironés during the running of the bulls. Hemingway added this scene into what became chapter XVII after he had already written that part in his fifth notebook.

INSERT BOOK V

Back in the town I went to the café to have a second coffee and some buttered toast. The waiters were sweeping out and mopping off the tables. One came up and took my order.

"Anything happen at the encierro?" he asked.

"I didn't see it all," I said. "One man was badly cogida."

"Where?"

"Here." I put my hands on the small of my back and on my chest where it looked as though the horn had come out.

The waiter nodded his head and swept the crumbs from the table with his cloth.

"Badly cogida," he said and nodded his head. "All for sport. All for pleasure." He went away and came back with the coffee and milk pots.

He poured the milk and coffee from the long spouts into the big cup. He nodded his head.

"Badly cogida through the back," he said, putting the pots down on the table and sitting in the chair opposite me. "A big horn wound. All for fun you understand. Just for fun. What do you think of that?"

"I don't know."

"That's the way. All for fun. Fun you understand."

"You're not an aficionado?"

He shook his finger.

"What are bulls? Animals. That's not fun." He stood up. "Right through the back. A cornada right through the back. For fun—you understand."

He shook his head and walked away.

Two men coming from the Plaza went by in the street. The waiter shouted to them. They were grave looking. One shook his head.

"Muerto," he called. It was a bad sounding word.

The waiter nodded his head. The two men went on. They were evidently on some errand. The waiter came over to my table.

"You hear? Dead. He's dead. With a horn through him. All for fun. Muy flamenco. You like that?"

"It's bad. Very bad."

"Not for me," the waiter said. "No fun in that for me."

Later in the morning we learned that the man who had been killed was named Vicente Gironés and came from near Tafalla. He was twenty-eight years old and had a farm, a wife and two children. His wife came in from Tafalla to get the body and after a service in the chapel of San Fermín the coffin was carried to the [manuscript ends]

7. Item 194, 6-13 to 6-20. The handwritten first draft of Romero's ultimate bullfight. Romero is still called Guerrita. Hemingway reworked this scene several times to improve the description and drama of the event to maximum effect.

Guerrita had the greatness. He loved bull fighting and I think he loved the bulls and then, at least, he loved Duff. Everything that he could control the locality of he did in front of her all that afternoon. Never once did he look up. He made it stronger that way and did it for himself too as well as for her. Because he did not look up to ask if it pleased he did it all for himself inside and it strengthened him and yet he did it for her too. But he did not do it for her at any loss to himself. He gained by it all through the afternoon.

His first <u>quite</u> was directly below us. The three matadors take the bull in turn after each charge he makes at a horse. Belmonte had the first. Marcial the second and then came Guerrita. The three of them were standing at the left of the horse. The picador, his hat down over his eyes, ~~his~~ the shaft of his pic angling sharply toward the bull, kicked in the spurs and held them and with the reins in his left hand walked the horse ~~a~~ forward toward the bull. The bull was watching, ~~Guerrita was~~ seemingly watching the white horse but really watching the steel shod point of the pic. Guerrita, watching, saw the bull start to turn his head. He did not want to charge. Guerrita flashed his cape so the color caught the bull's eye and the bull charged with the reflex, charged and found not color but a white horse and a man leaning far down shot the ~~stick~~ steel point of the long hickory shaft into the bull's shoulder and pulled his horse sideways as he pivoted on the pic, making a wound, enforcing the iron into the bull's shoulder, cutting him down further to size for Belmonte.

The bull did not insist under the iron. He did not really want to get at the horse. He turned and the group broke apart and Guerrita was taking him out with his cape. He took him out softly and smoothly then stopped and standing square in front of the bull offered him the cape. The bull wanted it and came and Guerrita ~~did not side step~~ moved one step to the side and swung the cape. The dampened, mud weighted cape swung open and full as a sail fills and Guerrita turned with it just ahead of the bull. At the end of the pass they were facing each other again. Guerrita smiled. The bull wanted it again and Guerrita's cape filled again, this time on the other side. Each time let the bull come so close that the man and the bull and the cape that filled out ~~ahead~~ pivoting ahead of the bull all were one mass. And it was all so slow and so controlled. It was as though he were rocking the bull to sleep. He made four veronicas like that and finished with a half veronica that turned his back on the bull and came away toward the applause, his hand on his hip, his cape on his arm and the bull watching his back going away.

In his own bulls he was perfect. His first bull did not see well. After the first two passes with the cape Guerrita knew just how badly the vision was impaired and worked accordingly. It was not brilliant bull fighting it was only perfect bull fighting. The crowd wanted the bull changed. They made a great row. Nothing very fine could happen with a bull with defective vision but the President waved not [to] order him ~~changed~~ replaced.

"Why don't they change him?" Duff asked.

"They've paid for him. They don't want to lose their money."

"One would think they'd have to give another for a blind bull."

"Yes," I said. "But he may have done it banging against the wall of the chiquero before he came out."

"It's hardly fair for Guerrita."

"Well," I said. "The crowd give him credit. Watch how he handles a bull that can't see the capes."

"It's the sort of thing I don't like to see."

It was not nice to watch if you cared anything about the person who was doing it. ~~Duff was right.~~ With a bull who could not see the color of the capes or the scarlet flannel of the muleta Guerrita had to make the bull consent with his body. He had to get so close that the bull saw his body and started for it and then Guerrita would shift the bulls charge to the flannel and finish out the pass in the classic manner. The Biarritz crowd did not like it. They thought Guerrita was afraid and that was why he gave that little side step each time as he transferred the ~~bulls lure~~ bull's charge from his own body to the muleta. They preferred Belmonte's imitation of himself or Marcial's imitation of Belmonte. There were three of them one row behind us.

"What's he afraid of the bull for?" one said. "The bull's so dumb he only goes after the cloth."

"He's just a young bull fighter. He hasn't learned it well yet."

"But I thought he was very good with the cape on the last bull."

"Probably he's gotten nervous now."

Out in the center of the ring Guerrita, ~~was~~ all alone, was going on with the same thing, getting so close to the horns that the bull could see him plainly, offering the body, offering it again a little closer, the bull watching dully, then so close that the bull thought he had him, offering again and getting the charge and then as the horns started giving the bull the red cloth to follow with that little almost imperceptible jerk that so offended the critical judgement of the Biarritz bull fight experts.

"He's going to kill now," I said to Duff. Duff gripped the rail.

"The bull's still strong," I said. "He wouldn't wear himself out."

Out in the center of the ring Guerrita profiled in front of the bull, drew the sword out from the folds of the muleta, rose on his toes and sighted along the blade. The bull charged as Guerrita charged, Guerrita's left hand dropped the muleta over the bull's muzzle to blind him, his left shoulder went forward between the horns as the sword went in and for just an instant he and the bull were one figure, he way out over the bull, the right arm extended high up to the high place between the bulls shoulders. Then the figure was broken, there was a little jolt as Guerrita came clear and then he was standing one hand up, ~~toward~~ facing the bull, his shirt ripped out from under his sleeve, and the white blowing in the wind and the bull, the red sword hilt tight between his shoulders, his head dropping and his legs settling.

"There he goes," Bill said.

Guerrita was close enough so the bull could see him. His hand still up. He spoke to the bull. The bull gathered himself, then his head went out and he went over ~~suddenly~~ slowly, then all over, suddenly, four feet in the air.

"That's not a stylish way to kill them," I said. "But it's one way."

They handed the sword to Guerrita and carrying it blade down, the muleta in his other hand he walked over to in front of the President's box, bowed, straightened and came over to the barrera and handed over the sword and muleta.

"Bad one," said the sword handler.

"He made me sweat," said Guerrita. He wiped off his face and put on his hat.

The sword handler handed over the water jug. Guerrita wiped his lips.

"Not so good," he took the cape. "All right if you like it."

He did not look up at us.

Marcial had a big day. They were still applauding him when Guerrita's last bull came in. It was the bull that had sprinted out and killed the man in the morning running. ~~It was on this bull that he cured his face~~ This bull made ~~us~~ Guerrita happy again. Also he made the crowd happy who had felt defrauded in Belmonte, incidentally he destroyed Marcial's triumph. That was only incidental. He did not care anything about Marcial or Marcial's triumph. Marcial was an imitation, a very wonderful imitation that many times looked better than the original. He was himself and he had the greatness and he felt whole again inside.

During his first bull his hurt face had been very noticeable. Everything he did showed it. All the concentration of the awkwardly delicate working with the bull that could not see well brought it out. It was the battered face of a fighter coming out of the side entrance of the old garden after a hard fight. The fight with Cohn had not touched his spirit. That in the end was what destroyed Cohn. But his face had been smashed and his body hurt. He was wiping all that out now. Each thing he did with the bull wiped that out a little. As he worked with the bull he wiped all that away. It was a good bull, a big bull and with horns and it turned quickly and re-charged easily and surely. He was what Guerrita wanted in bulls. When he had finished with the muleta the crowd made him go on and he went on. It was like a course in bull fighting, all the passes linked up, all completed, all slow, templed and smooth. They were all sincere, there were no tricks and no mystifications and each pass as it reach its ~~climax~~ summit, that instant when the man and the bull are in the position that has been led up to reached and each pass gave me that ache inside that only comes from greatness. Then the bull was calmed and squared on all four feet ~~away~~ to be killed and Guerrita killed directly below us. He killed not as he had been forced to by the last bull but as he wanted to. Not blinding the bull with the muleta but only indicating to him how he should go, executing perfectly the three tempos of the Volapié the ~~most beautiful~~ best thing I know to watch in bull fighting. ~~After~~ He profiled and sighted along the blade, ~~he~~ made the three steps, the one that takes the measure, the one that gets there and then the one that carries the left shoulder forward and drives in the sword, the left hand crossed in front of the chest gives the bull the sortie with the muleta and the swordsman, having been one with the bull is then alone, the bull having broken the figure himself because the man has planned it so.

Handkerchiefs were waving all over the stands ~~and~~ before the bull was dead. ~~He~~ The bull went down ~~to~~ on his knees and ~~the puntillero~~ Guerrita's older brother ~~went~~ leaned forward between him and drove a short knife into ~~his~~ the bull's neck just at the base of the horns. The bull went over, twitching and rigid. Guerrita's brother looked up at the President. All the handkerchiefs were waving ~~now~~. The President waved his and the brother leaning over cut the notched black ear from the dead bull and trotted over with it to Guerrita. Guerrita held it up toward the President. The President bowed and Guerrita, running to get ahead of the crowd came toward us. He leaned up against the barrera and gave the ear to Duff. He nodded his head and smiled. The crowd were all about him. Duff held down the cape.

"You like it?" Guerrita called.

Duff did not say anything. They looked at each other and smiled. Duff had the ear in her hand.

"Don't get bloody," Guerrita said and grinned. The crowd wanted him. Several boys shouted at Duff. They were the ~~kids~~ boys, the rough-necks and the drunks. Guerrita turned and tried to get through the crowd. They were all around him trying to lift him up and put him on their shoulders. He fought and twisted away and started running in the midst of them toward the exit. He did not want to be carried on people's shoulders. But they held him and lifted him. It was uncomfortable and his legs were spraddled and his body was very sore. ~~He felt suddenly very tired and hollow inside.~~ They were lifting him and all running toward the gate. He had his hand on somebody's shoulder and he looked around at us apologetically. The crowd, running, went out the gate with him.

8. Item 194, 6-25 to 6-55. The handwritten first draft of the last part of the novel, which would be designated Book III. Hemingway made considerable revisions to this final section of the book, which can be compared to the published version.

CHAPTER XXI

In the morning it was all over. The fiesta was finished. I woke about nine o'clock, ~~dressed, bathed~~ rang for a bath, dressed and went downstairs. The square was empty and the streets were deserted. The town was quiet. A few children were picking up rocket sticks in the square. The cafés were just opening up and the waiters were carrying out the com-fortable white wicker chairs and arranging them around the tables in the shade of the arcade. They were sweeping the streets and sprinkling them with a hose.

I sat in one of the wicker chairs and leaned back comfortably. The waiter was in no hurry to come. The ~~notices also~~ white paper announce-ments of the unloading of the bulls and the big schedules of special trains were still up on the pillars of the arcade. A waiter ~~came out with an apron~~ wearing an apron came out with a bucket of water and a cloth and ~~tore~~ commenced to tear down the notices, pulling the paper off in strips and washing and rubbing away that which stuck to the stone. The fiesta was over.

I had a coffee and after a while Bill came over. ~~and sat down too~~ I watched him come walking across the square. He sat down and ordered a coffee.

"Well," he said. "It's all over."

"Yes," I said. "When do you go?"

"I don't know. We better get a car I think. Aren't you going back to Paris?"

"No. I can stay away another week. I think I'll go to San Sebastian."

"I want to get back."

"What's Mike going to do?"

"He's going to Saint Jean de Luz."

"Let's get a car and all go as far as Bayonne. You can get the train up from there tonight."

"Good. Let's go after lunch."

"All right. I'll get the car."

We had lunch, paid the bill, Quintana did not come near us, one of the maids brought the bill, and the car was outside. ~~We took all the baggage~~ The chauffeur piled and strapped the bags on top of the car and put them in beside him in the front seat and we got in and the car went out of the square, along through the side streets, out under the trees and down the hill and away from Pamplona. It was a good ride. Mike had a bottle of Fundador. I only took a couple of drinks. We came down the white roads and through the over foliaged, wet green Basque country and finally into Bayonne. We left Bill's baggage at the station and bought him a ticket. His train left at seven ten for Paris. We came out of the station.

"What should we do about the car?" Bill asked.

"Oh bother the car," Mike said. "Let's just keep the car with us."

"All right," Bill said. "Where will we go?"

"Let's go to Biarritz and have a drink."

"All right. If money doesn't mean anything to you."

We drove to Biarritz and left ~~stopped~~ the car outside a very Ritz like place. We went in to the bar and sat on high stools and drank a whiskey and soda.

"That ~~one's~~ drink's mine," Mike said.

"Let's roll for it," I said.

So we rolled poker dice out of a deep ~~rolling~~ leather dice cup. ~~It was~~ Bill was out first roll. Mike lost to me and handed the bar tender a hundred franc note. The whiskeys were ~~fifteen~~ twelve francs apiece.

We had another round and Mike lost again. Each time he gave the bar tender a good tip. There was some good jazz music playing. It was a pleasant bar. We had another round. I went out on the first roll with four kings. Bill and Mike rolled. Mike won with four Jacks on the first roll. Bill won the second roll, on the ~~second~~ final roll ~~he~~ Mike had three kings and let them stay. He handed the dice box to Bill. Bill rolled the dice out and there were three kings, an ace and a queen. He pushed the three kings to one side and shook the two other dice in the leather cup and slanted them out onto the board. One of them was a king.

"It's yours, Mike," Bill said. "Four kings in two."

"I'm sorry," said Mike. "I can't get it."

"What's the matter?"

"I've no money," Mike said. "I'm stony. ~~Have~~ I've just twenty francs. Here, take twenty francs."

Bill's face sort of changed.

"I just had enough to pay Quintana," Mike said. "Damned lucky to have it, too."

"I'll cash you a check," Bill said.

"That's damned nice of you," Mike said. "But you see, I can't write checks. I'm an undischarged bankrupt."

"What are you going to do for money?"

"Oh some will come through. I've two week's allowance should be here. I can live on tick at this pub."

"What do you want to do about the car?" Bill asked me. "Do you want to keep it on?"

"It doesn't make any difference. Seems sort of idiotic."

"Come let's have another drink," Mike said.

"Fine. This one's on me," Bill said. "Has Duff any money?" he turned to Mike.

"I shouldn't think so. She put up most of what I gave to old Quintana."

~~"Well," said~~

"She hasn't any money with her?" I said.

"I shouldn't think so. She never has any money. She gets five hundred quid a year from Ashley and pays three hundred and fifty of it out in interest to Jews."

"I suppose they get it at the source," Bill said.

"Quite. They're not really jews. We just call them jews. They're Scotsmen I believe."

"Hasn't she any at all with her?" I asked.

"I hardly think so. She gave it all to me when she left."

"Well," Bill said. "We might as well have another drink."

"Damned good idea," Mike said. ~~You know~~ "One never gets any-where by discussing finances."

"No," said Bill.

~~We paid for~~

Bill and I rolled for the two rounds. Bill lost and paid.

We went out to the car.

"Anywhere you'd like to go, Mike?" Bill asked.

"Let's take a drive. It would do my credit ~~a lot of~~ good. Let's drive about a little."

"Fine. I'd like to see the coast. Let's drive down toward Hendaye."

"I haven't any credit along the coast," Mike said.

"You can't ever tell," said Bill.

We drove along the coast road. There was the green of the head-lands, the white red-roofed villas, the patches of forest and the ocean very blue with the tide out and the water curling at the edge of the wide beaches. We drove through the town of Saint Jean de Luz and passed through ~~several~~ villages further along the coast. Back from the rolling country and the headlands were the mountains we had come over from Pamplona. The road stretched on ahead. Bill ~~signaled for the driver to stop the car. He~~ looked at his watch. It was time for us to go back. ~~He~~ I knocked on the glass and told the driver to turn around. He backed the car into the grass to turn it. In back of us was woods, below a stretch of meadow and then the sea.

At the ~~pension~~ hotel where Mike was going to stay we stopped the car and he got out. The chauffeur carried in his bags.

"Well good bye you chaps," Mike said. "It was a damned fine fiesta."

"So long, Mike," Bill said.

"I'll see you around," I said.

"Don't worry about money," Mike said. "You pay for the car Jake and I'll send you my share."

"So long, Mike."

"So long you chaps. You've been damned nice." We all shook hands.

We got to Bayonne just ~~in time~~ before the train left. A porter carried Bill's bags in. I went as far as the inner gate to the tracks.

"So long fella," Bill said.

"So long Kid."

"It was swell. It was a swell fiesta."

"Will you be in Paris?" I asked.

"No, I have to sail on the seventeenth. So long fella."

"So long Kid."

He went in to the train. The porter went ahead with the bags. I watched the train pull out. Bill was at one of the windows. He waved and the window passed, the rest of the train passed and the tracks were empty.

I went outside to the car.

"How much do we owe you?" I asked the driver.

The price to Bayonne had been fixed at a hundred and fifty pesetas.

"Two hundred pesetas," he said.

"How much more will it be if you drive me to San Sebastian on your way back?"

He thought for a minute.

"Fifty pesetas," he said.

"Don't kid me," I said.

"Thirty five pesetas."

"It's not worth it. Drive me to the hotel Panier Fleure."

At the hotel I paid him and gave him a tip. ~~He drove away down the street.~~ The car was dusty. I rubbed a finger in the dust. It seemed the last thing that connected me with Spain and the fiesta. The driver put the car in gear and went down the street. I saw it turn off to take the road to Spain. I went into the hotel and ~~got~~ they gave me a room. It was the same room I had slept in when Bill and Cohn and I were in Bayonne. That seemed a very long time ago. I washed, changed my shirt and went out in the town. At the café I read the papers and a copy of the New York Herald. It felt strange to be in France again. There was a safe, suburban feeling. I wished I had gone up to Paris with Bill except that would have meant more fiesta-ing in Paris and I was through with fiestas. It would be quiet in San Sebastian. The season did not open until August and I could get a good hotel room and read and swim. It was a splendid place to swim. You could lie on the beach and soak in the sun and get straightened around inside again. Maybe I would feel like writing. San Sebastian was a good place. There were wonderful trees along the promenade above the beach and there were good looking children sent down with their nurses before the season opened. In the evening there would be band concerts under the trees across from the Café Marinas. ~~When the tide~~ There was a nice old port. It would be quiet and solid and restful.

Inside the café was a restaurant.

"How does one eat inside?" I asked the waiter.

"Very well. One eats very well."

"Good."

I went in and had a very decent supper. It was a big meal for France but it seemed very carefully measured and apportioned after Spain. I drank a bottle of wine for company. It was a Chateau Margaux. It was pleasant to be drinking slowly and lastingly and to be drinking alone. A bottle of wine was good company. Afterwards I had coffee and the waiter recommended a Basque liqueur called Izzarra. He brought it in the bottle and said it was made of flowers of the Pyrenees. The real flowers of the Pyrenees. It looked like hair oil and smelled like Italian Strega. I told him to take the flowers of the Pyrenees away and bring me a vieux Marc. The Marc was good. I had ~~two glasses~~ another after the coffee. The waiter seemed a little offended about the flowers of the Pyrenees so I tipped him a little. That made him happy. It seemed comfortable to be in a country where it is so simple to make people happy. You can never tell whether a Spanish waiter will thank you. Everything is on such a clear financial basis in France. It is the simplest country to live in. No one makes things complicated by becoming your friend for any obscure reason. If you want people to like you you have only to spend a little money. I spent a little money and the waiter liked me. He appreciated my valuable qualities. He would be glad to see me back again sometime and he would want me at his table. It would be a sincere liking because it would have a sound basis. I was back in France.

The next morning I tipped everyone a little too much at the hotel to make more friends and left on the morning train for San Sebastian. At the station I did not tip the porter more than I should because I did not think I should ever see him again. So I did not care about his good opinion. I only wanted a few good French friends in Bayonne in case I should come back there again. I knew if they remembered me their friendship would be loyal. At Irun we had to change trains and show passports. I hated to leave France. Life was so simple in France. Never in France have I had any trouble nor have I had any adventures. In Spain you could not tell about anything. ~~Spain was another country.~~ I felt I was a fool to be going back into it but I stood in line with my passport and opened my bags and bought a new ticket and went through a gate and climbed onto the train and after forty minutes and five tunnels I was at San Sebastian.

Even on a hot day San Sebastian has a certain early morning quality.

The trees seem as though their leaves were never quite dry. The streets feel as though they had just been sprinkled. It is always cool and shady on certain streets on the hottest day. I went to a hotel in the town where I had stopped before and the woman who ran it took me up in the elevator and gave me a room with a balcony ~~that~~ from which you could see the roofs of the town and a green mountain side beyond them. There was ~~running~~ a bath with the room and a reading light at the head of the bed. I unpacked my bags and stacked my books on the table at the head of the bed, put out my shaving things, hung up some clothes in the big armoire and made up a bundle for the laundry. Then I had a wash and enjoyed the luxuriousness of the bathroom and went down to lunch. Spain had not changed to summer time and so I set my watch again. I had recovered an hour by coming to San Sebastian.

As I went in to the dining room the concierge brought me a police bulletin to fill out. I signed it, asked him for a telegraph form and wrote a message to the Hotel Quintana telling them to forward all mail and telegrams for me to this address. I calculated how many days I would be in San Sebastian and then asked for another form and wrote a wire to the office asking them to hold mail but forward all wires to me here for six days. Then I went in and had lunch.

It was pleasant to have ~~too much~~ a great amount of food served again. You did not have to eat it and it was nice not to have that measured French feeling. There was only an old man in the dining room. He was eating a big lunch over against the window. He talked to his waitress when she brought him dishes and she seemed to be amused. I had Borrow's Bible in Spain with me and read through the meal and drank a bottle of Alta Navarra. Afterwards I went upstairs, read a while and went to sleep. When I woke it was half past four and I found my swimming suit in one of the bags, put Borrow and a comb in my pocket and went downstairs and out the door and up the street to the concha. The tide was about half way out. The beach was smooth and firm and the sand yellow. I went into a bathing cabin, undressed, put on my suit and walked across the ~~smooth~~ sand to the sea. The sand was firm and warm under bare feet. There were quite a few people in the water and on the beach. The tide was going out and out. ~~across the harbor of the concha there was a white line of breakers beyond the harbor where there was open sea.~~ beyond where the headlands of the concha almost met to form the harbor there was a white line of breakers and the open sea. Although the tide was going out there ~~was a~~ were a few slow rollers. They were like undulations in the water, ~~that~~ came in, gathered weight of water, and then broke smoothly on the warm sand. I waded out. The water was cold. As a roller came I dove, swam under water, and came up with all the chill gone. I swam out to the raft, pulled myself up and lay for a few minutes on the hot planks. A boy and girl were at the other end. ~~The She had~~ The girl had undone the top strap of her bathing suit and was browning her back. The boy lay ~~on his~~ face downward on the raft and talked to her. She laughed at things he said. I ~~dove off~~ lay on the raft in the sun until I was dry. Then I tried several dives. I dove deep once swimming down to the bottom, I swam with my eyes open and it was green and dark. The raft made a dark shadow. I came out of the water beside the raft, pulled up, dove once more, holding it for distance, and then swam ashore. I lay on the beach in the sun until I was dry and then went into the bathing cabin, took off my suit, sloshed myself with fresh water and rubbed dry.

Up under the trees I walked around the harbor to the casino and then up one of the cool streets to the Café Marina. There was music in the café and I sat outside on the terrasse, watched the people, enjoyed the fresh coolness in the hot day and the good feeling after swimming and had first an ~~lemon ice~~ Helados lemon, lemon juice and shaved ice, and then a long whiskey and soda.

San Sebastian was a good place. It was a good place to get all straightened inside again. I had a lot of books, a Turgenieff, two Mrs. Belloc-Lowndes, the Bible in Spain, I could get Tauchnitz if I wanted them. It would be fun to swim, to get up late, to eat good meals and read. Then I could go back to Paris and get to work again. Paris would be nice and it would be fun to eat out at the Parc Montsouris and at the Quatre Sergents de la Rochelle again. It was always fun to get back to Paris.

After the concert was over inside the café I paid for my drink and walked out to the old harbor. Then I walked all the way around the harbor, along the promenade and way beyond and then turned back and walked into the town and to the hotel to get supper. I was very hungry. It was beginning to get dark as I came away from the harbor and through the streets to the hotel. There was some sort of bicycle race on, the tour of the Basque provinces, and the riders were stopping that night in San Sebastian. In the dining room there was a long table of bicycle riders, their trainers and the managers of the bicycle firms they rode for. They were all French and Belgians and paid close attention to their meal but were having a good time. At the head of the table were two very good looking French girls with much Rue du Faubourg Montmartre chic. I could not make out who they belonged to. They all spoke in slang at the long table and there were many private jokes and jokes at the far end of the table which were not repeated when the girls asked to hear them. The next morning at five thirty o'clock the race would resume as the last lap from San Sebastian to Bilbao. The French riders did not think much of the competition given them by the Spaniards. They did not take the race seriously except among themselves. They had raced among themselves so often that it did not make much difference who won especially in a foreign country. It was only the money. That could be arranged. They drank much wine and were all burned and browned by the sun. The man who was a matter of two minutes in the lead in the race had an attack of boils which were very painful. He sat on the small of his back and his red brown neck with sun burned blond hairs slanted forward. One of the riders made a joke about his boils and said the leader would never be able to stand the saddle on the next day and the leader said "You think so? Tomorrow my nose is so tight on the handle bars that the only thing touches those boils is a lovely breeze."

One of the girls looked at him and he grinned and turned red. He did not want to turn red. He was the leader. He had two minutes and forty-five seconds advance. The Spaniards, they said, did not know how to pedal.

I had coffee and a brandy with the team manager of one of the big bicycle ~~companies~~ manufacturers. He said it had been a very pleasant race and would have been worth watching if Bottechia had not abandoned at Pamplona. The dust had been bad but in Spain the roads were better than in France. Bicycle road racing was the only sport in the world, he said. There were no other sports which called for as much from a man day after day. Had I ever followed the Tour de France? Only in the papers. The Tour de France was the greatest sporting event in the world. All spring and summer and fall he spent on the roads with the riders. It had made him know France. That is a thing few people know. It was a very ~~strange country. He knew~~ beautiful country. A very rich country. The number of motor cars now that followed the racers from town to town on the great circuit. It was a rich country and more <u>sportif</u> every year. It would be the most <u>sportif</u> country in the world. It was road racing did it, road racing and football. He knew France—<u>La France Sportif.</u> He knew road racing.

After all though it wasn't so bad to be back in Paris. Not so bad. There is only one Paris. Paris is the town the most <u>sportif</u> in the world.

Did I know the Chope du Negre. Did I not. I would see him there some time. I certainly would. We would drink another coffee and fine together. We certainly would. They started at six o'clock less a quarter in the morning. Would I be up for the depart? I would certainly try to. Would I like him to call me? It was interesting this early morning depart. I would leave a call at the desk. He would not mind calling me. I could not let him take the trouble. I would leave a call. We said goodbye until the next morning. I had meant to ask about the girls but we had only had one fine.

In the morning when I awoke the bicycle riders, their following cars, and all had been on the road for three hours. I had coffee and the papers in bed and then dressed and took my bathing suit down to the beach. It was pleasant walking to the beach, there were fine shops with sport clothes ~~behind and~~ in big show windows, there were many banks and there were big cafés and nurses in uniform and peasant costume with chickens walking under the trees. Everything was fresh and cool and damp in the early morning. Bootblacks sat together under the trees talking to a soldier back from Africa. The soldier had one arm gone. The tide was in and there was a good breeze and a surf on the beach.

I ~~dressed and~~ undressed in one of the cabins, it was not yet hot in the sun, and went ~~into the water~~ out and crossed the narrow line of beach and went into the water. I swam out, trying to swim through the rollers but having to dive sometimes when they broke and then in the quieter water turned and floated. Floating I could see nothing but the sky and feel the drop and lift of the water. I swam back to the surf and coasted face down on a big roller, then turned and swam along, trying to keep in the trough and not have a wave break over me. ~~The rollers were fun.~~ I felt a little tired and swam slowly out to the raft. The water felt buoyant and cold as though you could never sink. I swam slowly, it seemed like a long swim with ~~so much~~ a high tide and then pulled up on the raft and sat, dripping on the boards that were becoming hot in the sun. I ~~felt~~ looked around at the bay, the old town, the casino, the wonderful trees and the line of big hotels with their white porches and gold lettered names. ~~It was a fine place.~~ Off on the right almost closing the harbor was a green hill with a castle on it. I had seen lights in the castle last night. The raft rocked with the motion of the water. On the other side of the narrow gap that led out into the sea was another high headland. I thought I would like to swim across the bay but was afraid of a cramp. It would be fun alone out in the bay. I sat in the sun and watched the bathers, looking very small on the beach. After a while I stood up, gripped with my toes on the edge of the raft as it tipped with my weight and dove cleanly and deeply to come up through the lightening water to the air, blew out and swam steadily to shore.

After I was dressed and had paid for the bath cabin I walked back to the hotel. The <u>routiers</u> had left several copies of <u>L'Auto</u> on the tables of the reading room and I took them out and sat in an easy chair in the sun to read about, and catch up on, French sporting life. While I was sitting there the concierge came out with a blue envelope in his hand.

"A telegram for you, sir," he said.

I poked my finger along under the fold that was fastened down and read it. It had been forwarded from Paris.

COULD YOU COME HOTEL MONTANA

AM RATHER IN TROUBLE DUFF.

I tipped the concierge and re-read the message. A postman was coming along the sidewalk. He turned in to the hotel. He had a big mustache and a military bearing. He came out of the hotel again and the concierge just behind him.

"Here's another telegram for you, sir."

"Thank you," I said.

I opened it. It was forwarded from Pamplona.

COULD YOU COME HOTEL MONTANA

MADRID AM RATHER IN TROUBLE

DUFF.

The concierge was still standing there, waiting for his tip probably.

"What time is there a train for Madrid?" I asked him.

"It left at nine this morning," he said. "There is a slow train at eleven and the Sud Express at ten tonight."

"Get me a berth on the Sud Express. Do you want the money now?"

"Just as you wish," he said. "I will have it put on the bill."

"Do that."

Well that meant San Sebastian all shot to hell. I suppose, vaguely, I had expected something of the sort. Oh well it was the price one paid for knowing the aristocracy. Someone had to pay for the aristocracy. I was being very hard headed and disgusted about it. I saw the concierge standing in the doorway.

"Bring me a telegraph form, please," I said.

He brought it with a pen and ink. I took out my fountain pen and printed

LADY ~~ANTHONY~~ ASHLEY

HOTEL MONTANA
MADRID
ARRIVING SUD EXPRESS TOMORROW

Then I stopped. That handled the matter. There was nothing else to say. What else was there to say? I printed LOVE JAKE and handed the concierge the wire. There I was, doing it again. Why not let it alone. I knew there was not any use trying to let it alone. I felt perfectly hard about it. I had certainly acted like anything but a man. Send a girl off with one man. Introduce her to another to go off with him. Now go and bring her back. And sign the wire with love. Well I could not apply the rules to myself. I was not a man anyway. Oh stop that stuff. There was not going to be any of that stuff. All right though. I had felt so very fine swimming this morning too. Oh well, to hell with all of it. I could have a good time. I had been having a good time for two days. I would get this Madrid thing over with. There was no use belly aching about it. That was not the way "good people" acted. It was that ass Braddocks that started the good people plucese. Braddocks was translating his own works into French. He explained to me that he had been working all day to find a French equivalent for good people.

"Of course, being an American you can have absolutely no conception of what that means," he said. "The words good people could only have a meaning to an Englishman." He went on at great length about how an American could not understand it because we have no good people. It was one of Duff's and my favorite jokes for a long time. We always spoke of each other as good people. This was obviously an affair of good people. It was a sort of double acting noblesse oblige. It seemed so different from Braddocks's novels though. In them there was always a great deal of passion but it took sometimes two and three volumes for anyone to sleep with anyone else. In actual life it seemed there was a good deal of sleeping about among good people ~~and when there was any actual passion nobody believed in it~~ with more sleeping about than passion. Braddocks was very good on passion. He would probably be very good if he wrote about people of his own class. But he had this aristocratic obsession. It seemed to take Englishmen that way. Well they made money out of it. All the Jews and Americans and Welshmen and ex clerks and ex school teachers all wrote about the aristocracy. The aristocracy when they wrote wrote about the ~~natives of distant countries~~ Wallabies or about horses or salmon or other things. Of course the best ones did not either write or read and as fast as they commenced to think they usually shot themselves or if it only took them in a mild form they would contest seats as labor candidates or get themselves mixed up in Ireland.

Of course the best ones did not think, read nor write. They were nice people. What did I know about them? Nothing. Who knew anything about anybody? You didn't know a woman because you slept with her any more than you knew a horse because you'd ridden him once. Why pick on Braddocks and the Armenians then? Why not? To hell with Braddocks and all the smart Armenians. Besides you learned a lot about a woman by not sleeping with her. I ought to be glad I was the way I was. Oh yes very glad. Glad as hell. Nothing like recognizing your advantages. I went in to lunch.

There is a strange feeling in making a trip in luxury that you have once made before in discomfort and with difficulty.

It seems to kill something, in some way to kill a great stretch of country. The Sud Express always did that for me and I always avoided taking it. There was ~~no reason to~~ nothing to be gained by compressing and destroying country to save a little time and get some sleep. But I took the Sud Express and slept well in a compartment by myself and had breakfast in the morning and looked out of the window and saw the Escorial, grand and gray and cold in the sun with the cheerfulness of the little town below it and forty-five minutes later Madrid a compact white skyline on the top of a little cliff away across sun hardened country. The Norte station in Madrid is like a country town. The trains do not go on from there. It is the end of the line and they all stop. Outside were the cabs and taxis and a line of hotel runners. I took a taxi and we climbed up through the tropical seeming gardens and on up until we were in the high, hot~~, smooth streeted~~ town. We came down a ~~hill~~ smooth street to the Puerto del Sol and through the traffic and into the Carrera San Jeronimo. All the shops had their awnings down against the heat and all the windows on the sunny side of the street were shuttered ~~tight~~.

The Montana was a pension. The English translation of a pension is boarding house. But it is not a boarding house. It is a cheap hotel where you have to take your meals. The taxi stopped at the curb. I saw the sign Hotel Montana on the second floor. That meant you had to go up there to find the Hotel Montana. ~~There was an elevator but I could not make it work so I walked up.~~ The taxi driver left the bags by the elevator. I could not make the elevator work so I walked up. On the second floor was a cut brass sign Hotel Montana. I rang and no one came to the door. I rang again and a maid with a sullen face opened the door.

"Is Lady Anthony here?" I asked.

She looked at me dully.

"Is an Englishwoman here?"

She turned and called to someone inside. A very fat woman came to the door. Her hair was gray and stiffly oiled in a scallop about her face. She was short and commanding.

"Muy Buenos," I said. "Is there an Englishwoman here? I would like to see this English lady."

"Muy Buenos. Yes, there is a female English. Certainly you can see her if she wishes to see you."

"She wishes to see me."

"The chica will ask her."

"Is this female English a blood relation of you?"

"She is the sister of my sister."

"Clearly then you are her uncle."

"It is very hot."

"It is very hot in summer in Madrid."

"And how cold in winter."

"Yes. It is very cold in winter."

"Including that I find Madrid muy bonita."

"If Madrid had the sea what a place."

"That would be bonita."

Did I want to stay myself in person in the Hotel Montana? Of that as yet I was undecided. But it would give me pleasure if my bags were brought up in the elevator in order that they might not be stolen. Nothing was ever stolen in ~~Madrid~~ the Hotel Montana. In other Fondas yes. Not here. The personages of this establishment were rigidly selectioned. I was happy to hear it. Nevertheless I would welcome the upbringal of my bags.

The maid came in and said that the female English wanted to see the male English now at once.

"Good," I said. "You see. It is as I said."

"Clearly."

I followed the maid's back down a long dark hall. At the end she knocked on a door.

"Hello," said Duff. "Is it you Jake?"

"It's me."

"Come in. Come in."

I opened the door. The maid closed it after me. Duff was in bed. She had just brushed her hair back. The room was in that disorder produced only by people who have always had servants. Duff dropped the brush and held out her arms. I ~~held her close and kissed her.~~ kissed her and held her. Her arms were around me. She held me very tight. I was all aching inside and I held all of her body tight against me.

"I knew you would come."

"Oh yes."

I sat on the bed now with my arm around her. She turned and kissed me very suddenly and fiercely. I tightened my arms around her and held her against my chest where it ached. She felt thin.

"You hate me don't you?"

"Just a little."

"It's all right," she said. "I deserve it."

"No you don't."

"Do you love me still?"

"I guess so."

"You don't love me anymore. It's all right."

"I love you. But I try so damn hard not to."

She was thinking of something else. I could feel her heart beating under my hand. She was trembling too a little. She felt so small. I had always thought of us as about the same size.

"Have you got a cigarette?" Duff asked. She took one and lighted it. We were sitting side by side now.

"Oh Darling," she said. "I've had such a hell of a time."

"Tell me about it."

"Nothing to tell. He got ashamed of me. Ashamed of my looks. They ragged him about me at the Café I believe."

"How damned funny."

"Well I have a funny face you know."

"Dear face."

"You know where he learned English?"

She thinned the line of her lips on the cigarette. ~~and blew out smoke.~~

"He was a waiter in a hotel in Gibraltar when he was ~~sixteen~~ fifteen. He came down from Ronda. That's what made him ~~rather overvalue the title at the start~~ put so much value in titles."

I did not say anything.

"He only left yesterday. I made him go."

"You could have kept him."

"I should hope so. It isn't the sort of thing one does. I don't think I hurt him any."

"You were probably damn good for him."

"He shouldn't be living with anyone. I realized that right away."

"No."

"Oh hell," she said. "Let's not talk about it. Let's never talk about it."

"Only if there's anything you want to get off your chest."

"Oh no. It was rather a knock him being ashamed of me. He wanted me to grow my hair out. Me, with long hair. Can you see it? I'd look so like hell."

"That was funny."

"He said it would make me more womanly. I'd look a fright."

"What was it about being in trouble?"

"I didn't know whether I could make him go and I didn't have a sou to go away and leave him. He tried to give me a lot of money, you know. I told him I had scads of it. He knew that was a lie. I couldn't take his money you know."

"No."

"Oh let's not talk about it. There were some funny things though. He wanted to marry me finally."

"Really?"

"Of course. I can't even marry Mike."

"~~Perhaps~~ Maybe he had an vague idea that would make him Lord ~~Anthony~~ Ashley."

"No. It wasn't that. He really wanted to marry me. So I couldn't go away from him, he said. He wanted to make it sure I could never go away from him. After I'd gotten more womanly, of course."

"You ought to feel set up."

"I do. I'm all right again. He's wiped out that damned Cohn."

"Good."

"You know I'd have lived with him if I hadn't seen it was bad for him. We got along damned well."

"Outside of your personal appearance."

"Oh that would have come out ~~and~~ right enough."

"That was funny."

"I'm thirty-four you know. I'm not going to be one of these bitches that ruins children."

~~"Yes. In Paris you can't tell if whether a boy's with his wife or his mother."~~

~~"Yes. Well I'm not going to be that way. I feel rather good you know. I feel rather set up."~~

"Dear Duff."

"No."

"In Paris you can't tell whether a boy's with his wife or his mother."

"I know."

"I'm not going to be that way. I'm damned if I am. I feel rather good you know. I feel rather set up."

"Dear Duff."

I put my arms around her. She began to cry. I could feel her crying, shaking, crying. She wouldn't look up. She was crying and I held her close to me.

"Don't let's ever talk about it," she said. "Don't please let's ever talk about it."

"I won't."

"I'm going back to Mike." I could feel her crying as I held her close. "He's so damned nice and he's so very awful. He's my sort."

She wouldn't look up. I stroked her hair. I could feel her shaking.

"I won't be one of those bitches," she said. "But oh Jake. Please let's never, never talk about it."

CHAPTER XXII

We left the Hotel Montana. The woman who ran the hotel would not let ~~us~~ me pay the bill. The bill had been paid.

"Oh well. Let it go," Duff said. "It doesn't matter now."

We ~~took~~ rode in a taxi down to the Palace Hotel, left the boys, arranged for two berths on the Sud Express for that night and went into the bar of the hotel for a cocktail. We sat on high stools at the bar while the barman shook the martinis in an enormous ~~silver~~ nickeled shaker.

"It's wonderful what a wonderful gentility there is in the bar of a big hotel," I said.

"Barmen and jockeys are the only people who are polite any more."

"No matter how vulgar a hotel is the bar is ~~usually~~ always nice."

"It's odd."

"Bartenders have always been wonderful."

"You know," Duff said. "It's quite true. He is only nineteen. Isn't it amazing?"

We touched the two glasses. They were coldly beaded. Outside the window was the summer heat of Madrid.

"I like an olive in a martini," I said to the barman.

"Right you are Sir. ~~Some gentlemen do and some gentlemen don't.~~ There you are Sir."

"Thanks."

"I should have asked you, you know."

He retired far enough back of the bar so as not to hear our conversation. Duff had sipped from the martini as it stood on the bar. Then she picked it up. Her hand was steady enough to lift it after that first sip.

"It's good," said Duff. "Isn't it a nice bar."

"They're all nice bars."

"You know I didn't believe it at first. He was born in ~~1905~~ nineteen five. I was in school in Paris then. Think of that."

"Anything special you want me to think about it?"

"Don't be an ass. Would you buy a lady a drink?"

"We'll have two more martinis."

"Right you are Sir. Just as they were before?"

"They were very good," said Duff.

"Thank you Ma'am."

"Well Bung-oh," Duff said.

"Bung-o."

"You know," Duff said. "He'd only been with two women before. He never cared about anything except bull fighting."

"He has plenty of time."

"I don't know. He thinks it was me. Not just the show in general."

"Well it was you."

"Yes. It was me."

"I thought you weren't ever going to talk about it."

"How can I help it?"

"You'll lose it if you talk about it."

"I just talk around it. You know I feel rather damned good Jake."

"You should."

"You know it makes one feel rather damned good deciding not to be a bitch."

"Yes."

"It's sort of what we have instead of God."

"God's ~~rather good too~~ not too bad."

"He never worked very well with me."

"There's lots of time yet."

"Should we have another martini?"

"We'll have two more ~~martinis~~ cocktails," I said.

"Martinis Sir?"

"Yes."

"Right you are Sir."

"Where will we lunch?" I asked. The bar was cool. You could feel the heat outside through the window.

"Here?" asked Duff.

"It's rotten here in the hotel. Do you know the address of a place called Botin's?" I asked the barman.

"Yes sir. Would you like to have me write it out?"

"Thank you."

We lunched upstairs at Botin's. It is one of the best restaurants in the world if you like food. We had roast young suckling pig and drank rioja alta with it. Duff did not eat much. She never ate much. I ate a great quantity and drank three bottles of the rioja alta.

"It's funny how many things you can find comfort in."

"Yes. You like to eat don't you?" Duff said.

"Yes. I like to eat and I like to drink and I like to lead a quiet life and I like to read books."

"You're a little drunk," Duff said. "What else do you like?"

"Oh I like horse races and I like bull fights and I like to fish and I like to eat and drink."

"You said that."

"I know it."

"I like to sail," Duff said.

"Yes," I said. "I like to sail too."

"Sailing's rather wonderful," Duff said.

"Yes," I said. "Let's have another bottle of rioja alta."

"It's damned good."

"You haven't drunk much of it."

"Yes I have. You haven't seen."

"Let's go for a long ride. Out through the park and all around."

"Right," said Duff. "I haven't seen Madrid. Ought to see Madrid."

The last bottle of rioja alta came. I poured a little in my glass and, then a glass for Duff, then filled my glass. We touched glasses.

"Bung-oh," Duff said. I drained my glass and poured out another.

Duff put her hand on my thigh under the table.

"Don't get drunk Jake," she said. "You don't have to."

"How do you know?"

"Don't," she said. "You'll be all right."

"I'm not getting drunk," I said. "I'm just drinking a little wine."

"Don't get drunk," she said. "Jake. Don't get drunk."

"I'm not," I said.

Downstairs we came out through the ~~lower~~ first floor dining room to the street. A chasseur went for a taxi. It was hot and bright. Up the street was a little square with trees and grass where there were taxis parked. ~~The chasseu~~ A taxi came up the street, the chasseur hanging out at the side. I tipped him, told the driver where to go and ~~we~~ got in beside Duff. The driver started up the street. I settled back. Duff moved close to me. We were close against each other. I put my arm around her and she rested her body against me. It was very hot and bright and the houses looked sharply white. We turned out into the Grand Via.

"Oh Jake," Duff said. "We could have had such a damned good time together."

Ahead was mounted policeman in khaki directing traffic. The car slowed suddenly pressing Duff closer against me.

"Yes," I said. "It's nice as hell to think so."

The End.
Paris Sept. 21-1925

"Isn't it nice to think so"

9. Item 194, 6-56 to 6-57. Hemingway's notes to himself, written by hand at the end of the seventh notebook after the ending of the novel. This passage, starting from the second paragraph, was slightly revised and inserted in the typescript at the beginning of Book II after the second paragraph. The final statement "Not Love" (his emphasis) was omitted and ultimately Hemingway cut the entire passage.

There is now a ~~break~~ slackening in the emotional tightness of the story. That terrible taughtness did not come again until we were all in Spain. There could not have been a worse business than the five of us being in Spain together. ~~but~~ It was Cohn's fault. He had every chance to get out of it. So he took so much punishment and there is no question but that he took plenty of punishment, he had no one to blame but himself.

As I am writing this story exactly as it happened it probably loses much in credibility that I could have saved by molding the facts to certain accepted standards. Love, with the aid of the psychoanalysts, has become in literature either a very intellectualized business or else such a sort of you are my man I am your woman let us live together for ever mess that any sort of honest passion is quite suspect. The thing I would like to make my reader believe, however incredible, is that such a passion and longing could exist in me for Brett Ashley that I would sometimes feel that it would tear me to pieces and yet in the intervals when I was not seeing Brett, and they were the greater part of the time, I lived a very happy life. The world was to me a very fine and pleasant place and ~~I believe that I get as much or more enjoyment from it than nearly anyone I know~~ if I felt alone in it being alone was a comfortable feeling. ~~As for what Brett Ashley felt or how she looked at things~~ It was only when I had just left Brett Ashley that I felt all of my world taken away, that it was all gone, even the shapes of things were changed, the trees and the houses and the fountains, and that life was ~~just only~~ just something to be gone through. Brett Ashley could do that to me, and no doubt she could do it to other people, and no doubt she did it to other people. Women do it to men for amusement sometimes I believe. And men do it to women. Some men, I believe, enjoy having a number of women in love with them. Love always seemed such a very funny name for it.

As for how Brett Ashley felt and how the things that happened to her affected her, I am not a psychologist, I only put down what she did and what she said. You will have to figure that out by yourselves.

Not <u>Love.</u>

10. Item 202c. The following is a transcription of a first-draft, handwritten foreword that Ernest Hemingway penned after he had finished writing the book but was still undecided about the title. It is written in an eighth notebook that also contains a list of possible titles for the novel. Hemingway decided against using the foreword and never published it.

THE LOST GENERATION

A Novel.

FOREWORD

One day last summer Gertrude Stein stopped in a garage in a small town in the Department of Ain to have a valve fixed in her Ford car. The young mechanic who fixed it was very good and quick and skillful. There were three other mechanics all about the same age in the garage.

"Where do you get boys to work like that?" Miss Stein asked the owner of the garage. "I thought you couldn't get boys to work any more."

"Oh yes," the garage owner said. "You can get very good boys now. I've taken all these and trained them myself. It is the ones between twenty-two and thirty that are no good. C'est un generation perdu. No one wants them. They are no good. They were spoiled. The young ones, the new ones are all right again."

"But what becomes of the others?"

"Nothing. They know they are no good. C'est un generation perdu. A little hard on them," he added.

I did not hear this story until after I had written this book. I had thought of calling it Fiesta but did not want to use a foreign word. Perdu loses a little something by being translated into lost. There is something much more final about perdu. There is only this to say that this generation that is lost has nothing to do with any Younger Generation about whose outcome much literary speculation occurred in times past. This is not a question of what kind of mothers will flappers make or where is bobbed hair leading us. This is about something that is already finished. For whatever is going to happen to the generation of which I am a part has already happened.

There will be more entanglements, there will be more complications, there will be successes and failures. ~~There may be other wars. A few will learn to live perhaps one or two may learn to write or to paint.~~

~~But the things that are given to people to happen to them have~~
~~already happened. There will be many new salvations brought forward.~~
My generation in France for example in two years sought salvation in
first the Catholic church, 2nd ~~communism~~ Dadaism, third the movies,
fourth Royalism, fifth the Catholic church again. There may be another
and better war. But none of it will matter particularly to this generation
because to them the things that are given to people to happen have
already happened.

11. Item 197. One-page typescript fragment with a false start to the
    novel opening in Pedro Romero's room in the Hotel Montoya in
    Pamplona. This false start and the following (number 12) false
    start include the earliest use of the title that Hemingway settled
    on. Hemingway is still working out the possibility of beginning
    the book in Pamplona and Pedro Romero is the central charac-
    ter. It is notable that Hemingway is trying to write not from the
    perspective of Jake Barnes but from the third person. The pas-
    sage also emphasizes the material success of the bullfighter and
    his high compensation, which were eventually cut.

THE SUN ALSO RISES

A Novel.

It was half past three in the afternoon in a dark bedroom in the Hotel
Montoya in Pamplona, Spain. It was a cheap room because the boy who
lived in it had not yet learned to appreciate luxury. He stood under the
electric light in the center of the room and he seemed quite alone altho
there were five people in the bedroom. Two Spanish newspaper men sat
on the bed. They were amused. The boy, who was a bull fighter, was
talking English.

"You go to see the fight?" he asked the two Americans who had just
been introduced to him.

"You know English," one of the Americans said, feeling as he said it
what an idiotic remark it was.

"No. I only talk it a little," he smiled. The electric light shone on his
hair. He was twenty years old and very straight and handsome and

unsmiling. Each afternoon that he killed bulls he made seven thousand five hundred pesetas which is a little over a thousand dollars. This year if nothing happened he would make seventy thousand dollars. Montoya, the owner of the hotel made a little speech telling the boy what great lovers of bull fighting the two Americans were. Pedro Romero listened very seriously

12. Item 197a. A longer false start of five typed manuscript pages.

THE SUN ALSO RISES

A Novel.

It was half past three in the afternoon in a dark bedroom in the Hotel Montoya in Pamplona, Spain. It was a cheap room because the boy who lived in it had not yet learned to appreciate luxury. So far, that year, he had made sixty thousand dollars. The money represented the measure of his success. He had not yet had time to experiment with the things that money could buy. He had an idea that at the end of the season, if he did not go to Mexico, he would buy himself a motor car. He was nineteen years old and he stood very straight, and very handsome and quite alone although there were five people in his bedroom.

Pedro Romero was the boy's name and he was a bull fighter. Two Americans on their way to their room to get a leather wine bottle to take to the bull fight had met Montoya, the proprietor of the hotel, on the stairs.

"Come on," Montoya said. "You ought to meet Pedro Romero. He's just dressed for the bull fight."

The two Americans were named William Gorton and Jacob Barnes and they followed the proprietor of the hotel into the dark bedroom where the boy stood, dressed in his bull fighting clothes, except for his coat which lay on one of the beds. He stood, very straight and unsmiling and the electric light shone on his hair brushed very smooth and shiny from his brown face. He nodded seeming very far away and dignified when he shook hands with Barnes and Gorton. Montoya made a little speech about what great admirers of bull fighting the two Americans were and how they wanted to wish him luck. Romero listened very seriously. Then he turned to Jake Barnes.

"You go to see the bull fight," he said in English.

"You know English," Barnes said feeling like an idiot.

"No," Pedro Romero answered and smiled.

A newspaper man who had been sitting on the bed came over and offered, in French, to interpret. "Is there anything you would like to ask Pedro Romero?"

The two Americans thanked him. There was nothing that they wanted to ask. The bull fight was to commence in half an hour. They shook hands again, wished the boy "Much Suerte," and went out. Pedro Romero was standing, altogether by himself, alone in the room with the hangers on as they shut the door.

"He's a fine boy. Don't you think so?" Montoya asked.

"He's some boy," Bill Gorton said. "He's some boy."

"We'll see how he is in the ring," Montoya said. "Where you go now? The café?"

"One little drink," Bill said. Montoya stood in the doorway of the hotel and the two Americans crossed the hot square toward the Café Iruna.

In front of the café a Rolls Royce motor car was surrounded by a crowd. On the front seat was a courier in livery siting beside the chauffeur. In the back of the car were two women and a man. They evidently expected to be met by someone and sat ~~looking varying degrees of importance while they~~ waiting for the reception to begin. The man sat with the pompous democracy of the heavier American statesman. One of the women looked rather like a White House hostess and the other snuggled into the seat of the car and met the eyes of every man in the café who looked at her.

Bill Gorton and Jake Barnes went through the crowd around the gray, official looking car and joined their party at one of the café tables.

"I say," Brett called. "That's a shabby way to treat an Ambassador."

"He's only an American Ambassador." Bill sat down.

"They don't know that here though," Jake said.

"Go on, Jake," Brett said. Her name was Brett Ashley. Lady Brett Ashley. "You know him. Go out and say something to him."

"Give him the keys of the city," Mike suggested.

"Give him the key to my room," Bill said.

"Go on, Jake. You really ought," Brett urged.

"Go on yourself," Jake answered. "You've got all the noblesse oblige."

"Go on Brett. Tell him you're Lady Ashley and you make him very very welcome."

"Go on, Jake," Brett said. "Tell them to come and have a drink."

Jake Barnes went out to the car, shook hands with the Ambassador, a Mr. Ferdinand J. Watson from Ohio, met the White House hostess, who was the Ambassador's niece, met the snuggly lady with the eyes, the eyes looking at him from under the brim of the man's felt hat she wore pulled down over sun streaked blonde hair, she was the recently married correspondent of a fashionable American portrait painter, explained to a policeman that this was the American Ambassador and that he did not have to pay a tax on his car, sent another policeman for the Alcalde, sent the Ambassador's card over to the other hotel to reserve two rooms for a lady friend who was coming the next day from Biarritz and then talked. Jake Barnes knew Carelton, the husband of the lady in the car and had known, and been rather fond of the original Mrs. Carelton. It was therefore interesting for him to meet the present Mrs. Carelton whom he had hitherto known only through the newspapers. Mrs. Carelton was a very vivid lady. This was her first visit to Spain and she had attended thirty-four bull fights. Carelton was in Burgos. They were all going back to San Sebastian tonight after the bull fight and drive up again the next day to spend the night and see Belmonte. Jake Barnes told her Belmonte was going to stop at his hotel. She simply worshiped Belmonte—and Marcial Lalanda. Jake Barnes told her Marcial Lalanda was stopping at the same hotel.

"What hotel is it—the Grand?"

"No," Jake said. "The Montoya."

"Do tell Marcial I'm in town."

"Surely," Jake said. "I'll see him tonight in the dining room."

"And do tell me," she said. "Have you seen Pedro Romero? I think he is absolutely the most divine boy. Is he at your hotel too?"

"Yes. Do you want me to tell him you're in town?"

She turned down the vividness. She was afraid she was being joked. "Oh, no," she said. "I've never met him. I've only seen him in the ring."

"Where? At Madrid?"

"No. At Seville."

As Jake talked the Alcalde came up to the car. He had cigarette ashes on his vest, wore a brown slouch hat and seemed rather embarrassed. It seemed they had wired him for tickets to the bull fights and he had done nothing about it. But he could get them. Jake Barnes said good-bye. He was angry at himself for having gone out. Ambassador Watson had said he remembered him perfectly from Paris and Jake was sure he did not. Jake was angry at himself for having in any way played up to Mrs. Carelton. He wanted to say something that would annoy her. "Tell me," he said as he shook hands, "Do you really want me to tell Marcial you are in town?" She took it as a compliment, pursed her lips and became very vivid again. "Really. I don't know. Yes tell him I'm in town and tell him I'm quite angry with him because he didn't come out to Tovar's that last time."

Jake Barnes shook hands and went back to the table where his friends had been trying to ruin his social position by attempting to buy the Ambassador's chauffeur a drink. The chauffeur had refused very haughtily. Lady Brett Ashley had then tried to buy the uniformed equerry, or A.D.T. delivery boy or whatever the Ambassador's other attendant was, a drink. But he was even haughtier.

So they all went to the bull fight. It was not much of a bull fight. The Ambassador and the two ladies sat in a box with the Alcalde and Jake Barnes looked at them once with the glasses. The uniformed messenger boy was also in the box and Mrs. Carelton sat leaning forward very intent and earnest. The White House Hostess in the blue dress watched the fight too but did not seem to be seeing very much of it. The Ambassador was smoking a cigar so Jake supposed he was happy. The Alcalde looked miserable. The messenger boy looked very English and superior to it all.

Looking at them Jake was angry. He knew Brett had made him go out simply to devil him

13. Item 202D. Typescript fragment with handwritten emendations of a late false start to the novel.

This is a novel about a lady. Her name is Lady Ashley and when the story begins she is living in Paris and it is Spring. That should be a good setting for a romantic but highly moral story. As every one knows Paris is a very romantic place. Spring in Paris is a very happy and romantic time. Autumn in Paris, although very beautiful, might give a note of sadness or melancholy that we shall try to keep out of this story.

There were about twenty five more pages like that which have ~~now~~ been cut out of this novel which now opens with Robert Cohn who ~~will~~

may be a great disappointment to the reader who has just been promised Lady Ashley. But if the reader will stay around Lady Ashley will come into the story again in a little while and will stay in until the end. A large amount of material about the author has also been cut out in the twenty-five pages that have been eliminated and I feel sure that this will compensate the reader for any loss he may feel about Lady Ashley. We will now start with Robert Cohn.

14. Item 202B. Pencil manuscript fragments on two pages of another notebook. These remarks were likely made when the author was undertaking revisions of the first draft.

You must make fantastic statements to cover things.
It is like living with fourteen men so no one will know there is someone you love.
We can't do it. You can't hurt people. It's what we believe in in place of God.
I have to have it and I can't have what I want with you so I'm going to take this other thing.
I have never been able to have anything I ever wanted.
And I looked at you and I thought I wouldn't be able to stand it.
What a shame he put the top thing down just as we came up.
What are you so nervy about. What were you so nervy about the other day.

Appendix III

The Discarded First Chapters

The following chapters were cut from the novel by Ernest Hemingway at the final galley stage. The remaining part of the second chapter—from "Robert Cohn was once middleweight boxing champion of Princeton"— became the beginning of the book. Hemingway later decided to include a slightly revised version of the story about Braddocks and Hilaire Belloc in *A Moveable Feast*.

Item 202 of the Ernest Hemingway Collection, John F. Kennedy Library, Boston.

This is a novel about a lady. Her name is Lady Ashley and when the story begins she is living in Paris and it is Spring. That should be a good setting for a romantic but highly moral story. As everyone knows, Paris is a very romantic place. Spring in Paris is a very happy and romantic time. Autumn in Paris, although very beautiful, might give a note of sadness or melancholy that we shall try to keep out of this story.

Lady Ashley was born Elizabeth Brett Murray. Her title came from her second husband. She had divorced one husband for something or other, mutual consent; not until after he had put one of those notices in the papers stating that after this date he would not be responsible for any debt, etc. He was a Scotchman and found Brett much too expensive, especially as she had only married him to get rid of him and to get away from home. At present she had a legal separation from her second husband, who had the title, because he was a dipsomaniac, he having learned it in the North Sea commanding a mine-sweeper, Brett said. When he had gotten to be a proper thoroughgoing dipsomaniac and found that Brett did not love him he tried to kill her, and between times slept on the floor and was never sober and had great spells of crying. Brett always declared that it had been one of the really great mistakes of her life to have married a sailor. She should have known better, she said, but she had sent the one man she had wanted to marry off to Mesopotamia so he would last out the war, and he had died of some very unromantic form of dysentery and she certainly could not marry Jake Barnes, so when she had to marry she had married Lord Robert Ashley, who proceeded to become a dipsomaniac as before stated.

They had a son and Ashley would not divorce, and would not give grounds for divorce, but there was a separation and Brett went off with Mike Campbell to the Continent one afternoon, she having offered to at lunch because Mike was lonely and sick and very companionable, and, as she said, "obviously one of us." They arranged the whole business before the Folkestone–Boulogne train left London at 9:30 that night. Brett was always very proud of that. The speed with which they got passports and raised funds. They came to Paris on their way to the Riviera, and stayed the night in a hotel which had only one room free and that with a double bed. "We'd no idea of anything of that sort," Brett said. "Mike said we should go on and look up another hotel, but I said no, to stop where we were. What's the odds." That was how they happened to be living together.

Mike at that time was ill. It was all he had brought back with him from the two years he had spent in business in Spain, after he had left the army, except the beautifully engraved shares of the company which had absorbed all of the fifteen thousand pounds that had come to him from his father's estate. He was also an undischarged bankrupt, which is quite a serious thing in England, and had various habits that Brett felt sorry for, did not think a man should have, and cured by constant watchfulness and the exercise of her then very strong will.

Mike was a charming companion, one of the most charming. He was nice and he was weak and he had a certain very hard gentleness in him that could not be touched and that never disappeared until the liquor dissolved him entirely. Mike sober was nice, Mike a little drunk was even nicer, Mike quite drunk began to be objectionable, and Mike very drunk was embarrassing.

It was the boredom and the uncertainty of their position that made Brett drink as she did. There was nothing of the alcoholic about her. Not, at least, for a long time. They spent their time sleeping as late as possible and then drinking. That is a simple way of stating a very complicated process, and waiting for Mike's weekly allowance, which was always late, and therefore always spent and borrowed into a week or more in advance. There was nothing to do but to drink. The drinking was not done alone in their rooms. It was all at cafés and parties and each day became a replica of the day before. There were very few differences. You had been to bed late or gone to bed early. You felt good or you felt bad. You felt like eating a little something or you couldn't face the thought of food. It had been a good party the night before or it had been a bore. Michael had behaved abominably or Michael had been a model of admirable behavior. But usually it had been a good party because alcohol, either brandy and soda, or whiskey and soda, had a tendency to make everything much better, and for a time quite all right.

If Michael had behaved well it was probably a good party, and Michael had a strong tendency to behave well. In fact you could always count on him to behave absolutely as he should until the alcoholic process had taken place, which always seemed rather like that old grammar school experiment in which a bone is dissolved in vinegar to prove it has something or other in it. Anyway, the vinegar quite changed the bone and made it very unlike itself, and you could bend it back and forth, and if it were a long enough bone and you had used enough vinegar, you could even tie it into a knot.

Brett was very different from Mike about drinking. Brett had a certain grand vitality. She had her looks too. She was not supposed to be beautiful, but in a room with women, who were supposed to be beautiful, she killed their looks entirely. Men thought she was lovely looking, and women called her striking looking. Painters were always asking her to sit for them and that flattered her, because she considered that her looks were not much, and so she spent much of her waking time sitting for portraits, none of which she ever liked. She did not seem to mind how bad the painters were. The worse they were the more it amused her. It was the being asked to sit for her portrait that she liked. One painter was as good as another. Of course, the best portrait painters had done her a long time before.

Brett drank much more than Mike liked, but it never dissolved her in any way. She was always clear run, generous, and her lines were always as clear. But when she had been drunk she always spoke of it as having been blind. "Weren't we blind last night, though?" It was short for blind drunk, and the curious part was that she really became, in a way, blind. Drinking, and this does not mean the odd drink, or two or three cocktails before dinner and wine at the meal, but real drinking of the sort that kills off the good drinkers because they are the only ones who can do it, affected Brett in three successive stages. Drinking, say, whiskey and sodas from four o'clock in the afternoon until two o'clock in the morning Brett first lost her power of speech and just sat and listened, then she lost her sight and saw nothing that went on, and finally she ceased to hear. And all the time any one coming into the café would never know she had been drinking. To anyone greeting her she would respond automatically, "Hullo, I say I am blind," or something of the sort.

In sleeping and in drinking, playing bridge in the afternoon, usually having her portrait painted by some socially climbing artist who knew the value of a title on a portrait, a party somewhere every night, Brett and Mike passed the time in Paris. They were rather happy. Brett was a very happy person. Then Mike had to go to England, to London to see a lawyer about something connected with the divorce Brett was trying to get, and then to Scotland to visit his people and prove by residence that he was a dutiful son, in order that, among other things, they should not stop his allowance. Brett was left alone in Paris. She had never been very good at being alone.

CHAPTER II

I did not want to tell this story in the first person but I find that I must. I wanted to stay well outside of the story so that I would not be touched by it in any way, and handle all the people in it with that irony and pity that are so essential to good writing. I even thought I might be amused by all the things that are going to happen to Lady Brett Ashley and Mr. Robert Cohn and Michael Campbell, Esq., and Mr. Jake Barnes. But I made the unfortunate mistake, for a writer, of first having been Mr. Jake Barnes. So it is not going to be splendid and cool and detached after all. "What a pity!" as Brett used to say.

"What a pity!" was a little joke we all had. Brett was having her portrait painted by a very rich American from Philadelphia, who sent his motor-car around each afternoon to bring her from her hotel in Montparnasse up to his Montmartre studio. Along about the third sitting Brett stopped posing for a little while to have tea, and the portrait-painter asked her: "And when you get your divorce, Lady Ashley, what will you do then?"

"Marry Mike Campbell," Brett answered.

"And what will your name be then?"

"Mrs. Campbell, of course!"

"What a pity," the portrait-painter said. "What a pity!"

So my name is Jacob Barnes and I am writing the story, not as I believe is usual in these cases, from a desire for confession, because being a Roman Catholic I am spared that Protestant urge to literary production, nor to set things all out the way they happened for the good of some future generation, nor any other of the usual highly moral urges, but because I believe it is a good story.

I am a newspaper man living in Paris. I used to think Paris was the most wonderful place in the world. I have lived in it now for six years, or however long it is since 1920, and I still see its good points. Anyway, it is the only city I want to live in. They say New York is very fine but I do not care for night life. I want to live quietly and with a certain measure of luxury, and a job that I do not want to worry about. Paris provides all these things. Paris is also a lovely town to live in once you get an apartment and give up various American fetishes such as all the year round B. V. D.s and too much exercise.

In 1916 I was invalided home from a British hospital and got a job on *The Mail* in New York. I quit to start the Continental Press Association with Robert Graham, who was then just getting his reputation as Washington correspondent. We started the Continental in one room on the basis of syndicating Bob Graham's Washington dispatches. I ran the business end and the first year wrote a special war-expert service. By 1920 the Continental was the third largest feature service in the States. I told Bob Graham that rather than stay and get rich with him the Continental could give me a job in Paris. So I made the job, and I have some stock, but not as much as I ought to have, and I do not try to run the salary up too high because if I ever got up past a certain amount there would be too many people shooting at my job as European Director of the Continental Press Association. When you have a title like that, translated into French on letter-heads, and only have to work about four or five hours a day and all the salary you want you are pretty well fixed. I write political dispatches under my own name, and feature stuff under a couple of different names, and all the trained-seal stuff is filed through our office. It is a nice job. I want to hang on to it. Like all newspaper men I have always wanted to write a novel, and I suppose, now that I am doing it, the novel will have that awful taking-the-pen-in-hand quality that afflicts newspaper men when they start to write their own book.

I never hung about the Quarter much in Paris until Brett and Mike showed up. I always felt about the Quarter that I could sort of take it or leave it alone. You went into it once in a while to sort of see the animals and say hello to Harold Stearns, and on hot nights in the spring when the tables were spread out over the sidewalks it was rather pleasant. But for a place to hang around it always seemed awfully dull. I have to put it in, though, because Robert Cohn, who is one of the non-Nordic heroes of this book, had spent two years there.

The Quarter is sort of more a state of mind than a geographical area. Perfectly good Quarterites live outside the actual boundaries of Montparnasse. They can live anywhere, I suppose, as long as they come to the Quarter to think. Or whatever you call it. To have the Quarter state of mind is probably the best way of putting it. This state of mind is principally contempt. Those who work have the greatest contempt for those who don't. The loafers are leading their own lives and it is bad form to mention work. Young painters have contempt for old painters, and that works both ways too. There are contemptuous critics and contemptuous writers. Everybody seems to dislike everybody else. The only happy people are the drunks, and they, after flaming for a period of days or weeks, eventually become depressed. The Germans, too, seem happy, but perhaps that is because they can only get two weeks visas to visit Paris, and so they make a party of it. The frail young men who go about together and seem to be always present, but who really leave in periodical flights for Brussels, Berlin, or the Basque coast, to return again like the birds, even more like the birds, are not gay either. They twitter a good deal, but they are not gay. The Scandinavians are the regular, hard-working residents. They are not very gay either, although they seem to have worked out a certain pleasant way of life. The only really gay person during the time I frequented the Quarter was a splendid sort of two-hundred-pound meteoric glad girl called Flossie, who had what is known as a "heart of gold," lovely skin and hair and appetite, and an invulnerability to hangovers. She was going to be a singer, but the drink took away her voice, and she did not seem to mind particularly. This store of gladness made her the heroine of the Quarter. Anyhow, the Quarter is much too sad and dull a place to write about, and I would not put it in except that Robert Cohn had spent two years in it. That accounts for a great many things.

During these two years Robert Cohn had lived with a lady who lived on gossip, and so he had lived in an atmosphere of abortions and rumors of abortions, doubts and speculations as to past and prospective infidelities of friends, dirty rumors, dirtier reports and dirtier suspicions, and a constant fear and dread by his lady companion that he was seeing other women and was on the point of leaving her. Somehow during this time Robert Cohn wrote a novel, a first and last novel. He was the hero of it, but it was not too badly done and it was accepted by a New York publisher. There was a great deal of fantasy in it.

At that time Robert Cohn had only two friends, an English writer named Braddocks, and myself, with whom he played tennis. He beat me regularly at tennis and was very nice about it. Cohn gave the novel to Braddocks to read and Braddocks, who was very busy on something of his own and who, as the years went on, found it increasingly difficult to read the works of writers other than himself, did not read the novel, but returned it to Cohn with the remark that this was excellent stuff, some excellent stuff, but there was a part, just a small part, he wanted to talk over with Cohn some time. Cohn asked Braddocks what the part was, and Braddocks replied that it was a matter of organization, a very slight but important matter of organization. Cohn, eager to learn and with an un-Nordic willingness to accept useful criticism, pressed to know what it was.

"I'm much too busy now to go into it, Cohn. Come around to tea some time next week and we'll talk it over." Cohn insisted Braddocks keep the manuscript until they should have a chance to discuss it.

That night after dinner Braddocks called at my flat. He drank a brandy. "I say, Barnes," he said, "do me a favor. That's a good chap. Read this thing of Cohn's and tell me if it's any good. Mind you, I don't think it can be any good. But be a good chap and run through it and let me know what it's all about."

The next evening I was sitting on the terrace of the Closerie des Lilas watching it get dark. There was a waiter at the Lilas named Anton who used to give two whiskeys for the price of one whiskey owing to a dislike he had for his boss. This waiter raised potatoes in a garden outside of Paris, beyond Montrouge, and as I sat at the table with someone else, Alec Muhr, I think it was, we watched the people going by in the dusk on the sidewalk, and the great slow horses going by in the dusk on the Boulevard, and the people going home from work, and the girls starting their evening's work, and the light coming out of the bistro next door where the chauffeurs from the taxi line were drinking, and we asked the waiter about his potato crop, and the waiter asked about the franc, and we read the *Paris-Soir* and *l'Intransigeant*. It was very nice, and then along came Braddocks. Braddocks came along, breathing heavily and wearing a wide black hat.

"Who's that?" Alec asked.

"Braddocks," said I, "the writer."

"Good God," said Alec, who thereafter took no further part in the conversation, and does not again appear in the story.

"Hullo," said Braddocks. "May I join you?" So he joined us.

"Did you have a look at that thing of Cohn's?"

"Yes," I said. "It's a fantasy. Lot of dreams in it."

"Just as I thought," Braddocks said. "Thanks awfully."

We looked out on the Boulevard. Two girls went by.

"Pretty good-looking girls," I said.

"Do you think so?" asked Braddocks. "My word."

We looked at the Boulevard again. The waiter came and went. Braddocks was haughty with him, speaking literary French through his moustache. Along the sidewalk came a tall, gray, lantern-jawed man, walking with a tall woman wearing a blue Italian infantry cape. They looked at our table as they passed, saw no one they knew, and went on. They seemed to be looking for some one. Braddocks clapped me on the knee.

"I say, did you see me cut him? Did you see me cut him? Can't I cut people though!"

"Who is he?"

"Belloc. Hasn't a friend in the world. I say. Did you see me cut him?"

"Hilaire Belloc?"

"Belloc. Of course. He's absolutely done for. Absolutely through."

"What did you row with him about?"

"There was no row. Simply a matter of religious intolerance. Not a review in England will touch him. I tell you."

I was very impressed by this. I can see Braddocks's face, his moustache, his face in the light from the Lilas window. I did not know that the literary life could become so intense. Also I had a valuable piece of information and gossip.

The next afternoon I was sitting with several people at the Café de la Paix having coffee after lunch. Along the Boulevard des Capucines came the tall, gray-looking man and the woman wearing the blue Italian infantry cape.

"There's Hilaire Belloc," I said to the people at the table. "He hasn't a friend in the world."

"Where?" asked several people eagerly.

"There," I nodded, "standing with the woman in the blue cape."

"You mean that man in the gray suit?"

"Yes," I said. "There's not a review in England who will publish him."

"Hell. That's not Belloc," the man on my right said. "That's Allister Crowley."

So I have never felt quite the same about Braddocks since, and I should avoid as far as possible putting him into this story except that he was a great friend of Robert Cohn, and Cohn is the hero.

Appendix IV

List of Possible Titles

There exist a small number of alternate titles that Ernest Hemingway considered for his first novel. On the cover of each of the seven notebooks of the first draft of the manuscript appears the title *Fiesta: A Novel*, which was the working title. The short list transcribed below was written by hand in an eighth notebook, labeled on the cover "Ernest Hemingway, Chartres, September 27, 1925," shortly after he had finished the first draft of the novel. All five of the titles come from the Bible.

Item 202c of the Ernest Hemingway Collection, John F. Kennedy Library, Boston.

Titles
<u>The Sun Also Rises</u>
~~River to the Sea~~
For in much wisdom is much grief and he that increases knowlege increaseth sorrow.
Two Lie Together
<u>The Old Leaven</u>

Acknowledgments

I would like to thank Patrick Hemingway for his leading role in the creation of this new edition, and Susan Moldow for her steadfast support. Many thanks as well to Michael Katakis for his wise counsel and vision. I am most grateful to Tom Putnam, Director of the John F. Kennedy Library in Boston; Susan Wrynn, Curator of the Hemingway Collection; Laurie Austin of the Audiovisual Archives; Stacey Chandler of the Textual Archives; and their colleagues, without whose unfailing and generous assistance this project could not have been undertaken. For permission to publish quotes from my grandfather's letters in the United States, I am grateful to The Ernest Hemingway Foundation, especially Professor Kirk Curnutt. I am grateful to Princeton University Library, especially Gabriel Swift, Ben Primer, and AnnaLee Pauls. I am also thankful to my editor, Brant Rumble, and his colleagues at Simon & Schuster, particularly Nan Graham, John Glynn, Yessenia Santos, and Jeff Wilson, as well as the following individuals: Stacy Basko and Vic Gokuldas, Angela Hemingway Charles, Joseph and Patricia Czapski, Carol Hemingway, Valerie Hemingway, Liisa Kissel, John Michael Maas, Stephen A. MacGillivray and Hannah McCouch, James Moody, Sandra Spanier, my daughter Anouk Anji Hemingway, and Chloe, too. My greatest appreciation is for my wife, Colette C. Hemingway, who is a constant source of support and inspiration.

Notes to the Introduction

1 John W. Aldridge, *After the Lost Generation: A Critical Study of the Writers of Two Wars* (New York: McGraw-Hill, 1951), 23–24. See also Peter L. Hays, *The Critical Reception of Hemingway's "The Sun Also Rises"* (Rochester, New York: Camden House, 2011), 28.

2 The single most important study of the manuscripts of *The Sun Also Rises* is Frederic J. Svoboda, *Hemingway and "The Sun Also Rises": The Crafting of a Style* (Lawrence, Kansas: University Press of Kansas, 1983). Also of importance are Michael S. Reynolds, "False Dawn: A Preliminary Analysis of *The Sun Also Rises'* Manuscript," in D. R. Noble, ed., *Hemingway: A Revaluation* (Troy, New York: The Whitston Publishing Company, 1983), 115–34; and William Balassi, "The Writing of the Manuscript of *The Sun Also Rises*, with a Chart of Its Session-by-Session Development," *Hemingway Review* 6, no. 1 (fall 1986), 65–78. A complete facsimile edition of the first handwritten draft of *The Sun Also Rises* was published in 1990 in two volumes: Matthew J. Bruccoli, ed., *Ernest Hemingway: "The Sun Also Rises": A Facsimile Edition* (Detroit: Omnigraphics, Inc.). A list of the changes from the typescript setting copy of *The Sun Also Rises* to the published version appears in James Hinkle, "'Dear Mr. Scribner'—About the Published Text of *The Sun Also Rises*," *Hemingway Review* 6, no. 1 (fall 1986), 43–64, especially pages 58–62.

3 Hays, *The Critical Reception of Hemingway's "The Sun Also Rises."*

4 Peter Griffin, *Along with Youth: Hemingway, the Early Years* (New York: Oxford University Press, 1985), 169.

5 Gertrude Stein, *The Autobiography of Alice B. Toklas* (New York: Literary Guild, 1933), 261–62.

6 Hemingway fictionally describes how the bag and the novel it contained were lost in the posthumously published short story "The Strange Country." See *The Complete Short Stories of Ernest Hemingway: The Finca Vigía Edition* (New York: Scribner, 1987), 646–50.

7 On this period and Hemingway's involvement, see Michael Reynolds, *Hemingway: The Paris Years* (New York: W.W. Norton & Company, 1989). See also Michael S. Reynolds, *The Sun Also Rises: A Novel of the Twenties* (Boston: Twayne Publishers, 1988); Colette C. Hemingway, *in his time: Ernest Heming-*

way's Collection of Paintings and the Artists He Knew (Boston: John F. Kennedy Library, 2009).

8 Joyce Carol Oates, ed., *The Best American Essays of the Century* (New York: Houghton Mifflin, 2000).

9 Donald Ogden Stewart later stated that the report that appeared in the *Chicago Tribune* and elsewhere of his and Hemingway's being gored was wildly overstated. See Bertram D. Sarason, *Hemingway and the Sun Set* (Washington, DC: NCR Microcard Editions, 1972), 194, 196. See also Donald Ogden Stewart, *By a Stroke of Luck! An Autobiography* (London: Paddington Press Ltd, 1975), 132–33.

10 Ernest Hemingway, *A Moveable Feast: The Restored Edition* (New York: Scribner, 2009), 71.

11 Ernest Hemingway, *Along with Youth*, Ernest Hemingway Collection, Manuscripts, Item 239a, John F. Kennedy Presidential Library and Museum, Boston.

12 Reynolds, *Hemingway: The Paris Years*, 295.

13 In 1956, the notebooks containing the first draft of the novel were rediscovered by Hemingway in two steamer trunks stored at the Ritz Hotel in Paris. See Seán Hemingway, "Introduction," in Hemingway, *A Moveable Feast: The Restored Edition*, 1.

14 Ernest Hemingway, *A Farewell to Arms: The Hemingway Library Edition* (New York: Scribner, 2012), viii.

15 See Sarason, *Hemingway and the Sun Set*.

16 After Hemingway began with Harold Loeb, he switched the character's name to Gerald Cohn, and finally to Robert Cohn. It has been suggested that his use of Gerald was a reference to his friend Gerald Murphy. See Amanda Vaill, *Everybody Was So Young: Gerald and Sara Murphy: A Lost Generation Love Story* (New York: Houghton Mifflin Company, 1998), 175.

17 Bruccoli, ed., *Ernest Hemingway: "The Sun Also Rises": A Facsimile Edition*, v.

18 Letter from Ernest Hemingway to Gertrude Stein and Alice B. Toklas, August 20, 1925, in Sandra Spanier, Albert J. DeFazio III, and Robert W. Trogdon, eds., *The Letters of Ernest Hemingway, Volume 2, 1923–1925* (Cambridge: Cambridge University Press, 2013), 381.

19 Hemingway, *A Farewell to Arms: The Hemingway Library Edition*, 216.

20 It is interesting to note that Catherine Barkley, the heroine of *A Farewell to Arms*, is also a damaged person, having lost her first true love in the war. Yet Catherine is able to fall in love again and achieve brief happiness with Frederick Henry.

21 George Plimpton, "Ernest Hemingway, The Art of Fiction No. 21," Interviews, *Paris Review* 18 (spring 1958), 76–77. In contrast, Colm Tóibín notes seeing Hemingway's handwritten commentary on a film script of *The Sun Also Rises* where Hemingway writes in the margins that Jake had his testicles shot off in the war (Colm Tóibín, "PEN Hemingway Keynote Address Delivered at the John F. Kennedy Library 24 March 2013," *The Hemingway Review* 33, no. 1 (fall 2013), 8–14, especially page 13). So while the specific nature of Jake's wound is likely to remain a subject of debate, what is important is that Jake was physically wounded during the war.

22 See Reynolds, "False Dawn: A Preliminary Analysis of *The Sun Also Rises*' Manuscript," in Noble, ed., *Hemingway: A Revaluation*, 121. Reynolds theorizes that
the idea came from a World War I Navy pilot Hemingway had met who had lost
his penis in an airplane crash.

23 Hemingway, *A Moveable Feast: The Restored Edition*, 62.

24 For a powerful recent fictional account of the devastating psychological effects of
post-traumatic stress on an American soldier from the Iraq war, see Kevin Powers,
The Yellow Birds (New York: Little, Brown and Company, 2012).

25 The timing of the drafts written in the third person can be fixed by a January 14,
1926, letter from Pauline Pfeiffer addressed to Mr. and Mrs. Ernest Hemingway
in which she mentions that she hopes his revision to the third person is progress-
ing well. The letter is preserved in the Ernest Hemingway Collection at the John
F. Kennedy Library in Boston.

26 The first known runner to have died during the running of the bulls at Pamplona
was twenty-one-year-old Francisco García Gurrea, who was gored on July 7,
1910, and died on January 18, 1911. The second was twenty-two-year-old Este-
ban Domeño Laborra from Sangüesa, who was gored on July 13, 1924, and died
the next day.

27 Michael S. Reynolds, *Hemingway: An Annotated Chronology: An Outline of the
Author's Life and Career Detailing Significant Events, Friendships, Travels, and
Achievements* (Detroit: Omnigraphics, Inc., 1991), 42.

28 Matthew J. Bruccoli, *Fitzgerald and Hemingway: A Dangerous Friendship* (New
York: Carroll and Graf Publishers, Inc., 1994), 58–59.

29 Fitzgerald's undated letter is preserved in the Ernest Hemingway Collection at the
John F. Kennedy Library in Boston. It was published together with the original
beginning for *The Sun Also Rises* in *Antaeus* 33 (1979), 7–18. In *Antaeus* Fitzgerald's letter is dated to 1931, but this must be erroneous, as the letter certainly
predates June 5, 1926, when Hemingway wrote to Maxwell Perkins suggesting
the cuts to the beginning of the novel and stating that Fitzgerald agreed with his
decision.

30 Fitzgerald had revised and rewritten *The Great Gatsby* in the galley proofs with
much success, continually working to perfect his masterpiece. See Matthew J.
Bruccoli, "Preface," in F. Scott Fitzgerald, *The Great Gatsby* (New York: Scribner,
1992), 6. See also Richard D. Lehan, *F. Scott Fitzgerald and the Craft of Fiction*
(Carbondale, IL: Southern Illinois University Press, 1966).

31 See Bruccoli, *Fitzgerald and Hemingway: A Dangerous Friendship*, 76.

32 See Matthew J. Bruccoli, ed., *The Only Thing That Counts: The Ernest Hemingway–
Maxwell Perkins Correspondence, 1925–1947* (Columbia, SC: University of South
Carolina Press, 1996).

33 It is the kind of dialogue that likely made a strong impression on J. D. Salinger,
whose protagonist, Holden Caulfield, uses similar personal commentary so force-
fully in *The Catcher in the Rye*.

34 Svoboda provides an excellent and detailed examination of the many kinds of
revisions that were made to the original manuscript. See Svoboda, *Hemingway
and "The Sun Also Rises": The Crafting of a Style*, especially 43–110.

35 See Hemingway's letter to Perkins *ca.* November 16, 1926, in Bruccoli, ed., *The Only Thing That Counts: The Ernest Hemingway–Maxwell Perkins Correspondence, 1925–1947*, 48.

36 For a detailed discussion of the alternate titles, see Svoboda, *Hemingway and "The Sun Also Rises": The Crafting of a Style*, 106–10; Reynolds, "False Dawn: A Preliminary Analysis of *The Sun Also Rises*' Manuscript," in Noble, ed., *Hemingway: A Revaluation*, 116–17.

37 Carlos Baker, *Ernest Hemingway: A Life Story* (New York: Scribner, 1969), 337; Seán Hemingway, ed., *Hemingway on War* (New York: Scribner, 2004), xxxii.

ERNEST HEMINGWAY was born in Oak Park, Illinois, in 1899, and began his writing career for *The Kansas City Star* in 1917. During the First World War he volunteered as an ambulance driver on the Italian front but was invalided home, having been seriously wounded while serving with the infantry. In 1921 Hemingway settled in Paris, where he became part of the expatriate circle of Gertrude Stein, F. Scott Fitzgerald, Ezra Pound, and Ford Madox Ford. His first book, *Three Stories and Ten Poems*, was published in Paris in 1923 and was followed by the short story selection *In Our Time*, which marked his American debut in 1925. With the appearance of *The Sun Also Rises* in 1926, Hemingway became not only the voice of the "lost generation" but the preeminent writer of his time. This was followed by *Men Without Women* in 1927, when Hemingway returned to the United States, and his novel of the Italian front, *A Farewell to Arms* (1929). In the 1930s, Hemingway settled in Key West, and later in Cuba, but he traveled widely—to Spain, Italy, and Africa—and wrote about his experiences in *Death in the Afternoon* (1932), his classic treatise on bullfighting, and *Green Hills of Africa* (1935), an account of big-game hunting in Africa. Later he reported on the Spanish Civil War, which became the background for his brilliant war novel *For Whom the Bell Tolls* (1939), hunted U-boats in the Caribbean, and covered the European front during the Second World War. Hemingway's most popular work, *The Old Man and the Sea*, was awarded the Pulitzer Prize in 1953, and in 1954 Hemingway won the Nobel Prize in Literature "for his powerful, style-forming mastery of the art of narration." One of the most important influences on the development of the short story and novel in American fiction, Hemingway has seized the imagination of the American public like no other twentieth-century author. He died, by suicide, in Ketchum, Idaho, in 1961. His other works include *The Torrents of Spring* (1926), *Winner Take Nothing* (1933), *To Have and Have Not* (1937), *The Fifth Column and the First Forty-Nine Stories* (1938), *Across the River and into the Trees* (1950), and posthumously, *A Moveable Feast* (1964), *Islands in the Stream* (1970), *The Dangerous Summer* (1985), *The Garden of Eden* (1986), and *True at First Light* (1999).

THE SUN ALSO RISES

Ernest Hemingway

A masterpiece of the Lost Generation, *The Sun Also Rises* was Hemingway's first novel, and is one of his most enduring works. In spare, athletic prose, Hemingway tells the story of Jake Barnes, a journalist and American veteran of World War I who lives in Paris in the 1920s. Emasculated by a war injury, Jake must reconcile his love for Englishwoman Brett Ashley with the new realities of his life. *The Sun Also Rises* captures both the disillusionment and resilience of a generation haunted by the atrocities of modern warfare and the universal challenges of unrequited love.

TOPICS AND QUESTIONS FOR DISCUSSION

1. As Seán Hemingway suggests in his introduction, Ernest Hemingway believed that the role of a writer was to create absolute truths. What absolute truths do you think *The Sun Also Rises* attempts to locate?

2. Consider the novel's first epigraph: "You are all a lost generation." How do the characters in the novel seem lost? What can you extrapolate about the Lost Generation from Hemingway's portrait?

3. The characters in *The Sun Also Rises* were based on people from Hemingway's real life. In fiction, this type of narrative is known as a roman à clef. What responsibility does an author have—if any—when drawing inspiration from real people? How do you think relationships and life experience inform the creative process?

4. Why do you think this novel is one of Hemingway's most successful and enduring works? What about the story continues to resonate with readers? In what ways does the novel still feel contemporary?

5. Consider Jake's fishing trip to the Irati River. How is the natural world depicted in the novel? How does it echo and refract the larger themes of the book?

6. On page 9, Jake says: "Nobody ever lives their life all the way up except bull-fighters." How does the novel depict bullfighting from both an aesthetic and philosophical perspective? How does the novel's depiction of bullfighting function as social commentary?

7. Throughout the novel, Jake's war injury is alluded to but never described directly. Why do you think Hemingway chose to write "around" Jake's emasculation?

8. Jake and Brett are both haunted by the atrocities of war. How do their coping mechanisms differ? In what ways do their survival strategies overlap?

9. When we first meet Brett at the dancing club (page 17), we see that she is "very much with" a group of men. How does Brett upend gender mores? Despite being a woman, is Brett a masculine character?

10. The guiding principle of Hemingway's writing was the "iceberg theory" or the "theory of omission," in which deeper meaning is not stated explicitly but exists beneath the surface. How is Hemingway's iceberg theory on display in this novel? Were there any omitted moments that you wish had been included?

11. In what way are Count Mippipopolous and Jake similar? How are they different? What function does the count serve in the narrative? What ideas does he introduce?

12. Is *The Sun Also Rises* a tale of unrequited love? What does the novel have to say about the relationship between sex and intimacy? Can true love still exist between two people, even if it is never consummated?

13. On page 169, just before Pedro Romero's bullfight, Brett says, "Funny . . . how one doesn't mind the blood." Why is Brett the perfect muse for Romero? What does the novel have to say about our cultural attitudes toward violence?

14. What do you make of the final scene? Is this novel a tragedy? What glimmers of hope beckon within Jake's and Brett's revelations?

15. Why do you think Hemingway chose the title *The Sun Also Rises*?

Enhance Your Book Club

1. Read Hemingway's short story "A Clean Well-Lighted Place." Do you see any thematic overlap? Why is the café milieu so important to Hemingway? What is it about local coffee shops and hole-in-the-wall bars that we continue to find so compelling?

2. *The Sun Also Rises* is very much a novel from the Jazz Age. Watch Ken Burns's documentary miniseries *Jazz*. How does *The Sun Also Rises* reflect the adaptive values of jazz music?

3. Brett Ashley, like Daisy Buchanan in *The Great Gatsby*, embodies the flapper aesthetic. Read *The Great Gatsby* and talk about how Hemingway and Fitzgerald depict women of the era. Does the flapper archetype still exist today? How has it evolved?